MEG

GENERATIONS

MEG

GENERATIONS

STEVE ALTEN

A TOM DOHERTY ASSOCIATES BOOK ||| NEW YORK

MEG: GENERATIONS

Copyright © 2018 by Alten Entertainment of Boca Raton, Inc.

A Forge Book
Published by Tom Doherty Associates
120 Broadway
New York, NY 10271

www.tor-forge.com

Forge® is a registered trademark of Macmillan Publishing Group, LLC.

The Library of Congress Cataloging-in-Publication Data is available upon request.

ISBN 978-1-250-62152-8 (trade paperback)
ISBN 978-1-250-25159-6 (ebook)

Our books may be purchased in bulk for promotional, educational, or business use. Please contact your local bookseller or the Macmillan Corporate and Premium Sales Department at 1-800-221-7945, extension 5442, or by email at MacmillanSpecialMarkets@macmillan.com.

First Edition: July 2020

Printed in the United States of America

0 9 8 7 6 5 4 3 2 1

This novel is dedicated to my MEGheads,
a section of my fan base whose enthusiasm and support
over the past twenty–three years has been more than
any author could ask for.

MEG

GENERATIONS

Then again, perhaps he was paying back the good deed that had been bestowed upon his career when his own mentor, Dr. Carlos Jaramillo, had extended an invitation to join him on a dig in Colombia. Jiang had been working on his doctorate degree at the Smithsonian Tropical Research Institute at the time; the experience would be the major stepping-stone that launched his career.

The Colombian town of Cerrejón was located sixty miles from the Caribbean coast—a dusty coal mining region encompassing enormous pits fifteen miles in circumference, the sites connected by dirt roads. More than ten thousand laborers worked for Carbones del Cerrejón Limited, and the multinational company was not about to suspend operations for very long for a bunch of scientists collecting dinosaur bones.

"Jiang, Cerrejón is one of the most important fossil deposits in the world, in that it dates back to the epoch which immediately followed the asteroid impact sixty-five million years ago. After the resulting Ice Age passed, this entire region became an immense, swamp-covered jungle. The fossils unearthed on this expedition will give us a rare glimpse of the creatures that ruled the Earth after the dinosaurs perished."

Jiang Wei had spent six months at Cerrejón, helping collect and document more than two thousand plant specimens, along with several giant turtle shells and the fossil remains of at least three different species of crocodiles, each more than a dozen feet long. But it was another graduate student who would stumble upon the biggest find of Cerrejón—a monstrous snake measuring more than forty feet long, dubbed *Titanoboa cerrejonensis*.

―――――――

The jungle opened, the path leading them to the base of Sarigan's volcano, its summit replacing the cobalt-blue sky.

Jiang waited for Jie Chen to join him. "How are you holding up?"

"I am good . . . mostly excited. You never told me how you learned about the cave."

"It was discovered by Chunzi Wang, a seismologist who was assigned to investigate a recent seaquake two kilometers to the south. The cave leads to an ancient lava tube. Chunzi said the lava tube was blocked by

Sarigan Island, Northern Mariana Islands
Western Pacific

Located in the Western Pacific, the Mariana Islands are a relatively young by-product of volcanic activity that began with the formation of Guam thirty million years ago, the remaining landmasses eventually working their way around the archipelago to the north. The power train behind this geological entity, known as the Izu-Bonin-Mariana arc system, came into being hundreds of millions of years ago, when the massive Pacific Plate subducted beneath the Philippine Sea Plate to form the floor of the Mariana Trench—the deepest location on the planet.

————————

Professor Jiang Wei wiped beads of perspiration from his brow as his team of six men and his young female assistant followed their Filipino guide through the jungle-dense vegetation. It was a violation of the "old boys' school" to allow a woman to be part of an archaeological find but, as the head of paleontology at China's prestigious Peking University, Jiang had insisted that Jie Chen join them; she being the department's lone graduate student, he felt he owed her that much.

what appeared to be an immense fossilized skull. She reached out to me as an alumnus of Peking University."

"And she hasn't told anyone?"

"No. But all things considered, I felt it best we get to the site right away."

The team quickly set up camp and then repacked their gear, each person carrying a headlamp, flashlight, LED lamp, candles, lighters, radio, ropes, air mask, and a backpack in which to store their belongings. Two of the younger men carried a twelve-foot aluminum ladder.

It was late in the afternoon by the time they entered the cave.

Chunzi Wang had covered the four-foot opening with brush. Pulling it aside, Jiang adjusted his headlamp and knee pads and crawled in.

The cave was made of basalt; the volcanic rock carried a heavy scent of sulfur. The walls were damp, the ceiling alive with bats. Mosquitoes were everywhere, forcing the team to don their breathing masks.

They continued on, the cave floor descending at a thirty-degree slope until it merged with the entrance of the lava tube—a thirteen-foot-high opening, its entrance marked by a pair of curved, razor-sharp stalactites and stalagmites.

Jiang led his team inside, their headlamps revealing a bizarre lava pattern apparently left behind by the last eruption. Every six to eight feet, the flow of magma had paused in its ascent just long enough to harden, creating a series of eight-to-twelve-inch-thick archways that continued through the dark tunnel like buttresses in a cathedral.

After another seventy feet, the tube twisted to the left. Jie Chen took the lead, her light momentarily disappearing around the bend.

"Dr. Wei . . . here it is!"

The men joined her, their lights illuminating the fossilized skull and jawbone of an immense crocodile, the creature's remains wedged tightly between the floor and ceiling so that there was no way past it.

An open debate ensued between flashes from half a dozen iPhone cameras.

"What species is this?"

"It can't be a modern-day crocodile; the jaw alone is over two meters."

"How did it get here?"

"I imagine this tube connects with the sea. The creature must have gotten caught in the cave during the last eruption."

"Gentlemen . . . and lady . . . excuse me please. A two-meter jawline would equate to a body length in excess of fifteen meters. The biggest prehistoric croc was *Sarcosuchusimperator*—"

"It cannot be *Sarcosuchus,*" one of the scientists stated as he aimed his light at a crushed forelimb. "This animal possessed flippers, making it a prehistoric sea creature . . . a plesiosaur, no doubt. My guess would be . . . Kronosaurus."

Jiang shook his head. "Plesiosaurs died off forty million years before this island rose from the seafloor."

"Dr. Wei?"

"You are forgetting, my friend, *which* seafloor lies beneath us."

"He's right. Jonas Taylor documented the existence of Kronosaurus in the Mariana Trench more than twenty years ago."

"Excuse me, Dr. Wei!"

The men stopped talking, turning around to face Jie Chen.

"Sorry, but this creature did not die from the lava. If it had, there would be no fossilized evidence left behind. Look at its skull—it appears to have been crushed by the ceiling."

"What are you suggesting?"

"Sir, I don't think this is a lava tube."

Jiang Wei shone his light along the section of the ceiling, which appeared to be pressing down upon the creature's crushed skull. "Where is the ladder?"

The twelve-foot aluminum ladder was set up for Dr. Wei.

Retrieving a small pickax from their supplies, the paleontologist climbed the rungs until he was only a few feet from the curved ceiling. With all his might, he swung the tool in an arc, burying the flat blade into the smooth surface—

—which crumbled into soot-like flakes, unleashing thousands of bats, their flapping wings chasing the fossilized flesh from the vertebral column of a monstrous, hundred-fifty-five-foot-long creature.

PART ONE

SUNSET

I've reached the point where I hardly care if I live or die. The world will keep on turning without me, and I can't do anything to change events anyway.

—Anne Frank

|||||||||||||||||||||||||||||||||||||

Aboard the *Tonga*
Tanaka Oceanographic Institute
Monterey, California

The bull was lost.

For the entirety of its adult existence it had been the master of its domain—a domain defined by sound. A simple *clickety-click* and the silver-gray behemoth immediately recognized its territory, be it the subglacial lake in Antarctica where its kind had survived for eons, the shallows where its harem of cows had birthed their calves, or the now-accessible depths of the Southern Ocean where the dominant male had, up until recently, foraged for food.

None were present. Nor was there a memory of how the bull had come to be in this unrecognizable sea. And so it took refuge in the shallows in a semiconscious stupor, its blowhole remaining free of the water.

———

Jacqueline Buchwald adjusted the hood of her parka over her shoulder-length, strawberry-blond hair, the air temperature inside the bowels of the Malacca-class oil tanker kept at a brisk 42 degrees Fahrenheit. The *Tonga* and her sister ship, the *Mogamigawa*, no longer transported crude, their enormous holds having been scrubbed and refitted with seawater pens by their new owner—a Dubai crown prince—to stock Dubai-Land, his ambitious prehistoric aquarium theme park in the United Arab Emirates. The size of the tank was a necessity—the species targeted for capture were among the largest and most dangerous life-forms ever to have existed on the planet.

The twenty-six-year-old marine biologist stood dead center of the catwalk, a narrow expanse of grated steel connecting the two walkways anchored along the port and starboard bulkheads. The hold was purposely kept dark in order to accommodate the eyes of the nocturnal species they had been hunting over the past year, the only light coming from strings of Christmas decorations wrapped around the walkway's guardrails.

Jackie used the night-vision scope of her harpoon gun to search the dark waters forty feet below her perch for the lone animal that now occupied the *Tonga*'s hold. Jonas Taylor had dubbed the creature "Brutus," and the name was apropos; at eighty feet and a hundred eighty-seven thousand pounds, the *Livyatan melvillei* was certainly a brute. Unlike the other prehistoric species, the Miocene whale had been discovered in an ancient habitat somewhere in Antarctica, its location safeguarded by Jonas's colleague, Zachary Wallace, the marine biologist who, years earlier, had resolved the mystery of the monster that inhabited Loch Ness.

Capturing the Miocene whale had been an accident. Jonas's son, David, had set the *Tonga*'s nets at the exit point of an Antarctic bay to capture the adult Liopleurodon they had been chasing for nearly a year when Brutus showed up, springing the trap.

Three weeks had passed since the whale's capture. The feisty bull was not keen on being held inside the tight confines of the tanker, forcing Jackie to introduce phenobarbital into its pen to calm the beast. It was a tricky proposition; too little tranquilizer and the prehistoric mammal might go berserk, too much and it could drown.

Her employer, Fiesal bin Rashidi, had made it clear that he was in favor of the latter.

"Miss Buchwald, I did not spend tens of millions of dollars and eight long months at sea to capture a whale."

"This isn't just a whale, sir. *Livyatan melvillei* was a prehistoric sperm whale, only it possessed the lower jaw of an orca. Megalodon and *melvillei* were the two dominant predators during the Miocene era . . . maybe of all time. This creature's teeth are actually bigger than a Meg's teeth, and its bite is just as powerful. Your cousin just purchased the Tanaka Institute from the Taylors; the lagoon would be perfect for Brutus."

"And what happens when it dies? All our specimens are female, capable of internal fertilization. You know firsthand that we've been storing eggs to ensure our exhibits' longevity. This menace is a male. Without a female, the creature is a dead-end investment.

"The public also feels differently about penning a whale—even a prehistoric menace like this creature. Animal rights groups are staging protests outside the governor's mansion in Sacramento. The crown prince has agreed to release the animal during this afternoon's festivities aboard the *Tonga*. A special tracking device has been prepared. At precisely two o'clock, an hour before the prince makes his speech, I want you to tag the whale and prepare it to be released. Is that clear?"

"Two o'clock . . . yes, sir."

Jackie peered through the harpoon gun's night scope, which lifted the veil of darkness, rendering everything olive green. Bin Rashidi had given her an hour to tag the *melvillei* with the radio transmitter and then bring it out of its drug-induced state by adding fresh seawater to the tank so that it would be able to escape under its own power once they opened the tanker's keel doors.

An hour's not nearly enough time. Brutus has been drugged for three weeks; it could take several hours before he comes around. The last thing the crown prince wants is for the whale to go belly-up in front of the international news media.

She glanced at her cell phone to check the time before placing it in the ziplock bag and tucking it in the back pocket of her jeans.

Twelve-fifteen. Tag it and then wait another fifteen minutes before you add fresh water.

She located the semiconscious bull in the shallows where the keel angled to conform to the *Tonga*'s bow. Selecting a location between the whale's blowhole and its dorsal hump, she squeezed the trigger and fired.

The harpoon buried the transmitter four feet inside the Miocene whale's spermaceti organ, eliciting a stabbing pain accompanied by a burst of adrenaline that lifted the phenobarbital-induced fog.

Enraged, Brutus slapped its tail along the surface as it lurched ahead—beaching itself in twenty feet of water.

The sensation of being trapped sent the beast into full panic mode. Whipping itself into a barrel roll, it attempted to dive, only to end up stuck on its side, its fluke unable to strike the hull in order to gain leverage, its ninety-three tons crushing its lungs and internal organs.

Jackie watched the Miocene whale through the night scope as it flailed helplessly on its left flank, seconds from flipping over onto its back. She reached for the walkie-talkie held snugly inside a holster clipped to her belt. "Bridge, this is Buchwald—pick up, goddammit!"

"This is Ensign Slatford."

"Andrew, Brutus beached himself. Open the stern hatch; we need to raise the water level so he can swim free."

"Jackie, I can't add ballast without clearing it with the captain."

"Then ask him; just do it fast!"

"Stand by."

Jackie removed the night scope from the harpoon gun and faced the stern. Thirty seconds passed before a stream of bubbles and foam rose to the surface, indicating the keel doors were open.

She returned her gaze through the night scope to Brutus. The water level was rising about a foot a minute, gradually lifting the beached behemoth, which was wriggling furiously while desperately slapping its fluke against the steel hull to prevent itself from going belly-up.

The rising tide finally floated the behemoth. It rolled onto its belly and wriggled away from the bow's shallow incline until it slipped beneath the dark waters and disappeared.

"Buchwald to bridge—we're good. Andrew, close the keel doors."

"Roger that."

Zzzzzzzzzzzzzzzzzt . . . zzzzzzzzzzzzzzzzzzt.

The double blast of echolocation sent Jackie's skull reverberating as if it had been struck by a giant tuning fork. Looking down, she saw a ten-foot wake pass along the surface as Brutus accelerated toward the stern end of the hold two football fields away.

The water was rancid, permeated with the toxic scent and taste of phenobarbital, the acidic animal tranquilizer burning the delicate tissues of the whale's blowhole. The fresh ocean water entering the tanker's hold was a river of life.

The whale raced for it, homing in on its cooler temperatures.

Whomp!

The Miocene whale's squared-off skull impacted and popped open a seam of rivets connecting two steel plates along the stern's inner hull. Jackie registered the collision deep inside her bones. A moment later, she experienced a wave of nausea as the rusted grating beneath her feet began to shake and the darkness on her right squealed its final warning.

Dropping the harpoon gun, she grabbed for the safety rail and held on as the bolts connecting the bridge to the port bulkhead snapped and suddenly one side of the catwalk dropped, the grating sliding out from beneath her as it collapsed at a forty-five-degree angle.

"Oh God, oh God, oh God—"

The loose end of the bridge splashed down into the water, the starboard bulkhead holding tight.

Jackie pulled herself up, managing to straddle the rail. Realizing she had dropped the walkie-talkie, she looked down in time to see an undulating gray mass pass twenty feet beneath her unsteady perch—

—Brutus heading back to the bow to make another assault on the stern.

———————

The Bell 525 helicopter soared south above the Pacific coast on its short excursion from downtown San Francisco. Among its thirteen passengers was the CEO of the Emirates National Oil Company; one of the presidents of the National Bank of Fujairah; Ryan Skinner, the newly elected governor of California; a half-dozen chairmen representing three of the largest construction companies in Dubai; and a reporter with the Gulf News.

There were also two Arab security men, their Glocks bulging beneath the jackets of their dark suits.

The man seated alone in the last row unplugged his headphones, cutting off the voice of his first cousin. Crown Prince Walid Abu Naba'a had been pitching his entourage of financial backers about "his" aquarium and "his" juvenile Liopleurodon from the moment they had taken off from the rooftop of their hotel, and Fiesal bin Rashidi could not handle another word.

Your Liopleurodon? *Was it you who spent the last eight months aboard the* Tonga, *chasing that creature's mother across the Pacific Ocean? Was it you who had to deal with a mutinous crew after you threatened to cancel their bonus checks?*

The only reason we captured that monster's offspring is because I held the mission together . . . me, cousin. Not you. Instead, you've reduced me to an afterthought. Do you think that I cannot hear the whispers of deceit coming from back home . . . your discussions to buy out my twenty percent? To replace me as director of Dubai-Land?

Without me, there would be no aquarium . . . there would be no Dubai-Land!

Fiesal bin Rashidi massaged the tension knotting beneath his unibrow. The Dubai-Land Resort and Aquarium was on the verge of becoming the entertainment mecca of the world. Yet by the time the park opened, he would be as forgotten as Billy Wilkerson, the man who had lost the Flamingo Hotel in Las Vegas to Bugsy Siegel.

––––––––––

Like his father before him, Fiesal bin Rashidi was an engineer, earning his degrees from Cambridge, his field of interest targeting naval applications. He had been working on the Chunnel when a friend introduced him to a marine biologist in need of someone with his expertise.

Dr. Michael Maren had been as paranoid as he was brilliant—an odd chap who had avoided eye contact when he spoke and trusted no one. His mother had died recently, leaving him an abundance of wealth with which to pursue his scientific endeavors. Maren had been interested in exploring the deepest ocean trenches in the world and was looking to hire a naval engineer who could design a deep-water habitat possessing a submersible docking station capable of withstanding water pressures in excess of nineteen thousand pounds per square inch.

The challenge had been enormous, the requirement a bit baffling, since the Mariana Trench, the deepest known location on the planet, possessed sixteen thousand pounds of pressure. Still, the job paid well and Fiesal could work on it while he completed his work on the Chunnel.

Over the next three years the naval engineer had tested half a dozen different designs before coming up with one that had proved stable enough to flood and drain a docking station nine miles beneath the surface. Two titanium habitats had been built while Maren's research vessel was fitted with an A-frame, winch, and steel cable strong enough to lower and raise the enormous weight. After five years of construction and tests, the marine biologist had been ready to set sail to "an unexplored realm." Fiesal had been offered a position on the maiden voyage, but the thought of spending upward of a year at sea with the volatile scientist and his lover/assistant, Allison Petrucci, held no appeal. With the Chunnel complete, Fiesal had accepted an offer from his father's firm, returning to Dubai to work on the emirate's new airport.

Eighteen months later, he had been contacted by Allison Petrucci, who informed him Dr. Maren was dead. After coercing the engineer into signing a nondisclosure agreement, the woman had presented him with evidence of an unexplored sea that dated back hundreds of millions of years, possessing ancient marine life that could be captured and placed on exhibit. For a seven-figure sum she would provide Fiesal with the coordinates of an access point into the realm her fiancé had referred to as the Panthalassa Sea.

Bin Rashidi had needed more convincing. He got it when the woman had produced a map of the Philippine Sea Plate, indicating that the ancient sea actually resided *beneath* the Mariana Trench. Years earlier, Jonas Taylor had theorized that these same depths harbored a warm-layer habitat that supported a subspecies of Megalodon, a sixty-foot prehistoric cousin of the great white shark. He had proven it to the world when one of the monstrous sharks—a pregnant female—had risen to the surface. Taylor had been forced to kill the beast, but its surviving pup, Angel, had grown into a seventy-four-foot monster, and for years was the star attraction of the Tanaka Oceanographic Institute.

If Fiesal could bring such an attraction to Dubai . . .

The Middle East was a battleground. America's military interventions in Iraq and a failed Arab Spring had added only more fuel to that fire. Democracy had been subverted in Egypt, autocratic rule festered in Syria and Iran, and ISIS militants were threatening both Arab states and the West.

Three months after his meeting with Allison Petrucci, Fiesal bin Rashidi had presented his first cousin, Crown Prince Walid Abu Naba'a, with a business plan for Dubai-Land, a marine theme park featuring a dozen five-star hotels centered around massive aquariums stocked with real prehistoric sea monsters. The popularity of the Tanaka Institute had proven the public's love of aquatic beasts; Dubai-Land would take the concept multiple steps further, making their country the number one tourist destination in the world. Just as important, the aquarium would present Westerners with a more positive opinion of Muslims, while inoculating the UAE against the threat of radical Islam.

Bin Rashidi had designed the supersized aquariums himself. He had also identified two Malacca-class crude oil tankers, the *Tonga* and the *Mogamigawa*, that could be purchased from the Japanese. All that was needed was the crown prince's capital and someone to lead the underwater safari to stock their exhibits.

Jonas Taylor was the unanimous choice—only the former Navy submersible pilot and marine biologist had flatly refused. He and Dr. Maren had crossed paths before, the last time culminating in Michael's death. The Tanaka Institute did agree to sell two of Angel's four surviving Megalodon offspring to the crown prince, along with four of its deep-sea Manta submersibles.

But there was another Taylor who had captured Fiesal's eye—Jonas's son, David. The cocky twenty-one-year-old was not only a highly skilled Manta pilot, but he seemed fearless around the Megalodons. A lucrative summer job offer in Dubai to stabilize the two Meg runts in their new aquariums was the lure to bring David to the UAE; but it was a summer romance with one of their pilot candidates—Kaylie Szeifert—that would send him into the depths of the Panthalassa Sea searching for ancient prehistoric monsters.

Locating the Panthalassa life-forms had been easy; drawing them into the surface ships' nets had proved to be a bit more challenging. After several months, the submersible crews had managed to capture four different species, two of which perished inside their tanker pens.

And then Fiesal bin Rashidi had laid eyes on the Liopleurodon.

The creature was an aberration of evolution—a specimen that Fiesal knew would easily become the identity of the aquarium. While the rest of the crew aboard the *Tonga* remained mesmerized by the Lio, Fiesal had fired a tracking device into the animal's back as it surfaced, ensuring they would not lose their prized quarry.

For the next eight months, the aquarium director and his crew aboard the *Tonga* had chased after the hundred-twenty-two-foot creature as it trekked across the Western Pacific and south to Antarctica. The Lio had refused to surface, and Fiesal's team of submersible pilots had been too afraid to venture close enough to engage the goliath and lure it into the tanker's nets. Compounding the problem was the failure of bin Rashidi's second unit aboard the *Mogamigawa* to capture a pod of Shonisaurus that had escaped the Panthalassa Sea. With only three of the twelve exhibits occupied, the crown prince's initial excitement about the aquarium had waned, turning Fiesal's optimism into doubt, his joy festering into resentment, frustration, and bitterness.

A sense of gloom seemed to hang over the *Tonga*. Desperate, lacking a game plan, and clearly out of his element, Fiesal bin Rashidi had lost the respect of his crew. The driving force behind the aquarium had spent his days alone in his stateroom, a prisoner to his own ambition. Women no longer interested him, gold no longer shimmered. Stuck on a seemingly endless voyage of damnation, Fiesal bin Rashidi, once the favored cousin of the crown prince, had become his albatross.

And then David Taylor had arrived on board the *Mogamigawa* and lady luck had returned. Three prehistoric sea creatures had been captured within thirty-six hours, including a Mosasaurus.

It was as if the sun had shone for the first time in almost a year.

The crown prince arranged for a helicopter to transport David, his friend Monty, and the ship's female marine biologist, Jacqueline Buchwald, to the *Tonga*. A buzz of excitement had spread through the crew—David Taylor would take charge of the mission and capture the Lio. The *Tonga* would return home with its prize, families reunited, bonus checks cashed.

But was the son of Jonas Taylor to be trusted? The Liopleurodon had savagely taken the life of David's girlfriend, and the young man was clearly haunted by her death.

Was he out to capture the Lio . . . or kill it?

In the end, the answer had turned out to be both.

———

The disgruntled naval engineer plugged his headphones back in as the helicopter began its vertical descent over the *Tonga*'s helipad, their arrival having done little to slow down the crown prince's pitch.

". . . That's the beauty of internal fertilization. All the pups are female, each a genetic clone of their mother. That means our Liopleurodon pup will grow into a thirty-seven-meter monster, just as Angel's daughter, Zahra, will be her mother's mirror image."

A smattering of applause was followed by the chopper's landing gear touching down. One by one the men climbed out, crossing the tanker's enormous deck to where a set of bleachers had been set up before a three-story-high, five-hundred-thousand-gallon aquarium.

Bin Rashidi was the last person to deboard. As he stepped down from the helicopter he was met by the crown prince. His cousin's personal attorney, Kirsty Joyce, was standing two paces behind him holding a leather briefcase.

"Fiesal, things have changed. Our costs have skyrocketed, and I need to recapitalize the venture or we'll be bankrupt before we open." He turned to the British woman, who handed him two copies of a legal document. "I'm releasing another ten million shares of the company—"

"Diluting my twenty percent to . . . ?" Bin Rashidi scanned the five-page addendum, his hand shaking. "A buyout? I was the one who came to you with this idea . . . the location of the Panthalassa Sea . . . the design of the tanks. Cousin, how can you do this to me?"

"I am offering you ten million dollars for your stock. Most people would be grateful."

"Once it's open, the park will make that every hour."

"You mean, *if* it opens. My accountants estimate our start-up costs will exceed twenty-four billion before we book our first reservation. Will you be putting up that money, Fiesal?"

"We're already booked three years in advance."

"And those deposits must all be returned if I cannot recapitalize the venture. Sign the contract and Ms. Joyce will wire the funds into your account. Don't sign, and my next offer will be half that amount."

Fiesal bin Rashidi felt the blood rush to his cheeks. Taking the pen from the blond attorney, he signed the two signature pages, the crown prince's authorizations already stamped and notarized.

Kirsty Joyce filed one of the copies in her brief. Removing her iPhone, she quickly texted instructions to the crown prince's bank. "The funds have been wired."

"Plans within plans, eh, cousin?"

"Excuse me?"

"It's been nine days since the *Tonga* arrived, nine days since the blood sport occurred in the Tanaka Lagoon. And yet the Miocene whale has still not been released, the contract to sell the Taylors' facility to Agricola Industries is yet to be signed."

"As Ms. Joyce will tell you, there are still several deal points being negotiated."

The attorney nodded. "There is a legal question as to which party owns the teeth from the two deceased Megalodons, as well as the adult Lio. As you can imagine, each tooth can bring in quite a lot of money. Mr. Agricola is claiming owner's rights to the albino Megalodon, Lizzy, since he captured the shark after it had escaped—"

Fiesal held up his palm. "There is an old Arab saying, 'Avoid the company of liars, but if you can't, then be sure you never believe them.' I may not be royalty, Ms. Joyce, but do not take me for a fool." He turned back to his cousin. "I see Governor Skinner is among your entourage."

"Is it a crime to extend the courtesy of an invitation to a political ally?"

"You mean a future bedfellow, don't you, cousin? There will be no deal with the Canadian. You mean to keep the Tanaka Institute for yourself, along with the Miocene whale, which will occupy the lagoon."

"And will I also be spending half a billion dollars to place a dome over this thirty-year-old facility?"

"The sale of the two Megalodon siblings' teeth alone would cover that expense."

"And when the bull dies?"

"You have a living specimen and a modern relative in the sperm whale. Cloning the species would be a relatively easy task for our genetics team, on par with what the Russians are doing to bring back the woolly mammoth. The bigger concern is one of real estate. How much land will the governor make available for you in Carmel and Monterey to build your hotels and theme park?"

"An interesting theory, Fiesal—one I'd advise you to keep to yourself. You wouldn't want to violate the nondisclosure section of the buyout agreement you just signed."

"Is that it then?"

"I see no reason for you to attend tonight's festivities. Gather your belongings and the pilot will take you back to San Francisco."

The crown prince turned to his attractive personal attorney. "Come, Ms. Joyce . . . let us introduce the Lio to our new partners."

———————

At eleven hundred feet from bow to stern and a hundred ninety-six feet wide, the *Tonga* was as large as an aircraft carrier, and when her hold was filled to capacity, she displaced more weight. A floating steel island, the Malacca-class crude tanker was anchored less than a mile offshore, her starboard flank several hundred yards from the entrance of the canal that led into the Tanaka Institute's man-made lagoon.

The ship's superstructure towered twelve stories above the stern, the Lio's holding tank erected in its shadow. Sixty feet in diameter and thirty feet high, the circular Lexan aquarium had been flown in from the Dubai-Land resort and assembled by Jacqueline Buchwald and her staff to better care for the Lio pup during the anticipated three-week voyage to Dubai.

———————

Like excited children on Christmas Day, the crown prince's entourage hurried across the deck to join the other invited guests and members of the media, all of whom were busy snapping photos and taking video of the star attraction.

While the business pitch from their billionaire host had certainly been convincing, it paled in comparison with actually seeing the Liopleurodon circling within its tank. Only a month old, the pliosaur was already a dangerous predator, its jaws sporting two-to-five-inch dagger-like teeth, the largest of which jutted outside of its mouth. Flapping along its short, powerful neck were six gill slits. While the creature's ancestors that had dominated the Late Jurassic seas were air-breathing marine reptiles, the subspecies that had escaped extinction in the Panthalassa Sea had adapted to their new deep-water environment by growing gills, rendering them "reptilian fish."

What really surprised the crown prince's guests was how large the Lio had grown in such a short amount of time. When the public had last seen the pliosaur, it had measured eight feet from the tip of its crocodile-like snout to the point of its stubby tail and weighed just under two hundred and fifty pounds. Its transformation during this past week in captivity had been startling. While its length had increased by 50 percent, its girth had more than doubled. The marine biologists on board the *Tonga* theorized the pliosaur's incredible growth spurt could be credited to a diet much higher in fat content than the prey the juvenile might normally find in the Panthalassa Sea, combined with the aquarium's increased oxygen content. The latter also helped to explain the creature's hyperkinetic movements.

Lead-gray on top with a speckled belly, the juvenile killer glided around the tank on a single burst from its paddle-like forelimbs with the dexterity of a seal, using its hindquarters as a rudder from which to steer. With both sets of limbs pumping in open water, it could give a speedboat a run for its money.

The animal remained close to the inside of the glass, the dark pupil of its yellow right eye appearing cold and calculating as it circled counterclockwise, watching the watchers.

A few of the VIPs had brought their children to the event. When a six-year-old boy went running toward the tank, the Lio banked on a dime to intercept, its jaws wide and outstretched and ready to swallow the shrieking child down its hideous pink gullet, had the three-inch-thick, bulletproof Lexan glass not been in the way.

This reaction naturally spurred a dozen copycats, and within minutes, the videos had gone viral.

———

Fiesal bin Rashidi entered his stateroom, not surprised to find his belongings already packed, his two suitcases and duffel bag tagged, the airline ticket left ontop of his laptop. He checked the itinerary. *San Francisco to Dubai, leaving at eleven-thirty tonight, with a layover in New York. Not only does he have me on the red-eye, he has me flying coach . . .*

"No good deed goes unpunished, eh, cousin."

Whomp!

The jolt felt as if the *Tonga* had run aground, only Fiesal knew that was impossible, as the tanker was poised over the depths of the Monterey Bay Submarine Canyon. A quick glance at his watch confirmed it was only 12:52 p.m.

I told Buchwald 2 p.m. . . . I was very clear—

His walkie-talkie buzzed and he grabbed it off its charger.

"Bridge to Mr. bin Rashidi."

"I'm here. Go ahead, Mr. Slatford."

"Sir, did you feel that jolt? The captain's concerned the whale may be attempting to break out of the hold. I tried to raise Ms. Buchwald, but she hasn't responded. The skipper wants me to send an armed detail below—"

"That's not necessary. I'll check on Brutus; you can send one of the crew to my quarters to load my belongings on board the chopper."

Walkie-talkie in hand, Fiesal left his suite and headed down a corridor to the stairwell. He descended three flights, exiting to a small corridor which led to a watertight door set inside the bulkhead.

STARBOARD WALKWAY
Keep Door Closed at All Times

Fiesal selected one of the fur-lined parkas hanging from hooks along the wall and slipped the coat on. He grabbed a flashlight from a footlocker and tested it to make sure the batteries were good. Then he pressed down on the steel handle of the watertight door, wrenched it open, and entered the hold, pulling it closed behind him.

Stepping out onto the walkway, he was greeted by a howl of chilled air. The narrow steel path ran from the stern to the bow, hugging the starboard bulkhead.

Fiesal aimed the beam of his flashlight at the water, surprised to see an enormous wake rolling away from him toward the bow. *Why is there a wake in the hold? We're not moving; there should be no—*

"Hello?"

The voice was female and faint, coming from somewhere up ahead. He proceeded down the walkway, guided by the strand of Christmas lights until he reached the catwalk's bridge . . . or what remained of it.

"Down here!"

Fiesal aimed the beam of his flashlight below, where Jacqueline Buchwald was holding on to the guardrail.

"Get a rope!"

Before he could reply, an immense silver-gray mass raced beneath the collapsed catwalk—

—followed by a massive swell that swallowed the bridge, and the female biologist with it, the wave cresting three feet over the starboard catwalk, soaking Fiesal's lower torso as it rolled in the direction of the stern.

Whomp—boom!

The enraged whale struck the keel's steel plates with the force of a train hitting a brick building—

—while the swell climbed the far end of the tank to blast the underside of the deck five stories overhead, the displacement of ballast actually raising the *Tonga's* prow three feet out of the sea.

Fiesal ran toward the impact as the swell receded beneath his perch in the opposite direction, the retreating depths revealing the creature's midsection as Brutus squeezed through the gap it had created in the hull, its wriggling torso pushing the opening wider—

—until the leviathan's fluke disappeared into open ocean.

The Pacific rushed into the tanker, the water level rising quickly. Yanking open the watertight door, bin Rashidi stepped out into the corridor and resealed it behind him. He tossed the coat on the floor and hurried up six flights of stairs, his mind racing.

Get to the chopper; don't create a scene. As long as the watertight doors remain sealed, the ship will stay afloat.

He emerged on the main deck, realizing his pants and shoes were dripping wet. He slowed his pace to a natural walk, watching the producer of Dubai-Land's reality show stalking him in his peripheral vision.

"Mr. bin Rashidi!"

He struggled to recall the man's name. *Barry* . . . Tucker? *Barry Walker?* He spotted the Star of David hanging around his neck. "Yes, Mr. Zuckerman?"

"What just happened? It felt like we ran aground."

"Nonsense."

"Then what was it?"

"It was Brutus. Our marine biologist had to add seawater to his pen to bring him out of his stupor. He's getting a bit agitated; she may have to release him earlier than we planned."

"Why wasn't I told? There's a ton of shots we still need to get on video." He retrieved a walkie-talkie from his Windbreaker pocket. "Ponyboy, it's Barry. Get your second unit down to the hold—the whale is conscious. Is that British MMA actor on board yet?"

"Lee Shone? He's posing by the Lio tank."

"Bring him below and get his shots." He looked at bin Rashidi. "How much time do we have?"

"Not much. "Turning on his heel, bin Rashidi headed for his cousin's helicopter, his soaked shoes and socks leaving a trail of wet marks.

The swell had hit the catwalk like a thirty-foot-high tsunami, the current stripping the sneakers and socks from Jackie's feet as she held on to the guardrail for dear life—until the entire span of twisted metal was swept away, dragging her with it.

She released the anchor of steel and fought her way to the surface, only the wave refused to let her go, carrying her a hundred feet before lifting her straight up the stern bulkhead to the ceiling. Flailing blindly, she managed to grab hold of a ceiling strut and hold on as the swell suddenly fell back into the tank, leaving her dangling from a new perch—seventy feet above the retreating waters.

Grunting and shaking from the cold, she raised her right leg up to the ceiling's steel framework, her bare foot snaking its way atop a support beam until she was able to pull herself into a seated position.

Jackie looked down. As she watched, the water level rose above the starboard walkway's rail, causing the Christmas lights to spark and short.

Brutus must have punched through the hull. . . .

"Oh, Jesus, I'm going to drown."

She searched her pockets for her iPhone, blessing the instinct that had led her to seal it in a plastic ziplock bag. With trembling hands, she scrolled for a number. . . .

———————

David Taylor shifted uncomfortably on his assigned bar stool, fighting the urge to look at the camera looming directly in front of him. He despised interviews, but the *Hollywood Xtra* segment producer, James Gelet, had been an ally during his sea monster safari, and so he had reluctantly agreed.

At least the location of the shoot was convenient—the two bar stools set up at the north end of the Tanaka Oceanographic Institute's arena along the span of concrete separating the man-made lagoon from the Meg Pen. Still, he saw no purpose to the exercise. Both habitats remained vacant, the facility technically closed until he and its new owner, Paul Agricola, could capture one of Bela's or Lizzy's newborns— assuming any of the pups had survived the orca populations inhabiting the Salish Sea without the protection of their ferocious mothers.

Then there was the reporter.

Melissa Bell was a blue-eyed, raven-haired beauty hired to read from a teleprompter—or so he had assumed. It quickly became evident that she had come prepared and that David would need his "A" game to keep pace. It didn't help that his best friend, Jason "Monty" Montgomery— a former Army medic with an explosion-induced bipolar brain—was lurking off-camera like a hungry shark on lithium.

"Melissa Bell here. Today I'm visiting the world-famous Tanaka Oceanographic Institute with David Taylor, the son of Jonas Taylor, who, I think it's safe to say, is the foremost authority on *Carcharodon megalodon*. Did I say that right?"

"Yeah, that was perfect."

"Eight nights ago, you played ringmaster to an unexpected showdown between two adult Megs—Bela and Lizzy—and an absolute freak of nature, a one-hundred-twenty-foot female Liopleurodon. Is it safe to say that what happened in the Tanaka Lagoon was the scariest moment of your life?"

"Not really. I mean, don't get me wrong . . . that was scary, but when everything is happening so fast like it did, there's no time to be scared. You just react. To be honest, if I had to pick the absolute scariest moment of my life, I'd say it was when I was fourteen years old and Angel returned to California waters after being gone for seventeen years."

"Angel, of course, was the surviving offspring of the pregnant female that your grandfather Masao Tanaka had lured to the surface from the depths of the Mariana Trench."

"He didn't lure the Meg to the surface, it was an accident." David glanced over her shoulder at Monty, who was pretending to hang himself with his shirt collar.

"Tell us about that scary moment."

He pointed in the direction of the canal, which was blocked by the Canadian-registered hopper-dredge, *Marieke*, which belonged to his soon-to-be partner, Paul Agricola. "I was scuba diving just outside the entrance to the lagoon. . . . There's an underwater junction box that controls the canal doors and I was trying to fix it."

"Were you diving alone?"

"Yeah. Kinda stupid, I know. I was in about eighty feet of water when I felt this . . . *presence*. There's a section of the Monterey Submarine Canyon that is only about fifty yards from the canal doors. When I looked in that direction, I thought I saw Angel's tail moving off, heading into the depths."

"You're right, that's pretty scary."

"No . . . that wasn't the scary part. The scary part happened about a week later. To prove to my uncle Mac that Angel had returned, I powered up the lagoon's underwater loudspeakers and played the deep sounds the Meg associated with feeding time. I was alone in the observation post, which is this underwater viewing chamber set along the southern seawall, when Angel entered the lagoon. Keep in mind that up until then, I had never seen her except in videos. Well, she was an absolute monster . . . easily seventy-five feet long and fifty tons. She was as white as a ghost, her head was as big as a two-story house, and her jaws were opening and closing like she was talking. I could see water entering her mouth and slipping out her gill slits and I realized she was just breathing.

"We were as close as you and I are now, separated by seven inches of glass, and she was looking at me, and her snout was casually pressing up against the viewing chamber glass, and I could see that her sheer mass was causing the Lexan to bend inside the frame."

"What did you do?"

"There was an emergency button set along the chamber wall that dropped a steel plate in place to protect the glass. I hit it about two seconds before she charged—otherwise she would have flooded the viewing area and eaten me. Angel was a scary fish."

"But no match for the Liopleurodon."

"Not true. Me and another submersible pilot were trapped in a deep-water habitat in the Panthalassa Sea when they fought. From the viewing portal I saw that Angel had her jaws around that bitch's neck and was crushing its throat. It would have ended there, only the *Tonga* netted Angel and hauled her out of the water, and that's when the Lio . . ."

His words trailed off as the memory interceded.

He was treading water, Kaylie on one side of his father's submersible, David on the other, the bloodstained sea washing over the acrylic pod . . . the creature's fang-laced crocodilian jaws rising along either side of the girl, plucking her from below—

He jumped as his iPhone vibrated along his right butt cheek.

Reaching into his back pocket, he powered off the device.

"Let's talk about Bela and Lizzy. You seemed to have really cared about those two monsters."

"I raised them from birth. And the sisters weren't monsters."

"Come on, David—they killed at least three people."

"One was a fisherman who shot Lizzy from point-blank range in her eye. Another was some old lady who tried swimming with them in open water. Pretty stupid, if you ask me."

"People in the Salish Sea say they were afraid because the sisters hunted in tandem."

"Yeah, well, they learned to do that out of fear. From the moment they were birthed they were afraid of their mother. My father was actually in the lagoon, circling Angel in one of the old Abyss Gliders in an attempt to distract her. As each pup shot out of her birth canal, my uncle Mac would net them and haul them out of the lagoon and into the Meg Pen before she could kill them."

"Which is exactly why the public considers these sharks to be such a menace. I mean, come on—what species eats its own young?"

"Megs don't eat their young, Melissa. With Angel, it was a decision based on the limited capacity of her habitat. The same strategy applied to the sisters. The lagoon and Meg Pen are actually connected by an underwater tunnel. We kept it closed, of course, but the pups could still detect the presence of their mother. She was the Alpha-Meg and Bela and Lizzy were afraid of her, so they swam in tandem. Eventually they became co-Alphas in their own tank, which is why they were always bullying the three runts."

"Bullying? Angelica was eaten."

"Technically, she was eviscerated. Again, it was a territorial thing. As you can see, the Meg Pen is too small to support five adult females, so the sisters went after the three runts while they still had the size advantage. The triplets may have been born smaller, but they were genetic clones of Angel. The surviving runt in Dubai-Land will eventually be as big and as nasty as her mama. Make no mistake about it: The three runts would have eventually killed the sisters. Bela and Lizzy simply made a preemptive strike."

Glancing over her shoulder, he saw Monty sitting up, motioning to his iPhone.

"One last question, David. As you know, aquariums are being pressured to release their captive orca back into the wild. Even if you can locate another Megalodon pup . . . my question is, should you?"

He was about to answer her when Monty abruptly walked on camera, handing him his iPhone. "Your ex is blowing up both our phones . . . something about drowning."

David took the phone. "Jackie?"

"Brutus escaped and I'm trapped in the hold, which is filling up with water—David, help me!"

"Calm down. Did you say Brutus escaped?"

"And I'm trapped in the goddamn hold!"

"Okay . . . okay." He glanced around the deck. "Monty, the Manta's in the dry dock; I need to get there in a hurry. Can you find us a maintenance vehicle?"

James Gelet stepped forward, his camera still rolling. "Our van is parked outside the northern gate."

They followed him out the closest exit to the parking lot. The segment producer tossed the keys to Monty and climbed in back to film while David hopped in front, speed-dialing a number on his iPhone—

—hanging on for dear life as his friend accelerated, the van racing south across the arena's parking lot at eighty miles an hour. "Come on, Uncle Mac . . . pick up."

The call went straight to voice mail: "This is Mac. Me and the kid are busy soiling our diapers and taking naps. Leave a message if you want to annoy me, otherwise go to—"

Beep.

"Uncle Mac, Jackie just called. She said Brutus escaped and the *Tonga* is sinking. Call the Coast Guard."

Monty exited the lot and headed west down a private access road leading to a concrete pier. The security gate was unlocked and he bashed it open with the front bumper, accelerating along the one-lane concrete path while six-foot swells crested and broke between the pilings beneath them.

David glanced to his right. The pier ran parallel to the lagoon's canal, which extended into the Pacific two hundred yards to the west. Farther out, the *Tonga* dominated the horizon, its superstructure towering above the Pacific.

If the tanker was sinking, it certainly wasn't obvious to the naked eye.

David grabbed the dashboard as the van skidded to a halt in front of a single-story building at the far end of the dock. Exiting the vehicle, he hurried inside the submersible maintenance and launch area, known to the staff as the "Sub Shack," where he found the institute's chief engineer, Cyel Reed, seated at a large wood table, using a mounted magnifying glass to examine the inner workings of a pocket watch.

"Well, look who it is? Little Boss Man."

"Cyel, I need a Manta!"

"Do you now? Did you clear it with the Big Boss Man?"

"I'm a partner; I don't have to clear anything with anybody."

"You're a junior partner, Junior. That makes you a worker bee, just like me. And us worker bees don't collect honey until we're guaranteed the money . . . as in a new contract—*capiche*?"

David felt the blood rush to his face as Monty entered, followed by James Gelet with a camera perched on his shoulder.

"Well? What are you waiting for? Go save your Baby Mama."

David hurried past Cyel to the back room. There were four launch cradles poised over four sealed hatches on the floor. Three were vacant, and the fourth held Manta-7, a two-man submersible with a nine-foot wingspan and contours similar to that of Manta birostris, the aquatic species that had inspired its design.

The vessel's chassis was composed of a seamless layered acrylic that supported its cockpit, a spherical, clear, Lexan escape pod that could withstand nineteen thousand pounds per square inch of water pressure.

Powered by dual pump-jet propulsor units, the Manta was quiet, fast, and neutrally buoyant. The two hydrogen tanks mounted on its back added another gear—a forty-second burn that temporarily transformed the deep-water submersible into a rocket.

"Cyel, where's the remote? . . . Never mind." He saw the key fob hanging from its lanyard on a hook and placed it around his neck. Powering on the device, he pressed the green button labeled OPEN.

With a hiss of hydraulics, the dark-tinted acrylic top popped free from its assembly and yawned open, allowing him to climb down into the portside bucket seat of the two-man cockpit.

David powered up the engine and then quickly strapped his feet onto the two foot pedals, his eyes taking a brief scan of the wraparound control panel.

"Jesus, Cyel, the fuel cell's at nineteen percent! How hard is it to recharge the goddamn battery?"

"Tell your new partner that he'll get one hundred percent when I get a new contract . . . and don't blaspheme in my workshop."

"Ugh!" David resealed the cockpit and pressed LAUNCH on the keypad, causing the horizontal doors beneath the submersible to open. Gray-green swells rolled below the pier's pilings.

David's iPhone rang as the hydraulic cradle began lowering the Manta into the incoming surf. "Jackie?"

"David, where are you!"

"On my way." He waited for the next swell to pass before releasing the cradle.

The Manta splashed down on its belly. David quickly engaged both foot pedals, the twin pump-jet propulsor units accelerating the submersible into the next swell—

—his right hand pushing down on the joystick, diving the craft into deeper water as it shot out from between the last set of pilings.

"Jackie, what section of the keel is the hole on?"

"Somewhere in the stern." Jackie stood upon the steel framework, the crown of her skull pressed against the underside of the deck, the rising water already up to her knees. "David, please hurry."

———

Lee Shone followed the two cameramen, key grip, soundman, makeup artist, and second unit director down three flights of stairs to a small corridor that led to a watertight door set inside the bulkhead. The mixed-martial-arts-fighter-turned-actor had been hired by the crown prince as the master of ceremonies to introduce the Liopleurodon to Dubai-Land's VIPs. The footage taken in the hold with the Micocene whale would be used in an upcoming episode of the reality series . . . or so his agent was told.

Jon "Ponyboy" Cesario had directed half the reality show episodes aboard the *Tonga*. He was familiar with the hold, having shot six hours of worthless B-Roll of the dozing whale over the previous two weeks.

Three hours earlier his crew had mounted spotlights in half a dozen locations along the port and starboard rails in anticipation of some promised "action" shots. Having instructed his cameramen, he waited impatiently for the makeup artist to finish powdering Lee Shone's forehead.

"Okay, big guy, we'll get a few takes of you opening the watertight door, then it's up to Brutus. Hopefully he's more awake than he was earlier; otherwise we're wasting our time."

The British-born action star examined the steel watertight door. "So I push down on this lever and pull it open, yes?"

"Yeah, babe. Wait until we mark the scene and I say, 'Action.'"

An assistant stepped in front of the bearded fighter, holding up a Smart Slate that displayed the time code generated by the audio recorder. "Brutus hold, scene one—take one."

"Ready camera one."

"Ready live shot, sound full . . . and action."

Lee Shone pushed down on the handle and yanked open the watertight door—

—releasing an explosion of bone-chilling seawater that knocked the action star off his feet and blasted the film crew with the force of a fire hose.

The corridor filled within seconds, sweeping the director and his team out to the stairwell.

Still gripping the door, Lee Shone attempted to reseal the hatch, only there was nothing to brace his feet against for leverage, the water level already above his head.

Abandoning the effort, he released the door and swam out of the corridor to the stairwell to join the others.

———

David banked hard to starboard on a north-by-northwest heading. He descended to eighty feet, the silt-covered shallows suddenly dropping away to become a foreboding jagged crevasse, the keel of the *Tonga* emerging out of the murk up ahead.

Using the Manta's headlights, he searched the tanker's immense keel for a way in.

"Oh . . . geez."

The whale's impact had punched loose a forty-foot seam of rivets along the starboard side of the stern. The plates were still intact, but the gap was wide enough to drive a train through.

David guided the sub through the opening, his ears immediately assaulted by the sound of screeching steel.

The tanker's superstructure's in the stern. With all that weight, she'll roll bow-up and sink ass-first.

"Jackie, I'm inside. Jackie, where are you?" He glanced at his iPhone, the call having disconnected.

Easing up on the foot pedals, he halved his speed and rose along one of the hold's interior walls, his left hand redialing Jackie's number—

—his heart racing as the phone went straight to voice mail.

"Come on, show me an air pocket. . . ."

He jumped as the Manta's prow struck the steel framework supporting the tanker's enormous deck.

The entire hold's underwater. . . . I'm too late!

He caught the splash of bubbles in his peripheral vision and veered toward it.

The girl appeared pale in the sub's lights and then she was sprawled across his hatch, her blue eyes wide in terror, her strawberry-blond hair blown out, the herky-jerky limbs telling him she was drowning, with no air pocket in which he could surface to allow her inside the sub.

"No!" David released his harness and spun around in his seat to the storage compartment, his right arm stretching out, straining to reach the pony bottle of air. Snatching it, he twisted back around and reached for the launch controls dangling from the lanyard around his neck. He pressed the green button as Jackie burped out her last bite of air and went limp, her body floating away.

Asshole . . . it won't open underwater. You have to override the safety measures.

Ripping open the center console, he felt inside for the emergency override and twisted the control a half-turn counterclockwise before pulling it up—

—causing the hatch to pop loose from its seal and open, flooding the cockpit with frigid water.

David stood and pushed it open wider. Grabbing Jackie by her wrist, he dragged her limp body inside and resealed the hatch.

A yellow light labeled BILGE PUMP blinked on his dashboard. He pressed it with his left thumb as his right hand pinched Jackie's nose and held her mouth shut. The water level had already dropped below her neck by the time he slipped the pony bottle's mouthpiece between her purple lips and squeezed the purge button, releasing a blast of air inside her mouth that filled her belly—causing her to vomit out the seawater she had swallowed.

Continuing to pinch her nose, he opened her airway and pressed his lips to hers, expelling three quick breaths into her lungs. He paused to feel for a pulse along her carotid artery, then repeated the breathing ritual as the *Tonga* lurched and rolled around his vessel, sinking stern-first.

Fiesal bin Rashidi had returned to the helicopter to find his luggage stowed on board, but no pilot. He located Captain Gilbert Gregg at the Lio tank, the former Navy flight instructor standing with his back to the glass, attempting to take a selfie with his iPhone as the creature circled the aquarium.

"Pilot, the crown prince insists you fly me back to the hotel at once."

"Sure thing. Just do me a solid and take my picture with the Lio; I can't seem to time it right." The captain handed him his iPhone.

"This is ridiculous; we are paying you to service our group, not to take photos. Take me back now, or I'll toss this phone into the sea!"

"Captain, what seems to be the problem?"

Fiesal turned to see Walid Abu Naba'a and his entourage approaching.

The pilot snatched back his iPhone. "Your Highness, this man is insisting I fly him back to San Francisco."

"Those were *your* orders, cousin."

Kirsty Joyce inspected Fiesal's pants. "Why are you all wet?"

"A harmless prank . . . one of the crew hosed me down when he heard I was leaving. I'll change back at the hotel."

The crown prince was about to respond when the crowd *oohed* and *aahed*. Turning to face the aquarium, he realized the Liopleurodon had broken off from its circular pattern and was cutting sharp figure eights, bashing its head against the thick Lexan glass.

"Fiesal, why is it behaving this way?"

"I wouldn't know; you'll have to ask Ms. Buchwald."

"Summon her."

"I can't—I turned in my walkie-talkie. Cousin, my father is very sick; I am attempting to catch an earlier flight out of San Francisco. Please—"

"Stop whining, Fiesal." The crown prince turned to the pilot. "Get him off my ship."

The pilot pocketed his iPhone and headed back to the helipad, Fiesal walking ahead of him, mentally urging the man to quicken his pace.

"You'll have to change."

"Of course . . . as soon as I get back to the hotel."

"No, you'll change now; otherwise you'll get the seat all wet."

"It won't be a problem; I'll sit on my luggage. Please . . . I'm trying to catch a flight." Reaching into his back pocket, he retrieved his wallet and pulled out three soggy hundred-dollar bills. "Your tip . . . in advance."

The captain pocketed the cash in the breast pocket of his Windbreaker and climbed into his seat, starting up the engine. Fiesal ducked in back, sitting on his duffel bag. Buckling his seat belt, he placed a pair of headphones over his ears and glanced out the windows on the right side of the craft—his pulse quickening as he saw the reality show's second unit emerge from the *Tonga*'s superstructure, everyone dripping wet and in a state of panic.

He could not hear their shouts over the sound of the overhead rotors, but he knew what they were saying.

He closed his eyes and thanked Allah as the chopper mercifully lifted off—

—his heart sinking as it hovered ten feet off the deck before setting down again.

"Captain, what are you doing?"

Gil Gregg motioned to the left, where the two security men in dark suits had their guns drawn and aimed at the pilot. One of the men wrenched open the sliding door and hustled the VIPs in back while the crown prince climbed up front to occupy the vacant copilot's seat.

He turned to face Fiesal as the tanker lurched beneath them. "You would leave me to die, cousin?"

"One good turn . . ."

Walid Abu Naba'a motioned to the nearest bodyguard, who grabbed Fiesal by the wrist and dragged him off the chopper.

The engineer landed on his back on the helipad tarmac, the headphones ripped from his ears as the helicopter lifted off.

For a long moment Fiesal remained on his back, watching the airship disappear from view. And then he felt the tanker lurch beneath him as the *Tonga*'s bow rose slowly out of the sea.

The breaths aren't getting in; she must still have water in her lungs. . . .

Pulling her inert body onto his lap, David reached his arms around her waist and squeezed her belly in a Heimlich maneuver. The abdominal thrust released a mixture of seawater and cappuccino, the marine biologist's pale complexion flushing pink as she coughed and drew a breath.

"You okay?"

She nodded, hugging him around the neck. "Thank you."

"Don't thank me yet. Better buckle in—this could get rough."

He helped her snap the harness across her chest. Then he strapped himself in and engaged the starboard propulsor unit, descending in a vertigo-inducing, hundred-eighty-degree roll as the tanker began sinking stern-first into the Monterey Submarine Canyon.

The Manta's lights darted across endless walls of steel plates and dead ends.

"Shit . . ."

"David, get us out of here!"

"Really?" He reached across her chest for the sonar—only to find the controls covered in vomit. Wiping the debris from the screen with his right hand, he pressed ACTIVE.

Ping . . . ping . . . ping . . .

The sound reverberated around the hold, painting his surroundings on the screen. He rotated the three-dimensional image until a void appeared below and to his left. Wiping his palm clean on Jackie's pants, David reached again for the joystick—this time turning hard to port.

The Manta submersible shot out of the *Tonga*'s mortal wound—

—directly into the path of the eighty-foot *Livyatan melvillei*.

"Kess Ommak!" The Arabic curse was muffled by the dull beating of helicopter blades receding to the east and a long-drawn-out protest of steel.

Fiesal bin Rashidi jumped as the deck trembled beneath his feet. He ran to the starboard rail and looked forward in time to see the bow of the three-hundred-fifty-thousand-ton tanker slowly lift out of the Pacific, the deck shifting beneath his feet.

Five degrees . . .

Ten.

Screams rent the air as the hundred and thirty-nine invited guests suddenly realized what was happening.

He looked to the north for a Coast Guard cutter, but saw only vacant ocean, then grabbed for the rail as the deck listed twenty degrees.

He glanced to the east and saw the walls of the Tanaka canal a half-mile swim away. Looking down, he estimated the surface to be a good six stories below, the distance increasing as the bow rose higher.

Too high to jump. Get to the stern and jump before it sinks and sucks you below with it.

Twenty-five degrees.

He attempted to ease his way down the slanting deck to the stern by holding on to the rail, only to realize the *Tonga* was rotating vertically too quickly to manage his footing.

He stripped off his suit jacket and straddled the rail backward. Using the garment to protect his hands, he slid backward like a kid on a banister, quickly shooting past the mid-deck.

He looked to his left as he passed the aquarium.

Water was pouring over the lowering side of the tank. The Liopleur-odon was swimming back and forth against the angled glass, its habitat diminishing by a thousand gallons a minute.

———

Lee Shone had escaped the flooded corridor and stairwell, only to find the watertight door leading out to the main deck blocked from the other side. With the sea rising behind him, the mixed martial arts fighter had forced the gauntlet open just enough to squeeze his way out—

—emerging on a tilting deck buried beneath a labyrinth of metal.

Like a mountain climber buried beneath an avalanche, Shone had fought his way to daylight, battling not only an entanglement of alumi-num that had been the south bleacher, but a steadily increasing stream that was quickly turning into a waterfall.

Emerging from the refuse, he stood triumphantly—only to realize he had crawled out of the frying pan and into the fire.

Six hundred feet of deck rose before him like a steel mountain—the *Tonga* listing at forty degrees as it slipped backward into the Pacific. Water was pouring over the top of the Lio tank, the structure looming over him sixty feet up the slanted incline—

—its anchored base squealing in protest as it pulled away from the deck.

Move!

Lee Shone waded through the torrent as fast as his legs could carry him, his eyes never leaving the glass edifice barreling at him until he cleared the flood zone. He heard the crash of Lexan glass meeting alu-minum bleachers a second before a wave of water and shrapnel blasted him from behind and sent him hurtling face-first against the rail. The action star held on until gray sky and blue sea returned.

"Ugh . . . gad almighty, whit's next then?"

He turned to see the answer slithering his way, its crocodilian jaws snapping at him.

Without looking, Lee Shone climbed over the rail and leaped seventy feet into the Pacific.

Stamping down on both foot pedals, David wrenched the joystick hard to starboard, the Manta's port wing just clearing the closing jaws of the Miocene whale.

"It doesn't like the pinging. . . . Switch it!"

"Switch what?"

"The sonar!" David leaned across the center console, only to be flung back in his bucket seat by the harness.

Jackie reached for the sonar, shutting it off.

"No, don't shut it off—switch it from active to passive and tell me where he is."

She complied, pulling the headphones over her ears to hear a *clickety-click* sound amid the thunder of protesting steel. "Behind us . . . he's turning . . . sounds like he's heading deep."

"Keep listening." Pulling back on the joystick, David headed for the surface, keeping the sinking tanker off his starboard wing.

David leveled out the sub at thirty feet as the ocean became a deep blue tapestry of churning legs and arms and fresh bodies raining down randomly from above, each muted splash accompanied by a sinkhole of air.

A human torpedo shot past the Manta's left wing, the bearded man's eyes wide as he took in the dark blurred shadow of their vessel.

"Guy's pretty deep; I'd better help him up." David was about to loop beneath the terrified jumper when an immense object splashed down directly ahead of the sub in an eruption of churning brown limbs and receding bubbles.

The Liopleurodon righted itself and swam straight for Lee Shone, its jaws opening—

Whomp!

The Manta's left wing struck the Lio in its chest, stunning the plio-saur and pile-driving it twenty feet before it twisted away. With two rapid lunges of its forelimbs, it darted toward the depths and disappeared.

––––––––––

It was rare that Lee Shone tasted defeat, but the fighter knew it was over. His chest burned, his legs felt like lead, and he was no longer rising. With his last ounce of strength, he reached his hand futilely for a surface still thirty feet above his head.

And then, miraculously, he was rising! With a *whoosh,* he broke the surface to find himself straddling a dark object, his arms wrapped around a plastic bubble . . . and there were people in it.

The sub carried him east to one of the walls of the canal that led inside the Tanaka Lagoon. He pulled himself out of the water onto the top of the concrete barrier, the low tide exposing a footpath that led into the empty arena.

Distant screams caused him to turn. He saw the tanker's bow point straight into the air, towering six hundred feet above the sea. And then its twelve-story superstructure disappeared below the surface, drawing the rest of the eleven-hundred-foot-long ship with it.

––––––––––

Fiesal bin Rashidi quickly realized he had made a fatal mistake in not removing his shoes, dress shirt, and pants before leaping overboard. Not only were his clothes weighing him down, they were entangled around his limbs, restricting his movements. After only a dozen strokes he could barely keep his head above water.

He felt the *Tonga* grab hold of him as it began to sink. For an exhausting twenty seconds he fought back, his arms flailing at the surface to keep his face clear of the sea.

And then the ship went down, and he knew his life was over, the weight displacement dragging him under with a sudden ferocity that was terrifying. Water shot up into his nostrils, forcing him to pinch his nose. Within seconds his ears were popping, his head feeling as if it were in a vise, about to explode.

For a glorious second Fiesal actually thought it had exploded and that he had passed, his soul rising from the depths into heaven. And then he was out of the water, only he wasn't dead . . . he was sitting on a small island, bouncing along the waves.

Looking behind him, he thought he saw Jackie Buchwald and that maybe he really was dead. And then he was back in the water, a Coast Guard cutter close by, a motorized raft bearing down on him, filled with passengers from the *Tonga*.

———

David dove the Manta after the sinking tanker, but by now the ship's bow was seven hundred feet below the surface. Dozens of bodies were caught in its wake, chasing after the *Tonga* until they too disappeared into the darkness.

San Francisco Medical Center
San Francisco, California

The man was lost.

For the entirety of his adult existence he had been the master of his domain—a domain defined by the sea. He had joined the Navy immediately after graduating from Penn State University with the goal of becoming a SEAL, but the results on an aptitude test had convinced his commanding officer that the cocky twenty-two-year-old possessed the traits that would make for an outstanding Argonaut candidate.

Submersibles were a relatively new field at the time. The *Alvin* had recently returned from expeditions at the bottom of the Atlantic, presenting discoveries that had shocked the scientific world—entire communities of life living in darkness, having sprouted from chemicals gushing out of hydrothermal vents. The scalding 700-degree-Fahrenheit elixir of chemicals and minerals served as the bottom of a chemosynthetic-based food chain . . . a primordial soup that may just have seeded life on our planet.

The Navy hadn't been interested in discovering exotic new life-forms;

it had invested in a small fleet of submersibles specifically designed for rescue and salvage missions, and needed pilots with ice water in their veins. Over the next eight years, Commander Jonas Taylor had established himself as the military's most dependable deep-sea Argonaut, meeting his future wife, reporter Maggie Cobbs, in the process.

And then disaster had struck.

Jonas had been training for a top-secret series of dives seven miles down in the Mariana Trench. On his fourth descent in a week, the exhausted submersible pilot had panicked, racing the three-man craft too quickly to the surface. Pipes had burst, causing pressurization problems that led to the deaths of the two scientists on board. Jonas had survived—barely—only to learn his commanding officer blamed him for the incident. "Despite the fact that we had a competent backup pilot aboard the surface ship, Commander Taylor insisted upon making the last dive himself. Completing the descent, he experienced what our chief medical officer described as an 'aberration of the deep.' Taylor lost it down there, and his actions ended up costing the lives of two good men."

Jonas's testimony had described a different story:

"The Sea Cliff was hovering about ten meters above the hydrothermal plume. Dr. Prestis was working the drone's vacuum and the soothing vibrations of the motor were putting me to sleep. I must've drifted off because the next thing I knew the sonar was beeping—an immense object rising directly beneath us. Suddenly a ghost-white shark with a head bigger than our three-man sub emerged from the mineral ceiling, its gullet filling my keel portal."

The physician on duty had ordered Jonas to complete a ninety-day evaluation in a mental ward, after which he had received a dishonorable discharge—a parting gift from his commanding officer, who intended to deflect his own culpability for ordering the exhausted pilot to make the dive.

With his naval career over, Jonas had set out to prove the albino monster he had encountered was not a product of his imagination. Five years later he had graduated from the Scripps Institution with a doctorate degree in paleobiology. A published book followed, theorizing how ancient sea creatures living in isolated extremes could evolve in order to survive extinction.

Colleagues had panned his work, squelching his new career. Meanwhile, on the home front, Maggie had been secretly having an affair with his millionaire friend, Bud Harris.

While Jonas had been struggling to reinvent himself, world-renowned cetacean biologist Masao Tanaka had been completing construction of a new aquatic facility on the coast of Monterey, California. The Tanaka Oceanographic Institute was essentially a man-made lagoon with an ocean-access canal that intersected one of the largest annual whale migrations on the planet. Designed as a field laboratory, the waterway had been intended to be a place where pregnant gray whales, returning from their feeding grounds in the Bering Sea, could birth their calves. Masao had been so convinced his facility would bridge the gap between science and entertainment that he had mortgaged his entire family fortune on the endeavor.

Rising construction costs had forced the cetacean biologist to accept a contract with the Japan Marine Science and Technology Center—JAMSTEC. The mission: to anchor sensory drones along the seafloor of the Mariana Trench, creating an early-warning earthquake detection system. To complete the array, D.J. Tanaka, Masao's son, had to escort each drone to the bottom using an Abyss Glider, a torpedo-shaped one-man submersible.

When several of the drones had stopped transmitting data, Masao had needed a second diver to help D.J. retrieve one of the damaged aquabots in order to diagnose the problem.

He had sent his daughter, Terry, to recruit Jonas Taylor.

Jonas had accepted the offer, desiring only to recover an unfossilized white Megalodon tooth photographed in the wreckage—the evidence he needed to prove the monstrous sharks still existed.

The dive had ended badly, Jonas and D.J. coming face-to-face with not one, but two Megs. The first had been a forty-five-foot male that had become entangled in the surface ship's cable; the second had been its sixty-foot mate, a pregnant female that was accidentally lured out of the trench and into surface waters teeming with food.

The Tanaka Institute had taken on the task of capturing the creature; Jonas and Masao determined to quarantine the monster inside the whale lagoon. JAMSTEC had agreed to refit the canal entrance with King Kong–size steel doors to keep their would-be attraction from escaping.

The hunt had lasted a month, culminating in an act that would haunt Jonas's dreams over the next thirty years. All had not been lost—the Megalodon's surviving pup was captured and raised in Masao's cetacean facility—and a monster shark cottage industry had been born.

Angel: The Angel of Death
Two shows daily. Always your money's worth!

Jonas had married Terry Tanaka. Angel had grown into a seventy-four-foot albino nightmare that drew crowds from across the world, earning the Tanaka-Taylor family hundreds of millions of dollars. She had also managed to escape twice, birth two litters of pups, and devour no less than a dozen humans—five of them in her own lagoon.

Births and deaths, lawsuits, and around-the-clock stress. Jonas and Terry's daughter, Danielle, had nearly died as "Megalodon Bait" on a South Pacific–based reality show, while son, David—who seemed to have experienced more lives than a cat—had attempted suicide after he witnessed his first love, Kaylie, die the most gruesome death imaginable, literally having been eaten alive before his eyes.

The accumulated stress had taken a toll on his wife. Terry had been diagnosed with Parkinson's disease, and while the meds and natural extracts had kept the symptoms manageable, the recent voyage to the Antarctic to save her son was manifesting itself in severe stomach pains.

Jonas had taken her for a battery of tests, all while attempting to convince her—and himself—that it was just an ulcer. "The doc will prescribe meds, you'll feel like your old self, and then we're off to Boca Raton to meet with a Realtor and start our new life together."

They had been summoned to the medical center that afternoon.

Dani, who was in her second year of medical school at University of California San Francisco, had insisted on coming with them for support. Terry had not wanted her to miss class, but Jonas was relieved she was there. The three had been waiting in the exam room for nearly twenty minutes when Terry's physician, Dr. Katherine Simmons, entered . . . followed by a male colleague.

"Terry, this is Dr. Ethan Brennan. He'll be a consultant on your case."

"What kind of specialist are you?" Dani asked.

"I'm an oncologist."

Gravity in the small room seemed to increase. Jonas felt Terry squeeze his hand as the cancer doctor rendered his wife's verdict, his cadence calm but direct.

"All right, so this is melanoma. Melanoma is the one skin cancer that can spread to all our other organs. It's gone away from the original site, which was your cheek, and moved into your liver. There are nodules in your right lung and also the peritoneum, the lining that covers the abdominal cavity. It may have been there for a few weeks or a few months, but like all cancers, it reaches a critical stage where we start to see symptoms."

"What stage is this?" Jonas asked, praying for a low number.

"This is stage four."

Jonas felt his body sink as if the physician's words had punched him in the gut.

"There are a couple of things I think need to be done, and quickly. My recommendation is that we try to find a clinical trial. And the reason I say that is because standard therapies for melanoma are not very good. The success rate with chemo is only about fifteen percent. However, there are a lot of new and exciting drugs that are now being studied for melanoma. I've made a few calls to UCLA. Katherine, you had mentioned you have a colleague at Penn?"

"Yes, we'll try there as well."

"How long, Dr. Brennan?" Terry's question seemed to draw Jonas back into his body.

"It's hard to say. Everyone is different."

"How long?"

"Three months."

————————

Danielle walked her parents to their car. "Listen to me—this is a speed bump, not a wall. I'm going to see my adviser the moment I get back to school. He'll get me a list of every clinical trial in the United States. We'll get you through this."

"Thank you, Dani."

Danielle hugged her mother, registering the weakness in her upper torso.

Jonas opened the car door for his wife, then hugged his daughter. "Thanks, kiddo."

"Stay positive. And no stress."

"Drive carefully." He climbed inside the Lexus, only to see Terry staring at her iPhone in disbelief. "What?"

He took the device from her trembling hands and enlarged the image on the screen.

Miocene Whale Sinks Tanker
Outside Tanaka Institute
Forty-eight dead; Liopleurodon escapes

"Jesus . . ." He handed back her phone and removed his own from his jacket pocket. "Call David; make sure he's all right."

"Who are you calling?"

"Tom Cubit."

"Why do you need to speak with our attorney? This is Paul Agricola and the crown prince's problem, not ours."

"You're right—what was I thinking."

She reached out and held his wrist. "What aren't you telling me?"

Jonas exhaled. "That sleazeball prince never signed the contract with Paul."

"Then he still owns the institute."

"Technically his partner, Fiesal bin Rashidi, owns it. We've been waiting for the crown prince to fly in from Dubai to sign off on the deal. . . . He arrived last night. Tommy sent his paralegal to his hotel this morning with the final purchase agreement. The prince's attorney said he was in meetings, but she'd have him sign everything this afternoon before the press conference."

"The press conference on board the tanker that just sank?"

"I know what you're thinking. In a worst-case scenario, we'll simply sell the institute directly to Agricola Industries."

"He won't sign without immunity from this accident."

"What's the difference? We had nothing to do with the *Tonga*."

"Jonas, you know how these class-action lawsuits go—the attorneys sue everyone. We also helped capture the *Livyatan melvillei*. And if the Liopleurodon remains in coastal waters and adds a bather or two to its menu, you can bet we'll be blamed for that as well."

Jonas laid his head back and laughed, tears of frustration pouring from his eyes. For the past thirty-plus years he had been riding this same roller coaster day in and day out; always worried about someone getting hurt around these creatures . . . the liabilities . . . the toll it took on his family.

Hearing his wife's prognosis . . . the stress had finally broken him.

Terry wrapped her arms around her man and hugged him. She had always been the strong one. . . . Even when the oncologist had given her a death sentence, she was there to console Jonas and Dani. If this was to be her final chapter, so be it . . . she would face it on her terms—protecting her family, seeing to it they were well equipped to go on without her until the moment her soul finally shed the garment of flesh that now caused her so much pain and her soul could pass on in peace.

Tanaka Oceanographic Institute
Monterey, California

It was dark by the time David had secured Manta-7 in its berth, the sub's fuel cell indicator blinking red. Popping open the Lexan top, he inhaled the cool fresh air before unbuckling his harness.

Monty reached down to help Jackie out of the cockpit. "Ms. Buch-wald . . . nice to see you again. Good Lord, what is that stench? Smells like something up and died in there."

"Yes, that would have been me."

"In that case, welcome back."

David climbed out of the sub, waving off James Gelet, who was film-ing. "Don't, man. A lot of people drowned out there. The tanker liter-ally dragged them down into the canyon with it as they tried to swim ashore."

"Gonna be a lot of floaters," Monty said. "You'd better shut the canal doors, or the tide'll bring them right into the lagoon. Am I right, Cyel, or am I right?"

"Don't get used to it, Cuckoo's Nest. Even a broken clock is right twice a day." The engineer stepped down into the cockpit, trailing a long power cord. He opened a compartment on the center console and connected the charger to the fuel cell outlet. "Why's the damn carpet all wet? And who hurled all over my sonar? I'm sure as shit not clean-ing this up."

"Relax, old man, I'll do it tomorrow."

"It's my fault," Jackie said. "I drowned. David brought me back . . . he saved my life." She turned to him, her hair entangled, her clothing still wet. "Is there someplace we can talk in private?"

"Sure." He led her through the work area and grabbed an old hooded sweatshirt hanging on a hook, handing it to Jackie, who was shivering.

"Thanks." She removed her wet top and handed it to him, leaving on her bra. He admired her body as she pulled the sweatshirt over her head, recalling their first night together aboard the *Mogamigawa*.

He had been in the throes of a night terror when she had knocked on his cabin door, wearing only a loose-fitting, gray sleeping shirt offering tantalizing hints of her naked breasts pressing beneath the thin cotton fabric.

"What are you doing here?"

"My cabin's next door; you were screaming."

"Bad dream." He sat on the edge of the bed, shivering.

She searched through a pile of clothing, pulling out a clean shirt. "Put this on."

He pulled off the wet T-shirt, revealing an athlete's muscular upper torso . . . and the thick three-inch red scars embedded along the palm-side of each wrist. He re-dressed quickly, covering the evidence of his attempted suicide with the wet T-shirt.

"David, there's no need to be embarrassed. It's just a scar."

"It's a little more than a scar, don't you think?"

"Only if you continue to dwell upon it. Give yourself a break."

"You sound like my shrink."

"Been there, done that. Antidepressants . . . alcohol therapy. You'd be amazed how normal you are compared to the rest of us. Back at Brown, all I cared about was filling out my resume—scared to death I wouldn't be able to find a job after graduating. I spent three years as a professional dancer while I was an undergrad, just in case the whole marine biology deal fell through. I think the crown prince chose me more for my legs than my grade point average." She stood on her toes, her leg muscles flexing as she assumed a ballet pose, her raised arms causing her shirt to ride up her hips, revealing a flash of her shaved vagina.

David's heart pounded in his chest, the blood rushing to his groin.

"So, what was it about?"

"What was what about?"

"The nightmare. Do you get them often?"

"Yeah."

"I know a cure; guaranteed to get you seven hours of sleep a night."

"I don't like sleeping pills—they make me feel weird."

"Who said anything about a pill? I was talking about sex." In one motion, she pulled the gray shirt over her head, revealing her naked body.

"We work in a stress-filled environment, David, filled with very real scary monsters. At the end of a long day I need to let loose. I'm not interested in love; this is purely about preventing nightmares."

"By having sex?"

"No. By fucking each other's brains out before we go to sleep. Think you can handle that? Or would you rather take an Ambien?"

Jackie glanced at the University of Florida decal on the sweatshirt. "U of F—is this where you graduated from?"

"I came up one or two semesters short."

"You should go back and finish."

"When the time's right."

"Let's talk outside." She led him out the main entrance onto the pier.

Dark waves rolled beneath the dock. In the distance were two Coast Guard cutters, their powerful searchlights cutting white swaths across the sea, directing smaller vessels.

"David . . . when the whale went berserk . . . everything happened so quickly. But when I was trapped along the framework beneath the hold's ceiling, watching the water rise . . . I had time to think. I thought about my life . . . what would I change if I could? I thought about us.

"When the water rose higher, I had my face pressed to the ceiling. . . . I was so scared. I took my last breath—realizing it was my last breath— and that's when I saw the Manta's lights and swam toward them . . . not because I expected to be rescued—I honestly didn't know you could do what you did. I swam to you, because I wanted you to be the last person I saw before I died."

He hugged her, feeling her sob against his chest. "It's okay. Everything's going to be fine."

She choked out a laugh. "You're so young."

"Hey, I'm only three years younger than you."

"I didn't mean your chronological age. You're still so young in that the world hasn't shit on you yet. I've been on my own since I was fourteen. I've seen the ugly side of life. Believe me, with what happened today . . . things are going to get ugly."

"Whatever. We'll deal with it a day at a time. First thing we have to do is get you some clothes. We can go to my parents' house and borrow some of my sister's stuff."

She pulled his face to hers and they kissed briefly—David pulling away.

"Sorry, I forgot my breath still smells."

Carmel, California

The ride from the Tanaka Institute's parking lot to the home of Jonas and Terry Taylor took twenty minutes, the last two miles through a private neighborhood that hugged the cliffs overlooking one of the most breathtaking coastlines in the world.

A gated driveway wound around to a series of garages and the second-story entrance of the Taylors' forty-six-hundred-square-foot, four-bedroom, five-bath home. David parked his Jeep off to the side, then led Jackie to the solid oak front door.

He had a key, but he knocked anyway, not wanting to disturb his parents.

His mother answered, wearing a red kimono bathrobe and sadness in her almond eyes.

Her face lit up when she saw her son. "David, thank God. Where have you been? I've been calling you for the last five hours."

"My phone got a little wet. You remember Jackie."

"Hi, Mrs. Taylor. As you can see, everything got a little wet."

"Leave your shoes outside and come in. Your father and I have been worried sick. Did you hear about the *Tonga*?"

Jackie nodded as she untied her shoes. "I was on board when it went down. Your son saved my life."

"Did he now?"

"I happened to be in the neighborhood." David tossed his wet running shoes and socks by the stoop and entered his parents' home.

Terry watched the strawberry-blonde squeeze the water out of her son's socks and then set both pairs of shoes neatly by the stoop.

The Taylors' home was a U-shaped, glass-and-stone-walled structure perched on a bluff overlooking Otter Cove. The house was split into two wings, with nearly half its foundation built within the cliff, divided by a courtyard and a long connecting curved-glass hall that looked out onto the crashing Pacific.

The upper floor of the estate was decorated in polished marble, the main hall divided by a grand staircase. To the left were three bedrooms and two full bathrooms, to the right a master suite and gym.

David turned as his father made his way up the stairs. "Hey, Dad. Don't hug me, I'm all wet."

"I don't care." Jonas embraced his son, kissing him on the cheek. "Are you kids hungry? We just ate, but there's plenty left over."

"Thanks, absolutely. We'll shower and come down."

Terry took over. "Jonas, go change your shirt, you're all wet. Jackie, come with me, we'll find something of Dani's for you to wear."

She led Jackie down the hall to the left and inside the first bedroom on the right.

"Oh, wow."

A queen-size bed faced French doors leading out to a balcony—she could hear the waves crashing twenty feet below. To the right was a sitting area with a stone fireplace, to the left a walk-in closet and a large bathroom that connected with a guest room.

"You look to be about my daughter's size . . . help yourself. I'll put out some fresh towels; come downstairs when you are ready."

"Thank you."

Terry removed several body towels from a linen closet and left them on the double marble sink, exiting through the guest bedroom. Heading back down the hall, she entered the master suite.

The entire west wall of the Taylors' bedroom was made of glass, which looked out to a cove. Jonas was sitting on the edge of the king-size bed, talking to his son, who was seated on the polished wood floor across from the stone fireplace. He looked up as Terry entered. "I told him."

"Mom . . ." David's eyes were flush with tears.

"It's okay. We'll find a course of action that works, and that will be that."

"Are you guys still moving to Boca?"

"Once your mother is well."

"David, go shower. You're leaving wet marks all over my floor. When you're done, bring all of your wet clothes to the laundry room and I'll wash them. Will your girlfriend be spending the night?"

"Yes, only she's not my girlfriend."

"But I thought—"

"It's complicated, Mom. Jackie could have stayed here in California and worked with me; instead she decided to go back to Dubai to care for the Lio. I'm not sure the tanker sinking really changes anything."

Terry turned to Jonas. "David saved her life."

"And the Lio escaped . . . oh, boy."

"Exactly."

"Mom, don't start in with the karma stuff. Jackie's really upset; a lot of people died today and she's blaming herself."

"Why, David? What happened on board the *Tonga*?"

"Brutus went berserk, Mom . . . that's all I know."

Jonas glanced out the floor-to-ceiling windows as the waning three-quarter moon rose above a cluster of clouds, revealing dark swells rolling into Otter Cove. "Go shower, kid. We'll figure things out in the morning."

———

Shadows danced in the lunar light, causing a striped shore crab to scurry sideways on its hind legs and seek refuge beneath an outcropping of rock.

The seagull circled twice before landing on the wood rail of a narrow footpath. Steps led from a patch of lawn behind the Taylors' home, down the cliff face, to an oasis of beach nestled amid jagged formations of rock.

The bird stood vigil, waiting for the algae carried by the incoming tide to lure its meal out of hiding.

Well aware of its precarious place on the food chain, the crab fed as it waited for the incoming tide to wash ashore and conceal its getaway.

Ebb and flow . . . risk and reward . . . life and death—such was the balance of nature.

A mile to the north and four thousand feet below the surface, the members of a different food chain gathered to feast upon an unexpected bounty.

––––––––––

The Monterey Bay Submarine Canyon is an anomaly of geology. Fanning out over sixty miles of seafloor and extending as far west as the Farallon Islands, the trench runs deeper than the Grand Canyon and possesses twisting chasms more than a mile deep that slice through the shallows like the gnarled fingers of a groping hand.

One of these jagged channels stretches southeast across the subduction zone of the North American Plate and ends a mere hundred eighty-seven feet short of the entrance to the Tanaka Lagoon's canal. Follow the chasm's sheer vertical walls nearly two miles down and you'll arrive at a seafloor buried in sediment that dates back 1.8 million years to the Pleistocene Era.

––––––––––

The *Tonga* had plunged over nine thousand feet before her stern had struck bottom. The impact had collapsed her superstructure, leaving the tanker leaning bow-up against the chasm wall.

Spread out around the site of the wreck were the bodies of two dozen members of the supertanker's crew and another sixteen civilians. Unable to escape the sinking ship's weight displacement, they had been dragged underwater and drowned, their lungs filling with water, the depth's crushing embrace squeezing the air from their sinus passages.

For twelve hours, the *Tonga*'s dead had rested on the bottom, the corpses undergoing chemical changes from within.

Anaerobic bacteria originating from the large intestines decomposed protein and sugars within the tissues, releasing carbon and sulfur dioxide. These gases inflated the faces and abdomens of the dead, as well as the men's genitalia and the women's breasts.

By 6 a.m., the bodies began dancing off the bottom as if they were marionettes on a string.

The movement did not go unnoticed.

Since its capture a month before, the Liopleurodon had been fed daily at 8 a.m. and 6 p.m. To keep the creature "feisty" for his potential investors, the crown prince had instructed Jacqueline Buchwald to skip the prior day's feeding and provide its next meal at 4 p.m., when his guests were scheduled to be on board.

Daylight had chased the pliosaur and its sensitive nocturnal eyes into the depths; hunger forced it to feed. Having never hunted on its own, the twelve-foot-long, thousand-pound juvenile simply bull-rushed every life-form in its path—a strategy easily detected by its prey.

Fourteen hours after escaping captivity, the Lio barely had enough energy to propel itself along the canyon floor in order to breathe.

Instinct had led it back to the tanker, its senses homing in on electrical discharges generated by the shifting metal. It had been circling the wreck when the first body lifted away from the bottom.

The creature appeared to be injured; its movements slow and languished. Wasting no time, the Lio charged, its open jaws snatching the woman's corpse around the waist, its teeth puncturing clear through the soft, rotting flesh. Zigging and zagging along the seafloor, the pliosaur shook its head as it fed, trailing clouds of blood and unraveling intestines.

The sudden influx of fat and protein reenergized the Lio. Swooping back and forth through the debris, it snatched the severed lower torso by its left leg, gnawing its way through the buttocks and pelvic bone before it could swallow.

So consumed was the Lio with its meal that it failed to detect the threat entering its kill zone.

Moonlight had summoned the school of Humboldt squid up from the depths to feed upon krill. As large as an adult human, each cephalopod possessed eight lightning-quick tentacles, two longer sucker-equipped feeder arms, and a razor-sharp, parrot-like beak that could slash and devour its prey like a buzz saw. They were fast creatures, able to jettison either head-or tentacles-first at speeds up to 25 knots. Highly intelligent, the squid were ferocious fighters—especially when hunting in schools.

The arrival of dawn had chased the nocturnal creatures back into the canyon. Detecting the disturbance along the seafloor, they homed in on the source, their bioluminescent flesh flashing from red to white to startle their enemy.

Sensing the swarming pack, the Liopleurodon secured the remains of its meal in its jaws and sped away, its forward limbs churning up the bottom with each powerful stroke.

The squid were suddenly everywhere at once. Suctioned tentacles tugged at the human leg held tightly within the Lio's clenched jowls, stripping it down to the bone. Sharp beaks tore into the pliosaur's hide, causing it to snap at its attackers. It caught a six-foot Humboldt in its jaws and bit through the succulent flesh as the wounded creature released a burst of brown ink—a defense mechanism that chased off several attackers, which were quickly replaced by a dozen more.

The Lio fled, hugging the seafloor to protect its soft underbelly from being ravaged. It could not see, its sensitive eyes blinded by the squids' flashing bioluminescence and the silt it was stirring up with each stroke of its forelimbs. Through the chaos, its senses detected an electrical discharge, and it headed for that.

It was the *Tonga*, the ship's keel towering upright against the wall of the chasm. The pliosaur entered the tanker through the gap in its stern, the Humboldt squid in pursuit.

The predators quickly broke off the attack, the metallic surroundings scrambling their senses. Unable to relocate the hold opening, they bashed their bodies against the steel plates in an attempt to escape.

Banking in tight circles, the Lio charged through the swirling dervish of luminescent bodies, its stiletto-sharp fangs puncturing tentacles and crushing heads as the pliosaur gorged itself on squid.

Smacking its crocodilian mouth, it swallowed the morsels of soft flesh caught between its teeth as it rose through the *Tonga*'s flooded hold, gauging its new surroundings. Reaching the summit, it stroked its forelimbs along the metal surface of the bow, searching for a way out. Eventually it gave up and descended, urinating inside the tanker to mark its territory before locating the patch of seafloor that designated the opening of its new habitat.

Monterey, California

The law offices of Cubit and Cubit had locations in Fort Lauderdale and San Francisco, but the firm's founder and senior partner preferred to work out of a modest two-story stucco dwelling on Lighthouse Avenue in downtown Monterey. For the fifty-five-year-old attorney, convenience had always outweighed ego. His home was a seven-minute ride from his reserved parking spot. The high school gymnasium where his son, Matthew, played varsity basketball was a six-minute walk from his office. The dance studio his daughter, Kamilla, took classes at was located next to his favorite Italian restaurant—and his biggest client's aquarium was a ten-minute drive from everything. Depending on, of course, if the facility was open.

Open or not, with the Taylor family it always seemed like there was legal work to be done.

Thomas Mark Cubit waited patiently while his law clerk set up the four-way Skype call. "Hello? This is Heather Dugan with Cubit and Cubit."

"Hi, Heather. Alan Miller with the governor's office."

"Kirsty Joyce, counsel for Dubai-Land."

"Great. We're just waiting for Paul Agricola to join us and we can begin."

"I'm here," the Canadian marine biologist said. "I can hear you, but the damn video isn't working."

"Mr. Agricola, this is Tom Cubit. I've asked Jonas Taylor and his son, David, to join us this morning. Ms. Kirsty, is the crown prince with you?"

"Unfortunately, His Highness is still recovering from yesterday's harrowing events."

"Would that be the harrowing flight aboard his luxury helicopter that departed nineteen minutes before his supertanker sank into the Monterey Bay Canyon?"

"Killing forty-eight friends and members of his crew. Yes, Mr. Cubit. The crown prince is in mourning."

"And what about the crown prince's first cousin and partner, Fiesal bin Rashidi?"

"Mr. bin Rashidi was rescued; his whereabouts are presently unknown. However, you should know that His Highness bought out his first cousin's shares of Dubai-Land shortly after our arrival aboard the *Tonga*. Mr. bin Rashidi is no longer associated with the resort."

Tom Cubit held up a signed contract. "Twenty-six days prior to that termination, Mr. bin Rashidi, acting on the authorization of your client, signed this legal document with the Taylor family to purchase the Tanaka Institute, along with the Liopleurodon offspring held aboard the hopper-dredge *McFarland*, for a hundred and fifty million dollars. That broke down to a hundred million dollars for the facility and fifty million for the pliosaur. Do you need me to send you a copy of this signed agreement, Ms. Joyce?"

"We have our own copy, thank you, Mr. Cubit."

"According to the terms of the agreement, the Dubai-Land Corporation was legally bound to pay the Tanaka-Taylor, LLC when you took possession of the Lio offspring on Wednesday of last week. As of this morning, payment has yet to be received."

"It was my understanding that the money and official transfer of ownership would occur during yesterday's ceremony."

"Not true. Your marine biologist, Jacqueline Buchwald, asked my clients to move up the delivery date of the Lio in order to acclimate the creature to its new tank prior to the voyage to Dubai. Once you accepted delivery, the money should have been wired."

"Mr. Cubit, my client has every intention of completing the transaction once the Liopleurodon is in our possession."

"The Lio was delivered to the aquarium your team erected aboard the *Tonga*. There is video footage and dozens of eyewitnesses that will attest to that fact."

"The question is not about delivery, it is about transfer of ownership. Technically, since Dubai-Land has yet to pay for the Tanaka Institute, the Taylors still own it. The same can be said for the Lio."

"The *Tonga* and the Lio tank were part of Dubai-Land, not the Tanaka Institute. You took ownership the moment you housed the creature."

"Technically, Mr. Cubit, the *Tonga* was still in the Tanaka Lagoon's waters when she sank."

Jonas felt his blood pressure rising.

His attorney merely shook his head. "Technically, the inside of my navel is part of my mother's umbilical cord, but that doesn't make her liable for my actions. The Tanaka Institute isn't a country, Ms. Joyce. It doesn't own the waters outside the canal. The Lio was yours before the *Tonga* sank, and we expect you to pay for it."

"If your client wishes to complete the sale, Mr. Cubit, they'll need to recapture the Liopleurodon. Otherwise, there's nothing to talk about."

"See you in court, Ms. Joyce. Oh, and be sure to remind your client not to spend the *Tonga*'s insurance money . . . or the rider you added last week to cover the Lio."

Using his laptop's mouse, Tom disconnected Kirsty Joyce from the video conference call. "Mr. Miller, there's a rumor going around that Governor Skinner and the crown prince had a deal on the table that would have essentially turned Monterey into Dubai-Land West. New zoning laws to accommodate five-star hotels . . . two-lane off-ramps along the Interstate . . . a high-speed rail constructed between San Francisco International and the Tanaka Institute."

"The governor is interested in any venture that brings jobs to California."

"Hypothetically speaking, if my client *did* recapture the Lio, and who knows, a surviving Meg pup, would the governor commit to putting the same offer on the table?"

"I think we'd love to see that, Mr. Cubit, but it would take far more than two sea monsters housed in a thirty-year-old arena to replicate what the crown prince had proposed to build in Monterey. David Taylor would know far more about this, but from what I understand, they've already captured five or six different prehistoric species, plus they've started a breeding program that ensures the longevity of all exhibits in every theme park. Technically, they never needed your facility; all they ever wanted was the Liopleurodon—and, of course, her eggs."

"Mr. Agricola, are you hearing all this?"

"Yes."

"Your deal with Jonas Taylor was to purchase the institute for a hundred fifty million dollars, with ten percent down and eight-year terms on the balance. Are you prepared to complete that arrangement?"

"Things have changed. Bela and Lizzy are dead. With the sisters gone, the orca pods have returned to the Salish Sea, and I have serious doubts whether any of the shark pups could still be alive. Personally, I don't care about a Liopleurodon. But without a Meg, the facility's as useless to me as tits on a bull."

Tom Cubit disconnected the call. "Sorry, Jonas. I know you have a lot on your plate, but I thought you and the kid needed to hear this."

David slammed both palms on the conference table. "That lady lawyer is lying. Mac and I delivered the Lio. They took possession—it escaped on *their* watch. They owe us the money . . . fifty million dollars, according to the terms of the contract. I say we sue them."

"Suing them isn't the problem," Tom replied. "They'll drag it out in court and, if all goes well, in a few years we'll get a judgment. The problem is in actually collecting the money. The United Arab Emirates is not a member of the Hague Convention on Foreign Judgments. Even if they were, they'd never enforce a U.S. ruling against their own royalty."

"What about lawsuits from the victims' families?"

"Those they'll be forced to settle. The prince will be generous with the civilians; I doubt he'll toss more than a few bucks at the crew's families."

Jonas ran his fingers through his thick, silver-white hair, tugging at his roots. "So we went from two buyers to being stuck with an empty arena and aquarium that is costing me twenty-two thousand dollars a month just to maintain."

"Dad, I can fix this. All I have to do is recapture the Lio."

"Out of the question."

"Why? I chased its mother. Junior's nothing."

"David, the only reason you were able to track its parent was because it was tagged. The juvenile could be a hundred miles from here by now. It's also nocturnal; it will probably remain in deep water forever, and I don't have the funds to mount an endless expedition. Besides, the governor's assistant is right—the Tanaka Institute is a thirty-year-old white elephant. It would take a quarter of a billion dollars just to modernize, let alone make it state-of-the-art like the tanks in Dubai-Land."

Jonas turned to his attorney, his mind made up. "I'm done, Tommy. Go ahead and file Chapter Eleven."

Paul Agricola logged out of Skype before turning his attention to his guest. "Looks like that call went pretty much the way you expected. So, what happens now?"

Fiesal bin Rashidi closed his eyes, massaging the center of his unibrow with the tips of his index fingers. "Now, Mr. Agricola, we recapture the Lio."

Carmel, California

Jacqueline Buchwald awoke to the semimuted sound of pounding surf and the *ca-caw* of seagulls. Locating her iPhone on the night table, she was surprised to learn it was 11:27 a.m.

She kicked off the quilt and rolled out of bed onto her feet. The room was dark—she felt for the drape cord and gave it a downward tug, drawing open the curtains.

"Oh, wow."

The view from the second-story balcony looked out to dramatic cliffs and deep blue sea. She lost herself in the Pacific coastline until her bladder decided she needed to get on with her day. After using the toilet, she searched through the sink cabinets, locating a half-empty bottle of mouthwash and deodorant. She also found some of Danielle Taylor's makeup and put on her "face," then left the bathroom and entered the walk-in closet, locating an old pair of sweatpants and a matching hooded sweatshirt.

Barefoot, she left the bedroom and knocked on David's door, but found his room empty. She followed the hallway to the grand marble staircase, which looked out onto the first floor and another breathtaking view that wrapped around the back of the house.

"Hello? Anyone home?"

Receiving no reply, Jackie entered the kitchen. She found the clothes she had been wearing yesterday washed and folded in a neat pile on a chair, along with her tennis shoes. The remains of a buffet breakfast had been placed in Tupperware containers. Jackie helped herself to a plate of eggs and hash brown potatoes and heated everything in the microwave. She filled a glass with orange juice and sat at the kitchen table and ate while she checked the messages on her iPhone.

The text from the crown prince sent her pulse racing.

She stared at the Pacific, lost in thought. After ten minutes she finished her breakfast, washed off her dishes in the sink, and headed outside to locate David.

She was greeted by a cloudless cobalt sky and just enough flesh-warming sunshine to allow her to tolerate the cold gusts of Northern California air. A stone path cut through the courtyard and a small garden, leading her to a wooden staircase that hugged the cliff face as it descended to Otter Cove and a small patch of beach.

Seated cross-legged on a white towel, facing the ocean, was Terry Taylor.

Jackie hesitated to join her, unsure if David's mother was meditating and preferred to be alone. She was about to head back up the stairs when her host waved her over.

"Isn't this a glorious day? I left some food out for you. Did you eat?"

"Yes, thank you. Where's David?"

"With his father, at our attorney's office."

"Mrs. Taylor—"

"You can call me Terry. David told you about my health challenges?"

"Yes. I'm so sorry. But I'm sure you can beat this."

"Death doesn't scare me; as my father taught me when my mother left us long ago, it is merely the soul's transition into eternal bliss. It's dying that is hard. I remember seeing my mother with tubes in her arms and machines booping and beeping. . . . That will not happen to me. When it is my time, then . . . What is it, dear?"

"Yesterday . . ."

"You thought it was your time?"

Jackie shook her head, her eyes welling with tears. "It *was* my time. I drowned. It was horrible and terrifying, and then it was serene . . . no pain."

"No pain." Terry smiled. "I look forward to that. What else?"

"I saw David hovering over my body, fighting to bring me back. Your son . . . so brave."

"Like his father." Tears rolled down Terry's cheeks as she squeezed Jackie's hands. "You saw David giving you CPR, and suddenly *zap* . . . you were back in your body . . . back in the world of pain."

"Oh my God—how do you know?"

"A long time ago, when I was a little older than you are now, Jonas resuscitated me in a similar way. The Taylor men . . . they fight hard for the women they love."

"I don't think David loves me."

Terry's almond eyes beamed at her. "He does. He's just afraid to allow himself to feel again. You have to be patient with him. If you can do that . . . the two of you will have something special."

Jackie shook her head, biting her lower lip to maintain control.

"What's wrong? Tell me."

"Your son deserves better. I'd only drag him down."

"I don't believe that."

"That's because you have a big heart. I'm not the person you think I am."

"And who might that be?"

"The dedicated Ivy Leaguer . . . the ambitious female scientist, forging ahead in a man's world. You and Jonas raised your kids the right way . . . you gave them a foundation of love and integrity. Me? I'm a survivor. I've had to lie, cheat, and steal to stay alive, and I don't trust easily . . . especially men. The sperm donor responsible for half of my chromosomes was pond scum—a high school dropout who impregnated my mother just so she would feel obligated to take care of him.

"He bounced around a dozen minimum wage jobs and spent the few paychecks he earned on clothes and beer, which he drank to excess while he rented movies and pretended to watch me so my mother could work two jobs in order to keep the lights on and food on the table. He was a violent drunk, and my mother gave him far too many chances before she finally threw him out and completed a restraining order. He didn't like that, so he broke in one morning while I was getting ready for school and beat her into pulp until the cops showed up, and that was the last memory I have of my father."

"My . . . God. Did she survive?"

"It would have been better if she hadn't. She ended up in an institution. I visit her every so often, but she has no idea who I am."

"How old were you when this happened?"

"Eight, maybe nine. I spent the next six years in foster homes. I was a quiet kid who read a lot and was a pretty good student. One really nice couple I lived with paid for six months of ballet lessons. Unfortunately, my body developed early, and my last foster father took interest. The second time he forced himself on me, I packed my stuff and hit the streets."

"Does David know any of this?"

"No. He thinks I put myself through college as a ballet dancer. I was a dancer . . . in a strip club in Santa Rosa. I worked there until I was nineteen. The owner knew I was a minor, but he didn't care. The guy was a meth dealer and all of his girls were hooked—that was the rule. The cops finally raided the joint and found his lab in the basement. I spent a week in jail and two hard months in rehab. My counselor helped me to get my GED and she also tutored me for the SATs. My scores were very high, and I got accepted at Brown University, but my police record kept me from getting a scholarship.

"I couldn't afford tuition at an Ivy League school, so I enrolled at a junior college in the area my first two years and transferred to Brown as a junior. Between my financial aid and lap dances at the topless bar outside of Providence, I managed to pay for tuition and books."

"You went back to stripping?"

"You can't make seventy grand working at a McDonald's, Terry. But I was older . . . more mature. The second time around, I stayed away from the drugs and booze. My marine biology professor, Barbara Becker, took me under her wing. She was one of the leading experts in the field of ancient sea monsters and she was very kind. Eight months later, Fiesal bin Rashidi recruited her to set up his aquarium habitats. She agreed, but only if I could be her paid assistant. The job would count as my internship and would allow me to save about half the money needed to finish my education.

"Five months later, Dr. Becker was recruited by the Defense Department for some secret project in Miami. Her replacement kept me on as an assistant. Meanwhile, things were going badly aboard the two tanker expeditions . . . and then David showed up with his friend, Monty.

"The crown prince met with me a day later. He said he was transferring me to the *Tonga*'s sister ship, the *Mogamigawa*, where I would be in charge of maintaining the hold habitats for each prehistoric specimen that our sub pilots netted. I was really excited—for the first time I felt part of something important. Then the prince told me the real reason he wanted me on board. I was bait—the lone academic among a harem of exotic women, all of us hired to seduce your son and mend David's broken psyche so he could focus on his job. There was a hefty bounty—fifty thousand dollars—for whoever kept him occupied on the job long enough to catch the Liopleurodon.

"The offer repulsed me; I actually ended up insulting David aboard the prince's jumbo jet. But something unexpected happened our first night aboard the *Mogamigawa*. His cabin was next to mine, and at about 2 a.m. he let out a bloodcurdling scream. I broke into his room and found him in the throes of a horrible night terror. He told me he was having them a lot . . . all having to do with his girlfriend's death. I really felt bad for him—"

"So, you seduced him."

"Seduced? No, I'd say it was pure lust. And for a while it worked— he stopped having the dreams and we enjoyed spending our nights in bed together. The problem was that he started having feelings for me, so I ended it. David deserves better, and . . . well—I guess I felt a little guilty."

For a long moment Terry sat motionless, gazing at her hands in her lap.

"Please say something."

"Jacqueline . . . it's not my place to judge."

"But you think I should go."

"Did the prince pay you?"

"He paid me five thousand dollars to set up the habitats aboard the *Mogamigawa* for the three creatures David captured. I was supposed to receive a twenty-five-thousand-dollar bonus once the Lio arrived safely."

"He never paid you for sleeping with my son?"

"I've done a lot of things in my life I regret, Terry, but I'm not a whore." Jackie interpreted Terry's body language. "You don't believe me?"

"You're all alone in this world . . . trying to finish school . . . trying to change your life for the better. If accepting that money meant not having to work in a strip bar to pay for school . . . who could blame you?"

"If you believe that, then why would it matter to you if I accepted the money?"

"It matters because David is my son and I may not be around too much longer. Before I go I'd like to know the person he's with cares about him and not about his money."

Gritting her teeth, Jackie reached into her sweatshirt pocket and retrieved her iPhone. "I received this text this morning from the prince." She pulled up the message, handing it to Terry.

> $1 million reward to J.B. if you get D.T. to recapture the Lio.

"A million dollars . . . that's a lot of money to convince my son to do something he's probably already thinking about doing."

"David can have the money. I'm going back to Providence to finish school." She stood, brushing sand from her clothing.

"How will you pay your tuition?"

"Thank you for your kindness and hospitality, Terry. I'll be praying for you."

▐▌▌▌▌▌▌▌▌▌▌▌▌▌▌▌▌▌▌▌▌▌▌▌▌▌▌▌▌

Global Group International Holdings
Hong Kong, China

The bank of China Tower is a four-tiered, glass-and-steel structure intended to resemble growing bamboo shoots—a symbol of prosperity. Rising above the thousand-foot mark, the seventy-two-story skyscraper is one of the more easily identified office buildings on Hong Kong Island.

Located on the fifty-fourth floor was Global Group International Holdings, Ltd. Established in 1997 to provide venture capital for technology-based companies, the corporation quickly expanded into private banking, biomedicine, education, energy, media and entertainment, mining, and property development—the diversity of its growing portfolio reflecting the interests of its founder and chairman.

The oldest son of a banker and film actress, Dr. Johnny Sei-Hoe Hon received his early education in Hong Kong before relocating to the United Kingdom to study abroad, earning degrees in Biomedical Science and Korean Studies from the University of London, and a PhD in Psychiatry from Cambridge. Following in his father's footsteps, he began a career in private banking at ABN AMBRO bank in Hong Kong before launching Global Group. Multiple business and government appointments followed, expanding Dr. Hon's influence while making him the "go-to guy" to bridge cultural differences and relations between the East and the West. The father of three daughters, Dr. Hon divided his time between his work and his family, as well as philanthropy and racehorses, leading his friends and associates to wonder if the man ever slept.

———

Johnny Hon felt his eyelids growing heavy as he stared out his office window at a morning skyline overlooking Victoria Harbor. Twenty-two hours earlier he had been in Hollywood attending a red-carpet gala for the premiere of a comedy he was producing, entitled *Dog Training the American Male* and starring Zach Galifianakis and Kate Hudson. He had left the festivities at midnight, boarding his corporate jet at 2:20 a.m. for the fifteen-hour flight back to Hong Kong—all in order to make an 8 a.m. meeting.

To reset his body clock and avoid jet lag, the seasoned traveler had planned on remaining awake during the first six hours of the flight home and sleeping when the local time was 10 p.m. Unfortunately, he had dozed off within an hour after leaving Los Angeles, and now he was paying the price, his brain in a fog, his head and body experiencing something akin to a hangover.

The sound of chimes snapped him awake. He reached for the intercom. "Yes, Eva?"

"Dr. Jernigan has cleared security and is on her way up."

"Thank you. Please bring me another coffee and whatever our guest wants."

There were very few business associates in Dr. Hon's life who would cause him to leave a movie premiere early, but Sara Jernigan was certainly one of them. One of the most respected molecular biologists in the world, Dr. Jernigan's research focused on finding natural cures to diseases. The two had met as graduate students at Cambridge; four years later Global Group funded Jernigan's three-month expedition into the Amazon rainforest to collect samples from the flora and fauna along the shoreline of the Rio Negro. The trip had yielded twelve hundred samples and four drugs that were now involved in human clinical trials.

Dr. Hon stood to embrace the fit fifty-nine-year-old scientist.

"Sara, it is so good to see you! You've hardly aged. I never realized eating bugs and climbing trees could be so healthy."

"Eh. My bug-eating, tree-climbing days are over. Brazil has permanently shut down all foreign expeditions into the rainforest, and with it, thousands of potential cures for cancer and other diseases."

Johnny motioned his friend into one of the two chairs in front of his desk before occupying the other. "You must be disappointed."

"'Disappointed' is not the word, Johnny. What the Brazilian government is doing is a crime against humanity. You've never been to the rainforest, have you?"

"No. But I have seen photos."

"A photograph cannot do it justice. The jungle is so dense, it obliterates the sun. In a single acre of rainforest there might be four hundred different specimens of trees and tens of thousands of species. There are eighty thousand flower-bearing plants and a thousand microbes in a single teaspoon of soil . . . all waiting to be analyzed."

"You've discovered something new . . . that's why you are here?"

Grinning, Sara reached out and slapped her friend on the thigh. "I can't take credit for it. It's a different kind of jungle, unexplored by man . . . an oasis of evolution populated by species that have adapted in startling ways in order to survive for tens of millions of years."

"Tens of millions of years?"

"Some species even longer."

"This isn't a jungle, Sara. You're talking about the Panthalassa Sea . . . Michael Maren's discovery."

"Correct. Johnny, the sea is an incubator of potential cures."

"More like a purgatory for sea monsters."

"True. But just imagine these creatures' immune systems . . . the regenerative power of their stem cells and white cells when unleashed upon a cluster of cancerous tumors."

Dr. Hon shook his head as he retrieved his iPhone from the breast pocket of his suit. "Search for 'Panthalassa Sea.'"

A computerized male voice responded. *"Searching for 'Panthalassa Sea' . . .*

"The Panthalassa was an ancient ocean so vast it once covered everything on Earth except for the supercontinent of Pangaea. The Panthalassa Sea is a geological anomaly that formed a hundred eighty million years ago when Pangaea broke apart, separating into Laurasia—which eventually became North America, Europe, Asia, and Greenland—and Gondwanaland, which in turn became Australia, Antarctica, India, and South America. The Panthalassa Sea is located four hundred thirteen meters beneath the seafloor of the Mariana Trench, replacing it as the deepest location on the planet. The Panthalassa Sea was cut off from the Philippine Sea as a result of superhot liquid magma being released along the subduction zones that surround the Philippine Sea Plate. As the magma and mineralized water rose to meet the near-freezing waters three hundred fifty meters off the bottom, the hydrothermal plume solidified into a basalt shelf hundreds of kilometers long. Nutrient-filled currents ensured a perpetual food chain, while the warmth provided by the subduction zone's hydrothermal vents attracted a wide variety of prehistoric life to an abyssal sea that spanned more than eight thousand square kilometers. Over the next thirty million years, the magma spewing from this volcanic subduction zone gradually sealed up the shelf, isolating the Panthalassa Sea from the rest of the Western Pacific Ocean.

"Sixty-five million years ago, an asteroid estimated at eleven kilometers in diameter struck Earth in an area that is now the Gulf of Mexico. Atmospheric dust from this impact led to a planet-wide Ice Age, killing off the dinosaurs and most of the ocean's carnivores. With ocean temperatures plummeting, prehistoric sea life inhabiting the Western Pacific were drawn to hydrothermal vent fields along the seafloor of the Mariana Trench. Pliosaurs and other apex predators survived the Ice Age by entering the Panthalassa Sea from one of many volcanic tube access points along the seafloor; other species, including Kronosaurs, and later Carcharodon megalodon, *preferred to remain in the hydrothermally warmed vent waters of the Mariana Trench. The volcanic tubes eventually sealed, trapping the Panthalassa inhabitants beneath the seafloor.*

"The Panthalassa Sea was discovered eight years ago by marine biolo-

gist Michael Maren while he was tracking a male Carcharodon mega-lodon *inhabiting the Mariana Trench. Dubai-Land Expeditions, LLC is attempting to capture a variety of species from the Panthalassa Sea to stock their aquarium—"*

Dr. Hon ended the verbal stream of information. "Fascinating stuff. And what is it you have in mind? Surely you don't intend to explore this hellhole."

"Actually, I was hoping Prince Walid would handle that chore for us. Eight months ago, I met with the crown prince to see if we could collect a small sample of tissues from the specimens his team had already captured. A kilogram of liver enzymes would be enough to determine if a cancer-fighting effect was present. He flatly refused, citing the dangers of anesthetizing these beasts, fearing an invasive procedure could lead to infection. So I asked him if we might have access to the specimens that had died after being captured. Again, he refused."

"The crown prince is a businessman," Dr. Hon said. "If you were to discover a prehistoric specimen that could deliver a cure for cancer or some other disease, he could lose his monopolization of the Panthalassa."

"His nets are set up at one access point, Johnny. There must be others."

"Then your intention is to enter the Panthalassa Sea?"

"It is not necessary to risk human lives as the prince's expeditions have done; a remotely operated drone—properly baited—can be used to lure a targeted species up and out of an access hole into our nets. We could then draw blood and tissue samples and return the creature to the Panthalassa or sell it to the Dubai aquarium."

"Have you prepared a business proposal?"

"We are working on it, but I wanted to speak with you first. Hypothetically, what would it take for Global Group to fund an expedition into the Panthalassa Sea?"

"For starters, proof that the fang-filled flora and fauna in this hellhole actually hold the potential for cures. . . . You are smiling again. What have you found?"

Sara removed her iPhone and held it up to Dr. Hon, scrolling through a series of black-and-white photographs. "These were taken about six months ago inside the hull of the *Tonga*, the tanker that sank a few days ago. The images originated from a security camera, which explains the poor quality. Wait . . . here's a good one where you can see how big this creature is."

An immense ray-finned fish was lying on its side along a steel grating. Its grouper-like head, as large as a cement truck, was followed by flipper-like pectoral fins. The belly below its long, sleek body was being sliced open by two men using knives attached to reach poles.

"Incredible. What is this creature? How large was it?"

"This adult female measured twenty-eight meters. The species is a filter feeder that inhabited the oceans a hundred fifty million years ago. The scientific name is *Leedsichthys,* more commonly known as a Leeds' fish. It was named after Alfred Leeds, who discovered its fossils back in the nineteenth century."

"These two men . . . they are performing a necropsy?"

"Correct. The marine biologist who was in charge was a Filipino named Richard Hibpshman. I met him four years earlier while I was speaking at the University of Washington, and it was my recommendation that got him the job aboard the *Tonga*. To repay my kindness, Richard agreed to secretly send me lab reports on tissue samples taken during the Panthalassa expedition.

"One of the major breakthroughs in cancer research occurred in 1989, when it was discovered that the p53 gene functions as a tumor suppressor in human cells. Tumor suppressor genes are like the brakes on a car—they prevent tumor growth. When the p53 gene is absent, mutant oncogenes take over the cell, acting like accelerators that are stuck to the floor of the car.

"It turns out the liver enzymes of these giant Leeds' fish stimulate the release of the p53 gene; when Richard introduced them to cancerous tumors they not only attacked the tumor, they actually changed the DNA of the cell."

"Unlike chemo, which destroys everything . . . That's fantastic, Sara."

"Unfortunately, while these Leeds' fish thrive in the Panthalassa Sea, they perished within minutes of entering the Pacific Ocean. Once death occurs, the anaerobic bacteria originating from the fish's digestive system rapidly decomposes, destroying the liver enzymes responsible for the p53 enhancers. After forty minutes the enzymes become toxified with sulfur dioxide."

Dr. Hon sat back, closing his eyes to think. "What was the average extraction time from the nets to the tanker?"

"According to Richard, an hour and forty-five minutes. Remember, it's seven miles from the surface to the Mariana Trench seafloor where the nets were set in place around the borehole leading down into the Panthalassa Sea."

"Then we need to design a deep-water lab . . . a place where the liver can be extracted within minutes of the fish's death."

"Agreed."

"Perhaps your friend Dr. Hibpshman can help us in this effort."

"Sadly, Richard was killed two days after this necropsy occurred."

"I am so sorry. What happened?"

"Richard was standing inside the slit-open belly of another dead Leeds' fish when he was attacked by a species of prehistoric shark, called a Helicoprion. Apparently, the fish had swallowed the seven-foot shark whole. The creature's lower jaw was composed of a spiral configuration of teeth resembling the vertical blades of a circular saw. It bit Richard in his stomach. . . . He died of blood loss within minutes of the attack."

"How gruesome . . . and bizarre. What happened to the Helicoprion?"

"Believe it or not, the person assisting with the necropsy had the temerity to drag it into one of the saltwater pens as it lay on the grated deck, covered in Richard's blood. The shark survived and is currently residing in one of the display tanks in the Dubai-Land aquarium."

"Perhaps we should hire this assistant? Do you know his name or how to reach him?"

"The assistant was Jonas Taylor's son, David. And yes, Johnny, I know exactly how to reach him."

||||||||||||||||||||||||||||||||

Monterey, California

The two-bedroom townhouse was located between Route 1 and the Del Monte Center and its Monterey 13 multiplex, less than a fifteen-minute drive from the Tanaka Institute. Jonas had rented the place for his son and his friend Monty back in October, six weeks after David's attempted suicide. The boys had lived there less than three months before they left for Dubai to meet secretly with the crown prince. Haunted by memories of Kaylie Szeifert's death, David had made it his goal to convince his former employer that he could be trusted to capture the tagged adult Liopleurodon that had escaped from the Panthalassa Sea and killed his girlfriend four months earlier. Instead, Prince Walid had sent the young submersible pilot and his friend to the Sea of Japan, where the crew of the *Mogamigawa* were tracking three Shonisaurus—seven-five-foot prehistoric marine reptiles resembling giant dolphins with teeth.

Four months and eighteen thousand nautical miles later, the townhouse was once again occupied.

———

The candy-apple-red, 1959 Cadillac Series 62 convertible exited Cabrillo Highway on Soledad Drive. James "Mac" Mackreides had purchased the vehicle at an auction six years earlier and had lovingly restored the iconic high-tail finned classic with its dual bullet taillights. Mac had two simple rules about riding in the Caddie—no food or beverages, and be prepared to cruise with the top down, no matter how cold it was outside.

On this mid-April day, it was a "balmy" 53 degrees Fahrenheit.

Shivering in the front seat, Jonas pulled the collar up on his Windbreaker and blasted the heat. "Turn right on Pacific—it's about a mile on the left."

"Are you sure they'll be there?"

"I spoke to Jackie this morning. David and Monty were still sleeping; she said she'd make sure they didn't leave before I got there."

"How is Terry doing?"

"Not well. She's not eating. I'm really praying this specialist Dani spoke to at Penn can get her into a clinical trial."

"Trish and I are praying for her."

"Thanks, pal. There it is . . . Mar Vista Drive."

Mac turned into the development and followed the private road that circled to the left. He located a vacant visitor's spot and the two men exited the car, following the path leading to Unit 114-B.

Jackie answered the door on the first knock, dressed in jeans and a black V-necked sweater. She greeted Jonas and Mac with a quick hug and led them into the living room. "David will be back in a few minutes; he went for a run. Would either of you like some coffee?"

"No, thanks," Mac said.

Jonas looked around, peeking in the open door to his son's bedroom and the made queen-size bed. "I haven't seen the apartment look this clean since the day the boys moved in."

"It took a good week to make it livable. There were things growing in the refrigerator that I don't want to think about. I still refuse to set foot in Monty's bedroom."

Mac knocked on the closed bedroom door. "It's Uncle Mac. Get dressed and come on out. Jonas and I want to talk to you and David."

"Should I leave?" Jackie asked.

"No," Jonas said. "This involves you, too." He turned as David entered through the open door, his cheeks flushed.

"Hey, Dad . . . hey, Uncle Mac." He pulled off his blue University of Florida sweatshirt, exposing a gray T-shirt drenched in sweat. "*What involves Jackie?*"

The closed bedroom door opened, releasing a musky stench and Monty, who was wearing plaid wool pajama bottoms and a SpongeBob SquarePants T-shirt. "Yo, Dr. T—kinda early for visitors."

Jonas glanced at his watch. "It's eleven forty-three."

"Not in Honolulu. I'm on Hawaii time."

"Since when?"

Monty flopped on the couch. "Since your boy's woman moved in and he's been getting laid three times a day."

"Yo, dude." David removed his soaked T-shirt, accepting a clean towel from Jackie. "Dad, how's Mom?"

"She had a rough night. We're flying out to Philly on Wednesday; Thursday morning we're scheduled to meet with an oncology team at the University of Pennsylvania's Abramson Center."

"Do you want me to go with you?"

"No. Dani's going. Besides, we have something else in mind for you. "Jonas took out his iPhone and scrolled through his email. "The diver who survived the attack of Bela and Lizzy in British Columbia back in October recently did an interview. He claimed he was swarmed upon by six Meg pups—three pure albinos and three sharks with white heads and dark backs.

"Last Tuesday, I received this video from Nick Van Sicklen, the director of the Adopt An Orca program in British Columbia. Mac and I had met him after the sisters decimated one of the Salish Sea's residential orca pods."

Mac nodded. "The guy was Ahab-angry. He demanded the Coast Guard hunt down and kill Bela and Lizzy."

Jonas handed the iPhone to David, who pressed PLAY.

The video had been filmed in the Salish Sea, a predawn pink sky backlighting the snowcapped Olympic Mountains. The photographer was standing by the starboard rail of a boat that was keeping pace with a pod of orca, the taller black dorsal fins of the males out in front.

"Jonas Taylor, it's your old pal Nick Van Sicklen. Hey, buddy, take a look at what our returning orca are using as a volleyball."

The image zoomed as a white object went airborne in a froth of blood; the carcass of one of Lizzy's albino pups flipping head-over-tail, only the Megalodon's tail was missing, the caudal fin having been bitten off below the pelvic fin.

"Ha! Did you see that, Jonas? My whales have returned to vanquish your monsters' offspring!"

David watched, his hand shaking as a thirty-foot bull caught the dead pup in its mouth and took it underwater.

"Nah nah nah nah . . . hey hey hey, good-bye—"

David turned it off, handing the phone back to his father. "Van Sicklen . . . good name. Guy's a sick fuck."

"Agreed. The pup in the video was obviously Lizzy's. We know it was one of Bela's offspring that drowned in Paul Agricola's net. If the diver was correct, at most there's two pups left from each litter. With the resident orca returning to the Salish Sea, the transient pods won't be far behind. Time is of the essence; if you're going to do this, you have to leave now."

David felt the blood rush from his face. "Dad, are you saying what I think you're saying?"

Jonas nodded. "Your mother, Mac, and I held a board meeting yesterday without you. Your mom doesn't want us to declare bankruptcy . . . at least not yet. She asked us to give you three months to rescue as many of the sisters' pups as you can and bring them back to the institute.

"You'll take the *McFarland*; the hopper is large enough to transport four Meg pups. Cyel Reed is installing tow nets beneath the prow of Manta-7 that will allow you to capture the sharks . . . assuming any more managed to survive and you can locate them before any more orca can get to them."

"Dad . . . thank you."

"Thank your mother . . . and Mac. He and Trish will be going with you."

Mac winked. "The wife's always bitching that I never take her anywhere."

"You'll need a marine biologist on board to care for the pups," Jonas said, turning to Jackie. "My wife said you were planning on returning to Brown to complete your senior year. If you can stick around until then—"

"I wish I could. The dance studio where I used to work offered me my old job back. I have to start teaching next week in order to have enough money put away by the end of August to cover fall tuition."

"Your tuition's already been paid," Jonas said. "Terry contacted the university's bursar's office. That's a gift from us; there are no strings attached. You'll still be paid for your work aboard the *McFarland*."

Jackie's lower lip trembled, her eyes tearing up. "Honestly, I don't know what to say."

"Say yes," David answered.

"Yes. Thank you . . . only—"

"She needs clothes, Dad. She's been wearing Dani's stuff all week."

"Use the company credit card; get her what she needs."

Monty sat up. "What about me, Doc? I could use a job."

"You could use a shower," David said, flicking his sweaty shirt at his friend.

"I already have you down as first mate," Mac replied. "You'll take shifts in the wheelhouse along with me and Captain Mallouh."

Jonas nodded, adding, "So that the three of you know, we're running this expedition with a skeleton crew—people we trust. If word gets out that the institute is after the sisters' surviving pups, every fisherman in the Salish Sea with a boat bigger than a dinghy will be after them."

"Or a dinghy bigger than a boat," Monty said, rising off the couch. "Speaking of which—"

Shuffling into the hall bathroom, he shut the door and released a loud, steady stream of urine.

Aboard the Hopper-Dredge *Marieke*
12.5 Nautical Miles Due West of Monterey Bay

Paul Agricola stood on a starboard perch situated next to the three-story superstructure that held the pilothouse. The steel behemoth, known around British Columbia as the "Jolly Green Giant" because of its bright kelly-green paint job, was three hundred twenty feet long from her bulbous bow to her stern and displaced over five thousand tons. Classified as a Trailing Suction Hopper-Dredger, the *Marieke* was designed to keep deep-water channels clear of sand brought in by the tide. When in use, its two drag arms would be lowered over the side and directed to the channel floor in order to suction up slurry. The mixture of sand and water would then be stowed in the ship's hopper, a two-hundred-foot-long, fifty-foot-deep bin that ran the length of the deck behind the pilothouse like an aboveground swimming pool. Upon reaching the designated dump site, the hopper's giant horizontal steel doors would open outward, releasing the slurry to the sea.

A month earlier, Paul Agricola had converted the *Marieke*'s hopper into a "Megalodon trap." Using an underwater drone he had nicknamed *Sea Bat*, the marine biologist managed to lure Lizzy up from the depths. When the forty-six-foot shark passed beneath the empty hopper, he had opened the keel doors, causing the sea to rush in—the albino killer inhaled with it.

Agricola felt confident he could recapture the juvenile Liopleurodon the same way; what he wasn't so sure of was whether he could find it.

———

Paul Agricola hadn't been looking to trap ancient sea creatures when he had first crossed paths with a Megalodon thirty-five years earlier. The marine biologist, the only son of Canadian venture capitalist Peter Agricola, had been on assignment in the Philippine Sea aboard his father's two-hundred-seventy-five-foot research vessel, the *Tallman*, to gather data on NW Rota-1, a deep submarine volcano that towered twelve stories off the bottom of the Mariana Trench seafloor.

To explore the deepest location on the planet had required special equipment. Fastened to the *Tallman*'s keel like a twelve-foot remora was a gondola-shaped device that housed a multibeam echosounder (MBES), its dual frequency, deep-water sonar pings designed for mapping the abyss.

Paul's team had quickly discovered the presence of a hydrothermal plume hovering like a ceiling of soot a mile off the bottom. Perpetually fed by tens of thousands of deep-sea vents spewing 700-degree-Fahrenheit mineralized water, this dense swirling layer served as a boundary of insulation that separated the freezing-cold deep water above from a tropical warm-water layer below, seeding an entire chemosynthetic food chain.

Unfortunately for Paul and his crew, the plume had also interfered with their drone's sonar and clogged its sensor's intake valves.

Paul's solution had been to deploy the *Sea Bat*. Tethered to the MBES, the winged, remotely operated drone could pass through the plume, its onboard sonar gathering data that it relayed to the *Tallman*.

For three months the *Sea Bat* had gathered data about the thriving chemosynthetic ecosystem feeding off the submarine volcano. And then one day the drone's electronics had attracted a visitor.

It had been a biologic and it was big, estimated to be over fifty feet long. It had also been aggressive, chasing the *Sea Bat* above the hydrothermal plume before giving up the chase.

What species could it be?

The extreme depth eliminated any possibility of the animal's being a sperm whale, while the creature's weight, approximated at twenty-five tons, had ruled out a giant squid. The consensus among the three oceanographers on board was that it was most likely a very large whale shark.

Paul Agricola had vehemently disagreed. The aggressive nature of the species had clearly defined it as a predator. Having given it careful thought, the marine biologist had been convinced the creature had to be *Carcharodon megalodon*, a sixty-foot prehistoric cousin to the modern-day great white shark, whose extinction two million years ago had remained an unsolved mystery in the paleo-world. Excited about the impact of his discovery, the scientist had intended to prove his theory by using the *Sea Bat*'s electronic signals to lure the beast to the surface.

For three days the crew of the *Tallman* had tried, but the predator, while interested, had refused to abandon its abyssal warm-water habitat.

And then another object had appeared on sonar—this one a submersible.

Paul would later learn that the Navy vessel was the USS *Sea Cliff*, piloted by Jonas Taylor, and that the *Sea Bat* had led the Megalodon right to it.

———————

Only Jonas Taylor had survived the dive, telling a tale that earned him a short stay in a mental ward and a dishonorable discharge.

Seven years later, the former submersible pilot would prove to the world he was right. As for the man who had actually made the discovery, Paul Agricola had been forced to take a vow of silence by his father, who feared Agricola Industries would be sued by the Navy and the surviving families of the two dead scientists if they found out that the *Sea Bat* had actually led the Megalodon directly into the path of the *Sea Cliff*.

While Jonas Taylor had turned misfortune into millions of dollars and lived the life of a celebrity, the Canadian scientist had stewed in obscurity, eventually hanging up his lab coat to relocate to the San Juan Islands near British Columbia to live off his father's hush money.

Six months ago, everything had changed. Angel's two hellish spawns, Bela and Lizzy, had escaped from the Tanaka Institute. Following the whale migrations north along the Pacific Northwest, they had entered the Salish Sea, where both females would birth their young. As fate would have it, one of their offspring would end up being netted by Paul Agricola. The pup had died, but its presence in the Salish Sea had turned the locals against Jonas.

Paul had stepped in, negotiating a deal with his rival; if he was able to recapture the sisters, Jonas would sell him the Tanaka Institute at an agreed-upon price. Two months later the former scientist had discovered the location of the Megalodon nursery, and the pups' aggressive parents with it. Luring Lizzy up from the depths with the *Sea Bat*, he had trapped the albino Meg inside the *Marieke*'s hopper. As predicted, Bela had shadowed the vessel down the Pacific coastline, following them through the canal leading inside the Tanaka Lagoon.

And then the adult Liopleurodon had shown up, and a bloodbath had ensued. In the aftermath, it had been decided that Dubai-Land would get the Lio offspring and Paul would take over the Tanaka Institute—gambling that he and David Taylor could capture at least a few of the sisters' orphaned pups.

But as the days of negotiations turned into weeks, Paul's board of directors had soured on the deal. At forty-six feet and twenty tons, Bela and Lizzy were star attractions. An eight-to-ten-foot Megalodon pup, on the other hand, was years of growth away from becoming a major draw—assuming it survived in captivity. When Paul had learned that the orca pods had returned to the Salish Sea, he knew the Meg pups' chances of survival were slim at best. Realizing he could be stuck making payments for an empty, antiquated aquarium, he decided to pull out of the deal.

The *Tonga* sank less than twenty-four hours later.

As Paul had watched the live news report from his hotel room in San Francisco, he had received an unexpected phone call from Fiesal bin Rashidi, requesting they meet immediately. "Before you leave the hotel, I need you to go to the front desk and see the manager. He will give you a key to my room . . . suite 1007. Pack my belongings in a suitcase and pick me up as soon as you can."

"Where are you?"

"I am in the north parking lot of the Tanaka Institute with the rest of the survivors from the *Tonga*. Tell no one we spoke. . . . I promise you will be very interested in what I have to say."

———

An hour later the Dubai engineer had climbed inside Paul's rental car, soaked from head to toe and wrapped in a blanket.

"Geez . . . what the hell happened to you?"

"My cousin and former partner, the crown prince, forced me to sell my shares in Dubai-Land for pennies on the dollar; then he left me on board the tanker to die. I promise you, it was a mistake he will live to regret."

"And how does this affect me?"

"Prince Walid had no intentions of selling the Tanaka Institute to you. He and Governor Skinner have been in secret negotiations to re-zone twenty-six square miles of prime real estate in Monterey and Car-mel in order to build Dubai-Land West. Similar negotiations are taking place with the Chinese to build a theme park in Chengdu."

Paul nodded. "It's a smart move . . . not just from a business stand-point but in regard to sustaining these species. There's no telling how long these creatures can survive in captivity. Multiple locations mini-mize the risk of losing a major attraction to a modern virus or some other waterborne disease."

Bin Rashidi snapped, "It is *my* survival I am worried about! There would be no Dubai-Land without me. I did not dedicate years of my life to allow my cousin to squeeze me out of a trillion-dollar venture so that he can take all of the credit."

"No disrespect, but why should I care?"

"I thought you wanted to own the Tanaka facility?"

"Sure . . . if it had an attraction. Your damn monster killed my two budding stars."

"Forget the sisters and their pups. I spoke with Dubai-Land's head of marine biology last week. He confirms our Megalodon Zahra has asexually fertilized her own eggs and is pregnant. If she births three offspring like her siblings, we'll be able to bring at least one of the sharks to Monterey."

"We? As in me and you?"

"Correct."

"And how are 'we' going to convince your cousin to sell us a Meg pup? Even if he agreed, where would we get the money to pay for it? My board of directors has cut me off, and you don't exactly come off as a guy who has the kind of money the crown prince is looking for from a potential partner."

"We don't need money, Mr. Agricola. What we need is Dubai-Land's most irreplaceable asset . . . the Liopleurodon pup."

"You're a day late and fifty million dollars short. The Taylors already sold Junior to your cousin. Even if we managed to recapture it, all we'd be entitled to is a nice reward."

"Not necessarily. The papers were signed yesterday so that the Lio could be moved to the *Tonga* in order to acclimate to its new tank before today's ceremonies. But the fifty million was never wired; the banks were closed for *Leilat al-Meiraj*, a national Islamic holiday. Let me assure you—with the Lio gone, my cousin will pay Taylor nothing, despite any legal documents that were signed."

Paul's face broke into a wide smile. "Holy pliosaur turds—Jonas just got screwed out of a fifty-million-dollar payday."

"And if we were to recapture the Lio?"

"There's an old adage, Fiesal—possession is nine-tenths of the law. If your cousin had actually paid Jonas for the Lio, then I suppose the prince could file a claim against us if we captured it, in which case we'd probably go to arbitration to settle on a fair reward for our services. But if what you say is true, he has no rights to the Lio, and I can't see Jonas being able to claim ownership of a wild animal he no longer possesses."

"You hunted down and captured Lizzy; could you do the same for Junior?"

"I don't know . . . maybe. It would take a sizable investment. I'd need to hire a crew, stock the hopper-dredge with supplies . . . fuel . . . food . . . bait. Plus another dozen things I can't think of right now."

"How much money are we talking about, Mr. Agricola?"

"Including my time? I couldn't do it for less than a hundred thousand dollars a month, paid thirty days in advance . . . plus ten percent of whatever future action you work out with your cuz after we capture the Lio."

Fiesal reached his hand out from the blanket to shake on the deal. "Have your attorney prepare a deal memo; include your bank information and wiring instructions. How soon can we get started?"

"I don't know . . . maybe a week."

"Where will you begin your search?"

"The Lio needs to eat; we'll search where there's plenty of food."

Aboard the Hopper-Dredge *McFarland*
Salish Sea, British Columbia, Canada

The Salish Sea is an intricate inland waterway between the northwestern tip of the United States and the southwestern tip of the Canadian province of British Columbia. The Pacific Ocean entrance is through the Strait of Juan de Fuca, a deep-water channel that empties into Haro Strait and Puget Sound to the south, the Strait of Georgia and hundreds of islands and islets to the north.

There were multiple challenges to overcome if the crew of the *McFarland* were to have any chance at locating and capturing a Megalodon pup, not the least of which was the sheer size of the Salish Sea, which spanned over sixty-eight thousand square miles. With only eighty days allocated for the mission, the hopper-dredge would have to cover an impossible eight hundred fifty square miles daily. That, of course, assumed the shark (or sharks) cooperated by remaining in their chosen territory long enough for the ship's fish finder to pick them up on sonar.

Mac had met with David and Jackie on their journey north to come up with a strategy.

"We've got a major problem here, kiddies. The Juan de Fuca Strait is ninety-five miles long and about fifteen miles wide. If these Meg babies are in the strait, we could patrol up and down the waterway for months without locating them."

"Forget the strait," David said. "Assuming any of these pups are still alive, they stayed alive by remaining close to their nursery. Where did that diver report seeing the two litters?"

Mac enlarged an area of the Salish Sea map on his laptop, placing an X at the mouth of Orcas Island's channel.

"Obstruction Pass—only the sisters moved the nursery after that fisherman put a load of buckshot in Lizzy's eye."

"I suggest we concentrate around the less populated islands—the deeper the water, the better."

Mac switched to a bathymetric display. "Hate to tell you, kid, but Obstruction Pass is shallow water."

"Yeah . . . well, I'm not convinced that location was actually their nursery. Maybe the sisters were escorting their young to the real nursery when they ran into the diver. What do you think, Jackie?"

Jacqueline Buchwald stared off into space, oblivious of their conversation.

"Jackie?" David nudged her shoulder.

"What?"

"I was just asking you what you thought."

"About what?"

"The sisters selecting Obstruction Pass as a nursery."

She gazed at the bathymetric map. "I don't know . . . maybe." She glanced at her watch. "Sorry, I'm feeling a little seasick. I'm going back to the cabin to lie down."

Mac and David looked at each other as she stood and left.

"Seasick?" Mac smirked. "It's like a lake out there."

"She's been acting weird ever since we left the lagoon."

"Don't try to figure out women, kid. Their minds are far too complex for our simple, straightforward brains."

Southeast Farallon Island
27 Nautical Miles Due West of San Francisco's
Golden Gate Bridge

The Farallones consist of four groups of islands—Noonday Rock, North Farallones, Middle Farallon, and Southeast Farallon. Uninhabited by humans, this barren landscape of mountains and wave-battered rocks is home to harbor seals, Steller sea lions, California sea lions, northern fur seals, and the largest pinnipeds in the world—northern elephant seals.

Male elephant seals can reach lengths of more than fifteen feet and weigh upward of six thousand pounds, the females slightly smaller but still tipping the scales at two tons. The mammals spend their winter months onshore at rookeries where they copulate, birth, and fight for dominance. The alpha bulls are sexually dimorphic and will mate with as many as four dozen females. Come spring, the herds return to the Farallones en masse to laze about the rocky beaches, playing, sleeping, and molting.

The presence of these massive creatures entices another species to this remote island chain: *Carcharodon carcharias*—the great white shark. The seals are the predator's favorite delicacy, and as many as thirty to one hundred mature male sharks and their larger female counterparts frequent these waters, their presence giving this expanse of sea the nickname "the Red Triangle."

The seventy-four-foot yacht *Lost Angel* was designed by its owners, Andrew and Sally Bartolotta, as a means of paying homage to their favorite Megalodon, the ship's dimensions actually mirroring those of the deceased shark—from Angel's fearsome jaws, painted along the eleven-foot prow, to her seven-foot "dorsal sail," mounted atop the upper deck to complete the effect.

A studio session percussionist and artist on the Zildjian, Evans, and ProMark rosters, Andrew Bartolotta had made his fortune playing drums and composing songs for half a dozen successful heavy metal bands. When they weren't touring North America, Australia, and

Europe, the long-haired, heavily-tattooed, and pierced thirty-four-year-old and his wife lived on the yacht, which functioned as their primary dwelling and office. A fully equipped mastering studio—Angel's Lair Studios, LLC—occupied most of the upper deck.

In addition to being musicians and devoted "MEGheads," the Bartolottas were avid divers. With the Tanaka Institute out of business, the closest they could come to experiencing the adrenaline rush of giant sharks was to cage-dive with the Meg's modern-day cousins. Unfortunately, Andrew found the local great white excursions to be rather disappointing. Chumming the Farallones was strictly outlawed, forcing dive crews to rely on fake wooden seals to lure the sharks close enough to see through the murky water.

Desiring to better the odds and treat his guests to a mind-blowing cage diving experience, Andrew had met with several marine biologists who had discovered that when music was pumped through underwater speakers, the vibrations—especially those of the bass-heavy, drum-pounding sounds of heavy metal—attracted sharks. Sensing kismet, he had dry-docked the *Lost Angel* for two weeks in order to outfit the ship's keel with underwater speakers that could pump out music coming from Angel's Lair Studios.

With everything finally ready, they had set out from San Francisco in the early afternoon in order to avoid the commercial cage diving companies. Joining them for their first "Great White Jam Session" were members of September's End—bassist Justin Kleya, lead guitarist Jack Morefield, drummer Jeremy Saltis, and singer Scott Marucci. The band's engineer, Mike Burke, had passed on the offer—"Why would anyone serve themselves up as a meal to a two-ton animal with teeth?"

Sally's friends were more enthusiastic. Dr. Rebecca Bass and her husband, Judson McCurdy, were both certified divers, McCurdy having taken up the sport after an ATV accident that led to debilitating back problems. Servicing their guests during the two-day jaunt was Captain Jeffrey Ritter and his mother, Teresa—a master chef who was on a working vacation from her four-star restaurant in San Francisco.

An intermittent drizzle suddenly became a heavy rain, the wind-guided droplets battering the forward bay windows of the pilothouse. Jeffrey Ritter increased the wipers' speed before checking the weather report again.

Gray skies, light rain, clearing by 5 p.m. Five-to-eight-foot seas. Nothing out of the ordinary.

The mouthwatering scent of fried onions wafted up from the galley, causing his stomach to growl. A moment later his mother ascended the spiral stairwell behind him, carrying a dish covered by an aluminum hot plate.

"Everyone's eaten; I thought you might be hungry."

"You read my stomach." He removed the top, revealing a Philly cheesesteak, the melted provolone dripping off the sourdough roll. "Ma, you deserve a raise."

"Just remember, your boss owes me at least two cage dives. How far out are we?"

"About forty minutes. We'd be able to see the islands if it wasn't so overcast."

A light appeared in the distance, corresponding to a blip on his radar screen. Jeffrey adjusted the yacht's course and then grabbed his radio, speaking into the mike. "This is Jeff Ritter aboard the dive yacht *Lost Angel* . . . coming up on your portside."

"Afternoon, Captain Ritter. This is David Popowitch aboard the dive boat *Superfish*."

"How are conditions in the Farallones, Captain?"

"Six-to-eight-foot seas, coming in at twenty-second intervals. Water temperature's fifty-five degrees, visibility's only about two feet."

"Any sightings?"

"Nothing in the cages. Lots of Risso's dolphins when we crossed the channel. Leaving Southeast Farallon, we saw a pod of orca west through Maintop Bay; that might explain the missing great whites. If you're planning on doing any cage diving, you may want to try Fisherman Bay. Lots of sea elephants out on the rocks, barking up a storm. Our passengers complained about the stench, so we circled upwind."

"Appreciate the advice, skipper. Ritter out."

He turned to his left, the fifty-four-foot dive boat blasting its horn as it passed a hundred yards off the yacht's portside bow. Jeffrey returned the gesture before easing back on the wipers as the rain let up.

Teresa took the wheel, allowing her son to eat and use the head. By the time he returned, the sun was poking through the clouds and a gauntlet of sharp, gray islet peaks were visible along the horizon.

Maintaining a northwest heading, Jeffrey kept a healthy distance from a breakpoint marked by white water. The Farallones resided in "confused seas," meaning the waves came in from all directions. As they neared the shallows they would stack up, rise, and break a good two to five feet higher than the swells that had delivered them across thousands of miles of ocean.

———

Using his binoculars, the captain stole a quick glance to port. Sea lions dotted the cliff faces and frolicked in the foam-coated shallows. Up ahead loomed a windswept mountain of gray rock; rising from the sea to starboard was a weather-battered obstacle known as Seal Islands.

Jeffrey cut his speed to 10 knots as he guided the yacht between the two landmasses, feeling the ebb tide pushing his vessel to the west and an unforgiving shoreline.

Throttling up to 15 knots released the sea's grip on his keel. Satisfied with his level of comfort with the elements, he reached for the radio's handset, switching over to the ship's intercom.

———

Andrew Bartolotta scanned the soundboard and pressed the button labeled PLAYBACK, sending the musical track of his band's new song, "Millennial Brain," through his singer's headphones.

Scott Marucci offered him a thumbs-up from the other side of the soundproof glass. Focusing his gaze upon the sheet of lyrics clipped to the music stand, he leaned into the microphone to lay down the vocals.

*"No time for books or magazines . . . My thoughts are barbed,
    but extra lean.
Don't need no vowels, sacrifice the I . . . Retweet a link,
    update a lie.*

*"Twitter, Facebook, Instagram . . . It's followers that make a
    brand.
Servitude to the one-four-tee . . . Going viral is X-Stas-C.*

*"The iPhone is—a deadly new disease. Instead of talking, we
    text to please . . .
The poles are melting, good jobs are few. I earn my keep . . .
    with likes and views.*

*"Twitter, Facebook, Instagram . . . It's followers that make a
    brand.
Servitude to the one-four-tee . . . Going viral is X-Stas-C."*

Scott tapped his foot, the instrumental quieting for his solo at the bridge.

*"Truth is buried in the lies of the beholder.
Hate thy neighbor as we grow older.
Divide and conquer, the end is near.
Social media preys on our fears—
Alternative facts feed the Millennial Brain
Alternative facts feed the Millennial Brain!*

*"Twitter, Facebook, Instagram . . . It's followers that make a
    brand.
Servitude to the one-four-tee . . . Going viral is X-Stas-C."**

Andrew offered him a thumbs-up, then turned on his microphone. "Sounded great. I want to do the bridge again. This time build it to a

*"Millennial Brain" available for download at CDBaby.com

crescendo so that you're screeching right as Jack's guitar lick takes us into the final chorus."

A blinking red light on a wall panel caught his attention. He wheeled his chair over, pressing the intercom. "Andrew here. Go ahead, skipper."

"We've reached Southeast Farallon. Awaiting your orders."

Locating his iPad on a stack of albums, Andrew clicked on a link that located his yacht on a Google-Earth map.

"We're here to dive with the great whites, skipper. Any idea where they might be?"

"One of the commercial boat captains recommended Fisherman Bay. He said the elephant seals were abundant in the area. He did mention there'd be a nasty stench."

Andrew looked over at Jack Morefield.

The lead guitarist shrugged. "What's a little stench among friends."

"Good point. Fisherman Bay it is."

It was four thirty-five in the afternoon by the time the *Lost Angel* dropped anchor in a hundred sixty-five feet of water. With the engines off, the yacht rose and fell with each swell, the eight-foot waves rolling beneath the keel before breaking into white water fifty yards to the west.

A football field away, hundreds of elephant seals belched and snorted across an inaccessible shoreline marked by several caves. With the winds blowing in from the east, the captain's location spared the *Lost Angel*'s guests from the pungent scent of pinniped droppings.

The yacht's dive shed occupied the back twenty feet of stern along the main deck and held enough equipment and gear to accommodate a dozen divers. Mounted along the outside of the transom was an A-frame; dangling from this perch by steel cable was a shark cage large enough to hold four adult divers. Everyone on board had donned wetsuits, save for the captain and September's End's drummer, Jeremy Saltis, who changed his mind when he saw that the shark cage was made of aluminum.

"Ya'll are crazy. If it were me, I'd want titanium around me . . . at least steel."

Andrew laughed. "Steel's too heavy, dude. You'd need a crane to drag it in and out of the water. Plus steel rusts. Either way, there's nothing to fear—sharks hate the taste of metal."

"How about rock 'n' roll?"

"We'll soon find out." Andrew keyed open a large plastic storage trunk secured to the deck. He raised the lid to reveal four plastic face masks, each trailing fifty feet of hose attached to an air machine. He handed the mask attached to the yellow hose to Rebecca Bass, the red to her husband, Judson McCurdy, the blue to Teresa Ritter, and kept the green one for himself.

"This is an Integrated Dive Mask. As you can see, the IDM covers your entire face, allowing you to breathe naturally through your nose and mouth. Air circulates across the inside of the visor to prevent fogging, and I've never had one leak. If you do get water in your mask, just hit this purge valve. Best of all, the IDM has a built-in microphone. Channel-1 is linked to the boat; Channel-2 connects you to the other divers in the cage. Press this button by your chin to talk."

Andrew pressed the power button on the air machine, causing the four hoses to inflate.

Teresa placed the IDM mask on her face, adjusting its six straps to create a snug fit. "This is great. My jaw always gets so sore from having to bite down on a regulator."

Rebecca helped her husband adjust his mask. "See? No heavy air tanks to lug in and out of the boat; this will be fun."

Collecting his fins, Andrew joined his wife by the shark cage. "The CD's loaded. Give the sharks ten minutes to assemble on their own before you start pumping out the music."

"Understood." Sally kissed him on the lips. "Keep an eye on my friends, especially Judson. He was in horrible lower back pain on the ride out; I saw him popping opiates like they were breath mints."

Leaning on the transom, Andrew pulled the fins over his rubber boots before securing the mask over his face. He pressed the microphone button by his chin. "If you can hear my voice, raise your hand."

The three divers complied.

"Okay, let's pump some adrenaline." Sitting on the fiberglass transom, he spun around on his buttocks to the awaiting shark cage and lowered himself inside while Sally fed his hose over the side.

"Let's go blue next, then red and yellow."

Teresa Ritter awkwardly made her way to the transom in her swim fins. She sat down before twisting around to face the cage, which was suspended upright in the water by the A-frame's steel cable. Inching her way out, she dangled her fins in the open gap framed by the cage's four aluminum buoyancy tanks before easing herself over the side.

The frigid sea took her breath away, the gray-blue underworld causing her eyes to widen in wonderment. Visibility extended only a few feet in every direction except to the north, where the cage was too high out of the water to see the yacht's keel.

"What's on tonight's menu, Chef Teresa?"

She turned to Andrew and smiled. "Hopefully not us." She looked up as a pair of fins plunged between them, followed by Judson McCurdy. As the heavyset man's mask dropped to her eye level, she saw the contortions on his face ease into a blissful smile.

"Oh, God . . . this feels like heaven."

"Are you in that much pain?"

"You have no idea. I fractured my pars bone years ago in an ATV accident. The pars is the only bone in the body that doesn't heal. Without it, the vertebral discs systematically fail, causing my L-5 to press against my spinal cord. I know it's hard to believe, but I used to be an athlete. Over the last five years I've lost two inches in height and gained fifty pounds."

He looked up as his wife slipped into the cage next to him. She mouthed several sentences in silence until her husband pointed to the communication button by her chin.

"Sorry. I was just saying how cold the water is, even in a wetsuit."

"I love it," Judson said. "It feels great on my back."

"Well, I'm freezing. I may have to get out."

"Give your body a few minutes to acclimate," Andrew said. He switched channels on his communicator. "Sally, seal the cage and lower us to thirty-five feet."

"Thirty-five feet; will do."

They looked up as the top of the cage was flipped over. Andrew reached up to position the four air hoses through a gap in the bars before snapping the aluminum grill in place.

A dull mechanical whine was their only warning as the cage suddenly sank beneath them, forcing the divers to grab hold of the aluminum bars for the ride down. Judson found himself floating along the underside of the aluminum hatch, his wife and the other woman standing upright beneath his dangling legs.

Rebecca Bass looked up at the bottom of the boat—one moment the keel was visible, the next it was gone. A minute passed before the winch was shut down, leaving them suspended in silence, surrounded by a gray-brown haze. Had she not been in the cage, she would have lost all orientation, unable to discern up from down.

The physician jumped as the creature shot out of the murk and began circling them, its big black eyes watching her in silence.

Rebecca reached out to pet the harbor seal, her gloved hand palming its gray-and-white-spotted hide as it maneuvered close by.

The mammal pirouetted like a sleek ballerina and disappeared into the surrounding ether, only to be replaced by three more of its kind.

"They're so cute," Teresa said, aiming the lens of her underwater camera at the passing gray torpedo.

"They're our canary-in-a-coal-mine," Andrew shot back. "If the seals are here, then there are no great whites in the area." Reaching for his Comm Link, he switched channels. "Sally, start the CD, please."

"Stand by."

Judson tapped his wife's arm, pointing to a dark silhouette rising slowly beneath them. "Is that a shark?"

All eyes watched the twelve-foot, two-ton mass ascend out of the murk.

Andrew switched his communicator back to Channel-2. "It's an elephant seal. Looks like a young bull—"

The four divers jumped as the opening riffs of Metallica's "Seek and Destroy" pumped out of the keel's underwater speakers.

The baritone sounds reverberated through the sea, attracting prey and predator alike.

The oceans harbor many of our planet's highest peaks and deepest valleys. The longest gorge in North America resides off the California coastline. Spanning two-hundred-ninety-two miles, the Monterey Submarine Canyon is similar in size to the Grand Canyon, except that it is twice its depth, plunging more than two miles below the surface.

Monterey Canyon is the most prominent of a cluster of fissures that cut east to west along Northern California's continental shelf. These geological grooves serve as sediment conduits, channeling silt across more than thirteen hundred miles of seafloor.

Since its escape from captivity, the juvenile Liopleurodon had inhabited a seven-mile-wide, twelve-mile-long stretch of seafloor along the bottom of the Monterey Canyon. This limited the pliosaur's diet to deep-water denizens that belonged to a food chain derived from methane pumping out of cold seeps. This chemosynthetic environment was easily adapted to by the Lio, whose ancestors had spent the last seventy million years living in the perpetual darkness and colder temperatures of the Panthalassa Sea.

Unchallenged in its deep-water realm, the Lio would have remained there indefinitely, never to surface again, had it not been for the turbidity event.

It had begun as an underwater earthquake along the San Andreas Fault that had triggered an avalanche of silt. Racing through the ravine, this rapidly moving current of sediment-laden water buried cold seeps and hydrothermal vents. Lethal to all gill-breathing life-forms, it had chased the Liopleurodon to the north, where the pliosaur had taken refuge in the Soquel Canyon. When the biological communities in these deep-water channels failed to satisfy its dietary needs, the carnivore had continued its forced migration, exploring the Ascension and Nao Nuevo canyons farther to the north.

Eventually, the progression of gorges had led the pliosaur to the Greater Farallones National Marine Sanctuary.

As the Lio cruised the seafloor, the hydrodynamic pressure of its movements perpetually channeled water over the external nares of its directional nostrils and across its palatal grooves. Passing through the nasal ducts, the seawater was "tasted" by the organ's olfactory epithelia, eliciting an intoxicating potpourri of scents and chemicals, the likes of which the creature had never experienced.

Locking on to the pungent traces of mammal sweat and urine, the Lio altered its course, abandoning the canyon as it headed northwest into Fisherman Bay.

———

The elephant seal was a twelve-foot-long, forty-three-hundred-pound adolescent bull. It had spent the afternoon playing the polygamist to its herd of thirty-seven cows, mounting two. Hungry from the energy expenditures of copulation, it gyrated across the rock-strewn beach on its pectoral fins and undulating rolls of blubber, making its way down to the sea.

The male paused at the shoreline to scan the foam-laced shallows. The presence of the hyperactive seals was reassuring, but the bull knew that both its desired prey and the predators that stalked its kind resided well beyond the breakwater.

The tall, black dorsal fins belonged to orcas, which hunted in pods farther out in the bay. Being air-breathers, the killer whales preferred to hunt near the surface and rarely dove deeper than a hundred feet. On rare occasions a lone juvenile male might venture close to shore in an attempt to bull-rush an elephant seal wading in the shallows. But the maneuver was easily spotted, and the bull risked beaching itself.

Great whites were always a threat, the rogue hunters preferring to launch a bite-and-flee attack from below. For the elephant seal, the key to surviving these hunting excursions was to get deep as quickly as possible and bottom-feed. Fortunately, evolution had endowed the mammals with a thick layer of blubber and sinuses in their abdomens that were capable of storing large volumes of blood and oxygen. Combined with the increased concentrations of myoglobin in their muscles, bull elephant seals could remain underwater for up to two hours while diving more than seven thousand feet—far deeper than any orca.

The sea was rough, the eight-foot swells concealing any telltale fins.

Wading in up to its thick neck, the rotund behemoth ducked beneath the waves, shedding the confines of its two tons of ballast. Engaging its hindquarters—an undeveloped tail ending in a pair of five-fingered webbed feet—it quickly slipped beyond the breakpoint as it followed the seafloor to deeper water. It paused to empty its bladder and mark its territory before searching the bottom for food.

Its whiskers quickly detected vibrations coming from beneath the silt, its proboscis flushing out a two-foot-long squid.

The bull had slurped its meal down its gullet when a frenzy of movement suddenly surrounded the giant pinniped as half a dozen harbor seals shot out of the gray-brown mist and passed overhead before disappearing again into the ether.

Uncertain if the seals were being chased or just playing, the bull moved off. For twenty minutes, it continued to scour the silt for telltale propulsion trails, until it detected a presence circling the periphery . . . something large.

Whipping its lower limb up and down, it attempted to distance itself from the unseen predator, its senses unable to determine the species.

Whomp!

The Lio's open jaws snapped down upon the strange creature's tail with ten thousand pounds per square inch of bite-force. The four-inch fangs jutting out from the upper jaw beneath its snout punctured the elephant seal's soft flesh, while the curved posterior teeth acted as a ratchet, pulling the thick wad of blubber into its mouth.

Hot blood gushed down the pliosaur's gut, sending the Liopleurodon into a frenzy. Twisting sideways, it rolled over like a crocodile, ripping loose a foot flipper and thirty pounds of energy-restoring fat.

The wounded elephant seal wiggled its way free, writhing in pain and trailing gobs of blood as it struggled to reach the surface.

"It's an elephant seal. Looks like a young bull—"

The four divers jumped as the opening riffs of Metallica's "Seek and Destroy" pumped out the keel's underwater speakers.

"It's struggling as if it's hurt."

"It is hurt. That black stuff's blood."

Andrew flipped the switch on his communicator back to Channel-1, raising his voice to be heard over the blurred heavy metal singer's vocals. "Sally, we've got a wounded elephant seal down here; there's blood everywhere."

"That's excellent. Was it a great white?"

"Stand by, it's swimming toward the cage." Crouching as low as he could, Andrew pressed his face mask to the aluminum bars as the wounded mammal struggled to ascend. "Must have been a great white; the bite radius is huge. Half its tail is missing."

The harbor seals swarmed in and out of view as the music continued pumping out of the underwater speakers, the agile sea mammals anxious, as if they were being stalked from all sides.

"Running . . . on our way. Hiding . . . You will pay—"

Judson was the first one to see the great white, his eyes drawn to movement as the fifteen-foot male's triangular snout emerged from the mist. Its spine arched, its black eyes rolled back in its head as it accelerated with a flick of its caudal fin, grazing the elephant seal as it struck the cage with the impact of an SUV hitting a golf cart.

The four divers cried out. The aluminum bars were bent, but miraculously remained intact.

"Everybody okay?"

Judson wrapped his arm around his wife's waist, grabbing Andrew with his free hand. "Why did it attack the cage?"

Andrew switched over to Channel-2. "Say again?"

"Maybe the music screwed up its sensory array," Rebecca offered.

"Here comes another one!" Teresa pointed below as a second male appeared from out of the murk. As it rose on a forty-degree plane, its jaws widened to reveal a hideous band of gums above a row of triangular teeth that clamped down upon the elephant seal's gushing lower limb, sending the wounded mammal into convulsions.

"Dying . . . One thousand deaths—"

—as a third great white, this one an eighteen-foot, thirty-six-hundred-pound female, circled in and out of the gray periphery, making its presence known.

"There is no escape, and that's for sure—"

Rebecca screamed as the elephant seal forced its head inside one of the rectangular openings of the cage, its proboscis suctioning her mask, prying it away from her face.

"This is the end, we won't take anymore."

Judson ripped the yellow air hose free, guiding it into his wife's mouth as divers and beasts disappeared behind a cloud of blood.

"Say good-bye to the world you live in. You've always been taking, but now you're giving."

Andrew wheezed to catch a breath. His back was pinned against the rattling metal cage, his chest crushed by the wounded mammal, its twisting torso now filling his entire field of vision, its girth blocking the entire upper half of the aluminum frame, sealing off their escape.

Teresa was curled in a ball on the other side of their prison, her blue airline pinned behind an unyielding wall of blubber. Inhaling a final deep breath, she separated the hose from the bottom of her mask and shoved her head out of the nearest two-foot-wide rectangle of aluminum to make her escape—

—her eyes widening in horror as the largest of the three great whites suddenly charged the cage, just missing her as it clamped its triangular teeth upon the exposed remains of the elephant seal's gushing hindquarters, the female's fluttering gill slits so close to the chef that she could have shoved her fist into one of them. She could only hold on as the shark shook the dying mammal from side to side, causing the tortured elephant seal to buck like a bronco, its gyrations popping loose the bolts supporting the four sides of the aluminum frame.

Andrew grabbed the closest section of cage and used it as a shield as he kicked for the surface. A dark silhouette appeared overhead, forcing him to halt his ascent. Looking down, he saw Teresa trailing fifteen feet behind. He waved for her to join him—

—never seeing the big female that struck him from behind, his impaled lungs belching air and blood into his mask as the shark's jaws crushed his upper torso in one savage bite and release.

Teresa screamed into her mask, her eyes wide as she swiveled around in circles before paddling and kicking furiously. Reaching the surface, she reached her hands out of the water—

—two of the musicians dragging her onto the boat.

Judson attempted to lead his wife away from the collapsed cage, only both of their air hoses were entangled in the aluminum hatch. Inhaling several deep breaths, he pulled out his hose again, thankful for the plug that sealed his mask. Freeing his wife's line, he took her by the hand and kicked for the surface, the sea above them a purple haze of bleeding body parts and circling sharks. Air was up, but so was death, and so he swam as hard as he could in the direction of the music, praying they could make it to the other side of the yacht before they drowned . . . or were eaten.

Without her mask, Rebecca was effectively blind. He kept his head on a swivel, looking right, left, behind them, and up.

Looking down, he saw the creature rise out of the mist.

At first he thought it was a crocodile . . . until a stroke of its powerful forelimbs revealed the Lio's identity and its intended meal . . . his wife.

No.

For fifteen years Rebecca Bass had been his doctor and his nurse, his lover, companion, and provider. This nightmarish ending was not going to happen . . . not on his watch.

Reaching the yacht's keel, Judson pulled her up, slinging her toward the surface. Instead of following after her, he grabbed hold of one of the underwater speakers, using his free hand to pull off his swim fins. With his lungs screaming for air, he braced both feet against the bottom of the boat, his eyes locked on the Liopleurodon as it ascended with frightening speed, its jaws opening as it homed in on his wife—

Now!

Thrusting away from the keel with every ounce of strength left in his body, Judson launched himself directly into the creature's path, propelling his head and right shoulder into the monster's widening mouth while wrapping his left arm around its snout to prevent it from going after his wife.

Caught with its jowls stretched open, the Lio could not generate enough torque to bite down upon the strange life-form jammed inside its mouth. It tried to shake it loose, but the animal's tentacle refused to let go.

Unable to channel water into its gullet and gills in order to breathe, the pliosaur panicked, diving into the depths.

With every twist and shake of its skull, a hundred two-inch-long, stiletto-sharp ivory teeth bore their way deeper into Judson McCurdy's flesh. On the verge of losing consciousness from the pain and lack of air, he felt the monster dive, and knew Rebecca was safe.

And then he smiled as a strange calm passed over him . . . the pain of life vanishing with his pulse, his soul slipping free of its physical bonds long before the nightmare of nature delivered his carcass to the bottom of Fisherman Bay.

PART TWO

NIGHT

We cannot change the cards we are dealt, just how we play the game.

—Randy Pausch

‖‖‖‖‖‖‖‖‖‖‖‖‖‖‖‖‖‖‖‖‖‖‖‖‖‖‖‖‖‖‖‖

Peking University
Beijing, China

Considered by many to be the top educational institute in China, Peking University is made up of thirty colleges and twelve departments that offer ninety-three programs to its undergraduates. Honoring the region's history, the sprawling campus features Oriental gardens and landscaping, waterways, and traditional Chinese architecture.

The event was being held on campus at an auditorium inside the Arthur M. Sackler Museum of Art and Archaeology. The star of the lecture remained hidden from view behind a red velvet curtain; the first three rows were reserved for dignitaries and members of the press.

Professor Jiang Wei was greeted by a standing ovation as he crossed the stage and stood behind the podium. "Thank you. Much has been written about the find on Sarigan Island, leading to both conjecture and debate. Did we discover a new species? Was the immense size of this reptilian creature simply an adaptation necessary to survive the warm-water abyss of the Mariana Trench, or perhaps the deeper, more isolated habitat of the Panthalassa Sea?

"The answers to these questions, and many more, were provided by the fossilized remains of the predator and its prey . . . so, without further delay . . ."

The curtains parted, revealing an immense serpent-like skeleton. The head was as large as a cement truck, its jaws hyperextended open an astounding thirteen feet, sporting a pair of curved upper and lower fangs, each tooth in excess of eighteen inches. The skull was anchored thirty feet off the ground so that the rest of its vertebrae angled downward before twisting off to the right, where the pliosaur remains were wedged in tight, approximately forty-five feet from the jowls. From here the skeleton completed several S-shaped curves across the stage.

Workers wheeled the lectern to one side, allowing photographers and guests to snap iPhotos and videos. Dr. Wei permitted the chaos to go on for several minutes before retaking control of the room.

"Please . . . if everyone could be seated. I heard a few colleagues ask if these are the actual skeletons unearthed at Sarigan. The answer is no. This is a replica created from casted molds. As to its size, from snout to tail the creature measured forty-seven meters . . . approximately one hundred fifty-five feet. We conservatively estimate its weight to have been forty-five to fifty tons. The way it appears on stage matches the angle at which it was situated when it was discovered and excavated from the cave. Our working theory is that it captured its prey in the abyss, then retreated to land by way of this sea cave when its meal became lodged in its gill slits, preventing it from breathing. Unable to regurgitate, it eventually suffocated—a fate experienced by Florida pythons that swallow and attempt to digest an entire alligator whole.

"To the first question . . . is the animal a snake? Beyond its physical appearance, we found multiple similarities with *Titanoboa cerrejonensis* and concluded the animal was indeed a snake. As to the identity of its last meal, that animal has been confirmed to be a pliosaur that measured approximately eleven meters. Unfortunately, the snake's gastric juices burned through many of its prey's identifying characteristics, making it difficult to discern whether it was a Kronosaur or Tylosaur—either of which can only be explained from a timeline perspective using our working theory that has the snake entering the Panthalassa Sea in order to feed. Further, the presence of gill rakers aft of the creature's skull is a physical adaptation shared by many of the marine reptiles purported to inhabit the Panthalassa. As such, we officially name our species *Titanoboa Panthalassic*.

"As evidenced by the presence of the adult female Liopleurodon that escaped the Panthalassa several years ago, an increase in size and girth appears to be a necessary adaptation for survival in this prehistoric sea. Therefore, we have concluded that *Titanoboa Panthalassic* is not a new species, but most likely a deep-water adaptation, rendering *Titanoboa Panthalassic* a subspecies of *Titanoboa cerrejonensis*.

"Finally, we come to the two questions that the public wants answered most: Could these monstrous snakes still be alive? And if so, are they a threat to humans? With the existence of the Panthalassa Sea, the answer to the first question must be yes. As to the second, the age of these fossilized remains coincides with the formation of the Mariana Islands—a volcanic event that ultimately sealed the Panthalassa Sea from the Mariana Trench. Therefore, if *Titanoboa Panthalassic* still exists today, it is sealed within a purgatory that meets not only its needs, but ours as well."

South Florida Bone Marrow/Stem Cell Transplant Institute
Boynton Beach, Florida

Jonas circled the Bethesda Health City medical complex once before locating Building C. He pulled the rental car by the front curb and waited as Danielle climbed out to assist Terry into the complex, then he parked. They had arrived in South Florida two days before after spending a week in Philadelphia while his wife had undergone tests at the University of Pennsylvania's Abramson Family Cancer Research Institute, supervised by Dr. Michelle Briggs.

"Tell me about your symptoms, Mrs. Taylor."

"I've lost some weight. My husband and daughter keep pushing me to eat, but I can't . . . my stomach always feels full."

"What you're feeling is the tumor in your liver pushing against your stomach. It's also irritating the lower lobes of your right lung."

Jonas nodded. "Her lung has to be drained every three days. Yesterday, the technician removed seventeen hundred cc's of fluid—nearly enough to fill a half-gallon container. But we keep telling her that she has to eat . . . the weight's falling off of her—"

"I've lost my sense of taste, which doesn't help. I suppose not eating has made me feel weak."

"Mrs. Taylor, when you were younger, did you go out in the sun a lot?"

"Not a lot, and I always wore protection, sun block forty-five."

"Have you started any treatments?"

"Not yet."

"In reviewing your pathology, the cancer most likely originated from the melanoma they removed from your face five years ago. It was actually a very low-risk melanoma; when the pathologist measured it from the top of the skin down to the underlying skin, it was determined to be point-two millimeters deep. This type of melanoma is a lentigo maligna melanoma, which I was hoping it was going to be, in that it's the kind we're working on treating. It tends to appear on the parts of the body that have chronic sun exposure.

"Melanomas that have a low chance of traveling are less than point-one-millimeter deep; high-risk melanomas are greater than point-four. Again, yours was point-two, which was thin. I'm sure the surgeon told you this was going to have a great chance of being cured. In terms of melanoma, it can travel through the bloodstream, and the most common places for it to reappear and evolve is in the lungs and the liver.

"There are several different approaches to treat it. One is chemotherapy, and the most common chemo is a pill called Temodar. It's easy to take, it has very few side effects, and it's a pill you take five nights in a row, once a month. Another approach is with immunotherapy—medicines that stimulate the immune system. There are some new approaches with a medicine called ipilimumab, and that's a possible treatment. Ipilimumab requires that you've had some kind of prior treatment. It's administered by IV and it's given once every three weeks."

"I've been reading that ipilimumab had dramatic results," Danielle said, "but it seems to be effective in only a small percentage of patients."

"That's correct. A third approach is something called target therapy, and that's really where all the excitement has been." Dr. Briggs drew a circle on a pad of paper. "I'm taking you back to high school biology. Here's a cell, here's the nucleus. The way our bodies work is that there are receptors on the outside of the cell, there are growth factors that circulate and trigger these receptors, and then there are a series of genes here that get turned on—it's like the dominoes fall and the cells grow. In about forty percent of melanoma there is a broken gene called B-RAF. If you have this mutation, there are some pretty amazing drugs that target the B-RAF gene. So, if you have a broken B-RAF gene we give you a pill that blocks it—it's like putting the brakes on it.

"You had a lentigo maligna melanoma. The most common broken gene with a lentigo maligna melanoma is something called c-KIT. I don't know if you have a broken c-KIT gene; we'll test for it using a liver biopsy. There is an FDA-approved medicine called Gleevec that has helped melanoma patients who have a broken c-KIT gene. So our first step is to test you to see if you have either a broken B-RAF gene or a broken c-KIT. . . . Hopefully you have one or the other."

"Be honest with me, Dr. Briggs. Even under the best scenario, what are my chances?"

"With regular chemotherapy there's a ten to fifteen percent chance the melanoma will shrink. If you get one of these targeted therapies the average shrinkage rate can be fifty to eighty percent. With Gleevec, it could be as high as forty percent if you have a broken c-KIT gene. If you don't have a broken c-KIT gene the drug can still help, it just won't help as much.

"Given your symptoms, my suggestion is that we start you on Gleevec right away. The traditional chemotherapy can help, but the Gleevec can be more effective."

"With the Gleevec, how soon can we expect a response?" Jonas asked. "What are the goals here?"

"The goal is to reduce the symptoms and shrink the tumors."

"What about a cure?"

"I'm sorry. Even with the most dramatic drugs we have, at the ten-month point, patients start to regress. There are new therapies in clinical trials, but I think Gleevec is a good first step for you."

Dr. Briggs had started Terry on the Gleevec while they awaited the results of the tests. Meanwhile, Danielle had worked the phones, looking for alternative treatments outside of the standard cancer therapies.

They received bad news six days later: Terry's cancer did not involve the B-RAF gene or a broken c-KIT gene, eliminating Gleevec and the options they had discussed.

However, in slamming the door it seemed God had opened a window. Dani learned about a new therapy that had recently been approved for human clinical trials for tumorous cancers—including melanoma. An appointment was made with the oncologist/hematologist overseeing the protocol; the location of the research center was just outside of Boca Raton, Florida—the very place Jonas and Terry had hoped to relocate to.

The South Florida Bone Marrow/Stem Cell Transplant Institute consisted of office suites and private hospital rooms used to treat people on an outpatient basis, as well as labs and a cryogenic facility to store stem cells.

The Taylors were ushered inside a small, cheery conference room, the walls decorated with framed medical degrees and honors in the field of oncology, hematology, and stem cell research.

The first thing that impressed Jonas about Dr. Dipnarine Maharaj was an assured calmness that could have come only from decades of experience. There was a worldliness about the man; it was in his eyes and his mannerisms, the eloquence of his voice and the intelligence conveyed in his message. For patients with life-threatening illnesses, he was the real deal—a searchlight guiding one to a life ring tossed in tempest seas, and Terry trusted him immediately.

Dr. Maharaj introduced himself and then got right to business. "I've reviewed your medical records, and I concur with Dr. Briggs. The cancer probably originated from the melanoma surgeons removed from your face five years ago."

The oncologist/hematologist turned his computer's large flat screen monitor to face them. "Terry, cancer cells are stem cells. There are different kinds of stem cells, and every organ in the body has stem cells. A characteristic of a stem cell is the way it divides into twins. One of the twins will actually begin to form tissues, while the other twin does nothing; it lies dormant. What prevents it from growing further is the immune system. As we get older or if we're under a great deal of stress, our immune system weakens, and the cancers can grow."

Jonas glanced at his wife. "Stress . . . yeah, we've probably had more than our share."

Dr. Maharaj nodded. "I'm sure I can't begin to imagine. The standard therapy for treating metastatic tumors is chemotherapy. If you look at long-term survival using the best drugs we have now, it only adds about two to three months to the average person's survival. As a transplant physician in this outpatient setting, the chemotherapy that I give is ten times the standard dose Dr. Briggs would give. The question is, why isn't the chemotherapy working?

"The first reason is that cancer is made up of many different kinds of cells. We have cancer stem cells, but we also have cells that are differentiating as they are dividing. Chemotherapy is designed to kill cells if they are dividing, but the cancer stem cells that are not dividing are not touched by the chemotherapy. Chemo will kill a certain number of tumor cells and those cells will shrink, so it will look as though you're making progress, but actually curing you of the cancer requires a different approach.

"I've recently been approved by the FDA to begin a human clinical trial for solid tumor cancers. This protocol is based on a 1999 study conducted at Wake Forest University by my colleague, Dr. Zheng Cui. Dr. Cui discovered a cancer-resistant mouse. No matter how Dr. Cui attempted to infect this mouse with cancer, he couldn't do it; the mouse's immune system was simply too strong. Forty percent of this mouse's descendants inherited the same significant cancer resistance. The white blood cells of these mice were able to seek out and destroy cancer cells not only in cell cultures, but also in living mice. Dr. Cui designed a test to measure this cancer-killing activity, called CKA, and used those cells from cancer-resistant mice to cure other mice that had cancer.

"Further investigation showed that high levels of CKA granulocytes were also found in the white blood cells of some healthy people, specifically in the immune systems of young healthy humans your daughter's age, between ages nineteen and twenty-five.

"What I am doing is translating the basis of that clinical trial into humans. Instead of the mouse white cells, I'm using the white cells taken from the immune systems of healthy twenty-year-olds. If you take a twenty-year-old and you look at the incidence of cancer versus the incidence in a seventy-year-old, a seventy-year-old has a one hundred times greater risk of cancer. That's because the immune system of a twenty-year-old is so much stronger. Years ago, when the melanoma was removed from your cheek, those cancer stem cells were still there, lying dormant. When your immune system dropped, they flared up. Again, the approach here is to reverse that process.

"So, if you're looking for an oncologist who treats a lot of melanoma patients, that's not me. The approach I'm taking is to rebuild the immune system, because the immune system is what has broken down here. Chemotherapy further weakens the immune system. When we look at the CT scans of cancer patients using chemotherapy, the tumors are shrinking, so it appears as if we are winning the battle. In fact, we're actually suppressing the immune system, which, in the long term, is needed to win the war."

"Doc, how many melanoma patients have you actually treated?"

"None. But our clinical trials are for solid tumors, and this is what your wife has. To date, we've only treated eleven patients. Because it's a trial, I can't give you the results, as we're under the strict protocol of the IND—the Investigational New Drug program. If I were to tell you all eleven patients had done well, I could be prejudicing your decision to enter the clinical trial. At the same time, one of the most important things you can do is to think positive; we know the power of the mind and how it affects the immune system. Some people might say that it doesn't exist, but I would disagree. I have been treating cancer for a long time, and I know the people who survive are the people who say, I am going to fight this thing."

Terry smiled. "Tell us about the protocol. What does it involve, and how soon can we get started?"

"The treatment I am using is simple: I'm basically asking a group of young people to give me some of their white cells, which I will then transfuse into you. Within these white cells are cells that are part of the innate immune system and the adaptive immune system. The innate immune system is made up of a number of white cells that are the cancer prevention system, which is actually what prevents an individual from getting cancer in the first place. The treatment is four infusions, completed over a two-week period, with the patient tested at thirty, sixty, and ninety days."

"Are there any side effects?" Dani asked.

"With any type of transfusion, there are always some risks. Side effects can vary from a minor allergic reaction, which we can treat with hydrocortisone, to a rise in temperature. I actually prefer a rise in temperature, because the granulocytes work much better in a higher temperature, fever being the body's natural response to infection. As for major reactions, we can prevent these through proper donor screening, but they can occur. We'll be doing a full range of blood tests on you to find the right matches. I'm sorry, Danielle, blood relatives cannot be considered.

"As far as how soon you can begin, because this is a clinical trial we must wait until the Gleevec is completely out of your system before we can start the first treatment."

"How long is that?" Terry asked.

"Thirty days."

Jonas winced. "Geez, Doc, thirty days? She hardly took anything . . . four, maybe five pills tops."

"I understand, and we'll certainly utilize that time to find the best donors available. But I have to follow proper protocol procedures."

Terry squeezed her husband's hand. "Boca Raton is five miles to the south; maybe we could look for a place to live while we wait."

Aboard the Hopper-Dredge *McFarland*
Salish Sea, British Columbia, Canada

"Nine weeks . . . two days . . . seventeen hours . . . thirty-six minutes, and twenty seconds." Jason Montgomery held up his iPhone so that his aunt Trish could see the screen. "That's how long we've been stuck on this stupid boat, circling a bunch of stupid rocks covered in stupid pine trees. I'd like to meet the genius who named them the 'San Juan Islands'? Does this look anything like Puerto Rico to you?"

"Stop complaining." Trish Mackreides reached across the galley's aluminum prep table for the quart of milk, only to discover the container was empty. Turning down the burner under her pan of scrambled eggs, she crossed the kitchen to the walk-in refrigerator and yanked open the handle—the device falling apart in her grip.

"Monty, I thought you fixed this!"

"I did."

"With what, a paper clip and a rubber band?"

"No. Wait, would that work?"

"Some handyman you turned out to be. I'm down to two working burners, a blender, and an oven that shuts off every seventeen minutes. And when is Cyel going to fix the plumbing? I haven't had a shower in five days."

"You should use the hopper; it's just like a pool."

"It's salt water, Monty. Do you know what salt water does to my hair?" She turned as David entered the galley, his tinted sunglasses concealing the dark circles beneath his bloodshot eyes. "You look exhausted."

"I couldn't sleep. We received a report late last night that another Meg pup was netted and killed."

"How many is that?"

"Four."

"Another albino?"

"No, this one was one of Bela's. Any breakfast? I need to eat, hit the head, and get in the sub before these damn fishermen slaughter another pup."

"Sit." Trish reached for the stove controls, reigniting the flame beneath her pan of eggs. "David, I know your priority is locating the sisters' nursery, but you need to make time for your girlfriend. Last night, I passed by her stateroom and heard her crying."

"To be honest, I just figured it was her menstrual cycle."

Monty shook his head. "Junior, if that's her menstrual cycle, I know why the plumbing is clogged."

Trish smacked her nephew atop his head with her spatula. "Fix the handle on the walk-in and bring me a quart of milk."

"Yes, ma'am."

"David, she's depressed. I've tried to talk to her, but she's very guarded about whatever it is that's bothering her. Are you two having problems?"

"You could say that."

They looked up as a rusted speaker anchored to the far wall crackled to life. "David, rezzzzt to the pilzzzzt houzzzzt."

"I gotta go."

"Wait." She grabbed a plastic plate from a stack and scooped a large portion of eggs from the pan onto the dish. "Promise me you'll talk to her later."

David shoveled the eggs into his mouth and nodded. "Prom*ffff.*"

Captain Mohammad "Mo" Mallouh returned the intercom microphone to its stand, only to struggle to find his comfortable spot in the pilot's chair. The red vinyl seat was worn and frayed, the foam escaping out from several holes. He had covered it with a towel, but Monty had spilled coffee on it during his afternoon shift.

A Muslim of Palestinian descent, Mo Mallouh was a product of an arranged marriage. His parents had been born and raised in Jaffa, Israel, where his father had been a respected doctor. Dr. Mallouh had moved his family to Saudi Arabia after the birth of the couple's second child, where he ran a medical clinic in Dhahran—a compound for the Arabian American Oil Company: Aramco.

Mohammad had been born a few years later. Growing up on the Persian Gulf, the boy had spent most of his early years and summers working aboard his uncle's hopper-dredge, keeping the deep-water channels clear of silt for the oil tankers. When he turned fifteen, Mo's family relocated to the United States, where he graduated high school and attended Florida State University, studying to become a pharmacist. But Mohammad missed working on the water, and so he left school his junior year to join the U.S. Army Corps of Engineers, and received naval training. Three years later, he and his girlfriend moved to British Columbia, where he earned a decent living piloting hopper-dredges in the Salish Sea.

Mallouh had been recommended to Mac by the *McFarland*'s regular pilot, Matthew DeVictor, who had decided he'd had enough "thrills at sea" with the Taylor family, having spent the past three months tracking monsters in Antarctica.

David liked their new pilot, who was only twenty-seven years old and more of a peer. The fact that Mallouh knew the Salish Sea like the back of his hand made him a valuable asset . . . and yet, after more than two months searching the San Juan Islands south to Puget Sound, they were no closer to locating the Megalodon nursery than when they first started—

—and now another pup was dead.

The shark, one of Bela's, was a thirteen-foot, fifteen-hundred-pound female. Genetically identical to its mother, the juvenile killer shared the same bizarre pigment scheme—its head pure white, its dorsal surface, from its gill slits to the half-moon-shaped tail, lead gray.

According to eyewitnesses, a charter boat captain had hooked the shark for one of his paid guests while night-fishing off Orcas Island. After a three-hour struggle, they had managed to bring the big game fish to the surface and drop a net around it, only to discover they had hooked what they assumed was a great white. Unfortunately, the hook was in too deep to safely remove it. To free the line, the crew attempted to invert the shark and put it to sleep. The predator went berserk, dragging a passenger overboard, forcing the captain to kill it.

Taxidermies will not mount a protected species, and the charter boat captain couldn't afford a hefty fine, so he turned the shark's remains over to the Coast Guard. Suspecting it was another Megalodon pup, the authorities had contacted Nick Van Sicklen.

To demonstrate the threat the species posed to humans, the director of the Adopt an Orca program used a winch to suspend the dead shark upside down by its tail before eviscerating it with a chain saw, the contents of its stomach spilling out across a pier.

There were no human remains inside, but the YouTube video had gone viral, setting off a firestorm of protests from animal rights groups.

Exiting the galley, David made his way forward, ascending three flights of stairs to the pilothouse. The night before he had barely slept, unable to free his thoughts from the YouTube video.

Of late, it had been his girlfriend that kept him awake.

Two weeks into the voyage, Jackie had begun experiencing severe bouts of insomnia. Trish had offered her a mild sedative, but the deep sleep gave her horrible nightmares and she stopped taking them.

Ironically, their roles had been reversed when they had met six months before. He had made her the same offer of "therapeutic sex," only she had turned him down.

"*I love you, David, but I think we need to slow things down a bit . . . at least until I finish school.*"

"*What about me? I can't sleep with you up all night pacing the cabin. I need at least six hours of REM sleep or I start dozing off the next day in the Manta.*"

"*There are plenty of empty cabins aboard the ship—just move into one of them. I won't be insulted.*"

Of course, she *had* been insulted. Since then, they had barely been intimate. Jackie's perpetual state of exhaustion left her irritable—her "vampire hours," Monty called them—causing her to pace the lower deck's corridors until early morning, when she finally passed out.

David was worried about her, but his first priority was locating the sisters' remaining pups. A second albino offspring had been hooked in the San Juan Channel off Hadron Island ten days ago. With last night's kill, there were only two pups left at most—one of Bela's, one of Lizzy's.

He entered the pilothouse to find Mo Mallouh seated in the captain's chair, his gaze shifting from the windshield to the radar screen to the fish finder.

"Morning, Mo. What's up?"

"I received the location where that charter caught Bela's second pup from the Coast Guard and loaded it onto your laptop. I thought you should have a look at it before you set out in the Manta."

"Please don't tell me the nursery has to be along the north side of Orcas Island. I've searched every square foot of sea; it's all kelp forest and shallows . . . nothing deeper than ninety feet. Bela and Lizzy would have never chosen these waters to protect their young."

"I know, I know . . . but take a look. I have a theory."

David sat down at the chart table and wiggled the computer's cursor, causing a map of the San Juan Islands to appear. "Go on."

"See how the pups appear to stick by their own litter? What if this is just their hunting grounds? What if the nursery is located in the closest deep waters?"

"Which is where?"

"Boundary Pass."

"Maybe . . ." David stared at the map. Mallouh's theory made sense, and he certainly knew these waters better than most, but something felt wrong. "How long will it take you to get us to Boundary Pass?"

"Thirty minutes. The problem is remaining in the shipping lanes. Lots of oil tankers out there."

Oil tankers? Jesus . . .

"Mo, where's Mac?"

"Last time I saw him, he was on deck flushing out the hopper."

David closed the laptop and headed for the exterior starboard door.

"Wait. Should I take us into the Boundary Pass?"

"Not yet." Twisting the knob, David pushed the heavy door open with his shoulder, releasing a whistling gust of wind that ruffled the papers tacked to the cork bulletin board. Gripping the rusty steel rail with one hand, the laptop in the other, he descended the three flights of stairs to the main deck.

The sea was gray beneath an overcast sky, a 20-knot wind whipping up whitecaps. He spotted Mac standing by the rail next to the starboard draghead, which was positioned over the side. Seawater shot out of the five-foot-diameter pipe with the force of an open fire hydrant, slowly draining the hopper.

"Works good now," David shouted.

Mac nodded. "You wouldn't believe what we found clogging it—an empty sea turtle shell. The draghead must've pulled him off the bottom, only the shell got wedged halfway to the hopper. The force must've sucked the turtle right out of his home."

"Which means there's a buck-naked sea turtle swimming in my hopper." Cyel Reed joined them, carrying a scooper net attached to a long aluminum reach pole. "The Manta's charged and ready, except for your port-o-potty. You want that clean—clean it yourself . . . or else wear diapers."

"For the last time, I'm not wearing diapers. Mac, can I talk to you a minute?"

"Too much noise out here—let's go inside." Mac headed back to the

McFarland's superstructure, David slowing his pace to accommodate his godfather's hobbling gait.

"Damn arthritis. And this damp weather makes everything worse. You look tired, kid."

"I couldn't sleep. Why the hell did Van Sicklen have to eviscerate the dead pup like that?"

"He's sending a message."

"To who?"

"To us. You don't think he knows why we're here? The sisters butchered his orca, and he's not about to allow their offspring to turn the Salish Sea into a Megalodon spawning ground."

Mac's walkie-talkie squawked to life. "Mac, are you with David?"

"Yes, Trish. What's wrong?"

"Get down to Jackie's cabin . . . fast!"

Monty was hovering over her upper torso, the former Army medic administering five rapid chest compressions before pausing to allow Trish to blow air into Jackie's mouth.

"What happened?"

"We don't know," Trish said between breaths, pausing while Monty continued CPR. "I came down to check on her. . . . She wasn't breathing; no pulse."

"—two and three and four and go!"

Trish repositioned her mouth over Jackie's purple lips and tilted her head back to open her airway, giving her two more breaths.

"This is no good; she could have been out an hour before we found her." Monty dumped the contents of his black leather medical kit on top of the inert woman's bed. Locating the syringe, he pulled the cap from the four-inch needle and gripped it in his right fist.

Trish's eyes widened. "What are you doing?"

"Throwing a Hail Mary." Pulling up her T-shirt with his left hand, he plunged the shot of adrenaline next to her exposed left breast between her ribs and into her heart with no hesitation.

The lifeless, pale woman shot up in bed, gasping for air. She looked around the room wildly, then at her rescuers . . . and finally down at the empty syringe protruding from her chest.

"Ow!"

"That's a helluva shot, if I say so myself. Hit a rib and you bust the needle right in half."

"Get it out of me!"

Monty yanked it free.

"Ahh!"

Trish pulled down Jackie's T-shirt. "What did you take?"

"Was it this?" David held up an empty prescription bottle. "Percocet."

"How many pills were in there?" Trish demanded.

"I don't know," she moaned. Her eyes rolled back in her head as she fell asleep sitting up.

"We need to get her to the nearest medical facility," Mac said. "I'll get the chopper started; you and Monty carry her up on deck."

"I've got her." David handed his laptop to his friend, then cradled Jackie in both arms and carried her out of the cabin, following Mac up two flights of stairs to the helipad.

———

The PeaceHealth Peace Island Medical Center was located in Friday Harbor on San Juan Islands. It took longer for Mac to warm up the single-engine Robinson R44 Light Utility marine helicopter than to complete the actual flight.

David stayed with Jackie in the emergency ward while a team of nurses administered an IV along with oxygen via a nasal tube. An intern ushered him out to the waiting room when she started vomiting.

Twenty minutes passed before an ER doctor came out to speak with him. "Mr. Taylor? Dr. Abel Rivas; I'm the attending physician. Do you have any idea how many oxycodone Ms. Buchwald ingested?"

"I don't know. But the prescription said it was Percocet."

"Percocet is one of the brand names for oxycodone, which is a semi-synthetic opioid. The drug suppresses the central nervous and respiratory systems. About twenty thousand people die every year from opioid overdose."

"Geez, Doc, is she going to be okay?"

"We gave her a shot of naloxone, which is a fast-acting oxycodone antagonist. We're also giving her activated charcoal to prevent further absorption. She threw up, so we're not going to pump out her stomach, but we are going to move her to the ICU to monitor her closely over the next twenty-four hours. Once we release her, I recommend she seek counseling."

"Counseling? She's had bad insomnia, Doc. I really don't think—"

"Mr. Taylor, no one takes that much oxycodone because they can't sleep. Today you were lucky; next time who knows."

———

David exited the hospital feeling numb. *What could Jackie be going through that she'd want to kill herself?* Of all people, how had he missed the signs?

He spotted Mac and Monty seated on a park bench.

"How is she?"

"They're treating her with a bunch of drugs."

"Naloxone?"

"Yeah . . . How do you know?"

Monty smirked. "Think you're the only person who's ever been depressed? Naloxone and oxycodone got me through the first six months after the war."

"Are they keeping her overnight?" Mac asked.

"Yeah. I'm going to stay here with her."

"I figured you would." The white-haired Navy vet noticed David staring over his shoulder at their helicopter, which was situated on the manicured lawn adjacent to the visitors' parking. "What's wrong?"

"The guy in the white van . . . I think he's videotaping us with his iPhone."

———

Jerrod Mahurin had spent the past two summers interning with the Adopt an Orca program in Friday Harbor, the seventeen-year-old local hoping that adding the experience to his resume would help him get accepted into the University of Washington's marine biology program.

He had been working his usual Saturday shift at his father's hardware store when Nick Van Sicklen had called.

"Jerrod, a helicopter just set down at the medical center. I need you to get over there and let me know who's on board when it leaves."

"I can't leave the store until six."

"Mr. Mahurin, if you want that letter of recommendation from me, then I suggest you get your ass over to the Peace Health Center and do as I say."

"Okay . . . okay." Jerrod had hung the BACK IN 20 MINUTES sign on the front door before climbing into the white Mahurin Hardware minivan and driving to the medical center. Spotting the helicopter, he had parked and waited.

"We're being set up," David said, showing Mac and Monty the map on his laptop. "The local paper reported the location of the orca attack off Waldron Island, but that info could have easily been planted by Van Sicklen. Same with the last two nettings. What if they were set up to make it look like they occurred along the east coast of Orcas Island just to occupy us while Van Sicklen's team continues hunting for the remaining pups at the real nursery?"

"Which is where?" Mac asked.

"The Georgia Strait."

"How do you know that?"

"I've been saying it for a month; the waters around the San Juan Islands are way too shallow to have hidden Bela and Lizzy. The Strait of Juan de Fuca is to the west, but we spent three weeks there and I don't remember seeing any suspicious charters. That leaves Boundary Pass to the north and Haro Strait to the south—two deep-water channels used by oil tankers. When Kaylie and I were trapped in Maren's habitat on the bottom of the seafloor, do you remember how you forced the bathyscaphe up to the surface so we could swim free?"

Mac pointed at Monty. "It was your friend's idea. He had one of the prince's supertankers pass directly over the sphere. The displacement created a massive suction powerful enough to drag a Los Angeles–class attack sub to the surface."

Monty nodded. "In physics, we call it the 'vaginal effect.'"

"Venturi," Mac snapped.

"My point is that the Meg nursery couldn't possibly be in either channel—the tanker traffic is way too strong. It would suck the pups right off the bottom."

"Which leaves the Georgia Strait?"

"Correct."

"We're still talking about hundreds of square miles of sea to search. How do we locate the nursery before Van Sicklen kills any more pups?"

"It's not Van Sicklen; I'm sure he hired someone else to do his dirty work. But I think I have a way that we can quickly pinpoint the location of the nursery. If you or my father have a military connection that could get us access to satellite images taken last night in these waters, we could use them to locate the charter boat that supposedly hooked Bela's pup off Orcas Island. Rewind the images from there and they'll lead you back to the actual exchange I'm betting took place in the Georgia Strait between the fishing boat that took credit for hooking Bela's pup and the vessel that actually netted it. Once we identify *that* vessel, you'll be able to use the SAT images to track it back to the nursery."

Mac smiled. "Pretty sharp, kid. What about our junior spy in the van? Why is he here?"

David glanced at the parking lot. "Van Sicklen's no dummy. At some point he knows we'll use the SAT images to identify the real boat. Once that happens, you'd search the Georgia Strait using the chopper to locate the ship hunting the pups and direct the *McFarland* to the nursery—"

"—unless Van Sicklen knows I'm coming ahead of time," Mac said, "in which case he'd warn the captain to move the boat to a bogus location, baiting us to waste more time while a third boat is deployed to the real nursery to net the remaining pups."

"Assuming there are any remaining pups to net," Monty muttered. "Sorry. Nine and a half weeks . . . it's a long time . . . but a damn good movie. Kim Basinger's hot."

David ignored his friend's gust of bipolarism. "Mac, take my laptop and see if you can access last night's satellite imagery. Once you have the location of the nursery, text me and I'll sneak out of the hospital and get to a deserted stretch of coastline where Monty can pick me up in the Manta."

"Whoa, hold on, Junior. Do you honestly expect me to find my way back to the San Juan Islands all by myself aboard that coffin with wings? It's been over a year since I even piloted a Manta, and I sucked back then. There's a better chance of me ending up in Puerto Rico."

"Monty, you don't have to do anything. Cyel will program the coordinates into the sub's GPS; the automatic pilot will do the rest."

"Better let me program the GPS," Mac said.

"Why? What's wrong with Cyel?"

"David, think about it—how did Van Sicklen know we were on San Juan Islands so quickly?"

"You think Cyel Reed told him?"

"Maybe. I'm guessing there's a tracking device hidden aboard my helicopter, and someone aboard the *McFarland* had to have put it there. Either way, we have a traitor on board. I'm fairly confident it's none of us, and I'm willing to give my wife the benefit of the doubt."

"Which leaves our new captain, our disgruntled engineer—"

"And Jackie, who just tried to off herself."

"Doesn't make her a traitor, kid. Until we figure out who it is, I suggest we keep everything on the down-low. . . . Did I say that right?"

"You said it right, Uncle Mac. It just sounded ugly coming out of your face."

"Be careful about what comes out of your face, Monty, or that GPS might just beach you on an iceberg in Alaska."

||||||||||||||||||||||||||||||||

Strait of Georgia
Salish Sea, British Columbia, Canada

The Strait of Juan de Fuca and the Georgia Strait were created during the last Ice Age when massive glaciers advanced through British Columbia. These excavated canyons eventually filled with seawater, with any spared land formations becoming islands and islets.

Denman and Hornby were private islands along the east coast of Vancouver Island. Home to about a thousand residents, they had become popular retreats among the rich and famous, so it was no surprise to see the sixty-foot Hatteras sport yacht become a common fixture on the seascape.

The *Hot & Spicy* was two-thirds bow and one-third flybridge and tuna tower, stacked above a three-seat fishing deck that occupied the stern. Sleek outside, she was all luxury within, the contours of her four staterooms, heads, galley, and dinette decorated in gray leather and teak. Below decks, she harbored two 21.5 kW generators that supplied the electricity needed to run the latest in electronics and AV systems, and her twin engines were capable of cranking out the horsepower necessary to maintain a top speed over 40 knots.

For two months the gray-hulled ship could be seen trolling the Georgia Strait, the size of their lines indicating they were after serious game fish. After about five weeks the yacht settled upon the deep waters between the southeastern tip of Hornby Island and Flora Islet— a moonscape of rock inhabited by hundreds of sea elephants and seals. The mammals barked and belched and dove in and out of the emerald-green waters of the Georgia Strait, but none would venture far from land.

———————

Ben Smallwood awoke from his afternoon nap at 4:44, a minute before the alarm was set to go off. A framed photo of his wife, Shelly, and their two children greeted him on the teak night table. The yacht had been a gift from Shelly's family, but it came with one condition attached:

Kill every Megalodon pup in the Salish Sea.

Ben Smallwood had been born and raised in London, earning degrees in engineering and the marine sciences from Imperial College. Six years before, he had traveled to British Columbia to attend a two-week symposium in Vancouver, where he'd met Shelly Shelby, a thirty-year-old Texas native and marine biologist who was in town for the same event. By the third day they had become inseparable, attending lectures by day, the nights reserved for more intimate rendezvous.

Shelly's father, Heath, had flown in with his daughter on his private jet. The former associate vice president of operations at Enron Corporation was an avid fisherman and had chartered the forty-eight-foot fishing vessel *Bite Me-2* for the week, hoping to land a prize halibut to adorn the office of his new summer getaway in Prince Rupert Sound.

With the weekend upon them, Shelly Shelby had invited Ben to join her aboard the boat. They had flown to Vancouver Island Friday night and met her father for dinner at an upscale seaside restaurant in Victoria.

"Daddy, this is my friend, Ben Smallwood."

"Smallwood? Well, son, if I feel the boat rocking later, we may just have to change your name to Driftwood."

Two hours and five shots later, the two men were the best of friends.

It took most of Saturday for the crew of the *Bite Me-2* to hook Shelby his halibut. They had been cruising the Swiftsure Bank on the southwest coast of Vancouver Island between Port Renfrew and Sombrio Beach when the fishing rod's heavy Dacron line suddenly spun out on its reel.

Ben had done his best to stay out of the rain and the way of the first mate, who had quickly secured the billionaire into the deck-mounted chair. As the captain put the boat in reverse, the boisterous Texan was handed the rod and had begun taking up the slack on the six-hundred-pound fish.

"Christ, he's strong."

"She. We hooked you a big female. Just bring her in nice and easy."

Ben had feared Shelby might have a stroke as he watched the fifty-three-year-old's face turn from red to purple, the veins in his neck popping out like rope. "She's coming up a bit—I can feel her weakening."

The first mate stood ready with a gaff. "Keep the end of the rod in that steel swivel, Mr. S. Let the chair do the heavy lifting."

"Hey, Smallwood, make yourself useful and get Shelly's camera."

Ben had headed inside and made his way forward to the cabin where his girlfriend was sleeping. Locating the Nikon carrying case, he'd removed the camera.

"What are you doing?"

"Your dad hooked a huge fish; come take a look."

"I'm sick. Tell them to take me back to the dock."

Ben had emerged in the stern as a cloudburst of rain began to pelt the deck, the splatter of a trillion droplets cloaking all other sound. Using his T-shirt, he'd wiped condensation from the camera's lens and snapped several shots as the big Texan wrapped the crook of his arms around the rod.

Water had poured off the soaked bill of Heath Shelby's 49ers football cap. The man's arms were burning with lactic acid, his back and legs trembling from muscular exhaustion. Still he had refused to give an inch, knowing his daughter's new boyfriend was watching.

Locking down the tackle, he had straightened his legs and leaned back, drawing in line with his entire body—

—unaware that two hundred feet below and a quarter of a mile away, a far larger predator had entered the arena and was homing in on his would-be trophy.

The first mate patted Shelby on the back. "Stay with it; I'm going to get the bigger net."

"You do that, Gilligan. Smallwood, you getting this?"

"Yes—" Ben watched as Shelby fell back in the chair, the tension on the pole gone.

"No . . . no!"

"Did you lose him?"

"Shut up." Gripping the pole with his left hand and arm, he'd reeled in line rapidly with his right. "There you are . . . I can feel you. You're running to the boat, aren't you? Dumb bitch, I got you now! You're not getting away this—"

Ben had blinked. One moment Shelby had been there, the next he was gone—flying through the air and over the transom into the sea, along with the chair and the wood planks it had been bolted to.

In a state of shock, his mind unable to respond to what his eyes had just witnessed, the Englishman had walked around the hole in the deck and stood in the downpour by the back of the boat in a rain-muted white noise, the empty expanse of sea mocking him.

His eye had caught movement and the lens followed, the whir-ring clicks catching an impossibly large white dorsal fin just as it dis-appeared beneath the gray-blue waters . . . and then was gone.

They had searched all evening, the Coast Guard joining them, along with a dozen local crafts. Shelly had been inconsolable. Ben had stayed with her in her father's hotel room until Tuesday, when her cousin, Mark, announced that the search for his uncle was over.

Ben had kept the roll of film, waiting until he had returned to Lon-don before having it developed. Most of the shots of the water had been blurry, but in one he could see what appeared to be the upper half of a ghost-white caudal fin slapping the surface.

The story had broken on BBC One two nights later. Angel, the Meg-alodon shark raised in captivity that had broken free of her pen seven-teen years earlier, had returned to the Tanaka Lagoon . . . along with a sixty-one-foot, sixty-seven-thousand-pound male. From the vicious bite scars along Angel's pectoral fins, the two brutes had mated—an event the larger female was apparently none too happy about, as the dead male's remains had been found bleeding out at the bottom of the canal.

The results of a necropsy on the male a week later had revealed the contents of its stomach, which included a baseball, a six-hundred-twenty-five-pound halibut . . . and the remains of Heath Shelby.

Kill every Megalodon pup in the Salish Sea. . . .

Ben's first move was to seek help from one of the locals. Nick Van Sicklen had led the public outcry six months earlier when Lizzy and Bela had escaped from the Tanaka Institute and invaded the Salish Sea, wiping out an entire pod of orca. The director of the Adopt an Orca foundation informed him that a diver had been attacked by what he first thought were six small great whites—three albinos and three sharing Bela's bizarre pigment pattern. One of the dark-backed pups had been netted and killed by Paul Agricola, a retired marine biologist, leaving five Megalodon offspring to terrorize the Salish Sea. It was Agricola who had used his company's hopper-dredge, the *Marieke*, to capture Lizzy and return her to the institute.

Anthony Marcinkowski had been first mate aboard the *Marieke*; for $2,000 a week he agreed to carry out similar duties aboard the Englishman's yacht. Unfortunately, every island in the Salish Sea looked alike to the former paramedic; but he did manage to isolate their search for the Meg nursery to the Georgia Strait.

The yacht's fish finder had given them their first glimpse of their prey when one of the pups passed beneath the boat in the waters off Texada, an island just northeast of Hornby. Sonar had painted a predator that was thirteen-to-fifteen-feet in length, weighing an estimated thirty-five hundred pounds. If this was a Meg pup, then the sharks had doubled in size and tripled their girth over that of their seven-foot sibling that Paul Agricola had netted and accidentally drowned six months earlier.

That presented a problem—these juvenile killers were far too large to bring in on a rod and reel. Rigging a trawl net was a possibility; but the Megs seemed to prefer the deep. Enticing one to the surface without the sea drone Anthony Marcinkowski's former employer had used to bait Lizzy would be a challenge, and chumming in the Salish Sea was illegal. They would have to hook something on the order of a halibut as bait and drag it ahead of the open mouth of the trawl if they had any hope of netting one of these killers.

Nick Van Sicklen, a valuable ally, had introduced Ben to a commercial fisherman who sold him a used trawl and set of winches. The director of the Adopt an Orca program also arranged to have a number of charter boat captains on standby so that, when a pup was captured, it could be hauled off to another area in order to keep the actual location of the Meg nursery from the local media—and Jonas Taylor's expedition.

They had been searching the Georgia Strait for several weeks, focusing on the local seal population, when they had their first surface encounter—a midnight banquet in the waters off Flora Islet, the pups' albino hides appearing bioluminescent in the lunar light.

That the sharks were nocturnal hunters was not unexpected; after all, the subspecies of Megalodon inhabiting the Mariana Trench lived in perpetual darkness. What Ben had not considered was the effect of the moon's phases on the creatures' feeding schedule. Lunar light gave the hunters a decided advantage, in that it reflected off bait fish as they surfaced to feed. With the juvenile Megs, the full moon appeared to send them into an absolute feeding frenzy.

Releasing the trawl, the crew of the *Hot & Spicy* attempted to sweep the pups up into the heavy nylon trap. On the third pass they succeeded in netting one of Lizzy's albino offspring—along with a half-eaten sea lion and three adult seals.

Ben contacted Nick Van Sicklen, who quickly tracked a resident pod of orca congregating in the waters off the San Juan Islands. The two boats rendezvoused a half-mile northeast of Hadron Island just before dawn. As the sunrise blistered the horizon gold, the net holding Lizzy's thrashing offspring was raised halfway out of the sea, affording one of the crew armed with a chainsaw an angle to cut off the Meg's right pectoral fin. The bleeding animal was then released to the circling pod of killer whales, the bulls taking turns eviscerating the shark as they fought to claim its liver—

—the entire scene filmed by Nick Van Sicklen on his iPhone.

The second Meg was netted twenty-nine nights later.

A heavy rain and six-foot seas rocked the yacht beyond the point of nausea, while the full moon remained concealed behind dense storm clouds.

The weather let up at 4:20 a.m.; the skies cleared an hour later. With dawn approaching and both the full moon and their opportunities waning, two crewmen were set ashore on Flora Islet with clubs and burlap bags. Ten minutes later the trawl was baited with a freshly killed pair of sea lions. By 5 a.m. the bleeding carcasses had attracted a pup, which refused to enter the open net . . . until a second Meg appeared on the yacht's fish finder. Realizing it was about to lose its meal, the first juvenile—another albino—darted inside the trap and was captured.

Three 12-gauge shots to the brain killed the beast. An eight-inch barbed hook was then hammered with a rubber mallet into place beneath the lower jaw. The rod and reel were passed off to another charter boat, which towed the dead "game fish" into the shallows between Stuart, Waldron, and the west coast of Orcas Island. Two local news teams arrived just in time to film the catch as it was hauled in. According to several unidentified eyewitnesses, the monster had gone berserk, forcing the crew to kill it.

Few who saw the ghostly two-ton, fourteen-and-a-half-foot albino beast hanging from a construction crane thought to protest.

By now, the crew of the *Hot & Spicy* had the routine down pat—so much so that Ben ordered the yacht anchored off Vancouver Island, giving his men three weeks of paid leave while they waited for the arrival of the next full moon.

It was then that the Shelby family's personal mission of revenge turned into an international game of dead pool.

It began when officials on San Juan Islands confirmed a report from a local diver stating that he had counted six Megalodon offspring— three from each deceased "sister"—when he had been attacked in the shallows off Orcas Island. Since then, one of Bela's pups had been killed, and two of Lizzy's . . . and suddenly the hot topic of conversation was which sister—the cunning albino or the dark-backed brute—possessed the best traits to allow its pup to be the last shark swimming.

Odds were posted, Las Vegas covering the action. Within a week boating traffic in the Salish Sea doubled.

Thankfully, most of it was confined to the San Juan Islands, where the three Megs had supposedly been captured. A local expert was needed to handle interview requests, and Nick Van Sicklen stepped into the limelight to preach about the "evil trio" still stalking the Salish Sea. The press ate it up, and soon there were rumors of Van Sicklen running for mayor.

Realizing that things could easily get out of hand, Ben met with his crew before weighing anchor, reminding them that they had signed nondisclosure agreements and that wagering in the Dead Pool would not be tolerated.

Ben might have been worried, but last night's netting, kill, and staged capture had played out with military precision. With the Dead Pool tied at two, the next pup captured would win it . . . or lose it, depending upon the wager.

Then Nick Van Sicklen took things too far. Before a crowd of reporters, the amped-up orca advocate had taken out a chainsaw and proceeded to eviscerate the dead juvenile's belly, hoping to produce human remains. Instead, he galvanized a public backlash, led by protests from animal rights groups, who demanded that the Executive Council of British Columbia take action against those who were hunting a protected species.

It was five-thirty in the afternoon by the time Ben Smallwood entered the pilothouse. Keith Amato was on duty, the yacht's copilot occupying the captain's chair, his attention focused on the fish finder.

"Are you tracking one of the remaining pups?"

"No, boss. Something a lot bigger."

Ben joined him at the monitor, the sonar "painting" an object tracking slowly along the seafloor, moving south by southeast at 3 knots.

"Twenty-five feet, weighing nine thousand pounds. It's either a juvenile orca or a young humpback."

"It's not a whale. I've been matching its course and speed for forty-three minutes and it hasn't come up for air. It's gotta be a whale shark."

Ben shook his head. "Whale sharks prefer the tropics. These waters are way too cold."

"It's rare, but it happens. A few years ago, a dead female washed ashore not too far south of here in Lincoln Beach. Not sure how it died."

"Maybe it was assassinated." Ben reached for the cell phone vibrating in his front pocket. He read the text message out loud. "The pigeon is still in its coop."

"You raise pigeons?"

"It's code, Mr. Amato. It means the competition is still stuck in the starting gate. If you need me, I'll be in the galley. And stop shadowing that whale shark. It may not have any teeth, but its size could be keeping the Meg pups away."

PeaceHealth Peace Island Medical Center
San Juan Islands, Salish Sea

Jackie certainly looked better. The color had returned to her complexion and she had regained her appetite.

David sat in a cushioned chair next to her bed, watching her devour a cheeseburger. "I'm glad to see you're eating."

She nodded, her mouth full. "Thanks for smuggling this in, babe. I needed it."

"Like you needed the opioids?"

"Percocet. And I told you, I only took them because I've been having problems falling asleep."

"Jackie, you're talking to the reigning champion of insomnia; it comes from harboring fears that lead to nightmares and a whole lot worse. So why don't you quit lying and tell me the truth."

She crumpled up the remains of the burger in its foil wrap and threw it at him. "Now I'm a liar?"

He was about to respond when his cell phone started chiming "Pop Goes the Weasel." He glanced at the text message: "False Bay. Fifteen minutes."

He replied, "Okay," and then tossed the rolled-up sandwich in the wastepaper basket. "I gotta go."

"You're leaving me to meet Monty?"

"Who said that?"

"I know his ringtone, David."

"Jackie—and I can't believe this is coming from me—but you need counseling. The guy I was seeing back in Monterey wasn't bad—I can get you his number."

"David, don't go!" She lunged forward to grab his wrist, pulling her IV out in the process, the blood drizzling from her vein.

"Damn it, Jackie." He reached for a wad of paper napkins and pressed them to the back of her hand.

"Ow."

"Keep pressure on that," he said as he pressed the nurse's call button. "We need help; she pulled out her IV."

Leaning forward, she kissed him on the cheek, tears in her eyes. "I'll tell you, then you can go."

He nodded as the door opened and a Jamaican nurse entered. "What a mess; now why would you want ta do a t'ing like dis?"

"It was an accident."

Pursing her lips as if saying "Accident my ass," the nurse donned a pair of latex gloves, snapping each finger in place. She cleaned and dressed the wound, then selected a fresh vein on the back of Jackie's other hand. Using an alcohol swab, she sterilized the area and slid the needle into the blood vessel.

"Ow again."

She disposed of the needle and collected the trash. "The doctor will be in ta see you soon; try not to pull this one out."

Jackie waited for the door to click shut behind the nurse. "David—"

"Jackie, I already know."

Her hands started shaking. "You do?"

"You put a tracking device on board Mac's chopper."

"What? Why would I do that?"

"To give Van Sicklen a heads-up when we realized the Meg nursery is in the Georgia Strait."

"David . . . no. God, is that what you think? I'd never turn against you—you saved my life."

"Then what is it?"

"It's my fault the *Tonga* sunk. I'm to blame for all those people dying."

David felt the blood rush from his face. "What are you talking about? It was the *melvillei*."

"The whale was drugged until I shot it with a tracking device. The harpoon must have pierced its skull and struck a sensitive part of its brain. The next thing I know, it went berserk."

"Even if that's true, it wasn't your fault, it was an accident."

"David, I was the marine biologist in charge. It was my job to keep that monster from destroying the ship. I not only failed—it was my actions that caused it to flip out. What do you think a jury is going to decide? What will a judge rule? You can bet the prosecutors will go for criminal negligence. I'm not some rich CEO; they'll give me jail time. Then there's the civil lawsuits. Think we have much of a future together with that mess hanging over my head? Face it, David, I'm toxic."

She sniffed, fresh tears pouring down her cheeks. "All that . . . maybe I could deal with it . . . only I can't stop . . . I can't stop thinking about the people on board the tanker who died. I knew most of the crew. . . . Many of them were my friends. Some days I can't handle being in my own skin. Some nights . . . some nights I wish you would have just let me die."

David caught her as she rolled over and wept, stroking her hair as his cursed iPhone went off, chiming "Pop Goes the Weasel."

Danielle Taylor stared out of the passenger window at the billowy-white cloud formations casting their shadows across the uneven squares of farmland that divided the flatland like a quilt. Dirt roads connected acreage to an occasional dwelling, but for the most part it was just patches of green and brown and isolation. She wondered about what it must be like to live so far from towns and cities—and about the six-year-old who insisted on kicking the back of her seat.

Four hours out of Fort Lauderdale—another hour before they'd land. She imagined herself collecting her suitcase from the baggage carousel and wheeling it out to locate her Uber. They'd hit some rush-hour traffic before exiting to the UC San Francisco campus. The driver would follow the circular drive of her apartment building and she'd exit into the lobby, where she'd flash her student ID before catching the first elevator up to the sixth floor. The hall was always quiet during midterms and finals; otherwise the walls would have been throbbing with music. She'd key into Unit 623 and hug her roommates. She'd shower and change and then they'd hit Union Square for a quick bite before pulling an all-nighter in the library.

Her fellow med students would chastise her for ordering a few glasses of wine with dinner, but Dani needed just enough of a buzz to tuck away the last three weeks of doctor's visits and endless tests and nightly battles between her parents—her father urging her mother to eat, *"Just another sip of Ensure . . . just one more grape,"* her mother moaning, *"I can't, Jonas! Enough!"*—Only it was never enough; each ounce her mother took in was two less than the day before . . . one step forward, two steps back.

Cancer was a cruel game of whack-a-mole, and Parkinson's had become its bedfellow, draining what little energy her mother had left to the point where her father would simply swoop her up in his arms and carry her from the car to the apartment or the doctor's office. She'd fuss and roll her eyes, but she knew that he needed to do it—to be her hero again—and so who was she to argue? And at the end of each day they'd cross another box off the wall calendar in the kitchen of their rental apartment—*"Twenty-seven more days before your protocol begins. . . . Twenty-three more X's before the cancer meets its killer. . . . Only three more weeks, Mother!"*

Maybe the cancer knew its days were numbered; with twenty days to go before her mother would undergo her white cell cancer elixir, Danielle had received a 7 a.m. call from Dr. Maharaj. *"Dani, you need to bring your mother to our office right away—her last blood test shows her creatinine level has risen dangerously high."*

From her studies, Dani knew that creatinine was a chemical waste generated by muscle metabolism and transported through the bloodstream to the kidneys. The kidneys then filtered out most of the creatinine and disposed of it in the urine. Mom's creatinine levels had risen from a normal 1.2 to 2.1 due to her not eating or drinking enough fluids, a condition that could lead to renal failure.

Dr. Maharaj adjusted their game plan to include three hours every morning of IVs until her creatinine levels stabilized.

They had made it through two more days when the next domino fell—her mother's uric acid levels were too high and had to be reduced for her to qualify for the protocol. That meant daily blood work and more IVs.

Dr. Maharaj's main concern was that her mother was growing weaker from not eating. Despite their constant coaxing, Mom was still not co-operating, complaining that it hurt too much to swallow. With seventeen days to go, a physical exam revealed the cause—the inside of Terry Taylor's mouth and throat was covered with thrush.

Thrush is an infection caused by the candida fungus. Often contracted by infants, the yeast spreads quickly in adults with weakened immune systems. The medicated rinse prescribed by Dr. Maharaj burned Mom's mouth beyond tolerance levels, so it had to be diluted.

Dani had looked at the discovery of thrush as a positive development—if the meds could eliminate the cause of her mother's reluctance to swallow, then hopefully she could start eating again. And so, a new routine developed—blood tests every morning, followed by four hours of IVs along with thrush rinses three times a day, and every other day, a trip to nearby Lynn University to drain her mother's left lung of fluid.

With fifteen days to go before the protocol, Dr. Maharaj had good news—a suitable donor had been found. More good news turned out to be a double-edged sword—the medication had removed the thrush, but her mother still couldn't swallow without pain. An endoscopy was scheduled to determine if there was a blockage.

Dani had midterms scheduled at the end of the week. Her parents insisted she fly back to San Francisco so she wouldn't fall any further behind on her studies. *"Okay, Mom, but only if you promise to drink three cans of Ensure a day."*

"I'll try."

With exactly two weeks to go, her father awoke to discover that a red rash had spread over most of her mother's back, so thick that it looked like she was wearing a vest. Dr. Maharaj felt it was probably a reaction to all the thrush medication and reduced her dosage.

Today was Day Thirteen on the kitchen wall calendar. Dani had a noon flight scheduled; her mother had a 7 a.m. endoscopy. Thankfully, the gastrologist found no blockage, but he was extremely concerned. "Mrs. Taylor's lack of nourishment is taking a toll. She'll never last until the protocol unless she takes in at least five hundred to a thousand calories a day."

Before boarding the plane, Dani had called Dr. Maharaj. "I know it's against protocol, but my mother's wasting away to nothing. We need you to move the start day up."

"When will you be back in South Florida?"

"Friday."

"All right. We'll push everything up to Monday. But tell your father she has to eat."

Dani had wept at the news.

"We'll be arriving at Gate C-13. Please wait until the plane has come to a full stop before leaving your seat. Use caution in opening the overhead bins, as your personal items may have shifted during the flight. On behalf of Captain William Fields and our flight crew, we'd like to thank you for flying United. The local time is now four twenty-five p.m."

Danielle stretched in her seat before taking out her cell phone to check her messages.

"Dani, it's Dad. Mom's in West Boca Medical Center. Call me."

She speed-dialed her father's number, her heart racing. "Dad, it's me. What happened?"

"About two hours after you left she had trouble catching her breath. Dr. Maharaj told me to get her to the ER. She has fluid in her right lung; they think she may have aspirated the Ensure from her esophagus muscles being so weak and out of sync. They have her wearing this enormous mask that forcibly blasts pure oxygen into her mouth. It's torture."

"What does Maharaj say?"

"He wants them to treat her lung and get her out of here. We're waiting on a thoracic specialist, but he won't be here until tomorrow morning, so it looks like we're spending the night. They're waiting for a bed to open up in the ICU. Dani, one of the ER doctors wants to speak with me; I need to call you back."

She hung up, feeling numb. It seemed like yesterday that Dr. Brennan was reciting her mother's verdict. Dani wished she could go back in time to that day . . . to redirect her parents to reject the course of chemo offered by the Abramson Center and go with the slight Indian doctor in Boynton Beach offering the miracle they were praying for.

Realizing she was the last passenger on board, she climbed out from her window seat, grabbed her carry-on bag from the open overhead bin, and exited the plane, her legs shaking as she made her way up the ramp and into the terminal. She cursed her decision to leave her parents as she scrolled through her messages to locate Dr. Maharaj's cell phone number.

"Dr. M., it's Dani Taylor."

"Danielle, hello. How is your mother?"

"I don't know. I just spoke to my father; he said they're going to be admitting her."

"Yes, it's very important that they clear her lung with antibiotics along with the oxygen. I told your father to make sure they start her on nutrients as well; hopefully she can regain some strength. What's important is that they don't start treating her cancer. Clear her lung; nutrients as soon as possible. Nothing more."

"Understood."

She hung up, feeling slightly more hopeful. If the hospital could feed her mother intravenously, then perhaps this new setback would be a blessing in disguise.

She found her way to the baggage claim, feeling mentally and physically exhausted. Her roommates had volunteered to help her cram for midterms, but the thought of studying all night seemed overwhelming. She recalled her father quoting General George S. Patton while training her for track-and-field tryouts back in high school. *"Fatigue makes cowards of us all, Dani. Your body is telling you to quit, but it's really your mind. You're not just conditioning your muscles; you're disciplining your thought process to stay positive."*

She recognized her suitcase circling the carousel and ran to it before it disappeared through the exit. *Suck it up, soldier. Think of what Mom has to endure; think about Dad and the long night and days ahead for him. Ace your exams, then get back to South Florida in time to witness your mother's miracle.*

She headed outside looking at her iPhone to see where her Uber was located. An old poster of San Francisco's attractions stared her in the face, one of the photos featuring Angel, taken as the seventy-four-foot, fifty-ton Megalodon rose out of the southern end of the lagoon to eat.

This sucks. Why does David get to pursue his dream while I'm flying from coast to coast, taking care of our parents and pulling all-nighters?

She took out her phone and dialed his number, the call going straight to voice mail.

"Hey, superstar, it's your sister. You need to forget about your stupid sharks and get your ass to Boca—our parents need you!"

False Bay, San Juan Islands

Nearly encircled by land, False Bay resembled a giant bite mark taken out of the southwestern coastline of San Juan Islands. The shallow waterway might have been a popular tourist destination had it not been for the abundance of shellfish that washed up daily along the mud-laced shoreline, each low tide leaving behind a powerful, intolerable stench.

Shoes in hand, David stood ankle-deep in the bog, watching seabirds feast on oysters and clams. He had been waiting for nearly an hour, the sun having long since dropped behind the mountains that occupied the western horizon, bathing the predusk sky in an orange hue. The screwup was his; he had left the hospital forty minutes late for his rendezvous with the Manta and his iPhone had died on the jog over, severing all communication between his GPS and the missing sub.

Without that signal to home in on, Monty could be anywhere.

David felt his lower back tightening. With no place to sit, he could only shift his weight or continue walking along the shallows—an activity he ceased after stepping on a crab.

The sky had deepened to a scarlet burgundy by the time he saw the ripple appear on the placid surface, the two-foot wave moving steadily in his direction. A quick flicker of underwater lights revealed the Manta. David hurried to intercept the sub before it beached, frantically signaling Monty to kill the engines to prevent the vessel's twin pump-jet propulsors from getting clogged with mud. Grabbing the vessel by its prow, he slowed its forward inertia, then turned it around one hundred and eighty degrees before pushing it back out into deeper waters.

The hatch popped open, releasing Monty, who stood up in the cockpit, unzipped his shorts, and ceremoniously peed over the side. "I've been holding that in for two hours—what the hell happened to you?"

"My phone died." David stepped onto the portside wing to climb aboard, causing the sub to teeter and Monty to pee down his shorts.

"Hey!"

"Sorry. You know there is a built-in porta-potty connected to your seat."

"And have to listen to Cyel bitch about using it? No thanks."

David dried his feet off on the carpet before slipping his shoes on. He then secured his feet to the two foot pedals and buckled the harness across his chest while Monty sealed the hatch. Powering on the engines, he headed across False Bay at 5 knots, approaching the exit to the Salish Sea.

"I take it Mac located the vessel that caught Bela's pup?"

"She was in the Georgia Strait, just as you predicted. A big ol' yacht—the Hot & Spicy, registered in Texas."

"Texas? What's it doing in the Salish Sea?"

"Hunting Meg pups . . . duh. The owner is Shelly Shelby-Smallwood. Her father was some corporate bigwig. He died on a fishing trip in the Salish Sea when he was yanked overboard and eaten by the male Meg that impregnated Angel."

"Geez. Well, that explains his daughter's motive. Where's the yacht now?"

Monty pressed a control on the dashboard monitor, causing a GPS satellite image of two islands to appear.

"Denman and Hornby Island?"

"Yeah, but there's a small island that's not showing up. . . . Hold on." He magnified the image to reveal Flora Islet. "According to Mohammad—our hopper captain, not the prophet—the water's real deep. He thinks there might be a seal population living on that rock."

"The Meg nursery . . . Where's the *McFarland*?"

"On the way. Mac said they should arrive around midnight."

"Then we need to put the pedal to the metal." They had reached the choppy surf separating the shallow bay from the sea. David switched the cockpit glass to night-vision mode, causing the world to brighten to lime green before he pushed down on the joystick in his right palm.

The submersible plunged at a steep angle to one hundred feet before he leveled out and pressed both feet to the thruster pedals.

The Manta accelerated through the dark green void, its forward speed causing particles in the water to whip at them as if they were traveling in a blizzard.

David locked in their course on the autopilot, adjusting the sub's speed to 30 knots. "We'll follow Boundary Pass into the Georgia Strait. Better go active on sonar, Monty. I don't want to get us sucked into the vortex of a tanker."

"Yeah, that would suck." Reaching for the sonar array, he flipped the toggle switch from PASSIVE to ACTIVE. "You know, Junior, if my dad had been eaten by one your sharks—"

"That big male wasn't one of ours."

"Duly noted. But if one of my family members had been eaten by Angel, or Bela or Lizzy, one could see why they'd want to kill these sharks."

"What's your point?"

"Actually, that was my point."

"Monty, I'm not advocating allowing the Megs to use the Salish Sea as a breeding ground. The difference is that I don't want them killed, I want them held in captivity."

"Right. But you don't exactly have a great track history of keeping these monsters in their pens. Angel escaped; so did Bela and Lizzy."

"Bela and Lizzy were released—there's a big difference."

"Not to the people who were eaten. Listen, I'm on your side. But if it comes down to us or them, I need to know you'll choose us."

David closed his eyes.

"Kinda need an answer to that one."

"Yeah, yeah . . . us over them."

Aboard the Sport Yacht *Hot & Spicy*
2 Miles Northwest of St. John's Point, Hornby Island
1 Mile Southeast of Flora Islet

Keith Amato was tired. The Long Island native was on his second six-hour shift and his eyes were already bleary from staring at the fish finder. As the hour approached 11 p.m., dense gray patches of cumulus clouds quickly moved in from the east to obscure the full moon, deflating the crew's spirits and casting them into a dense, uncomfortable darkness.

The pilot had no need for the lunar light; his instruments told him exactly where he was. Even had his GPS failed, he could smell Flora Islet as they passed the tiny hunk of rock to port. The pinniped habitat carried a powerful stench, and the approaching storm placed the yacht squarely downwind—a place no one on board wanted to be.

Captain Amato had been waiting for the updated weather forecast before determining their new course. At 11:05 he received the report: *Thunderstorms likely before midnight . . . clearing by 3 a.m. Seas: six to seven feet.*

No sense circling back around Flora; best to tuck us in at Tribune Bay until this mess blows over.

He was about to change course when the fish finder alerted him to the presence of the whale shark. The twenty-five-foot fish had crossed into range about a hundred yards off the portside bow. They had crossed paths no less than a dozen times today, the docile creature navigating the deep waters between Flora Islet and St. John's Point, which was a nature preserve on Hornby Island's northern coast.

As the pilot watched, the whale shark suddenly rose on a near-vertical ascent, homing in on what appeared to be two seals swimming along the surface.

Seals? Wait a second . . . whale sharks are filter feeders!

Amato turned the wheel hard to port with his right hand as he reached with his left for his night binoculars where they were hanging from a peg. Stealing a quick glance at the fish finder, he thought he saw the blip split into two—

—as the two Megalodon juveniles exploded out of the sea less than thirty feet off the yacht's starboard bow.

Through the night glasses he zoomed in on the albino, its upper torso twisting above the surface as its massive head whipped the two-hundred-and-twenty-pound seal in its mouth from side to side, the serrated daggers of its lower jaw clamping down upon its writhing meal microseconds ahead of the thick, wide upper teeth, which tore the shocked pinniped in half.

The other killer wasn't interested in style points. Rising straight out of the sea with its ghost-white belly to the yacht, it took the entire second seal in its mouth and simply crushed it behind nine tons per square inch of bite-force—half that of its parent, but more than enough to blast mammalian bone and blubber into a crimson piñata, the remains of which trickled down its quivering gullet.

It wasn't until the boat passed the second beast that Keith Amato realized it possessed a dark back.

Clever fish . . . they were swimming in tandem. . . .

The pilot blasted the horn twice and then grabbed the handset to the squawk box. "Surface sighting—two Meg juvies to starboard. Stand by, I'm coming about!"

He was about to execute a hundred-eighty-degree turn to starboard when the pilothouse door was wrenched open and Ben Smallwood rushed in.

"We've got company."

"I know . . . both remaining pups—"

"No . . . listen." He held open the door.

At first Keith Amato thought it was thunder, until he heard the distinct beating of a helicopter's rotors. "Coast Guard?"

"No, it's Mackreides. Which means the *McFarland* is close by; which means David Taylor is probably already in the Manta looking for a way to lure those Megs beneath the hopper so they can capture them."

"What do you want me to do?"

"The crew is baiting the trawl net. Once it's deployed, I want you to sweep them up and drown them. This ends tonight."

"Ugh . . . dude, what did you eat?"

"Bratwurst and onions. And don't blame me; you're the one who told me to use the porta-potty."

David blasted the air vents on high. "I'm surfacing and you're gonna clean that—"

"C-1 to M-7, come in."

David reached for his headphones. "Manta here; go ahead, Mac."

"I've located the yacht . . . uploading her coordinates now."

David checked the GPS. "Latitude: 49.5172 degrees north; longitude: 124.5767 degrees west . . . got it. Where's the *McFarland*?"

"Twenty minutes out."

"We'll be there in half that time."

"That may not be soon enough. It looks like they're getting ready to deploy a trawl net. Get here as quickly as you can, I'll do my best to buy you time. Mac out."

David pressed both feet to the thruster pedals, pushing the submersible's speed up to 43 knots. The debris was blinding, forcing him to rely solely on their active sonar to avoid striking one of the hundreds of rock formations lying in clusters on the strait.

Monty's complexion was as white as a sheet. He let out a scream as David swerved around an islet that suddenly bloomed out of the blizzard.

"Slow down! You can't rescue them if we're dead."

"Okay . . . okay." He reduced the sub's speed to 30 knots.

"So what's the game plan?"

"The game plan is to get them close to the *McFarland*'s keel and then pop open the dredge door, sucking them up into the hopper."

"Which means we're bait?"

"I'm open to suggestions."

"How about we call this off and open a pet store?"

David was about to reply when another islet appeared on their sonar screen. He checked the coordinates on his GPS. "That's it . . . that's Flora." Pulling back on the joystick, he ascended to the surface.

Dark waves rolled over the cockpit glass; intra-cloud lightning illuminated the heavens. There were no ships in sight.

"M-7 to C-1; Mac, where the hell are you?"

"Engaged in battle. Where the hell are you?"

"I'm here . . . Flora Islet."

"You must be on the east end. Circle around, kid. You're missing out on all the fun."

Remaining on the surface, David accelerated to the north. As they circled around the one-mile-diameter moonscape of rock, lights appeared to the southwest.

The yacht was heading toward the islet, its stern lit up by Mac's helicopter. The former Navy pilot was hovering over the ship, his landing gear within a few feet of the transom, his overhead rotors blasting the crew, preventing them from deploying their trawl net.

"Way to go, Mac!"

"Junior—"

"How close is the *McFarland*?"

"Eight minutes."

"David!" Monty pointed to the sonar, where a large object was rising beneath them.

"Oh, shit." He jammed both foot pedals to the floor and wrenched the joystick hard to port, sending the Manta into a steep vertical dive—

—as a black-and-white blur torpedoed past them.

Rocketing toward the seafloor, he pulled the sub out of its nosedive and leveled out at a depth of two hundred thirty feet, his head on a swivel. "Do you see them?"

"I see them both." Monty pointed.

"Oh . . . wow."

The juvenile Megalodons were circling the sub, swimming in tandem. Bela's offspring was on top, her dark pectoral fins aligned with her albino cousin's head, the top of which was pressed against her belly, the two sharks moving effortlessly and as one.

"How did they learn to . . . you think from watching their mothers do it?"

David nodded. "It's a defensive posture; to another predator they appear much larger. What's interesting is that Lizzy was always on top . . . she was the instigator to Bela's enforcer. The cousins reversed it."

"Maybe the albino's the enforcer in this generation of monsters?"

"I don't think so. Both Megs are clones of their mothers; aggression and intellect are genetic traits."

"I'm no expert, but they seem agitated."

Noticing the downward angle of both pairs of pectoral fins, David switched the sonar from active to passive, shutting off the acoustic pings.

As he watched, the creatures' pectoral fins lost some of their downward rigidity.

"Monty, if you blur your eyes, what do they look like to you?"

"They look like a fat shark. Oh wait—they look like an orca. You don't really think they did that on purpose?"

"Lizzy was clever . . . she could reason."

"Then why was she always on top? The top dog does more work; the bottom shark gets a free ride."

"Think about it. The sisters were born in captivity . . . they shared a tank with three rival stepsisters, and all five of them feared Angel . . . an albino. In the Meg Pen, it made much more sense to have Lizzy on top, projecting her dominance. But these juvies . . . they've had to survive in the wild, where being an albino is a distinct disadvantage— which is why the dark-backed Meg is on top."

"So, what happens now?"

"Now, we lead them away from that yacht." Reaching for the sonar controls, he flipped the toggle switch from passive to active.

Ping . . . ping . . . ping . . .

As David watched, the Megs' pectoral fins pointed down, their backs arching—the telltale signs of a pending attack.

Anticipating their angle, he accelerated to the south.

"Watch it—they split up!"

"Huh?" He spun around to see the fifteen-foot albino closing fast, with no sign of the dark Meg. *Dumbass . . . she's leading you into an ambush!*

Pulling back on the joystick, David shot straight up to the surface as Bela's offspring charged at them from the east.

"Watch out for the yacht!"

"Shit!" Yanking back hard on the joystick, he inverted the sub, executing a two-hundred-seventy-degree loop, the belly of the Manta's sphere-shaped Lexan cockpit grazing the yacht's keel.

Whomp . . .

Whomp . . .

"What was that?"

David leveled off, his heart racing. "Sounded like the cousins' heads just smacked into the bottom of the boat."

"Here's hoping they knocked themselves out." Monty flipped the sonar switch back to passive.

"Do that, and we're blind."

"Not quite." He pointed to the surface a hundred twenty feet above their heads, now glistening like liquid silver. The clouds had parted, revealing the full moon, the lunar light casting cobalt-blue curtains into the depths.

The silhouette of Bela's offspring was circling ten feet below the swells with agitated sweeps of her caudal fin, waiting for her albino cousin, who appeared to be spy-hopping, her two-ton girth vertical in the water, the shark visible from her gills down to her swishing tail.

David tapped the controls on his headset. "Mac, where are you?"

"Hovering about two hundred feet over Lizzy's pup. Damn thing's staring at the moon. But she'd better move, because the yacht's circling back, and they just released the trawl net."

"Damn." David flipped the sonar back to active, the first series of pings painting the two Megalodons on the surface—

—along with the yacht, which was on an intercept course a hundred yards to the east.

———

Ben Smallwood stood in the bow of the *Hot & Spicy*, his left hand gripping the polished aluminum rail, his right holding the night-vision binoculars to his face. He wasn't sure which Megalodon was spy-hopping; he only cared that its attention was focused on something other than the yacht.

He reached for the walkie-talkie hanging from his belt. "Stay on this course, Captain. We'll either scoop this bitch up in the trawl or slice her to ribbons."

―――――――

David pulled back on the joystick, racing the Manta toward the two Megs as he attempted to draw the sharks away from the surface.

Bela's offspring broke first, descending on an intercept course, its freakish white head—luminescent in the moonlight—appearing disembodied from the rest of its dark hide.

Keeping his left foot down, David pulled up on the right thruster as he jammed the joystick to the three o'clock position—

—the Manta pulling a full G as he executed a wing-over-wing starboard roll that left the charging Meg snapping at empty sea—and caused Monty to vomit the remains of his lunch across the sonar display.

"Jesus, dude!"

"Urp . . . not my fault—"

"Wipe it off, I can't see."

Using his sleeve, Monty smeared the screen clean. "Good as new . . . Watch it, she's right behind us!"

David accelerated, distancing them from the aggressive shark. "Where's Lizzy's pup? I can't see her."

"Still at the surface . . . and here comes the yacht. I think it's going to hit her—"

David circled back in time to see the albino shark barely slip out of range of the keel's churning propeller—only to witness the juvenile female suddenly yanked sideways as she was swept up into the trailing net.

―――――――

Ben Smallwood knew they had landed the fifth pup the moment he heard the steel cable snap to attention around the two winches, tightening the noose around the neck of the trawl.

"We got her, boys! Draw her in close so I can put a bullet in her brain."

Two of the crew reversed the winches, retracting the lines of steel cable connected to the trailing net.

David punched the leather padding by his left shoulder, pissed off at himself. Lizzy's offspring was entangled sideways in the net and was thrashing wildly, unable to channel enough water into her mouth to breathe. It was just a matter of minutes before the albino creature drowned.

To make things worse, Bela's offspring was circling the net. Refusing to abandon her companion, she was quickly moving into range of their hunters' weapons.

They'll die together, just as their mothers did, only months ago. . . .

He saw the blip appear on the sonar array a second before Mo Mallouh's voice shouted out over the radio, "*McFarland* to *Manta*—get deep!"

David slammed the joystick down as he punched both feet to the pedals, sending the submersible on a steep dive beneath the *McFarland*'s massive bulb-shaped keel—

—the hopper-dredge passing over them as it crossed through the yacht's wake, its bow towering over the *Hot & Spicy*'s transom as it snagged the two lengths of steel cable, snapping them in half a split-second before the trawl's winches were wrenched free of the stern, ripping open large sections in the wooden deck.

As the commercial vessel plowed through the gap, Trish Mackreides opened the keel doors, the suction inhaling the sea, the trawl net, and the albino Megalodon into its vacant hopper.

West Boca Medical Center
Boca Raton, Florida

Jonas Taylor balled his fists, wondering how many of the male nurse's teeth he could knock out with one punch.

Their night together had begun at 6:50 p.m., when the thirtyish physician-wannabe had declared, "Sir, have you seen your wife's CT scan? She shouldn't be here—she should be in hospice."

Hearing these words, Terry had panicked. "No hospice . . . I don't want to go to hospice!"

"Baby, don't listen to that bedpan scrubber, he has no idea about Maharaj's protocol. Wait here while I set him straight."

Jonas had stalked the man down the corridor. "Hey, asshole—where do you get off saying something like that in front of my wife?"

"Sir, she's dying."

"We're all dying, douche bag. My wife is scared enough without her overhearing you tell me she needs to be in hospice. Next time you see her, you'd better be all warm fuzzies or they'll be prepping you for surgery to remove my foot from your ass, you got me, Sunshine?"

An ER doctor overheard the conversation and quickly stepped

between them, pulling Jonas aside. "My apologies, Mr. Taylor. And you're a hundred percent right—that nurse overstepped his boundaries. Let's talk about how we can help your wife."

"Thank you."

"I've summoned a thoracic surgeon to look at your wife's last CT scan, but he's in surgery. While we're waiting, we're going to start her on a strong antibiotic, as well as a machine that will help clear her lung. She's not going to like it, but she needs to leave it in."

The machine connected to a mouthpiece that blasted air into Terry's mouth and down her esophagus into her lungs every twenty seconds with the force of a leaf-blower.

Unable to speak, she beckoned to Jonas for pen and paper to communicate. She wrote *"This is torture! How much longer?"* as her cheeks rippled away from her teeth.

The first two hours were as hard for Jonas to watch as they were for Terry to endure. By 11 p.m. she was drifting in and out of sleep, each violent expulsion of oxygen threatening to jar her awake.

At midnight, Jonas learned the thoracic specialist would not arrive until 7 a.m.

At 4:15 a.m. an orderly arrived with a tray of food, oblivious to the device in his wife's mouth.

At 7:44 a.m. a man in green scrubs entered her room. "Mr. Taylor? Jason Bradley—I'm the thoracic surgeon. May I speak with you in private?"

Jonas offered Terry a thumbs-up and followed the physician outside.

"Mr. Taylor, I read your wife's X-rays, and I don't think much Ensure had been aspirated. There's a large tumor in your wife's stomach pushing against her left lung, and that is most likely the reason she's struggling to catch her breath. The hospital wants to admit her; they're waiting for a room to open in the ICU."

"Admit her? No, no, no—we just want to get her stabilized and out of here as quickly as possible." Jonas explained Dr. Maharaj's white cell therapy protocol.

"If you want her stabilized, the ICU's still the best place for her."

"Fine . . . okay. But can you take that tube out of her mouth? She's had it in for twelve straight hours—she can't handle it anymore."

Soon, Dr. Bradley reentered the private room and removed the device from Terry's mouth, instructing the male nurse to place a far more humane oxygen tube in her nostrils.

Relieved, Terry laid her head back against the pillow, her breathing shallow.

Jonas ran his palm gently over her forehead, brushing back strands of her silky black hair. "You did it, babe. Your lung is clear. Rest easy and we'll get you out of here."

The male nurse jumped in. "Excuse me, Mr. Taylor, but your wife isn't going anywhere. She's being moved into the ICU." He pointed to the digital display on the oxygen device. "And if her breathing capacity drops below ninety percent, I'm putting the mask back on."

As Jonas watched, Terry's numbers dipped to 88 percent.

"I'm sorry, but the mask goes back on—"

Jonas balled both fists. "She's exhausted—give her a chance." He turned back to Terry and took her hand. "We've been through a lot worse than this—just breathe nice and easy. That's it . . . much better."

Terry's numbers rose to 92 percent.

"Good job. See that, Meg-bait? Sometimes you just need to give the patient a chance."

The nurse left.

Terry squeezed her husband's hand.

Jonas leaned over and kissed her, then took out his iPhone and called Dr. Maharaj.

"Hey, Doc. Rough night, but she's breathing better."

"Are they giving her nutrition?"

"I don't know. She's got an IV going but—"

"Jonas, you must insist they get Terry a nutritionist and start feeding her intravenously right away, or she could go into renal failure."

Jonas forced a smile for Terry before chasing after the male nurse who was going off-duty. "My wife needs a nutritionist. How do we get her one?"

"The ICU physician has to see her first; that's why we're admitting her."

"Then what?"

"That's not for me to say."

Aboard the Hopper-Dredge *McFarland*
Strait of Georgia, Salish Sea

For David Taylor, seconds seemed like minutes as he kept the Manta along the starboard side of the *McFarland*, waiting for the hopper-dredge's speed to drop under 5 knots so that Cyel Reed could deploy the submersible's docking platform. Two more excruciating minutes passed before the rubberized triangular object appeared along the starboard rail, beginning its fifty-foot descent.

"Come on, Cyel! A little faster!"

"The winch has two speeds: slow and slower. You want something faster—give me the money and I'll buy it."

David punched the radio, switching channels. "Mac, give me an update. What's the Meg doing? Is she moving? Are her gills fluttering?"

"She's still lying on the bottom of the hopper; she's too entangled in the net to move. I can't see her gills, but her mouth is opening and closing like she's gasping."

David laid his head back against the bucket seat in frustration. *She's dying. . . . I gotta get up there.*

The lift splashed down ahead of them. David accelerated, sending the Manta lurching forward onto the triangular object, the sub's belly fitting snugly into the platform's six-foot-diameter doughnut hole, its prow pressing snugly against the forward netting.

David switched channels. "We're in. Cyel, get us topside—and fast." Not waiting for a reply, he switched back to Mac—suddenly finding himself lunging for the control panel as the docking station lifted out of the water and began to sway.

Monty covered his mouth.

"Dude, don't you dare puke until I pop open the hatch. Mac, you still there?"

"Go ahead."

"I need you to attach a hose to one of the dredges so I can pump seawater into the Meg's mouth. I'll also need diving gear, and something that can slice through that netting."

"Christ, you're as reckless as your father."

"Mac—"

"All right, all right."

It took ninety seconds for the winch to hoist the docking platform up to the main deck. David had already popped the cockpit open; the moment Cyel dragged the sub through the gap in the rail he was off and running.

Mac was standing by the hopper's starboard dredge, attaching a length of hose to the suction device. Next to him was a tank of compressed air and a snorkel and mask. A pair of rusted bolt cutters was lying on the deck.

David climbed to the hopper's rail and looked down.

Underwater lights mounted sporadically along the inside of the Olympic-size tank revealed the captured Megalodon. The fifteen-foot, two-ton shark was lying on its side along the bottom of the flooded enclosure in forty-five feet of water, its pectoral fins hopelessly entangled in thick yellow cords of plastic netting. The creature's gills were clamped shut, its lower jaw open but barely moving. Its cataract-gray eye appeared vacant.

David jumped down from his perch. He quickly secured the air tank's harness to his back, tested the regulator by hitting the purge button, and then grabbed the mask, tossing the snorkel aside.

"You need to listen to me, kid. The only reason I'm going along with this insanity is because that mini-monster is trapped and most likely dead. But if you do manage to resuscitate it—"

"I'll be topside before she recovers." David kicked off his shoes. Grabbing the end of the hose from Mac in one hand, he picked up the bolt cutters in the other and climbed back up to the rail, swinging his legs over the steel barrier. "Don't wait for me; get the dredge into the water."

Without waiting for a reply, he spit into his mask, adjusted it over his eyes, and then jumped feet-first into the hopper—the frigid water robbing him of breath. Holding the bolt cutters away from his body, he used them as a dive weight as he kicked for the immense albino shark lying on the bottom, the hose trailing behind him.

Moving to the dredge controls, Mac lowered the suction arm over the side of the ship and into the sea.

David felt the pressure squeezing his ear canals. Pausing his descent at thirty-nine feet, he shifted the nozzle of the hose to the hand holding the bolt cutters, freeing his right hand to pinch his nose while he blew air into his cheeks in order to equalize the pressure in his sinus cavity.

Without warning the hose jumped to life, tearing loose from his grip as it whipped around in wild figure eights behind sixty pounds per square inch of pressure.

Precious moments passed before he was able to reel it back in. Aiming the stream of water at the surface, he rode it down to the Meg's head, slipping his bare feet into the nearest loop of net in order to keep the buoyant air tank from floating him topside.

The sheer bulk of the juvenile surprised him, its girth twice that of a female great white of comparable length.

By all appearances, it was dead.

David wedged the nozzle of the hose inside the Meg's lifeless maw, anchoring it in the gap between the two immense three-inch serrated teeth located dead center in its upper jaw as he directed a steady stream of seawater into its gullet.

After thirty seconds the gills opened, channeling the flow of water.

Only the Meg wasn't breathing. A full minute passed . . . then another . . . and still there was no response.

Growing more desperate, David reached out to the underside of the Meg's snout and began vigorous downward strokes along the peppered pores, hoping to stimulate the sensory cells known as the ampullae of Lorenzini.

Twenty seconds passed when the shark's massive head shuddered, as if the Meg was trying to revive itself.

That's when David realized the creature wasn't actually positioned on its side; it was angled more on its back. If it had been rolled over *before* it had ceased breathing, then there was a chance it wasn't dead . . . that it was in a zombie-like state of sleep known as tonic immobility.

Leaving the hose in the Megalodon's mouth, David swam with the bolt cutters to the albino predator's right pectoral fin and started snapping through the entanglement of netting. He quickly worked his way across its belly to the other fin, then down its caudal keel.

As he pulled the severed sections of net free from the dormant creature's tail, the Meg rolled onto its side, its jaws snapping shut over the end of the hose as it shook its massive head and righted itself.

David froze, his heart racing as the four-thousand-pound animal slowly regained its faculties, its tail swooshing past his face as it propelled itself forward—

—its snout colliding with the inside of the hopper. Disoriented, the Meg spun around, its ampullae of Lorenzini homing in on the electrical impulses of David's pounding pulse.

Stay calm . . . it's curious but it's not in attack mode.

With a flick of its half-moon-shaped caudal fin, the ghostly creature halved the distance between them and kept coming.

Oh, shit.

David reached out with both arms as the fifteen-foot juvenile was upon him, his hands gripping the Meg's snout as the albino monster drove him backward in the water.

He heard the distant splash seconds after the Meg detected new vibrations in the water. Whipping its head around, it swam off to investigate the disturbance, David having to backstroke rigorously to avoid being swatted by the shark's flicking tail. Releasing the bolt cutters, he rose quickly as the Meg homed in on the bleeding hunk of salmon being dragged along the surface in the far end of the hopper.

Snatching the morsel of food, the albino went deep, nearly pulling Monty over the hopper rail before the rope snapped.

David was hoisted out of the tank seconds later, greeted by his godfather, who looked as angry as the skies overhead.

West Boca Medical Center
Boca Raton, Florida

By 8 a.m. Terry had been moved to a private room in the Intensive Care Unit and was breathing normally with the aid of a small device fastened over her nose. Too exhausted to speak, she wrote a note instructing Jonas to return to their apartment to get some rest.

"Sorry, boss, but I'm not going anywhere without you. Our next order of business is to get you a nutrient bag, which will make you strong enough to start Maharaj's protocol on Monday."

Staking out the nurses' desk, he waited for the ICU administrator to make an appearance.

———

It took Debby Calvert several seconds to match the last name on the patient's chart with the onetime B-list celebrity. "Professor Taylor, in order to feed your wife intravenously we need a specialist to install a tube called a PIC line into her arm."

"How long will that take?"

"First, we want an oncologist to look at her."

"We have our own oncologist. Haven't you spoken to Dr. Maharaj?"

"I left him a message. But Dr. Maharaj is not affiliated with this hospital and your wife is very sick."

"Yes, I know. She also hasn't eaten anything in two days and her creatinine levels were already at two-point-two when I brought her in."

Dr. Calvert turned to Terry's nurse. "What's her level now?"

The nurse checked her chart. "She's elevated to two-point-nine."

"Then we're going to need a renal specialist to approve the PIC line."

Jonas could feel his blood boiling as another hurdle was placed in front of Terry's survival. "Why do we need a renal specialist?"

"Your wife could go into renal failure."

"Yes . . . which is why you need to hydrate her immediately and feed her nutrients. Doc, please—"

Dr. Calvert nodded to Terry's nurse. "Page Dr. Urso. Tell him I need him in ICU right away."

"Thank you."

Dr. Calvert scrolled through her iPhone photos. "My husband and I were out to your facility a few years ago; we had to wait sixteen months just to get tickets. But it was worth it just to see Angel." She held up a video taken of the seventy-four-foot albino Megalodon as it leaped out of the water to snatch a raw side of beef to the crowd's *oohs* and *aahs*. "Scary, huh?"

He pinched away tears. "Not as scary as watching my wife suffering like this."

"You have my word—we'll do everything we can."

Feeling himself losing his composure, Jonas nodded his thanks and returned to Terry's room. She was lying back at a forty-five-degree angle, her eyes partially open in a vacant stare, her breathing labored behind the mask. She was weak and malnourished, clearly in a downward spiral as the cancer gained new footholds on her depleting immune system.

The PIC specialist arrived a short time later, a caring woman determined to do her job as quickly and as efficiently as possible. She had already ordered the nutrient bag, which had to be specially prepared off-site. She promised it would arrive between eight and nine o'clock that night, but she could not install the feed line into Terry's emaciated arm until the renal doctor signed off.

Forty minutes passed before the renal specialist arrived. Dr. Anthony Urso reviewed Terry's chart before engaging in yet another exchange that made Jonas feel like he was Lou Costello arguing with Bud Abbott in a nightmarish medical version of "Who's on First?"

"Mr. Taylor, your wife's kidneys are failing."

"Yes, we know. She needs nutrients right away." (*Who's on first?*)

"We can't do that without a PIC line." (*Yes.*)

"Yes, we know. That's why we called you." (*I mean the fellow's name.*)

"Before I sign off on a PIC line, she needs a CT scan." (*Who.*)

"Why does she need a CT scan?" (*The guy on first.*)

"Her creatinine levels are very high; she could go into renal failure." (*Who.*)

"That's why we need the PIC line!" (*The guy playing first base!*)

"Fine. But I'll need to consult with an oncologist." (*Who is on first base.*)

"Why do you need to consult with an oncologist?" (*I'm asking you who's on first.*)

"To read the CT scan." (*That's the man's name.*)

"We don't want a CT scan; we want a nutrient bag." (*Who?*)

"We can't do that without a PIC line." (*Yes.*)

Dr. Calvert finally intervened, proposing that Dr. Strong sign off on the PIC line if Jonas agreed to allow the ICU to take a CT scan of Terry's lungs.

Aboard the Hopper-Dredge *McFarland*
Strait of Georgia, Salish Sea

The midnight cloudburst had released a deluge that forced everyone inside.

Mac led David and Monty up three flights of stairs to the bridge, chastising his godson in between grunts of pain from his arthritic knees. "I should have never allowed you *uhhh* into the hopper. If Monty hadn't *uhhh* tossed that fish in, you would have *uhhh* been dinner."

"She wasn't in attack mode, Mac. She was . . . curious."

"Curious? Well, I've eaten plenty of *uhhh* things just because I was curious and paid the price. What are you snickering about, Monty? From the stench coming out of that sub, I'm guessing you didn't exactly follow my dietary instructions, did you?"

"No, sir."

They entered the bridge. Rain was punishing the windows, the wipers on high speed, battling to provide visibility to Mohammad Mallouh, who was standing at the wheel, squinting to see through the storm.

"Report, Mr. Mallouh."

The pilot stole a quick glance over his shoulder at Mac. "The yacht's staying with us; she's right in our wake. As for the other Meg, it's still hanging out beneath our keel."

"No shit?" Dripping wet, David slogged his way over to the fish finder. Sure enough, Bela's last surviving pup was darting back and forth beneath the sealed steel door of the *McFarland*'s hopper.

"Mac, we have to find a way to get it on board."

"How? Open the hopper doors and you'll lose the albino."

Monty nodded. "A Meg in the hopper is worth two in the strait."

"I just don't want those fishermen to butcher it."

"You destroyed their trawl net—it'll take them some time to replace it. Bela followed Lizzy all the way back to Monterey when Paul Agricola caught her; maybe her offspring will do the same. The two of you look exhausted. Get some sleep and in the morning we'll pick up Jackie."

———

"David? David. Wake up."

He opened his eyes to find Trish standing over him. "What time is it?"

"Four a.m. Something's wrong with the Meg. Mac said it's struggling to breathe; he doesn't think it will last the night."

"Shit." David rolled out of bed, his muscles aching from having spent most of the night piloting the Manta. He dressed quickly and then followed her out of his cabin and up a flight of stairs to the main deck.

It had stopped raining. The air was thick with humidity, the full moon low in the western sky, luminous behind a formation of white cumulus clouds.

Mac was standing on the hopper's rise. David joined him, the captive creature nowhere in sight. "Where is she?"

"Lying on the bottom of the tank, barely moving. Take a look. I rigged a GoPro to the keel of my kid's remotely operated toy motorboat." Mac turned his laptop so David could see the monitor. "She's been swimming erratically, bashing her head against the insides of the tank. There—can you see her mouth?"

Mac zoomed in on the shark's lower jaw, which was opening and closing rapidly as if the Meg was under extreme duress.

"She's acting as if she can't breathe. Mac, how long has this been going on?"

"Hard to say. I had to wait until the rain stopped before I could use the motorboat—it's been coming down in buckets. At least twenty minutes."

"The rain . . . I wonder if it diluted the saline levels in the hopper to the point where her gills can't handle the freshwater?"

"Only one way to find out."

Climbing down from the rise, Mac lowered the starboard dredge over the side, David doing the same with the portside device. Thirty seconds later the two hoses jumped to life, shooting seawater into the tank along either side of the hopper.

Several minutes passed before the Meg rose away from the bottom, circling back and forth between the two streams.

"Good call, kid. There's only about a foot of freeboard. Will that be enough?"

"The salt water's denser; that's why she's staying deep. Let it overflow. We'll push the freshwater right out of the . . ." David paused. "Mac . . . look."

The Meg had surfaced and was spy-hopping between the two streams, its massive triangular head held upright, her mouth remaining open below the waterline. The creature's right eye appeared luminous as it caught the full moon, which had poked free of a cloud bank.

"Tell me that shark isn't staring at the moon."

"That's what it looks like to me."

"Any of the other Megs ever do that?"

David shook his head. "This one's definitely the first."

They walked around to the west end of the hopper to where the Meg's head was within ten feet of the starboard rail. Cast in the lunar light, the albino's alabaster hide appeared to glow.

"Mac, I know this sounds crazy, but I think it thinks the moon is Lizzy."

"You're right—that does sound crazy. Where are you going?"

"She wants her mama—maybe she's hungry?" David crossed the deck to where he and Monty had set up a five-foot-deep, twelve-foot-diameter aboveground wading pool. To feed any captured pups, they had brought along a half-dozen sides of beef, which were hanging from hooks in the walk-in freezer. Jackie had nixed the plan, recommending live fish. Upon entering the Salish Sea, they had used the fish finder to track schools of salmon. As they fed in the shallows, the *McFarland* would pass over the cluster of fish, its empty hopper inhaling a dozen or more at a time. From there, they simply drained the tank and placed the captured Chinook in the pool.

David heard the fish getting agitated as he approached. Using a landing net attached to a short pole, he scooped up a forty-five-pound Chinook and carried it over to the hopper, aligning himself within the field of vision of the Meg's right eye.

"Hey, you! Are you hungry?"

Mac scoffed. "That fish is way too fast for your shark to catch."

"Yeah, you're probably right. Can I borrow your bowie knife?"

Mac pulled the six-inch blade from the sheath attached to his belt and handed it to David. Laying the fish on the rail's two-foot-wide ledge, he proceeded to slice through the salmon's thick caudal peduncle two inches below its tail.

Blood rolled down the fish's pelvic fins, the droplets pooling along the surface of the tank.

"Not very sporting."

"No, but it should do the trick." David looked up at the Megalodon—

—only it was gone. He searched the tank but was unable to see below the surface, which was refracting the full moon's lunar light.

"Mac, where'd she—"

In one motion Mac lunged at David, dragging him away from the rail's ledge as the Megalodon's triangular head burst clear of the water, its open jaws gnawing at the top of the barrier where David had been standing before it managed to clamp down on the wriggling salmon, swallowing it whole.

For a frozen moment in time, the shark seemed to stare at David with its soulless gray eye. Then it slipped back beneath the surface and was gone.

Aboard the Hopper-Dredge *McFarland*
Strait of Georgia, Salish Sea

The thundering chorus of helicopter rotors beating the airspace above the ship woke David from a deep sleep. Reaching for his iPhone, he checked the time.

Seven thirty-eight? Damn helicopters . . . what the hell do they want? Oh, yeah . . .

The captured Megalodon was the lead story. David tracked several news updates on his iPhone until he located a video clip taken by one of the news choppers flying overhead. For the next ten minutes he sat on the toilet and watched the bird's-eye view of the *McFarland*'s hopper. Then he showered, brushed his teeth, dressed, and left his cabin—

—only to be intercepted by Trish. By the look on her face, he knew the news was bad.

"Jackie?"

"She's fine. Mac's on the way back with her."

"The Meg—"

"David, it's your mother. She's in the hospital. They don't think she'll make it through the night."

Trish's words struck him like a blow to the gut. He felt his knees buckle as the blood rushed from his face. "I don't understand? Dani said there was a protocol . . . that Mom was less than two weeks away."

"Pack a few belongings. Mac will fly you to Vancouver. You'll catch a connecting flight in San Francisco. Dani's already en route; she'll pick you up at the Fort Lauderdale airport tonight outside the baggage claim."

He staggered back to his cabin, the excitement about having captured Lizzy's offspring gone.

Over the past eight weeks he had received text updates every few days from his sister. He knew his mother's health was spiraling from not eating; he also knew that he had been so consumed with locating the Megalodon pups that he had ignored the possibility that she could actually die.

She might not make it through the night. . . .

Sitting on the edge of his bed, he broke down and cried.

Jackie was waiting for him by the helipad. She hugged him tightly, then spoke loud enough in his ear to be heard over the din of rotors. "Be with your family; I'll handle things here."

David nodded, then walked to the chopper and climbed in the copilot's seat next to Mac. He secured his seat belt and placed the headphones over his ears as the helicopter lifted away from the deck.

Mac headed east, scattering the three news choppers—

—the airship passing over the superyacht *Hot & Spicy*, which was following in the *McFarland*'s wake.

Aboard the Hopper-Dredge *Marieke*
Southeast Farallon Island
27 Nautical Miles Due West of San Francisco's
Golden Gate Bridge

Paul Agricola circled the hopper deck, iPhone in hand as he searched for a signal. It had been several weeks since the *Marieke* had been close enough to land to use his cell phone, and while the ship-to-shore line worked, when it came to accessing his bank account he didn't trust the system or his new employer.

Three months at sea with this lunatic. If the deposits aren't there, I'll leave him on the most desolate hunk of rock I can find, and he can swim back to Dubai. . . .

The signal flirted with his phone as he headed forward to the bow. In the distance he could make out the three pyramid-shaped summits of the South Farallon Islands, one of the four groups designated as a National Wildlife Refuge.

Their arrival at bin Rashidi's unscheduled stop sent a twinge of tightness down Paul's left arm.

For the first time since their voyage had begun, the former marine biologist had been making progress, having located a series of sea elephant kills along the northwest coast of Oregon that he was convinced belonged to the Liopleurodon. A few more attacks and he'd be able to narrow down the creature's feeding schedule—the most important variable he needed to track down the elusive beast and capture it.

And then, out of the blue, bin Rashidi had ordered the *Marieke*'s captain to chart a course for the South Farallones, wasting months of Paul's hard work.

"Why are you doing this? The Lio's close—we actually have a legitimate shot at capturing it!"

"Something important has come up . . . a necessary task that requires my immediate attention. I will explain everything when we arrive."

The iPhone's signal indicator jumped from no bars to three. Paul immediately pressed the preprogrammed number.

"You have reached Bank of America's small business services. Please enter the number of the account you wish to—"

He typed in the memorized info, followed by the last four digits of his social security number, and waited to hear the balance.

"Your available balance is 426,712 dollars."

He disconnected the call and exhaled a toxic breath. Bin Rashidi had wired his fourth monthly payment as promised, buying him another thirty days of Paul's services.

Still, this ridiculous detour to the Farallones better make sense, or I'll insist on being dropped off in San Francisco. . . .

He was about to power off the iPhone when his eyes caught the news blip:

Remaining Albino Meg
Pup Captured!
Shark En Route to Tanaka Institute

Paul gritted his teeth, once again registering the stress running down his left arm. *David's resilient, I'll give him that. Unfortunately for him, he's playing in the adult league now, where we keep aces up our sleeves. . . .*

Southeast Farallon is the largest island in the chain and the only one accessible by boat. In addition to a lighthouse perched atop its three hundred-twenty-eight-foot summit, there are several structures on its flatland, including a storage facility and two houses, all of which have been maintained over the years, though they remain vacant.

Per Fiesal's orders, Captain Robert Gibbons had entered Fisherman Bay to the north before circling to the eastern side of the seven-hundred-acre island.

Paul joined his employer by the starboard rail. Peering through his binoculars, he gazed at an inaccessible shoreline. Then, as they rounded a rock face harboring two sea caves, he saw something else—

Brutus . . .

The eighty-foot-long, hundred-eighty-seven-thousand-pound *Livyatan melvillei* had beached itself in the shallows and died.

Paul stared at the prehistoric sperm whale for a long moment before turning to Fiesal. "How did you know it was here? How long has it been dead?"

Fiesal lowered his binoculars to consult the GPS locator programmed in his iPhone. "I instructed Jacqueline Buchwald to tag it before she was scheduled to release it. According to its bio scan, the beast died two days ago."

"How did it die?"

"Perhaps you could determine the cause of death after we retrieve the tracking device. It was my team's latest design . . . very high-tech. I wouldn't want anyone else to have it, especially my cousin."

Paul scanned the eastern coastline. "There's no access from here. We'll have to make land along the south side of the island and walk around."

———

The sun was a brilliant golden hue by the time the motorized raft was lowered along the starboard side of the ship. Cold gusts greeted its three passengers, along with a six-foot swell that rolled beneath the craft as it settled in the water, nearly sending Fiesal bin Rashidi headfirst into the sea. Paul grabbed hold of the back of his life jacket and thrust him into his seat as Robert Gibbons started the outboard, the *Marieke*'s captain heading for the shoreline half a mile to the north.

Boarding an inflated raft to negotiate great white shark–infested waters was not something Paul would normally have suggested, but there was an advantage in using the lightweight Zodiac—it could be dragged out of the water with them, as opposed to a lifeboat, which would have had to be tied off and left exposed to the jagged shoreline and the sea's unmerciful pounding.

Paul grabbed the bowline as they approached the island's outlying rocks. Climbing out, he held the raft steady for Fiesal and Captain Gibbons. The three men then lifted the craft out of the water and onto a four-foot-high cliff face, allowing the outboard motor to hang over the side.

Spread out before them was a lime-green, moss-covered flatland that rose majestically into a mountain summit. The latter was made accessible by several long flights of steps that zigged and zagged their way up to a lighthouse perched atop the deserted island.

Captain Gibbons looked around. "I thought these islands had large elephant seal populations?"

"They do," Paul replied, "only you won't find them on this kind of geology. They prefer sandy beaches with rocky shallows, which help protect their pups from predators. The adults use the sand as sunscreen. I'm sure we'll find them where we're headed."

Fiesal activated his iPhone's tracking system. "This way."

They followed a footpath past a pair of identical two-story homes, the windows shuttered. Up ahead was a prefabricated warehouse with several roll-up garage doors. A side entrance was unlocked, allowing Paul to take a quick peek inside. Tools hung from pegs along one wall, dust covered two workbenches, and a plastic drop cloth protected an old gasoline-powered generator. By the heavy musk scent and cobwebs, he guessed it had been years since a scientific team had visited.

They continued until they came to the east side of the island—three acres of rock squeezed between the mountain to their backs and the Pacific, hidden from view by the *Livyatan melvillei*, its girth running almost the entire shoreline. The front of Brutus's massive squared-off head was wedged against a twenty-foot-tall escarpment, the towering rocks blocking their access to the sea. The carnivore's orca-like lower jaw towered two stories above them and remained open enough for them to see the points of its fourteen-inch teeth.

Paul zipped up his jacket, the temperature in the shade at least ten degrees cooler. "All right, Fiesal, find this tracking device of yours and let's get the hell out of here."

Fiesal held up his iPhone, tracing the GPS signal to the predator's skull, the dorsal portion of which was underwater. "Where is it? Do you see it?"

"What does it look like?"

"A four-foot-long harpoon."

The three men searched, finding nothing.

"Must be on the other side of its head." Captain Gibbons attempted to climb over the wall of blubber, only to slide down off the slick rounded surface.

"Forget it, Fiesal," Paul said. "There's no way to get to it, and you'd need a crane to move this carcass. Write off the loss and let's get back to hunting the Lio."

Fiesal turned to the two men. "Twenty thousand dollars . . . that is the reward money I am offering to recover the device. Find it together and split the money or one of you do it on your own. Either way, I am not leaving this island until the device is in my possession."

Captain Gibbons looked at Paul. "What do you think?"

"I don't know, Robert. Only you can put a price on your own life."

"What do you mean?"

"Have you ever seen a great white attack a whale carcass? It's not a sight for the faint at heart. These are the Farallones; there could be twenty sharks on the other side of this creature tearing fifty-pound chunks of blubber from its flank as we speak."

"Ridiculous," Fiesal rebutted. "The whale is lying in the shoals—it is not that deep."

"You don't know how deep it is."

The captain inspected the rock formation blocking their way. "For twenty grand, it's worth taking a look." Gibbons attempted to establish a handhold to climb the rock, only to slice his right palm on the sharp surface.

Removing his denim shirt, he used the rocky edge to cut off the sleeves. He wrapped his hands in the lengths of the thick cloth, then started to climb, quickly reaching the twenty-foot-high summit.

Looking below, he saw the surf washing up against the dead whale's upper torso, the water dark and ominous.

"Well?"

"Paul's right . . . it's definitely deep enough for great whites to feed. I don't see any dorsal fins."

"What about the tracking device?"

"I'm too high up—stand by." Turning around, he lowered himself feetfirst, struggling to find a secure toehold on the algae-covered rockface.

"It's too slippery—I can't climb back up!"

"Don't climb back up. Jump in, grab the tracker, and we'll toss you a rope."

Paul shot Fiesal an angry look. "We don't have a rope."

"There must be one in that maintenance shack."

They both turned—Robert Gibbons yelling out as he fell into the sea.

"Captain? Captain, are you all right?"

Gibbons surfaced, fighting to catch his breath in the frigid water. "I'm okay. Water's freezing . . . need that rope."

"You heard the man," Paul said. "Get him a rope."

Fiesal took three strides, calling back, "Find that tracking device."

Paul watched bin Rashidi disappear around the base of the mountain. "Robert, can you hear me?"

"Yeah."

"Are there any bite marks visible on the carcass?"

"Not above the water . . . oh, shit—"

"What?"

"I just felt something swim beneath me—ahhhhh! Ahhhhh!"

Paul's heart raced as the captain's screams were suddenly muted, replaced by heavy splashing and the distinct sound of a large caudal fin slapping the surface.

"Robert? Are you okay?"

Gibbons surfaced in a panic. Stroking for the moss-covered rocks, he dug his fingers into any nook and crag he could locate and dragged himself out of the ocean, balancing on the toes of his left hiking boot—

—his right foot gone, the leg bitten below his calf muscle, his severed Achilles tendon dangling from the gushing wound.

The great white surfaced out of a swell, its nostrils snorting his blood.

"Paul, it bit off my foot!"

"Jesus . . . Okay, stay calm. Can you get out of the water?"

"I'm on the rock, only I can't hold on and the blood's just pouring out of me."

"Are you wearing a belt?"

"A belt? Yeah."

"Use it as a tourniquet." Paul looked to his left—no sign of Fiesal. Looking to his right, he spotted a small gray shack nestled among the boulders at the base of the mountain.

"Hang on, I'm going to find something to reach you." Scrambling over the rocky terrain, he headed for the shack, only to find himself immersed in a thick swarm of flies.

"Ugh . . . What the hell—oh, God."

The elephant seal had been a mature female. Its lower torso was gone, bitten in half just below its front flippers by a force so powerful it had popped out both of the pinniped's eyes. The gaping wound had flushed the cow's innards from its remains, pooling between the rocks.

Hearing Gibbons cry out, he hurried on his way, only to discover more elephant seal carcasses, each kill as gruesome as the last. He counted a dozen half-eaten animals before he reached the shack, his mind demanding answers to questions that were delaying his completion of the task at hand.

What land creature could have done that?

Dumbass . . . it wasn't a land predator. The remains must have washed up with the tide. It was either orca or great whites.

Satisfied he had resolved the mystery, he yanked open the shack's warped wooden door, only to be greeted by an outhouse and the putrid scent of human feces. He pinched his nose and looked around, searching for anything he could use to reach Gibbons.

Hanging from a hook on the back of the door was a towel. He grabbed it and exited, following a narrow foot trail that ran along the base of the mountain. He saw Fiesal coming around the bend, the coils of a frayed length of rope slung over his left shoulder.

"Here—let me have that!" Taking the rope, Paul made his way back down to the beached sperm whale. The dusk had receded into night, the darkening sky dusted with stars.

"Robert, can you hear me?"

No response.

He tore the towel down the middle and wrapped the cloth around his hands. With the rope coiled around his neck, he started to climb, kicking toeholds in the brittle rock face as he ascended.

Straddling the summit, he looked down, searching for the captain.

"Well?" Fiesal asked.

"I don't see him—wait! There's something in the water by the whale's head." Paul removed the rope from around his neck, tossing one end to Fiesal. "Tie that to one of those rocks; I'm going to work my way down and try to reach him."

He waited for bin Rashidi to secure the rope and then tested it. Satisfied, he wound it around his wrists and half-climbed, half-slid down the algae-covered rock face, jamming the heels of his boots to brake before he reached the water.

He heard a splash somewhere beneath the whale carcass. Bracing his feet against the escarpment, he bent over to improve his sightline. "Robert, is that you?"

A three-foot swell rolled over his ankles.

"Damn it." He walked himself higher—

—the soles of his shoes slipping, causing his legs to slide out from under him.

Paul dangled from the rope, knee-deep in water. Pissed off, he fought to regain a foothold while he turned to his right, searching for Robert Gibbons.

The tide was out, revealing the underside of Brutus's head. A twelve-foot great white was gnawing on it, the bloodshot white of its eye showing as it fed. As he watched, another shark attacked the banquet of blubber farther down the carcass, exposing the whale's spine.

There was no sign of the captain.

And then he saw it—an antennae-shaped device protruding two feet behind the *Livyatan melvillei*'s blowhole.

"Fiesal, I located the tracker."

"Excellent. Bring it to me!"

"There are sharks everywhere, including some really nasty great whites. If I risk my life to get this for you, I want twenty-five thousand dollars for me and another twenty-five thousand for Gibbons's fiancée."

"The captain is dead?"

"One of the sharks bit off his foot. I can't see him."

A long moment passed. "Twenty-five thousand for you; fifteen thousand for the captain's fiancée."

"Agreed."

Paul stared at the white three-foot-diameter craters of shark bites lining Brutus's dorsal surface. In order to retrieve the tracking device, he'd have to let go of the rope and swim over, then yank the four-foot pole free and swim back, climbing out of the water before he was attacked.

Fast or slow? Slow and deliberate might work best. Gibbons probably startled one of them when he fell in.

He released the rope and eased himself into an incoming swell. Sculling forward, he waited for the twelve-foot male great white to swim off before replacing it at the feeding trough.

Paul's heart raced as he felt for the tracking device in the darkness.

Come on . . . where the hell is it?

Got you!

The former marine biologist tugged the aluminum shaft as hard as he could, but it was in good, having pierced the *Livyatan melvillei*'s skull.

And suddenly Paul Agricola was being dragged underwater, his rib-cage crushed in a vise-like grip as the air was forcibly expelled from his lungs. He struggled to remain conscious while a dozen stiletto-sharp teeth punctured his internal organs, his primordial scream choked off by a geyser of warm blood rising up his esophagus.

The Liopleurodon shook its crocodilian head from side to side and then released its prey to die.

The pressure eased. Paul willed himself to the surface. He spit out a mouthful of blood and quickly inhaled a gurgling breath, the pain driving him insane, the need to remove himself from the sea flooding his muscles with adrenaline. He kicked until he reached the rope and then gripped it in both hands and dragged himself out of the water, blood draining from a dozen or more puncture wounds.

The Liopleurodon was circling eight feet beneath its wounded prey when its vibrations suddenly ceased.

Hand over hand, Paul pulled himself up the slippery rock face. Each breath was a wheeze, his punctured right lung all but collapsed. Somehow he reached the top of the escarpment without losing his footing and collapsed to his knees, his lower extremities having gone numb from the loss of blood. Only the excruciating pain prevented him from losing consciousness.

Fiesal could not see the extent of his bounty hunter's injuries in the darkness, only that both his hands were gripping the rope instead of holding his tracking device. "Where is the bio-implant? You were instructed to bring it to me. Are you listening? What the hell is wrong with you?"

Paul Agricola's eyes rolled up as his heart stopped and he fell forward, his body tumbling down the opposite side of the rock.

Fiesal knelt by the twisted pile of limbs. He checked for a pulse and confirmed the man was dead.

Sensing a presence, the marine engineer looked up.

The Liopleurodon was staring down at him from atop the escarpment, its jaundice-yellow eyes reflective in the cloud-veiled moonlight, its gill slits hissing as its tongue squeezed the sea from its gullet.

In that instant of clarity, Fiesal knew what had happened, just as he knew the creature would interpret his proximity to the dead man as an attempt to steal its kill.

He took three steps backward and then turned and ran.

The thirty-foot-long pliosaur launched its eight-ton girth down the escarpment, its fore flippers absorbing the two-story drop, its jaws snapping at air.

Fiesal scrambled through, over, and between a labyrinth of beach, rocks, and boulders, refusing to stop until he felt the moss-covered flatland beneath his feet.

Pausing to catch his breath, he turned, and was shocked to see the enraged beast still in pursuit, its jaws snapping wildly with each forward thrust of its crocodilian head, its hind flippers fighting to maintain balance. Despite being on land, the alpha predator refused to cease its attack, its self-preservation overruled by its desire to kill its challenger.

Fiesal forced himself into an awkward jog. His throat burned, his muscles—drenched in lactic acid—felt like liquid lead. Desperately out of shape, he knew it was just a matter of time—thirty seconds at the most—before he'd collapse in a sacrificial heap and be eaten.

The insanity of his predicament made him furious, giving him the release of adrenaline he needed to make it to the maintenance shack. He pushed open the side entrance and slammed the door behind him, but the bolt was jammed inside the lock, allowing it to swing freely on its hinges. He tried once more to force it shut—

—only to be knocked sideways as the Lio's snout bashed open the metal door, sending Fiesal scampering blindly on all fours in the darkness, knocking over unseen objects as he searched for a place to hide.

Ducking beneath a worktable, he watched in horror as the creature attempted to squeeze the shoulder girdles of its forelimbs through the narrow opening . . . its movements noticeably labored.

Its blood oxygen levels are dropping . . . it needs to get back to the water.

Unable to enter through the door frame, the pliosaur retreated and then circled the one-story building to find another access point.

Fiesal's eyes locked on to the pair of sealed garage doors, quickly evaluating their construction. He surmised that two direct charges from the Lio would flatten either aluminum barrier. When that happened, he could always slip out the side door and continue to avert being eaten—at least until the crazed beast collapsed the entire prefabricated structure.

Unless . . .

He stared at the emergency lights mounted above each door and remembered the creature's sensitivity to bright lights.

If there was power, I could open the garage doors remotely and allow her inside, then confine her with the emergency lights. How long would it take the crew to get here . . . ten minutes? We could shoot her with tranquilizers and load her into the hopper, then cover the top of the tank with the cargo net so she couldn't climb out.

He climbed out from beneath the worktable and tried turning on the desk lamp—

—nothing.

Find the fuse box!

Fiesal located it on the wall separating the two roll-up garage doors. He heard the animal snorting as he pried it open and scanned the panel. Locating the main switch, he flipped it on—

—causing the generator to double-click and power up. Searching the double row of circuit breakers, he located the one labeled GARAGE DOOR and flipped the switch. Then he searched the interior walls for anything that resembled a garage door opener.

Finding nothing, he returned to the side entrance and closed the door, revealing three light switches and a pair of vertical buttons that he knew had to be the automated garage openers. He pressed one of the buttons—

—causing the garage door's chain to raise the immense panel on the left.

The creature entered, baring its fangs, saliva dripping from its lower jaw.

Fiesal's heart raced as he waited for the juvenile pliosaur to clear the garage door frame before pressing the button again, causing it to reverse directions and lower to the cement floor.

The sixteen-thousand-pound goliath was about to strike the moving object when Fiesal turned on the warehouse lights, the twin beams chasing the beast away from the garage doors and into the center of the warehouse.

"Ha! Not so tough in the light, are you? Now you are my dog."

The Lio moved toward Fiesal, who backed his way quickly to the side entrance in order to escape—

—only to find the metal door locked.

Son of a bitch! The bolt was electronic—that is why it wouldn't remain closed.

Abandoning his plan, he pressed both garage door controls, reopening the panels. "Go on . . . get out of here!"

Instead of escaping, the Liopleurodon advanced. It paused six feet in front of him, its nostrils snorting mucus as it struggled to breathe.

"Look at you . . . you're dying. Stupid animal—"

The Lio leaped forward, its hellish jaws snatching him around the chest.

Fiesal screamed as the needle-sharp fangs in the creature's upper jaw punctured his lungs and rib cage, the lower teeth shredding his calf muscles. The beast raised him off the ground and violently shook him, the pain causing him to momentarily black out—

—the lava-like acids of the pliosaur's digestive enzymes burning through his flesh as he regained consciousness in a pit of darkness. He lashed out at the stomach lining, clawing at it with his melting fingers—

—and suddenly he was being propelled back into the light, the Lio regurgitating him onto the cement floor.

He thrashed about in agony, blind and gagging, begging Allah to take his soul.

As if it comprehended his prayer, the crocodilian jaws snatched Fiesal bin Rashidi off the ground, its teeth grinding flesh, bone, and sinew into a bloody pulp with every crushing chew until its prey ceased all resistance.

A half a dozen more smacks of its jowls determined that the human was an insufficient energy source, and the Lio spewed what was left in its mouth onto the cement floor.

Exiting through one of the open garage doors, it headed back to the water.

———

The man dragged himself out of the sea and squeezed himself between two boulders, seeking shelter from the breaking waves. The heavens spun in his head, the pain driving him toward delirium, yet he refused to stop—not now . . . not when he was so close.

Moaning in agony, he stood on his left foot, moving from rock to rock until he reached the motorized raft. He rolled over its starboard side, careful not to bang his right leg.

The world was still spinning in his vision, so he closed his eyes and felt for the emergency kit. Removing the gun from the plastic container, he loaded it.

Lying on his back, Robert Gibbons fired the flare into the night sky, signaling to his crew that he needed help. He contemplated adjusting the belt strapped around the remains of his right calf muscle, only the wave of pain pulled him under and he blacked out—

—never seeing the Liopleurodon. Hobbling on its four finned appendages, the creature entered the dark surf and disappeared.

Fort Lauderdale International Airport
Fort Lauderdale, Florida

It was 8:18 p.m. on the East Coast when David Taylor stepped out of the air-conditioned terminal and into the South Florida humidity. He sat on a concrete bench and waited while his sister finished circling the airport for the fourth time—the uniformed police officers refusing to allow any cars to linger more than sixty seconds in the passenger pickup lanes.

He stood as the rental car approached the curb. Opening the rear passenger door, he tossed his bag in back and then climbed up front with Dani.

"You look tired," she said, leaning over to give him a quick hug.

"You look worried. How bad is she?"

"They don't think she'll last the night. Of course, they said that yesterday too, and she hung on."

"Geez . . ." David laid his head back, tears welling in his eyes. "What happened to that whole white cell thing?"

"We waited too long. I called the doctor yesterday and I told him to bring in the donor to initiate the protocol. As of two hours ago there's an IV bag at his clinic filled with cancer-killing granulocytes waiting to save mom's life."

"That's great!"

"No, it's not. Dr. Maharaj doesn't feel Mom's strong enough to handle it. He's probably right, but if we don't give it to her, she's going to die anyway."

"Then give it to her."

"It's complicated," Dani said, turning onto the ramp leading to the Florida Turnpike. "Dr. Maharaj isn't affiliated with the hospital, so he can't just walk in and hook up an IV."

"So we'll bring her to him."

"She's not strong enough to travel."

"Ugh! So what are we supposed to do?"

"If we can get the granulocytes, I can hook the bag up to her IV."

"Maharaj will give it to you?"

"No. But I know where it is; I saw them place it in a refrigerator while I was filling out releases. There's no lock and—"

"Hold it, Dani. You want to break into this guy's office and steal an IV bag?"

"I never said break in, and technically it's not stealing since Dad paid for it. I called the clinic an hour ago and said I needed to stop by tonight and pick up some info about the protocol to show the hospital administrator. There's only one nurse on duty at night. While you ask a million questions about the treatment, I'll excuse myself to use the bathroom—all I'll need is two minutes, tops."

David shook his head. "This is crazy."

"No, little brother—crazy is what you did when you tried to save Bela and Lizzy. This is an attempt to save our mother's life. Maybe it's a long shot, but it's the only shot she has."

"Take it easy . . . I didn't say I wouldn't do it."

West Boca Medical Center
Boca Raton, Florida

Jonas stared at the latest CT scan of his wife's right lung while Dr. Calvert pointed out several large masses. "What we had hoped was merely pneumonia is the spreading cancer. I'm so sorry."

She powered off the screen and removed a sheet of paper from a manila folder. "This is an order instructing our staff to either resuscitate or to not resuscitate."

"Resuscitate her." Jonas reached for the pen to sign.

"Mr. Taylor, before you sign, it's important you understand what you are committing us to. When your wife's heart stops, we'll be jumpstarting it with paddles or using CPR. When she stops breathing, we'll be intubating her."

"Intubate? You mean you'll shove one of those tubes down her throat?"

"To keep her breathing, yes, sir."

Jonas peeked in at Terry. She was in a morphine-induced, semiconscious state, lying in bed at a forty-five-degree angle, her breathing made possible by a mask.

He recalled how his wife had fought against a less invasive breathing apparatus the night they had arrived. "No, I can't do that to her . . . it's not what she would want."

Taking the pen, he signed the DNR order. Then he entered Terry's room and closed the door, wiping the tears from his eyes.

She was restless, fighting death in a semiconscious state.

Jonas held her hand, whispering, "It's all right, baby. You don't have to hold on any longer. Everything will be okay—we'll do this together."

She squeezed his hand so tightly he felt pain, then watched as she kicked and spasmed, her blood pressure rising from 73/40 up to 102/53 on the digital board behind her bed.

Her almond eyes opened, releasing a tear.

Dani introduced David to the nurse on duty at the South Florida Bone Marrow/Stem Cell Transplant Institute. "Roseanne Serrone, this is my brother—"

"David Taylor, oh my God!" She removed her iPhone from her pocket, her fingers dancing across the screen until the desired YouTube video began playing—a night scene taken from the Tanaka Lagoon's east bleachers.

"See! I was there the night that Lio-whatever-you-call-it killed Bela and Lizzy." She held up the device—the crowd on their feet as a dark dorsal fin cut across the lagoon, the juvenile Meg chased by a massive creature more than twice its size.

Dani nudged her brother. "Watch it with her, David, while I use the bathroom."

He took the iPhone from Nurse Serrone, feigning interest. "That was scary, huh?"

"Oh my God, you have no idea." She laughed. "What am I saying—of course, it was much scarier for you. Would you mind if I took a photo?"

Without waiting for a reply, she held up the iPhone and leaned in next to him, snapping several pictures.

They turned as Dani came running down the hall. "Dad called; we have to go."

David waved to the nurse and then hurried out the front entrance after his sister to the deserted parking lot. "That was quick. Did you get it?"

"I got it. You drive." She climbed in the passenger seat.

"What's wrong?"

She shook her head, unable to speak.

David started the car and slammed it into gear, racing through the deserted complex.

David followed his sister off the elevator, the two siblings jogging down an empty white corridor to the double doors of the ICU.

Their father was waiting outside of the first room on the left. Unshaven, with dark circles under his red-rimmed eyes, he looked visibly shaken. A blue light was flashing above the closed door, the curtains drawn as an emergency team worked furiously inside.

"Dad . . . what happened?"

"She stopped breathing. I signed a Do Not Resuscitate order about two hours ago, but . . ."

"You changed your mind." Dani hugged him.

"She's fighting it. Let's give her one final round." He looked up to see his son. "That's what we Taylors do, right, kid?"

David nodded, a lump in his throat as he hugged his father.

Dr. Calvert exited the room ten minutes later, followed by the paramedics. "All right, Mr. Taylor, she's been intubated. You and your family decide what you want to do next."

"Thank you." Jonas and his children entered the room, Dani closing the door behind them.

Terry was lying flat, the breathing tube in her mouth—the machine beside her pumping air in and out of her lungs. The digital vital signs behind her bed showed her pulse was 48, her blood pressure 78/56.

David stared at his mother, barely recognizing her. "How much weight has she lost?"

"Too much," Jonas said, returning his chair to the right side of her bed. He stroked her hair gently. "Terry, David's here. He came all the way from British Columbia to witness your miracle." He motioned for David to sit in the chair.

"Hey, Mom."

Jonas joined Dani, who was inspecting the two intravenous bags feeding into her mother's frail arms. "What do you think?"

"This thick elixir running below her armpit is the nutrient bag; we don't want to disturb that. I can run the granulocytes through the morphine drip, but I think we should wait until after the nurse comes in to change out the bag so they don't notice it. It should drain in the next fifteen or twenty minutes."

"Okay . . . good."

"Dad, as these granulocytes make their way through her body and start attacking the cancer cells, it's really going to take a toll on her. Dr. Maharaj said it will induce a high fever. She's already so weak . . .

what happens when she goes Code Blue again? How many times can you keep starting her heart?"

"Are you having second thoughts?"

"I just . . ." Dani wiped away tears. "I don't want to torture her because we're not ready to let her go."

"Let's just get this stuff flowing in her veins."

———

It was 10:15 p.m. when the nurse entered to swap out the empty IV bag with a new one. She took note of her patient's vitals and left.

David followed her out, closing the door behind him. He waited for her to enter another room and then tapped on the outside of the window of his mother's ICU room.

Dani removed the clear bag of fluid from her purse. She waited while her father unhooked the new bag of morphine from the stand and then hooked the donor bag of granulocytes in its place.

Jonas rehung the morphine bag, positioning it so it partially concealed the new IV.

Dani started the drip. "Okay, we're in."

"How long will it take to drain into her system?"

"I don't know . . . three or four hours."

Jonas checked the wall clock. "Maybe you should go back to the apartment with David."

She shook her head. "If something goes wrong with the drip—"

"Dani, if they discover that IV then I don't want you here. This could get you kicked out of medical school."

She hesitated, weighing his words. Then she checked the IV, hugged her father good night, and left.

Aboard the Hopper-Dredge *McFarland*
Strait of Juan deFuca, Salish Sea

Cycl Reed stood by the stern rail, glancing from the cloudless night sky aglitter with stars to the blinking yellow bow light of the *Hot & Spicy*, which was trailing the *McFarland* half a mile to the east.

Three months at sea, stuck on this damn garbage scow. Smallwood better go for this or I'm contacting that prince.

The cell phone in his front pants pocket vibrated. He checked the time—3:59 a.m.—then glanced around to make sure he was alone before answering it. "I'm here."

"Have you completed the job?"

"Not yet."

"May I remind you, Mr. Van Sicklen has no influence with the Coast Guard outside of the Salish Sea. At your present course and speed, you will be leaving the strait in eighty-three minutes. If you wish to be rescued from the wrath of your crew—"

"I wish to be paid in full."

"Our arrangements were clear. We sent you twenty percent of your fee as a down payment."

"Things have changed. I want the balance of the fifty wired now . . . unless you're not interested in having me eliminate both remaining pups."

"Bela's offspring? You know where it is?"

"It's beneath our keel. Somehow it knows the albino is inside the hopper, but it's there for the taking."

"How would you bring it aboard?"

"I'd have to kill the albino first, then drain enough water from the hopper to reestablish a negative pressure differential powerful enough to suction Bela's pup into the tank. Once that monster's in, I'll drain the tank and suffocate her."

"I assume you want another fifty for Bela's pup?"

"Seventy-five."

"No deal. I can go as high as sixty."

"Then you'd better call the missus, because I'm not risking my neck for anything less than seventy-five thousand."

"Stand by, I'll call you right back."

Cyel pocketed the iPhone and headed forward. *Three months without a new contract . . . I gave the institute twenty years of my life and this is how Taylor and Mackreides repay me? Old man Tanaka would have never left me twisting in the wind like this—even when he was on the verge of bankruptcy he'd always take care of his key personnel.*

And placing David in charge . . . What the hell does a kid know about running a business? I'll give him credit for capturing the albino, but what are the chances this juvenile manages to survive in captivity . . . one in five at best? When it dies, I'll be out of a job. Even if it lives, it'll be years before it's large enough to draw decent-size crowds. Meanwhile the lagoon's falling apart and the filtration system needs to be replaced. Does Taylor think a bank's going to loan a twenty-two-year-old the millions needed to turn this thing around?

Screw 'em. Better to get off the Titanic now before we hit the iceberg.

Arriving at the hopper, Cyel stayed to the right, following the starboard rail to the control station that operated the dredge. Powering the system was a 50-kilowatt generator anchored to the deck, the unit as large as a minivan. Situated next to the device was a plywood storage trunk, its brass latch sealed with a padlock.

Cyel removed the silver chain that held the key from around his neck. He popped open the lock and raised the lid, removing a ten-foot-long bamboo fishing pole. A copper pulley was attached at the tip. Mounted beneath it was a copper block and matching metal plate.

He laid the wood pole by the generator and then slid open the minia-ture power plant's side panel, exposing two lengths of insulated copper wire. The longer wire ran from the unit's positive terminal to the bamboo pole like fishing line, passing over the contactor en route to the leader.

The second line ran from the generator's negative terminal to a cop-per plate that was the approximate size of a legal pad.

Cyel carefully lowered the copper plate into the hopper, allowing it to sink several feet below the surface. Donning a pair of rubber work gloves, he slipped them on just as his iPhone vibrated in his pants pocket.

"Speak."

"The balance of the first fifty has been wired. You'll receive an ad-ditional twenty-five thousand in your account after you send us footage of the dead albino. The Coast Guard cutter is standing by to pick you up after you capture the dark-backed pup and send us the image."

"And the remaining twenty-five large?"

"When the second pup is dead."

"Terms accepted, with one caveat—the moment I send you photos of the dead Megs, you call for the B.C. Coast Guard to get me off the ship before Mackreides and his loony-tunes nephew throw me overboard."

"No worries. Now get to work."

Cyel carried the bamboo fishing pole to the wading pool holding the live fish. Wearing the rubber gloves, he managed to grab one of the cir-cling salmon by the base of its tail and dragged it out of the container with two hands, laying it on the deck. Pressing the bottom of his right sneaker to the writhing fish's gill slits, he proceeded to bait the copper hook.

The engineer's invention was simple but deadly: When the Megalodon took the bait, the action would cause the copper block to connect with the copper plate on the bamboo pole. This would close the connection on the electrical circuit and zap the albino predator with 56,000 volts of electricity. The beauty of the plan was not just the ferocity of the assault but the lack of evidence implicating Cyel. A necropsy would indicate only that the shark's heart had stopped, not the cause.

He carried the pole and the thirty-five-pound fish up to the tank's retaining wall—

—and was startled to find the ghost-like Megalodon's triangular head sticking out of the water, its snout level with his perch, the moon reflecting in the creature's soulless cataract-gray eyes.

"Evening, Cyel."

He turned to find Jackie watching him from the generator, the two ends of the copper wire that had been attached to the generator now dangling from her hands.

The engineer was caught red-handed, his mind racing.

"How much is Van Sicklen paying you?"

"Van Sicklen's all about protecting the orca. This is about protecting innocent people. Six years ago, the big male that tracked Angel along the coast entered these waters. A man was killed . . . his name was Heath Shelby. The guy had a wife and kids—they're the ones who asked us to intervene."

The engineer lowered the fish into the tank, feeding out copper wire. "You and Shelby's daughter are about the same age. Imagine witnessing your father eaten alive by a sixty-foot monster. Imagine the nightmares this family has had to endure."

He laid the pole down and approached the marine biologist. "The Shelbys can't bring Heath back, but they can prevent other innocent people from suffering a similar fate. The facts are the facts, Jackie. The Tanaka Lagoon has yet to hold an adult Meg captive. Angel escaped and killed a bunch of innocent people. Bela and Lizzy did, too. One day this juvenile will weigh fifty tons and be as big and as nasty as her grandmother. There's a good chance she'll bust through the lagoon's rusted steel doors and more innocent people will die—only this time, their deaths will be on *your* head."

Jackie's heart pounded in her chest, her cheeks flushing.

Cyel saw the fear in her eyes. "Drop the wires and go back to bed; let me handle this."

The marine biologist hesitated. Then she released the two insulated wires and walked away.

Cyel smiled. Moving quickly to the generator, he bent to retrieve the wires—

"Arrrghhh!"

—and collapsed, writhing on deck like the baited salmon.

Monty stepped out from behind the far wall of the tank, the two wires feeding out from the Taser in his right hand embedded in Cyel Reed's back.

"How's that feel, you old fart?"

The former Army medic reached into the pocket of his sweat suit and removed his walkie-talkie. "Uncle Mac, you awake?"

"I am now. Where are you?"

"On deck, by the hopper controls." Monty retrieved the bamboo pole and tossed it over the starboard rail into the sea. "You were right about Cyel. He's on Smallwood's payroll."

"What about Jackie?"

"That's more complicated."

"Monty, yes or no . . . can she be trusted with the Meg?"

Cyel Reed attempted to sit up, only to be rewarded with a swift kick to his solar plexus.

"In my opinion, they both need to be put ashore."

Southeast Farallon Island
27 Nautical Miles Due West of San Francisco's
Golden Gate Bridge

Chief Petty Officer Sean Ogden stood in the bridge of the *Mighty Hawksbill*, gazing at the rocky eastern shoreline through his night-vision binoculars. The eighty-seven-foot Coast Guard cutter had been the first ship to respond to the *Marieke*'s distress call, but once the former English teacher from Elizabeth, New Jersey, realized the nature of the emergency and the parties involved, he requested their homeport in Monterey to dispatch a forty-seven-foot motor lifeboat and rescue chopper.

Dawn was still several hours away, which Ogden considered a blessing. When word spread about the hopper-dredge's mission and the dead Miocene whale, every tour boat operator in San Francisco would be congregating around the cluster of islands, media helicopters crowding the skies.

The Coast Guard chopper had located Captain Robert Gibbons lying inside a motorized rubber raft along the southern shore. Ogden's medical officer, Danielle Letina, had treated him for shock before instructing the chopper to transport him to San Francisco. From the patient's feverish testimony and the inch-wide puncture marks encircling the flesh above the missing foot, the physician confirmed Gibbons had been attacked by a shark.

The twelve-year veteran had been hesitant to make the same pronouncement about Paul Agricola. Contacting her CO by radio, she had described the deceased man's eviscerated remains and the carcasses of the elephant seals that blanketed the area, making the search for Fiesal bin Rashidi difficult. "I'm certainly no marine biologist, Mr. Ogden, but this doesn't look like any shark attack that I've ever seen."

"Could it have been the whale?"

"I seriously doubt it. By the smell of things, the monster's been dead for a while, and some of these seal kills are fairly fresh. I'm guessing the attacks happened in these coastal waters and the seals' remains washed up with the incoming tide; I won't know for sure until the sun comes up. But if I didn't know better, I'd say we're standing in a killing field. And frankly, sir—"

"Stand by, Letina." The CPO switched radio channels. "Ogden here. Go ahead, Mr. Blount."

Seaman Ryan Blount sounded visibly upset. "Sir, I'm standing in one of the structures . . . looks like a maintenance shack. Something happened in here—there's blood everywhere."

"Secure the area, Mr. Blount, I'm on my way." He switched channels.

"Dr. Letina, get your team over to the maintenance building on the southern part of the island; I'll meet you there."

West Boca Medical Center
Boca Raton, Florida

Jonas had remained by his wife's side all night, applying cold compresses to her forehead and neck. Her flesh was hot to the touch, her internal temperature hovering above 105 degrees Fahrenheit. Now as the wall clock's minute hand inched its way toward seven o'clock, he felt his eyelids growing heavy, his head bobbing—

—the pain in his fingers snapping him awake as his wife violently squeezed his hand, her voice in his head. "How could you do this to me, Jonas? We talked about this!"

"I couldn't bear to lose you . . . I wanted to give the white cell protocol a chance."

"By turning me into a vegetable? By placing my soul in purgatory, preventing me from moving on? This is not living."

"I'm sorry. What can I do?"

"Let me go."

His head snapped back, his eyes opening as the blue light flashed above Terry's vital signs and an emergency team of doctors and nurses rushed in.

"Mr. Taylor, you'll have to leave!"

"Nurse, I changed my mind—I'll sign the DNR."

She turned to the physician, who continued working on his patient. "Don't look at me. I'm not stopping until the form is signed."

The nurse quickly exited the room as David entered, carrying a cardboard tray holding two cups of coffee and several breakfast sandwiches. "Dad?"

"Say your good-byes, son—we have to let her go."

"No—" He left the food on a table and squeezed past his father to check on the white cell IV. The bag was drained. "See? It's in her! We can't give up now."

The nurse returned, handing Jonas a clipboard with a Do Not Resuscitate form attached. "Sign here and here."

"Dad—"

"She didn't want this, David . . . to be kept alive hooked up to a bunch of machines. She made me promise." Jonas signed the form, then he hugged his weeping son as the doctor removed the tube from his mother's throat.

Terry's vital signs went into free fall, plunging to zero—

"Time of death . . . 6:52 a.m."

—and then she took a breath.

‖‖‖‖‖‖‖‖‖‖‖‖‖‖‖‖‖‖‖‖‖‖‖‖‖‖‖‖‖‖‖

Aboard the Hopper-Dredge *McFarland*
Strait of Juan de Fuca, Pacific Ocean

James Mackreides trudged up the three flights of steel stairs leading to the pilothouse, each push-off generating a stabbing pain in his knees. Three months on the *McFarland* were eleven weeks too many for the former Navy chopper pilot's arthritis. Having to deal with the fallout from last night's activities on two hours of sleep only compounded his misery.

Reaching the rusted steel door, he twisted the knob and put his shoulder to it, fighting the pressure differential caused by the wind.

Mo Mallouh was in the pilot's chair, watching the fish finder. Mac's wife, Trish, was seated on the vinyl sofa next to Jacqueline. Both women glared at him.

Uh-oh . . . they've formed a coalition.

"You're firing me?" Jackie said, beating him to the punch. "I'm the one who stopped Cyel from frying your fish."

"And then you walked away. If Monty hadn't been there, the Meg would be dead."

"I made a mistake . . . I was confused. But I knew Monty was there."

"They were both keeping an eye on Cyel," Trish said, playing the part of her legal counsel.

"It doesn't matter. After last night, I don't trust you around the Meg. If I see you anywhere near that tank, we'll put you ashore."

"And who's going to take care of it?"

"Monty and I can handle it."

Trish rolled her eyes.

"It's not brain surgery. We toss in a few salmon every hour and pump in fresh water a coupla times a day, no big deal."

Jackie turned to Trish. "He thinks he's taking care of a goldfish."

"The Meg's in shock, Mac. Listen to your marine biologist."

Jackie nodded. "The hopper's metal walls are sending the albino's ampullae of Lorenzini into a twenty-four/seven spin cycle. The only reason it isn't dead from bashing its head against the side of the tank is because I've been adding and regulating animal tranquilizer in its water supply. Remove me from the equation and Monty has a better chance of getting into Harvard than that fish has of making it back to Monterey alive."

Defeated, Mac stared out of the pilothouse window. Looking aft, he noticed that the superyacht had halved its distance to the *McFarland*. "Mr. Mallouh, why have you allowed that yacht to gain on us?"

"It's not my choice; they're a lot faster than this bucket of bolts."

"Cyel called them," Trish said. "He told them you were putting him ashore on Vancouver Island. I think they intend to pick him up."

"Damn it, I don't want that yacht anywhere near us. Mr. Mallouh, can you get them on the radio?"

"I can try." Returning to his chair, Mo reached for the radio receiver. "This is the United States hopper-dredge *McFarland*, attempting to speak with the owner of the sport yacht *Hot & Spicy*. Come in, *Hot & Spicy*."

The static was followed a moment later by a man's voice. "This is Ben Smallwood of the *Hot & Spicy*. Go ahead, *McFarland*."

Mac took the radio handset from Mo. "This is James Mackreides aboard the *McFarland*. State your intentions, Mr. Smallwood."

"We received a distress call from a passenger aboard your vessel who claimed your crew was planning on casting him adrift in a lifeboat.

This is incredibly dangerous. As you're well aware, Bela's offspring is in the area, last detected beneath your keel."

"The Meg left us over an hour ago. As for Mr. Reed, if you want him you can have him—after all, you bought him. We'll cut our engines and allow you to close to within a hundred yards of our ship. You can fetch him from our lifeboat in your Zodiac."

Mac handed the radio receiver to his pilot. "Cut the engines and allow them to rid us of Mr. Reed."

"I'd be careful," Jackie said. "While I was in the hospital, one of the nurses told me her nephew had spent four weeks aboard the *Hot & Spicy*. Word is, Smallwood only gets to keep the yacht if all six of the pups are killed."

———————

Cyel Reed stood by the starboard rail, the morning sun blinding as it reflected off the dark blue surface. The shoreline of Vancouver Island beckoned to the north, the gray-hulled superyacht now less than a quarter of a mile to the southeast.

Suspended along the opposite side of the starboard rail was a wooden lifeboat, its paint worn with age.

Mac stood close by, his binoculars aimed at the yacht. He watched as a third crewman climbed over the transom to join the other two men waiting in the motorized inflatable raft.

"Is that him?" Mac nudged the engineer in the small of his back with the business end of his 12-gauge shotgun.

Cyel squinted in the direction of the craft now making its way to the *McFarland*. "I never met Smallwood. All of my dealings were with Nick Van Sicklen."

Mac spoke into his walkie-talkie. "Mr. Mallouh, any sign of Bela's offspring?"

"Perimeter is still clear."

"All right, Cyel. Over the side with you—your elevator awaits."

"Come on, Mackreides, we've known each other twenty years. Confine me to quarters for the duration of the voyage if it makes you feel better, but don't leave me in Canada with these yokels."

"Should have thought about that before you spent the yokels' money. Now get off of my boat."

"Asshole." Swinging his right leg over the rail, Cyel climbed down into the lifeboat. He held on as Monty engaged the winch, lowering the boat along the starboard side of the *McFarland*. "Screw you and the Taylors, Mackreides! I'll be back in California in time to dance on Terry's grave."

Monty watched as his uncle's face became a mask of rage. In one motion Mac flipped the locks on both winches, sending the lifeboat free-falling the last twenty-six feet into the sea.

The plunge separated Cyel from his seat, the impact slamming him backward against the hard wooden bench seat. He sat up painfully, waiting for the motorized raft to reach him.

———

The *Raja binoculata*, known more commonly as "big skates," were four-to-seven-feet-long, weighing upward of two hundred pounds. Numbering in the hundreds, the school of rays had been buried beneath the sediment, feeding on worms and mollusks, when the lifeboat had splashed down on the surface almost directly overhead. The sudden explosion of sound startled the creatures, chasing them from their feeding grounds in an avalanche of flapping wings.

Two miles to the south, Bela's remaining pup had been stalking a six-foot thresher shark when the sensory cells along the predator's flanks began vibrating. These fluid-filled subcutaneous canals, known as the lateral line, contained tiny hair-like features designed to detect frequencies and fluctuations in the water over great distances.

The impulses racing through the Megalodon's nervous system to its brain identified the source of the disturbance seconds before its ampullae of Lorenzini alerted it that the thresher shark had already diverted to the north to intercept the skates.

Bad move.

Ingrained in the Megalodon's DNA was thirty million years of aggressive behavior honed from the species' dominance as an apex predator. As if that were not enough, Bela's lone surviving offspring was a genetic clone of its mother—a hyperactive female with a nasty disposition. As far as the Meg was concerned, every territory had its own rules come feeding time, and the thresher shark had just violated the number one law of the jungle: Among predators, the biggest and meanest always eat first.

Whipping its caudal fin at a frenzied pace, the juvenile killer quickly closed the distance between itself and the thresher shark.

Sensing the fifteen-foot Megalodon, the smaller hunter darted left and then right along the bottom, attempting to avoid its larger adversary—

Chomp!

The thresher spasmed in pain. Attempting to swim faster, it wiggled its tail harder—unaware that its caudal fin, clear up to its pectoral fins, had been bitten off and were now in the Megalodon's mouth.

A paralyzing numbness swept past the thresher's gill slits, forcing it to expand its jaws open and closed to inhale more water. A moment later it toppled forward, a crimson cloud of blood pouring from the back of its severed body as it nose-dived snout-first to the sandy bottom like a downed fighter jet.

The Meg continued on its northwesterly trek, the skates' migration once more bringing it in close proximity to the strange creature that had consumed its cousin. It did not sense the presence of the lifeboat until it was practically upon it, its attention focused on the challenger moving along the surface on an intercept course with its intended meal.

———

Ben Smallwood sat in the bow of the inflatable motorized raft, commonly known as a Zodiac. Using his binoculars, he bypassed the boisterous engineer, whom he could see ranting from inside the still-tethered lifeboat.

Smallwood didn't care what happened to Cyel Reed; however, in failing to kill the last of Lizzy's pups, the engineer had unwittingly presented his team with a second, less costly alternative.

Smallwood's primary responsibility during this exercise in justice was simply to keep the raft aligned with the aerial drone that was currently flying three hundred feet directly above their heads. The quad copter's control box was down to 22 percent, and there were no spare batteries to be had. If the signal strength fell below 15 percent, they might not be able to initiate the signal for the small craft to drop its three-pound payload into the *McFarland*'s hopper.

Seated behind Smallwood was Thomas Moore, the only member of the yacht's crew with any real experience flying drones. Using his boss's body to shield the control box in his lap from the *McFarland*'s onlookers, he focused his attention on the live video shot of the Zodiac being transmitted from the quad copter's onboard gimbal-mounted camera.

The inflatable had moved beyond the video's frame, the drone struggling to keep pace.

Damn headwinds . . .

Thomas turned around to face his cousin. Charlie Moore was seated on the last bench, his right hand gripping the tiller of the outboard motor. "Cut your speed. The drone can't keep up."

"Cut my speed? Dude, we're barely moving as it is."

"I'm dealing with twenty-mile-an-hour wind gusts and my controller's battery has dipped below nineteen percent. Just do it."

The sudden shadow of movement across the fish finder caught Mo Mallouh's attention. He stared at the blip until it disappeared behind a screen covered in electronic snow.

"What is it?" Jackie asked.

"I don't know. I think it was the other Meg, only something's interfering with the fish finder."

Trish tried her walkie-talkie. "Mac, are you—"

The sonic squeal of electronic interference forced her to power it off.

The high-pitched whine of the Zodiac's outboard engine was reduced by half as the raft slowed beneath them.

Charlie Moore's peripheral vision caught movement. Turning to his left, he glanced overboard—and was shocked to see hundreds of skates soaring past the inflatable just below the surface. "Look at all the rays! They're passing beneath us like bats outta hell."

Ben Smallwood ignored the crewman as he attempted to calculate the distance between the raft and the *McFarland*. "Thomas, how much longer?"

"Wind finally let up; I've got the drone hovering two hundred feet above the *McFarland*'s superstructure. Now I just need to locate the damn hopper."

"Two hundred feet's way too high; if you miss the hopper there's a chance you could accidentally hit someone with this stuff."

———————

Monty had been watching the approaching Zodiac through his binoculars when the raft's bow wake all but disappeared. "That's weird—they're slowing down."

Mac was about to respond when something large passed beneath the lifeboat, snagging on one of the thick ropes keeping it tethered to the *McFarland*. For several seconds the wooden craft was dragged sideways, until the tension became too great, causing the lifeboat to flip.

———————

"Whoa!" Ben Smallwood saw the lifeboat toss their would-be passenger overboard. Using his binoculars, he searched for the Tanaka Institute's engineer—

—while in the seat directly behind him, his drone operator struggled to operate the camera's zoom button. The video finally jumped, revealing an attractive woman standing on the *McFarland*'s deck—and she appeared to be pointing up in the sky at the drone.

Thomas widened the frame and found himself looking down on an older man—and the business end of a 12-gauge shotgun.

"Crap, we've been—"

And then the world went topsy-turvy as an unseen force struck the inflatable's bow, slingshotting Thomas Moore and his cousin Charlie through a cloudburst of blood before depositing them into the sea.

Mac's first shot had missed. The second shattered the aerial drone like it was skeet, the impact sending fiberglass shrapnel raining upon them—

—along with a softball-size object that struck the edge of the wading pool Monty and David had stocked with live salmon. The contents of the small balloon splattered open, a third of its pink residue adhering to the outside of the curved aluminum structure, the rest of the powdery substance spilling inside the pool, bubbling as it spread across the surface of the water.

"What the hell is that?"

"I don't know," Jackie said. Covering her nose and mouth, she moved closer to inspect the inside of the pool.

The water was frothing, churned by the salmon, which were under obvious duress. Several fish flung themselves out of the container and flopped on deck, their mouths sucking in air until they ceased moving, blood and fish guts leaking from their gills and mouth.

"It's some kind of acid . . . very concentrated."

"Jackie, if this had gotten inside the tank—"

"The Meg would have ingested it, and its internal organs would've eventually bled out."

"And what if that pouch had struck one of us?"

"Second-and third-degree burns at a minimum. Blindness, I suppose, if it got in your eye. A direct hit . . . who knows? This Smallwood is either very desperate or very dangerous."

"Not anymore."

They turned to find Monty standing by the starboard rail, pale and shaken. "Smallwood's dead. . . . I saw the whole thing. One second he was sitting in the front of the inflatable; the next he exploded like he had stepped on an IED."

Mac and Jackie scanned the Salish Sea.

"Monty, the Zodiac . . . where did it go?"

"The Meg got it. You know, the dark one—Bela's kid. That bitch is as mean and nasty as her mother."

Jackie turned to Mac. "Cyel?"

Mac hurried to the starboard launch and looked below. Cyel had righted the lifeboat, but the craft was filled with water. The disgruntled engineer remained inside the flooded craft, yelling at someone swimming toward the boat.

"No! You're leading it right to me!"

A gray dorsal fin trailed the swimmer, its pale white head zigging and zagging just below the surface.

———

Charlie Moore swam with a desperation born from having witnessed Ben Smallwood's gruesome demise. He knew the Megalodon had been after the Zodiac and not those on board, but now all bets were off. Having struck the inflatable, the shark's forward inertia had propelled it up and over the raft's bow, its open mouth reflexively clamping down on Smallwood with the force of a pickup truck striking a pedestrian, bursting the man's internal organs like a ripe tomato, even as its three-thousand-pound girth flipped the boat engine-over-bow, sending Charlie flying over his cousin and through the air.

He had surfaced to screams. Thomas was attempting to tread water twenty feet away, his legs churning the blue sea crimson as he kicked at a massive pale head that insisted upon rising directly beneath him.

The Meg drove its snout straight into his cousin's ravaged belly, snorting gouts of blood deep into its nostrils like a coke addict.

Fighting the urge to puke, Charlie turned and swam. He heard Cyel Reed yelling at him and adjusted his course.

"No! You're leading it right to me!"

Three more strokes and his knees collided with the side of the swamped lifeboat. He attempted to climb in—

—only Reed pushed him back out again just as the Meg veered off, its lead-gray tail slapping at the surface, the upper lobe cracking across the back of Charlie Moore's skull like a rubber mallet, knocking him woozy.

He must have gone under, because he heard gunfire as his head broke the surface. The hull of the *McFarland* spun sideways in his vision—blotted out a moment later by the rubber sole of a shoe that stepped on his forehead with a dull thud.

He sank beneath the swamped boat, which rolled upside down, depositing Cyel overboard.

The engineer panicked and swam toward the *McFarland*.

Charlie stayed with the boat, kicking his way onto its curved bottom, hitching a ride as it rose beneath him like a giant turtle. He sucked in a deep breath of air as it broke the surface, spreading his limbs out wide and hugging the bottom, desperate to stabilize the craft.

He heard people yelling and raised his head.

The life ring had been tied to three different lengths of rope in order to be long enough to reach the sea from the deck of the *McFarland*. Cyel had grabbed it and was being dragged through the water to the starboard side of the ship.

An experienced bass fisherman, Charlie held his breath and waited.

They just turned him into top water bait.

———

The Meg rose through azure curtains of sunlight, its back arched, its tail thrashing in short powerful bursts, its senses locked on to its prey—

—which abruptly disappeared.

Cyel had squeezed his head and chest inside the life ring, his armpits wedged around the flotation device. He held on as he was hauled out of the water, his rate of ascension slowing as his rescuers struggled to drag his two-hundred-twenty-seven-pound frame up the side of the ship.

"Ahhh!"

He looked down as the Meg fell back into the sea, its clenched teeth stained red.

The engineer suddenly felt light-headed. His flesh tingled, his will weakening as he spun in circles at the end of the rope, his eyes rolling up in his skull.

———

Mac and Monty stopped tugging on the rope when Jackie screamed, but not before Cyel's head struck the pulley. The engineer's mouth was open, his face frozen and pale, his upper torso wedged inside the life ring—

—his lower torso gone, both legs having been bitten clean through at midthigh.

Jackie covered her mouth as she witnessed the life gurgle from the engineer's purple lips.

For a long moment, the three simply stared at the remains of their former colleague, until Monty motioned for them to look down.

"Oh my God . . ."

Four stories below, the Meg had surfaced. The creature was spy-hopping directly beneath Cyel Reed's remains, its ghostly white face and mouth splattered with the blood dripping from the dead man's corpse.

"Like I said, that fish is the devil," Monty muttered.

"Just like its mother," Mac agreed.

Before they could react, the engineer's corpse slid out from the life ring and plummeted forty-seven feet into the sea, barely missing the shark's open maw.

Twisting its head, the creature accepted the offering and disappeared just as the approaching superyacht idled its engines, slowing to rescue a lone survivor.

Omni San Francisco Hotel
San Francisco, California

Stefanie Smith had served as Governor Ryan Skinner's personal assistant for the past four years. During that time, she had dealt with everything from defending the governor against accusations of sexual misconduct to delivering secret child support payments for a "love child" born to Skinner's former housekeeper—an illegal immigrant. And yet nothing seemed as nefarious as the cover-up she had been placed in charge of seventy-two hours earlier.

The cab circled through the Nob Hill neighborhood and pulled into the hotel's private cul-de-sac. She paid the driver in cash, collected the long rectangular flower box from the seat next to her, and exited the car into the grand lobby, taking the elevator up to the top floor.

The doors opened to a Secret Service agent dressed in the requisite black suit, a communication device visible in his right ear. He checked her credentials and then pointed down the hall to the King Suite, where an Arab man dressed in a similar outfit stood outside the last set of double doors.

Stefanie approached and handed the guard her identification. He glanced at it, but was more interested in inspecting the contents of the flower box.

"These flowers are a special gift from the governor. No one handles this box except the crown prince."

The security guard spoke Arabic into a handheld device. A moment later the suite door opened, revealing Kirsty Joyce, the personal attorney of Prince Walid Abu Naba'a.

"Mrs. Harmon, so good to see you again."

"Actually, it's Stefanie Smith. I went back to using my maiden name after the divorce."

"I'm so sorry."

"I'm not. May we?"

"Of course." Kirsty spoke Arabic to the guard, who nodded and allowed Stefanie to enter.

The suite occupied a corner section of the top floor—six hundred fifty square feet divided between a living area, bedroom, and two bathrooms. The crown prince was situated in an easy chair by a floor-to-ceiling window looking out onto the city, his attention focused on his iPhone.

The women waited an uncomfortable forty seconds before he spoke, his eyes remaining fixated on the tiny screen.

"Three days, Mrs. Harmon. For three days I have been kept a prisoner in your city, my private jet denied our takeoff orders. And all the while, the governor has avoided my calls."

"My apologies, Your Highness. He's been extremely busy."

"Am I a suspect in my cousin's death?"

"No, Your Highness. As the police stated, the deaths of Paul Agricola and your cousin have officially been listed as shark attacks."

"Is this the governor's retribution for my decision to pull out of the Monterey project?"

"Not at all, though we'd certainly love for you to reconsider."

"Then why is your boss risking an international incident by refusing to allow me to return to Dubai?"

"Your cousin, Fiesal, was killed by a sea creature, but it was not a shark. Of course, you already knew that, having seen his remains."

"My apologies," Kirsty said. "We were not informed as to who was given security clearance."

"Understood."

The crown prince looked up. "What is in the box?"

"The reason your cousin ordered the *Marieke* to the Farallones."

"I assumed he was hunting the Liopleurodon."

"They were hunting the Lio. Paul Agricola had tracked it to the northwest coast of Oregon—or so he believed. Your cousin ordered his ship to the Farallones because the *Livyatan melvillei's* homing device indicated the whale had died and beached itself on one of the islands."

"Why would he care about that brute?"

"He cared because the brute's bio-tracker contained this." Stefanie opened the flower box, removing the transmitter—a four-foot-long hollow harpoon designed to accommodate its three-foot-long, seven-inch-diameter hollow insertion tube.

"This tube fits inside the harpoon. It contained trace amounts of doxapram, a powerful veterinary stimulant designed to accelerate an animal's heart rate."

"I don't understand," Kirsty said. "Why would Fiesal want to inject the whale with a stimulant . . . unless? Oh my God—"

The prince stood, crossing the room to the minibar. He removed a small bottle of Jack Daniel's and handed it to his attorney. "Fiesal knew we were terminating our partnership. Sinking the *Tonga* offered him a means to get back at me while putting ownership of the Lio back in play. You have to give him credit—in the end he proved himself to be quite resourceful."

Kirsty took a swig of whiskey, choking on the gulp. "'Resourceful'? More than forty people died."

The prince shot back a disparaging look. "I did not say I approved of his methods, Ms. Joyce."

"Understood. But approval or not, as a former partner and employee of Dubai-Land, his actions leave the company, and you personally, responsible for everything that happened."

"Nonsense. I had nothing to do with the *Tonga's* demise. It was

Fiesal who prepared the tracking device, and the girl who shot it into the Miocene whale."

Stefanie looked up. "Girl? What girl?"

"The female marine biologist . . . what was her name, Ms. Joyce?"

"Jacqueline Buchwald. She's David's girlfriend."

"David? As in David Taylor?" Stefanie circled the small room, thinking aloud. "The Lio's still out there; it's worth a lot of money to you . . . correct?"

"Go on," the prince said, returning to his chair.

"Who better to recapture the Lio than David?"

"He won't do it," Kirsty said, draining the whiskey sampler. "We already approached him through the girl—we offered her a million dollars. He only wants to deal with the Megs."

"He might change his mind if this evidence implicated his girlfriend in the drowning deaths of forty people, and the only way to keep it out of the public's eye was to capture Junior."

The prince smiled.

Kirsty looked aghast. "You can count me out—I want no part of this."

"Perhaps you should leave then, counselor." The prince motioned to the door.

The attorney's eyes went wide. Exiting the living area, she entered the bedroom, returning a moment later wheeling out a small suitcase. "You'll receive my firm's final invoices in your email. Be sure to pay them promptly—I wouldn't want to jeopardize the attorney-client relationship."

She exited the suite, briskly shutting the door behind her.

"What a bitch." Stefanie crossed to the minibar, helping herself to a drink. "Of course, recapturing the Lio doesn't help the State of California. Then again, now that we know the pliosaur is somewhat amphibious by nature, it sort of makes more sense to design a habitat that encompasses both land and water. We can easily do that using the parcels of land the governor had set aside for the new Monterey exhibit."

"Mrs. Harmon, you are proving yourself to be far more resourceful than I knew."

"It's actually Ms. Smith: I'm divorced."

Monterey, California

There were two patient relocations scheduled on this blustery Satur-day in mid-February, both ending along the Northern California coast. Each involved members of the Taylor family, neither of whom had been given much hope of surviving their arduous ten-day journey.

The *McFarland* was first to arrive, its task to bring Lizzy's lone surviv-ing albino pup to the Tanaka Institute. The feisty female—named Luna, after her unusual habit of spy-hopping to watch the moon—had arrived by hopper-dredge thirty minutes before daybreak and a full twelve hours ahead of her announced ETA. In sharp contrast to the sold-out event that had occurred six months earlier, the institute would remain closed to the public this time around—the deception an attempt to avoid the chaos as-sociated with the expected fanfare, as well as potential threats from pro-testers. A heavy police presence took over the access roads, beachfront, and empty parking lots, the Coast Guard securing Monterey Bay.

At 6:27 a.m., the submerged King Kong–size doors of the canal opened, allowing the *McFarland* to enter the Tanaka Lagoon.

For nine out of the past twenty-five years, the lake-size, man-made waterway had been home to Angel, Luna's seventy-four-foot, fifty-ton maternal grandmother. The discovery that the monstrous Megalodon had been pregnant had forced the institute to construct a separate facility to house her pups. The result: a state-of-the-art, sixty-million-gallon, saltwater aquarium featuring an underwater gallery.

Though designed as a separate self-contained habitat, the Meg Pen was connected to the larger lagoon by way of a twenty-foot-diameter access tunnel—a feature deemed necessary to relocate at least a few of the pups as they became young adults and the Meg Pen grew too crowded. Still, Angel had made it clear that she had no interest in sharing the lagoon, reminding her offspring on a daily basis who the "Alpha" was by slapping her caudal fin against the grated steel barrier that separated the two habitats.

Did adult female Megalodon sharks possess maternal instincts? Angel's behavior had clearly demonstrated an adversarial relationship with her offspring. This was in sharp contrast to the recent discoveries of ancient Meg nurseries located in close proximity to one another along prehistoric coastal areas, which indicated cooperative parenting among the sharks.

By way of an explanation, Jonas Taylor pointed out the unique circumstances involving Angel's mother and her ancestors—a subspecies of Megalodon that had lived in isolation for millions of years in the Mariana Trench. Food would have been scarce, leading to cannibalism among the adults. Having escaped her purgatory, Angel's mother would still have considered her newborn pups a threat—any offspring spared at birth might grow into tomorrow's killer.

Housing five Megalodon pups in one tank had come with its own set of problems. There had been two distinct litters: Bela and Lizzy in one, the smaller triplet "runts" in the other. Angel's terrifying round-the-clock presence had bound Bela and Lizzy to each other, while the three smaller triplets had kept to themselves. The litters had coexisted like rival gang members in a prison yard. Though the "sisters" were larger, Lizzy realized the runts were growing bigger and more aggressive—which is why she unleashed her dark-pigmented sister on one of the triplets, thereby reducing the future threat of their rivals.

Had the two remaining triplets not been shipped to Dubai, they too would have met their demise—such is the law of the jungle.

Despite their ruthless nature, the sisters had possessed a strong maternal instinct, which they had passed on to their own offspring. The six newborns had quickly learned that the Salish Sea was filled with predators, and that safety came in numbers within the scent-established borders of the Meg nursery.

Before Lizzy's capture, the sisters had divided their pups into pairs, teaching them through cooperative parenting how to swim and hunt in tandem, with Bela's pups on top to camouflage the white hides of their cousins—a major detriment in the wild.

With their parents gone, two of the three tandems gradually expanded their hunting grounds. The third pairing had been reduced to one of Lizzy's pups, after its "Bela-mate" had been netted and drowned by Paul Agricola.

Left on its own, the albino had been the second Meg offspring to die.

Luna and her Bela-mate had been the last pair to remain intact. After the albino's capture, the dark-backed pup had remained within its cousin's sensory range . . . right up until the moment the ship had left the Strait of Juan de Fuca. The Pacific Ocean was flush with orca scent trails. When Bela's offspring detected several pods of killer whales patrolling the outskirts of the Salish Sea, the Meg returned to the strait, abandoning its cousin.

The realization that her partner was no longer around sent Luna into a frenzy. The moment one of its human captors was revealed, the one-and-a-half-ton shark attacked that area of the hopper, slapping its tail along the surface and beating its head against the wall—a behavior that led Monty to rename the Meg "Lunatic." Mac sent footage of these attacks to David via iPhone, hoping he could suggest a course of action, but the new owner of the Tanaka Institute could not be reached. In the end, Jackie had no choice but to increase the flow of sedatives into the tank—a dangerous maneuver that required a round-the-clock vigil in the event the shark lost consciousness, ceased swimming, and drowned.

Mo Mallouh docked the *McFarland* along the stretch of concrete walkway that separated the Meg Pen from the lagoon. Waiting for the ship were three men wearing wetsuits and a thirteen-year-old boy in street clothes.

Alan Cox had been the head orca trainer at *Sea World*, his eldest sons, Mason and Jalen—ages twenty and eighteen—having served as his assistants. Cox's youngest son, Ashton, was placed in charge of the team's equipment, but would not be joining the members of his family in either the hopper or Meg Pen.

Each member of Cox's crew was armed with a rubber tripod attached to a six-foot reach pole that was used for prodding and pushing the shark. At the center of these rubber pads was a metal probe that could disperse an "attention-grabbing" electrical charge.

Mac would man the crane; his job was to transport Luna from the hopper into the Meg Pen once the shark had been secured within its twenty-by-twenty-foot reinforced canvas pouch. Suspended beneath the hoist, the sides of the shark harness contained adjustable Velcro side panels that opened to accommodate the Meg's pectoral fins.

Jackie had increased Luna's tranquilizers over the last hour to make sure the animal was heavily sedated. To further minimize the risk to Cox's team, both the hopper and Meg Pen had been drained to five feet—a depth sufficient to allow the Meg to swim and breathe, but too shallow for it to establish neutral buoyancy, forcing the shark to bear a third of its own weight, which handicapped its movements.

Jackie zipped up her wetsuit and followed the three men down a ladder into the hopper. Moments later, the crane's boom appeared along the portside of the *McFarland*, positioning the canvas harness over the tank. Steel cable fed out, lowering the device to the water.

The pouch was quickly retrieved by Cox's team and laid out flat along the bottom of the tank in the path of the semilucid, fifteen-foot Megalodon. Alan positioned himself in front of the shark, pressing his tripod to the shark's snout as it attempted to move forward, occupying its attention while his sons positioned the side vents around Luna's pectoral fins.

Alan tightened the harness and then offered a thumbs-up to Jackie.

Reaching for the radio strapped to her left shoulder, she called Mac. "We're good. Take her up."

Mac pulled back on one of the crane's half-dozen control levers, causing the winch to retrieve steel cable, raising the three-thousand-pound preda-tor out of the *McFarland*'s hopper. Circling the cab counter clockwise in its track, he swung the shark slowly over the concrete walkway while extending the boom until it was positioned directly over the Meg Pen.

Jackie and Team Cox deboarded the *McFarland* just as the captive creature began its four-story descent into the nearly drained aquarium.

Monty stood by the west end of the tank, where he had secured the top of a forty-foot ladder to the railing. Jackie leaned out and looked down, the rungs disappearing along the sleek curved sides of glass, the descent daunting.

Alan was the first one up. "Just take your time and don't look down. Mason, wait until I'm at least halfway down before starting your descent . . . then Jackie and Jalen."

"What about me?" Ashton asked.

"We're counting on you to be our eyes and ears from above. Remem-ber, when you use the radio, we're all on Channel-1."

"Yes, sir."

Checking his radio, Monty switched his channel from CH-2 to CH-1.

Mason waited until his father had descended twenty rungs before swinging his legs over the rail one at a time, onto the ladder.

Jackie looked down, forcing herself to take slow, deep breaths. Alan was already wading in the water; Luna was suspended ten feet above his head.

"Ma'am." Jalen Cox tapped Jackie on the shoulder, indicating it was her turn.

Gripping the top of the rail, she swung her right leg over, her rubber-boot-covered foot, feeling for a ladder rung before her left leg followed.

The descent was nerve-racking but uneventful, and she soon found herself chest-deep in cold salt water. She waded out to Alan and Mason, who were flanking the Meg.

Jackie approached the albino, all but its head and tail sandwiched within the canvas hoist. The first step in releasing the Meg was to es-cort it around its new environment to allow the heavily drugged shark to come out of its stupor; but from Luna's thrashing, the drugs clearly appeared to have worn off.

"I don't understand—I gave her heavy doses of phenobarbital. I thought we'd have to walk her around the tank for at least a few hours."

Alan pointed to a twenty-foot-diameter grate along the top half of the southern wall. Water was streaming in through its porous steel surface, the incoming flow matched by the Meg Pen's drains. "What is that?"

"That's a tunnel connecting the Meg Pen with the lagoon."

"The two tanks share the same water supply?"

"Correct."

Alan shook his head. "The same water supply that accommodated Angel for all those years?"

"Angel's been gone since last July. And both tanks have filtration systems."

"But her scent is everywhere. Chemical traces from her urine have seeped into the pores of the lagoon, as well as into the algae and moss that coats the inside of the canal's walls. Luna detects the presence of an adult female, and even though it's her deceased grandmother, she's none too happy about it."

Opening its mouth to breathe, the juvenile predator inhaled a river of salt water into its nostrils and gullet . . . and once more went berserk, whipping its tail back and forth while twisting in an attempt to free itself and flee.

Jackie grabbed for her walkie-talkie. "Monty, lower the flex-tube, I need to administer more drugs."

As she watched in horror, the agitated shark rolled over several times, each rotation causing the harness to squeeze tighter around its sharp denticle-covered skin, the razor-sharp edges cutting into the thick canvas fabric.

The tearing sound caused everyone to back away.

"Get to the ladder," Alan warned as he suddenly found himself being dragged sideways into the Meg's chaotic vortex.

Jalen Cox extended the grip end of his reach pole to his father. Alan grabbed hold of it and held on as his son pulled him out of harm's way while his brother Mason struck the creature above its left pectoral fin with his bang stick, the 3,000-volt charge causing it to arch its back as it reared its head out of the water.

The Meg spun around, its tail unleashing a seven-foot swell that rolled over Alan's head.

Jalen managed three bounding strides toward his submerged father before he was forced to duck under the incoming wave. Opening his eyes underwater, he saw blood pooling around the monster's gnashing jaws and realized his father was under attack.

His head cleared the water as the wave rolled past him. "Mason, strike it again!"

Ducking underwater, Jalen grabbed his father by his armpits and dragged him away from the Meg, which had freed itself from its harness.

Mason moved in to attack—

—and his reach pole was slapped free from his grip by the creature's lashing tail.

Jalen left his father with Jackie to help his brother. Blood was in the water, pooling around the trainer, seeping from a jagged wound. Alan's right arm was gone, bitten off below the elbow. Pink tendons and sinew dangled from beneath a flap of skin matted in dark hair.

Alan looked down. "Oh, God—"

"Alan, stay calm, I'm going to make you a tourniquet." Retrieving her dive knife from its ankle strap, Jackie used its serrated edge to slice through the right sleeve of his wetsuit. Then she wrapped it around his right biceps and tied it as tightly as she could.

"That should hold for now, but we need to get you out of here."

He nodded, fighting to keep from blacking out. "The harness . . . is there anything left of it?"

She looked back where Mason and Jalen were retreating from the advancing Meg, the harness still dangling from its hoist. "It's torn, but salvageable." She waved to the boys. "Circle back and grab the harness; we'll need it to get your dad out of here."

"It can't turn."

Jackie looked around before pinpointing the voice to her left shoulder. "Ashton?"

"The Meg can't turn—the water's too shallow. It can only go forward."

Jackie realized the teen was talking to Jalen, who was struggling to stay ahead of the surging shark. Cutting hard to his right, he launched himself into a frenzy of swim strokes and kicks to avoid the lunging shark's snapping jaws—

—and its belly suddenly grounded, preventing it from pursuing Ashton's older brother.

Mason retrieved the canvas sheath and dragged it through the water to his father and Jackie. "Contact Mac. Have him raise the hoist so we can climb inside what's left of the harness."

Using the Velcro straps, he fashioned the torn fabric into a giant sling while his brother occupied the incensed Meg, preventing it from going after the others.

Jackie reached for the radio strapped to her shoulder. "Mac, this is Jackie . . . do you read me? Mac, come in! Are you kidding me?"

———

Unable to reach Monty on his radio, Mac had left the crane's cab to see what was happening inside the Meg Pen. He joined his nephew by the outer rail.

"Mac, what are you doing? Didn't you hear me yelling at you to raise the hoist? The Meg's awake—"

Mac grabbed the radio from the frantic man. "Idiot! You're on Channel-1, the shark crew's channel. I'm on Channel-2!" He switched the dial, stole a quick glance into the Meg Pen . . . and took off in an awkward jog, each pounding stride on the cold concrete surface sending shooting pains through his arthritic knees.

———

Jackie and Mason helped Alan into the harness. She scooted in beside him and wrapped her arm around his waist as the hoist rose above their heads, pulling up the slack.

Mason called out to his brother. "That's far enough!"

Jalen had led Luna thirty yards in the other direction. Circling back, the slender eighteen-year-old found himself out of breath, struggling to move quickly in the chest-deep water.

The Meg shook its head, its flared directional nostrils snorting the water—

—locking in on the scent of blood. Whipping its caudal fin into a wide arc, the Meg thrashed and twisted itself into a hundred-eighty-degree turn, its snout pointing directly at the canvas sling holding the three humans—

—Jalen Cox directly in its path.

Mason stood up and yelled, "Run!"

Alan opened his eyes. Weak from the loss of blood, he knew he was going into shock, but seeing the white dorsal fin advancing on his son snapped him out of it.

"Jalen! Stop trying to outrun the damn thing and start swimming!"

Hearing his father's order, the teen dove forward into a crawl stroke, and now it was a race, the teen two body lengths out in front, the shark picking up speed as it adapted to moving through the shallows with short, quick swipes of its tail.

The harness had risen three feet out of the water when Jalen righted himself and jumped, grabbing his brother by the hand—

—his right boot actually stepping on the Meg's snout as he used it to boost himself out of the water onto the canvas perch.

———————

The steel cable retracted, lifting the harness out of the Meg Pen. Thirty seconds later it was set down on the concrete deck, where EMTs quickly worked on Alan Cox.

Mac looked out the open cab door to see Jacqueline Buchwald heading his way, her wetsuit unzipped and dangling around her waist, revealing a red bikini top.

As she reached the cab, he realized her top was actually white, the thin spandex material soaked in blood.

Jackie signaled for him to shut down the crane's motor, then handed him her radio.

"I quit."

‖‖‖‖‖‖‖‖‖‖‖‖‖‖‖‖‖‖‖‖‖‖‖‖‖‖

Monterey High School
Monterey, California

The gymnasium carried the heavy scent of perspiration that only comes with age. Wood bleachers rattled beneath a foot-stomping crowd that easily surpassed the fire marshal's twenty-five-hundred-person capacity as the pregame clock ran down to 0:00. Cheerleaders scurried onto the basketball court, led by the home team's mascot—a toreador, replete with a red bullfighting cape.

The visitors' starting five were introduced to a chorus of boos. And then the band's trumpet section played the Toreador theme.

"... and now, for your Green Machine! Starting at center ... a six-foot, seven-inch junior—number thirty-three, Jim Tiknor. At power forward ... a six-foot, five-inch senior—number twenty-one, Joel Benavides. At small forward ... a six-foot, three-inch junior—number thirty-two, Kyle Lancaster. At point guard ... a six-foot senior—number twelve, Michael Davies. And at shooting guard ... a six-foot, five-inch All-Conference senior—number eleven, Matthew Cubit."

The dark-haired teen hustled to center court and was surrounded by his teammates as the crowd chanted, "Green Machine ... Green Machine."

Twenty rows up, Tom Cubit occupied the last two seats in the upper row of the center aisle. As the referee tossed the ball for the opening tap, the attorney and former two-guard at the University of Central Florida casually scanned the crowd, identifying clusters of Division I college coaches pretending to scout his son. In reality, every coach in the country knew what Matt could do; at this juncture they were simply using the game as an excuse to "court" Tom, hoping to gain an edge in signing his son to a Letter of Intent.

Michael Selby was the first to approach. The third-year coach at UCLA and his assistants had been engaged in a "full-court recruiting press" ever since Matt's Facebook post stating that he might be interested in playing closer to home after all. This had sent waves of panic through the staffs at the former front-runners, Duke and North Carolina, and both schools' assistant coaches were in attendance.

Tom Cubit watched Selby make his way up the rickety bleachers. "Tommy?"

"Hey, Coach."

"Mind if I join you?" Without waiting for a reply, Selby squeezed himself onto the last two feet of wood bench. "Tom, you know how much we want your boy to come to UCLA—we're a perfect fit. As a friend, I just wanted you to be aware of some nasty rumors being floated out there."

Cubit's hazel eyes grew fierce. "What rumors?"

"Something about a secret surgical procedure that enhanced Matt's shooting range. It's crazy, I know, but I had to ask. I mean, the kid wasn't on anyone's radar as a junior; suddenly he's averaging thirty-eight points a game while shooting NBA threes."

As if on cue, Matthew buried a three-pointer from five feet beyond the top of the key, sending the bleachers reverberating with stomps.

"Coach, Mattie was born with *pectus excavatum*; it's a condition where the breastbone is sunken in the chest. He could have lived with it, but as an athlete it was affecting his wind and workouts. When he turned fourteen he begged us to have it fixed. We took him to a surgeon, who performed something called a Nuss procedure. Basically, they inserted a concave steel bar beneath his breastplate and then flipped it over, popping out his chest. It's secured with stabilizers, but you have to wear it for four years, and I know it had to affect him. Mattie never complained; he just worked harder. This past summer his surgeon removed the bar, and suddenly the kid's shooting the ball like he's Stephen Curry."

The crowd roared again as number eleven hit a jump shot from deep in the corner.

"Tom, that's an amazing story; I think we should publish it the day Matt signs with the Bruins. As for those rumors, don't say I said anything, but the guy spreading it . . ." Selby nodded in the direction of Chris Carter, the head basketball coach at USC, the local competition.

Cubit was about to reply when he saw a young woman enter the gym, her hair tucked beneath a San Francisco Giants baseball cap. "Hey, Coach, there's someone here who needs to speak with me . . . you don't mind?"

"Sure, no problem." Selby shook Cubit's hand and left, passing Jacqueline Buchwald on the way down.

She held out her hand when she got to Tom. "I'm Jackie. Thank you for agreeing to meet with me, Mr. Cubit. I'm curious—why here instead of at your office?"

"This isn't on the clock. We're simply engaging in a casual conversation."

"Casual? How's this for casual: The crown prince claims he has evidence that his cousin and I conspired to sink the *Tonga*."

"What evidence?"

"The transmitter bin Rashidi gave me to tag the *Livyatan melvillei* . . . it wasn't a tracking device, it was an injection cartridge. The prince showed me results of a lab report that indicated the cartridge contained traces of a powerful stimulant. Mr. Cubit, Fiesal bin Rashidi told me the harpoon held a tracking device. He ordered me to use it on Brutus. I swear, I didn't know about any of this."

"I believe you. But why would he purposely sink a tanker, killing so many innocent people?"

"To get back at his cousin for forcing him out of the company. The guy's a sociopath. He also has his own reasons for releasing the Lio. A few weeks before the *Tonga* arrived in Monterey, I overheard one of the other marine biologists talking about a new start-up venture coming out of China. That gives bin Rashidi a major buyer should he manage to recapture the Lio."

"Bin Rashidi's dead. So is Paul Agricola. Their remains were found in the Farallon Islands—their raft was attacked and sunk by great white sharks that were feasting off the dead Miocene whale. That's the official story. My contacts in the Coast Guard told me what really happened. Agricola's remains were found near the shoreline; bin Rashidi was attacked inside a maintenance building."

"By what?"

"The Lio. Looks like your former boss was devoured and then regurgitated, with his flesh melted down to the bone by the creature's digestive juices."

"May his soul rot in hell. Are you sure about the Lio venturing on land? I mean, I realize these monsters were once amphibious, but they've clearly evolved gills."

"According to one of the Farallon marine biologists, the Lio decimated the elephant seal population—that's why it left the water. David believes the creature has functional lungs, which simply remain deflated until it breathes air. The governor's keeping this quiet—the last thing he wants is to panic the public."

"Where is David? I've been trying to reach him since he returned to Monterey. Why is he avoiding my texts and calls?"

"David's in a precarious position, Ms. Buchwald. As of last week, he officially took ownership of the institute. As you know, we're suing the prince and his corporate entities. You worked for Dubai-Land before and during the transfer of the Lio to the *Tonga*. Prince Walid's accusations won't hold up in court, but once the story breaks, the families of the survivors will go after you, too."

"There's nothing you can do to help me?"

"I wish there were. Again, it's a conflict of interest."

"Sounds to me like my whole relationship with David Taylor is a conflict of interest." She stood to leave—

—and Cubit grabbed her by the wrist. "David asked me to give you something." Reaching beneath the bench, he pulled out a decorative gift bag, a cardboard box inside.

"What's this?"

"Two five-inch Megalodon teeth: one from Lizzy, the other from Bela. David included a list of private dealers as well. He says the pair should pull in close to a million dollars each."

"Tell the new owner of the Tanaka Institute I don't need his blood money . . . that I'll manage on my own." She handed the package back to the attorney and stormed down the bleachers.

Tom Cubit waited until halftime. Then he stepped outside the gym and placed the call.

"David, bad news: She turned down the package."

David sat in the dark galley, watching the albino Megalodon as it circled counterclockwise around its new habitat. Having spent most of her existence being towed through the water by her dark-pigmented cousin, Luna had developed a lazy caudal fin, a condition that caused her to sink every twenty feet until she lashed her tail to compensate.

He could have stayed all evening in the Meg Pen's bleachers, but hearing the news from the attorney sent him heading for the exit, cursing under his breath.

"If she didn't take the teeth, that can only mean one thing: The crown prince is blackmailing her."

"To do what?"

"To go after the Lio."

Carmel, California

Jonas entered his master bedroom. Sitting in his wife's favorite wicker rocking chair, he gazed out the floor-to-ceiling windows at the emerald-green swells rolling into Otter Cove.

How long has it been since I was home? Three months?

It seemed a lifetime ago that he had agreed to relocate to Boca Raton with Terry to enjoy their retirement years together in peace.

"The Pacific gave us a tempest life; the Atlantic offers us serenity. I know you love this house, Jonas, but you'll see . . . the change will do us good. We'll make new memories."

She was right. Over the last three months they had made many new memories—all of them nightmares.

———

Nearly two weeks had passed since he had been summoned to Dr. Calvert's office, feeling like a teen about to be expelled from school.

"We've met with Dr. Maharaj, who provided our medical board with a complete breakdown of what was in the IV bag. He stated emphatically that he had spoken to both you and your daughter about Terry's high creatinine levels . . . that he had told you she was far too weak to handle the granulocytes in her present condition. He also made it quite clear that he never authorized his staff to release the donor cells to your children."

"I paid for them; they were ours. My son took them as per my instructions. In football it's what we call a 'Hail Mary pass.' Terry was dying; the cancer had—"

"Introducing an alternative medical protocol without the knowledge of your wife's physician or our staff violates every rule in this facility. Under normal circumstances, these cancer-killing agents elevate the patient's internal temperature. In Terry's case, her elevated creatinine levels caused a massive swelling of her brain tissues."

"The results from the last blood tests seem to indicate the cancer is gone."

"Yes, but at what cost? Instead of passing in peace, your actions have left your wife in a coma."

"People awaken from comas. Terry's breathing on her own; isn't that a positive sign?"

"Mr. Taylor, your wife is in a persistent vegetative state . . . a state of severe unconsciousness. With a persistent vegetative state, there is breathing, circulation, and sleep-wake cycles, but she is unaware of her surroundings and incapable of voluntary movement. While there is a slight chance of her one day progressing to wakefulness, she'll never recoup her higher brain functions, meaning she'll remain in a permanent vegetative state until the day her organs finally shut down and she dies."

"For better or worse, that was the deal." Jonas pinched away tears. "Whatever it costs to take care of her, I'll pay it. Whatever it takes, I'll do it."

Dr. Calvert shook her head. "Not here you won't. My assistant is putting together a list of facilities where she can be remanded."

"That won't be necessary. Tell your staff to get her ready to travel. We're taking my wife home, where she belongs."

The knock on the open bedroom door snapped Jonas back into the moment. He turned to Dani, who was standing in the hallway.

"Dad, the medical team is here; they need to bring in mom's stuff."

"Thanks, Dani. Have them set up her bed so she's facing the ocean."

Two men entered, wheeling in a hospital bed. Three more trips yielded medical monitors, IV stands, a small refrigerator, and a supply cabinet.

The EMTs arrived twenty minutes later. They wheeled Terry in on a gurney through the second-story entrance—the end of a harrowing three-thousand-mile journey. Jonas had hired two private nurses for during the week and one for weekends, along with a rehab specialist who would move her limbs.

"Mr. Taylor, your wife is all set. The medical supplies and nutrition bags are being delivered this afternoon and we changed her diaper about an hour ago, so you should be good until tonight. We just need your signature on a few forms and then we'll be on our way."

"Thank you, fellas." He scribbled his name without reading the legalese and led them out, handing each man two folded hundred-dollar bills.

He reentered the house to find Dani on her cell phone.

"That was Kelly Rollyson, the first weekday nurse. She'll be here in an hour. Do you want me to wait?"

"That's not necessary. Besides, you need to get back to school. Mom and I will be fine."

She gave her father a long hug, then left.

Jonas carried his wife's wicker rocking chair from the other side of the bedroom and positioned it on the left side of the hospital bed. Sitting down, he took Terry's right hand in his, comforted by her pulse.

"Take your time and heal, babe. When you're ready to come back to me, I'll be here."

PART THREE

SUNRISE

All you need is love.
 —John Lennon/Lennon-McCartney

15 months later . . .

Quatsino Sound
Vancouver Island, B.C.

The waterway known as Quatsino Sound lies at the mouth of an inlet located along the northwest coast of Vancouver Island. As it moves inland, it branches off into several bays and harbors, with sparsely populated hamlets nestled along shorelines accessible only by boat and gravel-covered backroads.

The Canadian government's decision to ban fisheries from the area had revitalized the salmon stocks. There was a healthy abundance of coho, sockeye, and humpies, as well as offshore species like halibut and lingcod, making the destination one of the most popular among sports fishermen.

This was Peter Traxler's first fishing trip to Quatsino Sound, and he quickly realized that driving to Winter Harbour had been a mistake. It took him three hours and twenty minutes to negotiate the forty-two miles of bad road, he broke a shock on his boat trailer, and a brief encounter with two black bear cubs went sour when mama bear charged his car. Upon arriving at his destination, he discovered the boat launch was literally a hole bulldozed into the bank that could be used only during high tide.

Naturally, it was low tide.

With three hours to kill, he decided to check in at the Outpost, which served as a marina, general store, and lodge. Confirming his reservation, the desk manager proceeded to run the charges on his credit card—

—as two attractive women entered the facility. Both were blondes, decked out in fishing vests and tight jean shorts, and they were heading his way.

"Hi. I'm Katey Robinson and this is my friend Sasha Moulder. Are you here for the fishing?"

"Of course he's here for the fishing," Sasha chided, her British accent easy on the ears. "What else is there to do out here?"

Sasha's wink caught Peter off guard. "Yes, fishing . . . I love fishing. I have an eighteen-foot Bayliner out in the parking lot, only I can't launch it for another three hours."

"Then you're free to join us," Katey said. "We rented a charter that accommodates four, but one of our girlfriends didn't show and we need the fourth to split the costs."

"How much are we talking?"

"Three hundred . . . dollars, not pounds." Sasha smiled, turning on the charm.

"You can pay here," the manager said. "I can add it to your bill."

The two blondes nodded.

"Okay, what the hell."

The women clapped.

The manager ran his credit card and printed his receipt. Peter signed it and took his room key. "I want to stow my stuff and change. How about I meet you ladies outside in fifteen minutes?"

"That's perfect. It's the second-to-last boat on the right dock. We're stocked with food and beer, so don't worry about a thing."

They waved and hurried off.

The manager directed Peter to his room, which had a kitchenette and small living area. He took a quick shower, brushed his teeth, and changed into a fresh T-shirt and his favorite fishing shorts, one with Velcro pockets. Checking his breath one more time, he left the room and exited the building to the docks.

He located the ladies standing aboard a twenty-four-foot, aluminum, center-consoled boat, powered by twin ninety-horsepower, Yamaha four-stroke engines. As Peter approached, he saw a bearded male in his thirties wearing a captain's hat passing down supplies to another man standing in the boat.

Sasha waved him over. "Sorry, I can't remember your name."

"Peter."

"Peter, this is Kenny Powell, the best charter boat captain on Vancouver Island."

"Thank you, babe." Kenny wiped the sweat from his palm on his pant leg and playfully swatted Sasha on her rump. "Fish have been biting all week—we'll hit our allotment in a few quick hours."

Before he could react, Katey was introducing a second fellow passenger. "Peter, this is my fiancé, Sam Ramer."

"Sup, dude?"

"Yeah, you know what—I think maybe I'll just rest for a few hours until the tide comes in and go out myself."

"Suit yourself," the captain said. "But you've already spent the money; why not come out with us."

"What are you talking about? You haven't left yet—just refund my money."

"Sorry, Pete, there's no refunds. I actually turned down an older couple while you were paying Sasha."

"Really? Where'd they go? I'll sell them my seat."

"Too late—they caught another charter." Kenny climbed down into the boat and then reached up to help Sasha down. "So, what's it gonna be?"

Gritting his teeth, Peter stepped down into the vessel and took a seat next to the cooler, helping himself to the first of what he suspected would be many beers to come.

Four thirty-pound Chinook, a forty-five-pound halibut, and three more beers later found Peter feeling much better about life. A fading July sun drenched the pine-covered hills before them in orange as they trolled east on their return trip at 10 knots, the boat's bow wake rippling across a glass-like surface, their four fishing poles secured in small outriggers.

Seated across from the control console, Peter leaned over to speak with the captain. "So, be honest: Did you send the ladies inside as bait?"

"Hook, line, and sinker." Kenny reached out and clinked his beer bottle with Peter's. "You paid for the fuel and bait. But we'll make it worth your while. I'll have everything you caught filleted, packed in ice, and stored at the Outpost for when you check out. And tonight, you'll join us back at my place for fresh halibut and a Quatsino version of a luau."

"I like it—whoa!" Peter pointed to starboard, where dozens of salmon were leaping out of the water, the school of Chinook keeping pace with the boat. "I've never seen that before. What could be—"

He looked at Kenny. The guide's face had gone pale, his laid-back attitude instantly gone.

Reaching into his vest pocket, he pulled out a Swiss Army knife. "Peter, we need to cut bait and run. Take this knife and cut the lines. Do not reel them in."

The fear in the man's eyes eliminated all questions. Peter took the knife, used his thumbnail to release a blade, and moved to the nearest of the four outriggers, which was situated on the portside by his seat. It took some effort to slice through the thirty-pound super braid, which quickly disappeared when the heavy line finally snapped, dragged overboard by the leader and bait.

Kenny glanced at Sasha, who was curled in a ball in the bow. "Sasha, wake up." He buckled his seat belt and pressed down on the throttle, edging ahead of the leaping salmon.

Peter made quick work of the two starboard lines. The last outrigger was situated in the stern along the port gunwale. Sam was seated on a padded bench, his back to the sheathed fishing pole. Katey was asleep in his lap.

Peter stumbled toward him, knife drawn as the boat accelerated.

"Easy there, boss. What are you doing with that knife?"

"Cutting the line, as ordered."

"The hell you are. That's my rig." He turned to inspect the fishing pole, the top half of the fiberglass rod nearly bent in half. "There we go! Hey, Kenny, I got a hook in something big—ease up while I bring it in."

"Dude, Kenny wants all the lines cut—"

Sam rolled out from under Katey and stood, removing the pole from the outrigger, the drag nearly pulling him overboard. "Oh baby, she's gotta be seventy pounds. Hey, Kenny—"

Peter and Sam both turned to the captain for help—only Kenny couldn't hear over the twin engines, and his gaze was focused on the fish leaping out of the sea to starboard.

"Screw it." Placing one foot on the transom, Sam braced himself and leaned back, quickly leaning forward again to take in line. "God, what a brute. Katey, tell your buddy Kenny to slow down."

Bracing herself, Katey moved up the center aisle to speak with the captain, who was seated sideways with his back to her so that he could see everything to starboard, from bow to stern.

"Kenny, Sam needs you to slow the boat down."

"That's too bad. Now go sit down."

"But he caught a fish . . . he said it's a brute."

"What?" Kenny swung around to his left to find Sam engaged in battle, his effort causing a fifty-pound Chinook salmon to leap out of the water thirty yards behind the boat.

"Damn it!" He grabbed an empty beer bottle from a cup holder and tossed it at Sasha.

"Hey—"

"I need you to take the wheel." He stood, allowing his girlfriend to slip behind him into his chair. "Keep us ahead of the salmon."

"Salmon?" She looked to starboard. "Oh, wow . . ." She glanced back at Kenny. "You don't think . . . ?"

"Just watch the salmon." Kenny pushed past Katey and made his way to the back of the boat. Taking the knife from Peter, he secured the fishing pole with his free hand as he pressed the business end of the blade beneath the line, the sharp edge snapping the twenty-five-pound test, sending Sam sprawling backward into an empty seat.

"What the hell, Kenny?" Sam was about to confront the captain when he saw a massive triangular white head surface thirty yards behind the boat's diminishing wake, his fish flapping between the shark's clenched four-and-a-half-inch serrated teeth.

Sam looked at Kenny. "Was that?"

"Bella-donna? Yeah." Kenny hurried forward to take the controls from Sasha. He looked to starboard to check on the school of salmon, only to find a glass-like surface. "What happened to the damn fish?"

"I don't know."

"I asked you to stay ahead of them!"

"Well, they went deep—what am I supposed to do? And don't yell at me!"

"Sorry." He switched on the fish finder, his head on a swivel. "Watch the screen. Everyone else watch the water."

Peter looked around nervously, his heart pounding in his chest. "What are we looking for?"

"There!" Sasha pointed behind the boat's wake and to port, where a five-foot, lead-gray dorsal fin was cutting across the surface on an intercept course.

Peter balled his fists. "A Megalodon? Your governor or mayor or whatever he is announced you had killed them all. That was over a year ago—I remember watching it on TV!"

"Politicians lie; who knew?" Sasha turned to Kenny. "If the reports are true, she'll never allow us to make it back to Winter Harbour."

"We're not going to try for Winter Harbour." Cutting hard to port, he pushed down on the throttle, aiming for a cluster of rocks and uninhabited landmasses in the distance.

"The Gillams?"

"It's our only shot." He signaled everyone to gather around. "Guys, here's the deal—that dorsal fin that's chasing us . . . her owner doesn't like boats, especially ones that enter her feeding grounds. Our only chance is to put ashore on one of the islands—"

"Islands?" Peter stared at the cluster of sheer rock formations jutting out of Quatsino Sound a quarter mile ahead. "All I see are tall, jagged rocks. There's no beach—how do we climb out? Where will you land?"

"There are shoals shallow enough to abandon the boat . . . and let's be clear—we need to abandon the—"

The sudden heave from below sent the boat caroming to starboard.

Kenny veered back to port. "Everybody buckle in. Sasha, get on the radio and report our position to the Coast Guard!"

She took the seat next to him where Peter had been sitting, strapped herself in, and then leaned over and grabbed the handset, powering on the device. "Mayday, Mayday, Mayday. This is the fishing boat *Sea Robin-III* out of Winter Harbour, reporting a Code Red BD encounter. Our position is one-point-three kilometers southwest of the Gillam Islands. We will attempt to land there. . . ."

Peter held on to the bottom of his seat, the blood rushing from his face.

This is insane. . . . This isn't happening. . . .

The nearest island appeared ahead—a mound of gray rock three stories high, its sheer vertical sides impossible for anyone but a professional free-climber to negotiate.

Peter's peripheral vision caught a white object torpedoing in from starboard a second before the boat's hull was rolled beneath it. For a frightening moment the vessel teetered on its port gunwale—

—until the starboard's engine's rudder caught shark hide, purging blood before bending apart, the damaged outboard grinding, spewing thick black smoke.

The fishing boat slowed, its power cut in half, forcing Kenny to execute more radical turns in order to avoid another direct hit.

The towering gray rock loomed larger, its cliff face turning swells into white water.

Kenny never gave the landmass a second thought. Instead, he circled around the right side of the island—

—revealing a second cluster of rock formations situated in the shadow of a far larger island, its outcroppings offering white-water narrows, each a potential harbor.

Without slowing, he aimed for a twelve-foot-wide channel separating the big landmass and an eight-foot wall of basalt jutting out from the sea to its right.

"Hang on!"

The rocks appeared to leap at them, the incoming swells heaving them sideways—the boat's bow somehow finding its way in before the rudder of its remaining outboard bit rock and everything went silent, save for the sound of a heavy sea lapping against rock.

For a long moment the captain and his four passengers just held on as rolling waves battered the vessel from side to side like a cowboy strapped to a bull in its holding pen.

"We can't stay here." Sasha pointed behind them.

The Meg was spy-hopping, its ghost-white triangular head poised upright and free of the water, its right eye clearly watching them.

Katey's lower lip quivered. "My God . . . it's staring at us."

"Not just us," Sam said. "I think it's actually studying the pattern of the swells, timing its next attack."

"Well, I'm not waiting around for that." Moving to the bow, Kenny scanned the ten-foot-high barrier of rock ahead of them, searching for a way to use it to reach the shallows of the island towering on their left. "Okay, our target is the rock's perch.

"I'll go first, then Sasha, Katey, Peter, and Sam you're last. Time your jump so you're in the water just before the next swell hits—it'll lift you halfway up the rock face. When that happens, grab on to anything you can and start climbing. The Coast Guard's on the way, but like Sam said, we stay in the boat and we're dead."

Glancing back at the Megalodon, he watched the next incoming swell lift the boat's stern as it rolled toward the rocks . . . and jumped.

Kenny submerged, the frigid water stealing his breath—and then he was rising, the wave levitating him even as it slammed him chest-first against the sheer wall of rock. His hands groped for something to grip as the water receded, and for a moment he hung on, his fingertips clutching an outcropping, his feet searching and finding a narrow ledge to support his weight, only the surface was slick with algae and he quickly lost his balance, falling sideways back into the sea.

Seeing her boyfriend tumble, Sasha looked back to check on the Meg. The shark was gone.

"Oh God—Kenny, get back in the boat! Get out of the water—"

He attempted to grab on to to the bow—too late—as the next swell rolled beneath the vessel and suddenly he was back against the rock face, his hands and feet refusing to relinquish his frail grip. As the wave dropped away, he spotted a flat, dry perch three feet above his head. All he needed was a boost up . . . another foothold for his left shoe. He searched for one—

—and let out a scream as he stepped on something incredibly sharp that punctured the rubber sole of his sneaker straight up into the arch of his foot.

Looking down, he was shocked to find himself standing inside the Meg's lower jaw. Crying out, he wrenched his left foot free and attempted to climb—

—only the creature's upper teeth were puncturing his shoulders, the deadly points of its palm-size teeth just missing the top of his skull, pressing flat against his forehead as its mouth pried him from his perch and dragged him with it back into the sea.

Sasha screamed.

The others looked at one another, unsure of what to do next.

Katey was the first to spot the fishing boat captain as he surfaced, gagging and flailing in a pool of his own blood. She was about to alert the others when the world suddenly went topsy-turvy—the boat above, the crimson sky below—and then she was floundering underwater and someone's shoe was kicking her in the back of her head.

The swell restored a sense of direction as her face broke the surface and she saw Peter climbing up the ten-foot wall of basalt on her right.

She headed that way—and screamed as something grabbed hold of her from behind.

"Easy, babe, it's me!" Sam swam her to the jagged rock face, which was actually a series of boulders. He wrapped his arms around one of them and held tight as Katey climbed his back and got onto his shoulders, Peter reaching down from his perch to help her up.

"Wait—"

Sam turned to find Sasha towing Kenny through the swirling white-water. He was pale, and if he wasn't dead he was certainly dying, but she refused to abandon him.

"Sasha, climb onto my shoulders—"

"Promise you won't leave him."

"Jesus—fine." He grabbed the gurgling man by his shirt collar and held on as the girl scaled his back.

Somehow Sam managed to climb up to the others while dragging the boat owner's gushing remains with him—only to be shocked when Kenny reached up and took Peter's hand.

Straddling the top of the escarpment, the survivors looked below in stunned silence as the forty-five-foot long, twenty-five ton monster continued to attack the inverted submerged wreckage that three minutes earlier had been a boat.

Carmel, California

Jonas Taylor carried his clothing from his closet into the master bathroom, part of a routine that was now second nature. With Terry's nurse camped out on their bedroom love seat watching Netflix, privacy was out of the question, so he changed in the bathroom and took naps downstairs in his home office, where he spent his days designing a next-generation Manta submersible.

He knew his kids and Mac were concerned about him, that he was blaming himself for Terry's vegetative state. In truth, seeing the woman he loved in a comatose state unnerved him, bringing with it all the bad memories of her illness, and as the weeks turned to months, he found himself struggling to remember the good times they had shared. And so he took to ending each workday watching the sunset from his wife's favorite spot on the beach behind their home, often not returning to the house until after midnight.

Jonas dressed quickly, conscious of the time. Today David was being featured in a behind-the-scenes media event intended to whet the public's appetite for things to come at the Tanaka Institute as it attempted to compete with the tourism mecca known as Dubai-Land.

He heard the outer gate bell ring as he brushed his teeth.

Kelly Rollyson, one of Terry's weekday nurses, knocked on the bathroom door. "Mr. Jonas, do you want me to get it?"

He rinsed out and spit. "No, it's probably my driver. Tell him . . . Ah, never mind." He slipped on his shoes and exited the bathroom, pausing at the hospital bed to kiss the frail figure on the cheek. Today was a big day for their son, but he knew his wife would not have approved of what David was going to attempt, or the direction he had taken with Luna over the last year.

"Kelly, I'll be gone most of the afternoon; if you need to reach me, I'll be on my cell phone."

"Yes, Mr. Jonas."

Mr. Jonas . . . No matter how many times he had corrected her, she still insisted on the "Mr."

Heading down the hall, he opened the front door to leave—

—and was surprised to find a barrel-chested Asian gentleman waiting outside. He was in his early thirties, dressed in a blue surgeon's scrubs and carrying a physician's bag.

"I take it you're not my driver."

"Dr. Taylor, my name is Dr. Yun-Long Chi. I was sent by a great admirer of your work to help your wife."

"What great admirer?"

"A man of influence who will make himself known at the appropriate time. As for me, I have successfully revived more than a dozen comatose patients. May I see your wife?"

"Uh, yeah . . . sure. I mean, if you came all the way from China."

"Your admirer resides in China. I arrived this morning from Loxahatchee, Florida."

"Florida? Exactly what kind of doctor are you?"

"I am a licensed acupuncture physician. I received my training in China and was taught by masters in the art of Eastern medicine."

A ray of hope cut through the dark clouds of Jonas's psyche as he led the man to the master bedroom.

"Kelly, this is Dr. Chi. He's here to see Terry."

The nurse looked up from the small sofa. "What's he going to do to her?"

"I am going to attempt to awaken her."

Dr. Chi spent the next thirty minutes examining Terry, checking her pulse, eyes, and meridian lines. When he was through, he opened his bag and removed two small bags of needles, a small plug-in power pack, and a larger bag filled with electrodes, then placed them on the bed tray.

"I studied Acupuncture Channel Theory under Dr. T. H. Huang. Upon examining your wife, I found an obstruction blocking the Governing Vessel, which connects with and nourishes the brain and spinal region and intersects the liver channel at the vertex. Qi deficiency in the Governing Vessel often causes a heavy sensation in the head, vertigo, and shaking. Using acupuncture, I am going to attempt to remove the blockage and return the flow of Qi energy to your wife's brain."

Jonas and the nurse watched as the acupuncturist used a small pronged device to embed wooden needles along Terry's scalp and temples, switching to metal needles for her fingertips. Pinching the copper clips on each electrode, he connected the tips of the metal needles with the power pack and turned on the power.

"Doc . . . assuming this works . . . how long—"

"It could take several sessions a day for a few months, or it could happen much quicker. Every person is different."

"And if she does awaken . . . will she be mentally impaired?"

Dr. Chi placed a thick palm on Jonas's shoulder. "Have faith, my friend. It makes all the difference."

Tanaka Institute
Monterey, California

The concrete deck separating the lagoon from the Meg Pen resembled something more akin to a Super Bowl telecast than an aquarium. News vans jammed the exits leading out to the northern parking lot, their camera crews jockeying for position topside around the circular tank. Most of the media were camped out three stories below in the gallery's stadium-style seating, the hard bleachers having been replaced with the new recliner chairs found in movie theaters.

A podium had been set up for a question-and-answer session.

The star of the show circled lazily around her tank, mesmerizing her audience. Just over two years old, the surviving offspring of Lizzy had already equaled her mother's forty-six-foot length and—at twenty-six tons—had easily surpassed her girth, even though she was only half her deceased parent's age.

Why the huge disparity? David had a simple explanation—living space. Lizzy had shared the same tank with her four siblings; Luna had the Meg Pen all to herself. The bigger the aquarium, the larger the fish inside grew.

This afternoon, if all went well, she'd be occupying an even larger habitat—her grandmother's former haunt.

———

The desire to move Luna had taken on a sense of urgency three months before, following a huge growth spurt that marked the shark's adolescence. The tunnel connecting the Meg Pen with Angel's lake-size bowl was only large enough to accommodate a young adult. Luna was growing so fast that David feared she'd soon be too big to squeeze through the accessway, and Mac wanted no part of attempting to lift a hundred-thousand-pound, seventy-foot adult Megalodon by crane—even if he could locate one powerful enough to lift that much weight.

"Move her now while you can, kid. Otherwise she's stuck."

From that day on, the access way was kept open. The problem was that Angel's lingering scent frightened Luna, the shark's survival instincts preventing her from venturing through the connecting passage.

In an attempt to lure her out, David baited the tunnel's lagoon-side exit with salmon while skipping the shark's daily feedings. Six days later, Luna was visibly agitated, but still refused to enter the passage to eat.

On the seventh day, David donned a wetsuit, scuba gear, and a bright orange rubber-lined vest. After loading four freshly killed salmon into a burlap bag, he headed for the lagoon.

Monty intercepted him. "What are we doing?"

"I don't know what 'we' are doing, but I'm going to swim through the tunnel and lure my pet into the lagoon before she's too big to squeeze through."

"Sorry . . . did you just refer to that monster as your pet?"

"That's right. After feeding her every day, I'd say we have a connection. She knows me . . . she watches me whenever I'm in the gallery or up on deck. I've stood on the feeding platform with Luna spy-hopping as close as we are right now; it's just a matter of time before she responds to my hand signals."

"What I'm hearing is that it associates you with food, and that somehow tossing her said food gives you the confidence to swim down that passage despite the fact that it hasn't fed in a week. And just to make it more challenging, you'll be hauling a sack of dead salmon. Geez, Junior, I thought I was the one with the damaged brain."

"Chill out. I'm crazy, but I'm not stupid." David unzipped the rubber-lined vest, exposing a series of battery-powered electrodes.

"That tiny battery is going to stop Luna? Please . . ."

"Pay attention—Monty and you might learn something you'll forget by tomorrow. All sharks possess highly sensitive electrical receptors beneath their snouts called ampullae of Lorenzini. These gel-filled sacs can detect electric currents in the water that are generated by their prey's moving muscles, or the electrical discharge coming from a pounding heart. While these lower frequencies attract sharks, higher electrical waves hit the animal's sensory array like a live wire, repelling even something as large as a Megalodon. If Luna gets aggressive, I'll power up the device, which will generate an elliptical field that extends about eighty feet in all directions, leaving a nasty taste in her sensory organs."

"How do you know it will work? Have you tested it?"

"Not on myself, but I rigged a smaller device to a live salmon and left it swimming around the tank for a day."

"What happened to it?"

"Luna eventually ate it, but not until the battery died."

Monty waited while David climbed over the lagoon's guardrail and adjusted his fins and face mask before passing him the heavy burlap bag holding the salmon.

David gave him a thumbs-up and submerged in the 54-degree water—

—his departure sending Monty hustling to the supply shack to get a 15,000-volt bang stick and dive mask—just in case his friend had grossly miscalculated his place on Luna's food chain.

David released air from his buoyancy control vest, the weight of the dead fish dropping him feetfirst along the algae-covered concrete wall. Nearly a decade had passed since the first and last time he had entered the lagoon in scuba gear. The memories of Angel came flooding back as he descended thirty feet to the mouth of the passageway, and for a long moment, he contemplated surfacing.

No wonder Luna's spooked—hell, I'm spooked.

The tunnel was twenty-eight feet in diameter and sixty feet long. A soft azure light emanated at the end of the dark shaft. As he drew closer, he could see a shadow passing back and forth beyond the exit.

Luna can sense me coming.

He paused fifteen feet from the Meg Pen entrance, one hand gripping the burlap bag, the other poised over the controls to his electronic scrambler. From his vantage he could see that Luna was clearly agitated, her back arched.

Monty was right: I should have fed her first. . . .

Deciding it was best to turn back, he was about to reverse directions when the albino entered the passage.

David's heart pounded hard enough that he wondered if it would crack a rib. The Megalodon's head was so massive it filled his entire field of vision, its girth so wide it obscured the azure-blue aquarium. Barreling ahead, it was upon him so quickly that all he could do was squeeze his eyes shut, his muscles paralyzed in fear as he awaited death.

When the sharp teeth didn't skewer his flesh from the bone, he opened his eyes to see the Meg's nostrils inhaling his scent three feet from his facemask.

He realized it hadn't stopped to smell him—its dorsal fin was chafing along the top of the tunnel, its pectoral fins pinched against the interior walls.

Move!

David shoved the bag of salmon at the Meg's mouth and backstroked and kicked as hard and as fast as he could. He knew the immense creature could not turn around in the tight passage, that once he had lured it in it would have to continue until it entered the lagoon—that had been his plan all along.

Now he needed to reach the exit before Luna. Having torn apart the satchel of salmon, he watched the shark transform burlap and fish into pulp.

David had made it to the halfway point when he saw Luna attempt to turn around, only to realize it was trapped. Panic set in, causing the twenty-five-ton shark to bash its head from side to side while slapping its tail wall to wall, the action propelling it forward.

There was nowhere to hide, no place for David to escape to. As the furious beast lurched ahead, he grabbed on to its snout and held on— never realizing that the immediate area in front of the Meg's bullet-shaped nose was a blind spot and that the shark couldn't see him.

Enraged by the presence of its unseen challenger, Luna surged through the tunnel, the sudden rush of water tearing the dive mask from David's face and depositing it around his neck. Unable to free up either hand to pinch his nose to breathe through his regulator, he could only hang on as the Meg shot through the last twenty-eight feet of tunnel, entering the former habitat of its deceased legacy.

Luna shook him loose and immediately circled back to attack, its back arched, the pink bands of its upper jaw jutting forward.

David powered on the electric vest, delivering a high-frequency charge that chased the Megalodon through sunlit curtains of gray-green water. Pinching his nose, he drew a mouthful of air from his regulator. Then he repositioned the mask over his eyes and nose and blew air forcefully out of his nostrils, expelling water from the upper portion of the rubber seal.

Hovering forty feet below the surface, he searched for Luna. She was circling, her left eye watching him, her back no longer arched.

David powered off the electronic device.

The Meg moved closer, reducing the distance between them with each pass until it stopped circling and approached, its cataract-gray left eye identifying him.

It was an extraordinary moment. Moving closer, David reached out with his right hand and allowed his palm to run across the Megalodon's albino hide as it passed by.

If the creature felt it, she never responded. Instead, she circled back to the tunnel entrance and returned to her tank.

David was surrounded by cameramen as he made his way across the concrete deck in his wetsuit. He headed straight for the perimeter fence surrounding the Meg Pen, Monty waiting for him by the entrance.

"You sure about this, Junior?"

"She's ready. Where's Mac?"

"Standing by in the control room." Monty spoke into his radio. "Uncle Mac, any last words you want to say to your godson?"

"Yes. There's seven hundred and forty pounds of fish on the feeding platform. Make sure Luna eats all of it before you jump Snake River, Evel."

David turned to Monty, who shrugged. "Have you seen my father?"

"Not yet."

"Okay, let's do this." David entered the gate and circled to the north side of the tank. Looking to his left, he saw Luna's white dorsal fin break the surface, the Meg having been conditioned through reward and repetition.

The feeding platform resembled a high dive, its concrete base towering twenty feet, supporting a narrow walkway that extended fifteen feet over the azure-blue water. Anchored to the aluminum guardrail was the framework of a hydraulic lift, a winding track of steel cable that ran from the supply shack to the end of the feeding platform.

David ascended the circular stairwell and proceeded to the end of the short walkway, where a dozen freshly killed tuna were suspended by their tails from hooks rotating along the steel cable. Moving to the control console, David engaged the system, using a joystick to rotate the first fish into position along the conveyor belt.

Luna was already in position, her triangular head out of the water, her lower jaw opening and closing, her eyes fixed on David, the news cameras rolling.

"Luna . . . up!" His left arm rose above his head as his right index finger pressed the release button.

The Meg elevated twenty feet, its pectoral fins clearing the water as it snatched the eighty-five-pound fish in midair. Then it slipped silently back into the tank to a rousing applause.

Luna swallowed the snack as she circled the Meg Pen, giving the spectators in the gallery a show. Returning to its feeding spot, it awaited its trainer's command.

Twenty minutes and eleven tunas later, David looked out from his perch at the expressions on the faces of the cheering members of the media. Most of the eyewitnesses were stunned. Having witnessed Angel's pulse-pounding feeding ritual, few, if any, would have imagined one of these monsters could actually be trained. In the public's mind, sharks were eating machines to be feared—especially the most fearsome species of the lot.

David smiled to himself. *They haven't seen anything yet. . . .*

He descended from the platform to where a throng of reporters had gathered, everyone calling out questions.

"Guys, if you'd head down to the gallery, I'll answer all of your questions downstairs."

He watched them head for the exit leading below as Monty joined him with his scuba gear.

"Just the vest and snorkel—she doesn't let me get as close with the air tank."

"At least take a pony bottle; I charged two of them in case you wanted one." He reached into a backpack and handed David a small container of compressed air. "You can clip it onto your weight belt."

"Yeah . . . okay. That's actually a good idea."

"I guess Luna's not the only dumb animal that can be trained around here."

"I never called you a dumb animal, Monty."

"I know. I was referring to you. But no worries, you're not the first fool to tempt Mother Nature. Take Tania Cruz. She decided to go for a swim with Lizzy in the Salish Sea."

"What happened?"

"Bela ate her."

"Bela had a nasty streak."

"And knowing Lizzy, she probably baited the woman into entering the water."

"Enough. The main reason I'm doing this is to lock her down inside the lagoon. Once we widen the access tunnel, she can move freely between the two tanks."

David spit inside his mask and smeared it around to prevent fogging. Slipping on his swim fins, he swung his right leg over the guardrail and glanced at Luna.

The shark was spy-hopping twenty feet away, the Meg watching his every move.

Are you suckering me, Luna?

Swinging his left leg over the rail, he placed the snorkel into his mouth and eased himself into the water.

He remained close to the surface so he could breathe, his mask underwater so he could see.

Luna submerged and circled twenty feet below him as if beckoning David into deeper water.

She's aware of the audience in the gallery. Does she mean to kill me as a warning to the others not to invade her space?

He heard a strange sound . . . like a flock of birds flapping their wings. Looking down, he realized people were banging on the glass three stories below, attempting to get the Meg's attention.

Oh, geez . . . they must think I fell into the tank by accident.

He removed the pony bottle of air, spit out the snorkel, and placed the built-in regulator in his mouth. Heart pounding, he drew in a deep breath and descended.

He paused in thirty feet of water as Luna rose to meet him. He could see his reflection in her volleyball-size eye as she passed within five feet, her gill slits fluttering in his face.

Seeing the approaching pectoral fin, David attempted to hitch a ride by grabbing on to the one-foot-thick, winglike appendage. But the Meg's hide was too rough and he let go, tumbling sideways.

Stop trying to ride the damn thing and get it inside the tunnel.

David swam over to the entrance to the passage, beckoning Luna to follow. The Meg circled twice, and then entered the tunnel.

"The passage was sealed after Luna entered the lagoon. She doesn't like being there; she can detect Angel's scent. But now we'll be able to drain the Meg Pen and widen the tunnel so she'll be able to move from one tank to the other."

David was in the gallery, dressed in jeans and a Tanaka Institute collared shirt, standing at the podium before several hundred reporters.

"Okay, now I'll be happy to answer any questions. . . . Yes?"

"Lauren Haight, CNN. That was a pretty dangerous stunt. Is this going to be a regular part of the new shows?"

"There will always be some kind of human-Megalodon interaction. I can't promise I'll be taking a dip with Luna every feeding, but I am teaching her some wild new tricks. Once she gets settled into her new home, I'll be able to work with her more. Angel's scent makes her nervous."

"Steve Chyborak, *San Francisco Chronicle.* Could you give us an update on what's going on with the Liopleurodon?"

"Honestly, I haven't spoken with Jacqueline Buchwald in over a year. Locate the *Mogamigawa* and you'll find the expedition."

"The tanker's last reported position was off the Channel Islands. That was nine months ago; she hasn't been seen since."

"And neither has the Lio, so that's a good thing." He turned to a gentleman seated in the first row. "Yes, sir—did you have a question?"

"Indeed. Dolf van Craanenburgh, *Süddeutsche Zeitung—Southern Germany News*. Our readers wish to know if the purpose of your dive with the Megalodon was an attempt to sway the Canadian government to call off the hunt for Luna's mate following the recent attack off Vancouver Island?"

"First, it's not Luna's mate—it's Bela's surviving offspring. As for my dive with Luna . . . sure, part of my motivation was to dispel the public's fear about Megs and sharks in general. Yes, these are apex predators, but they are not cold-blooded killing machines; they have a place in the ocean's hierarchy."

"Don't you mean they *had* a place?" a woman shot back from the third row. "These monsters went extinct; they serve no purpose on the food chain, other than to kill off the orca pods in British Columbia."

David read her name tag: Heather Kitchens, *Washington Post*. "Ms. Kitchens, every year great white sharks kill surfers; every summer bull sharks attack bathers in the shallows. And yet there's no public demand to hunt them down. Humans sit at the top of the ocean's food chain, not a solitary Megalodon. Man is decimating the oceans; commercial fishermen are ruthlessly slaughtering millions of sharks by cutting off their fins for shark fin soup. If you added all of these shark incidents together, they wouldn't amount to one percent of the population who are killed or crippled by people texting while driving. Is the Canadian government planning a ban on iPhones?"

Diana DeBoer, a Canadian journalist, stood to be called upon. The woman with the striking red hair and green eyes was clearly perturbed by David's attitude. "This monster isn't just killing the occasional civilian, Mr. Taylor, it's going after any craft that dares to venture into her territory. Do you know what they're calling her now?"

"Not really. My friend calls her Lunatic—sort of a play on 'Luna.'"

"A Hispanic teen named her Bela Diablo, as in 'Bela the devil,' after he witnessed her sink a charter boat and dismember three of his friends. Notice I didn't say 'eat.' Apparently, this particular Meg doesn't like the taste of humans; she just wants them dead. The same thing was reported by the woman whose boyfriend was killed three days ago. Since then, the B.C. media has been calling her Belladonna. Do you know what belladonna is, Mr. Taylor?"

"I don't know . . . a porn star?" He shrugged as his response drew a few laughs.

The redhead was not amused. "Belladonna is a dark, poisonous berry so toxic that ingesting even a small amount can kill you. The Tanaka Institute is responsible for Belladonna's poisoning the Salish Sea. And judging by the size of her albino cousin, it won't be long until she internally fertilizes her eggs like her mother and spreads her demon seed throughout the waters of British Columbia. Before that happens, she needs to be hunted down and killed, Mr. Taylor. And you appear to be the one most qualified to handle that."

A flutter of camera clicks froze the moment in time, the flashes momentarily blinding David's eyes with purple spots.

"I agree something has to be done about Bela's offspring populating the Salish Sea with Megs. Our resident marine biologist, Carmen Rodriguez, is working on a drug that, when injected using a hypodermic dart, would sterilize the shark's . . ."

David paused as he saw his father enter the gallery, pushing someone in a wheelchair.

"Oh my God . . ."

David left the podium and dashed up the center aisle to embrace his mother.

||||||||||||||||||||||||||||||||||

Emmett Industries, Tanaka Pier
Monterey, California

The black Toyota Corolla made its way to the security gate at the end of the private pier, the driver rolling down her window to show her identification to the guard.

"Morning, Dr. Emmett. I didn't expect to see you on a Sunday. Guess there are no days off for the boss."

She ignored the comment, her eyes focusing on the Harley-Davidson motorcycle parked by the front entrance of the building. "I see Dulce's here. What time did she arrive?"

"I'm not sure she ever left. The Harley was here when I started my morning shift."

Helen Emmett waited impatiently for the gate to swing open wide enough to drive through without scratching her side-view mirrors. She parked in her reserved spot at the front of the building, her blood pressure ticking up a few points higher at the sight of her assistant's motorcycle in a spot reserved for the handicapped.

Pick your battles, Helen. . . .

The CEO of Emmett Industries grabbed her purse and brown-bag lunch and exited the vehicle, heading inside the building.

———————

Helen Emmett was born in Christchurch, New Zealand, her parents eventually relocating the family to Auckland. Her earliest memory was when she was six and her older siblings had locked her in a room, forcing her to watch *Jaws 2*. From that moment on she had become a shark fanatic. By the time she was nine she had been certified to dive; a year later she was swimming with seven gilled sharks in the Napier Aquarium. At home in the water, she remained an introvert on land, a trait no doubt influenced by her slight five-foot-three-inch stature and librarian looks.

Her world had been rocked during her freshman year in college when a pregnant Megalodon rose from the depths of the Mariana Trench, its lone surviving pup captured and raised in the man-made lagoon at the Tanaka Institute.

If there was one Megalodon in the trench, there had to be more. What other exotic prehistoric life-forms were down there? She had to know! The challenge, of course, was getting there. Intent on being at the forefront of this new "monster industry," she switched her studies from premed to engineering in order to design deep-water craft that could withstand the titanic pressures of the abyss.

Two decades and six patents later, Emmett Industries was the go-to company for sea exploration. When Jonas Taylor's Submersible Designs Inc. was placed on the market, she purchased the company, despite protests from her business advisers that she was paying far too much for the antiquated workshop.

It was Luna's capture two weeks earlier that had motivated her to buy Taylor out. To observe this magnificent creature on a daily basis . . . she had actually insisted that a clause for twenty-four-hour access to the Meg Gallery be added to the buyout agreement. She began each morning and concluded every workday watching the albino creature circling its aquarium—the exception being the past few days, ever since Luna had been exiled into the lagoon.

Is it any wonder she was in such a dour mood?

And then there was her assistant. Dulce Lunardon was everything Helen was not—cocky, athletic, outgoing, and alluring. The moment David Taylor had set eyes on the twenty-three-year-old submersible pilot with the long brown, blond-highlighted hair, he had been smitten.

Wouldn't surprise me if he told the girl he had named Luna after her.

Was Helen jealous? In truth, she was envious. For the better part of a year she had played the role of Jonas Taylor's confidante, their relationship expanding from shoptalk about his Manta sub design to his depression over his wife's vegetative state, as their friendship showed signs of developing into something more.

Last week she had emboldened him into a passionate kiss.

Three days ago his wife had awakened . . . almost as if she knew what was coming down the road.

Helen had not seen Jonas since; but David had told Dulce that the Chinese acupuncturist was rigorously rehabbing Terry, and that her husband had not left her side.

So much for their past twelve months of friendship.

In truth, what had set her off this morning was not Jonas Taylor, or Dulce's motorcycle, or even the missing hours of tranquility watching Luna in the Meg Pen. It was the text message she had received from her business partner and investor at six-fifteen the night before:

"Be available to receive my call, 0900 hours Pacific—J.H."

Helen moved through the small lobby and entered her security code, accessing the administrative offices. She continued down the marble corridor to the double doors of her suite and keyed in by pressing her right eye to the optical scanner.

The bolt clicked open and she entered.

Helen's office was more live-in apartment than office. A floor-to-ceiling window made up the north wall, providing an ocean view of the back end of the Tanaka arena and canal. There was a kitchenette and small eating area, and a second door led into a bathroom, replete with Jacuzzi, shower, and a sleep pod. Helen's work space encompassed the south side of the suite—a horseshoe-shaped enclave that surrounded her with virtual screens. Though she lacked Dulce's piloting reflexes, within this portal she was in command, able to test any new design element in a virtual three-dimensional environment.

As she sat in her desk chair, her presence activated her computer assistant, Roland.

"Good morning, Helen. I wasn't expecting you until Monday."

"Business call from Hong Kong. Where's Dulce?"

"Dulce Lunardon is in the simulator."

"Give me a visual."

The array of computer monitors activated, each displaying a different angle of her naked assistant, curled up in the arms of David Taylor.

"Dulce!"

The girl woke. "Helen, is that you?" Instead of covering up her nudity, she held her left hand up to the monitor, a diamond ring poised on her fourth finger. "Guess who proposed last night!"

David opened his eyes. "Oh, shit—"

The monitors went blank.

Christ, that's just perfect. What else can you pile on me, God?

"Incoming call from Hong Kong . . . Dr. Johnny Hon."

I had to ask. . . .

"Put it through." She forced a smile. "Good evening, Johnny. How are things?"

"We'll cut through the small talk. Have the new defense systems been field-tested yet?"

"Not yet. We're tentatively scheduled for Thursday."

"Push them up."

Helen felt the blood drain from her face. "You had another encounter?"

"Sting Ray-3. No survivors."

"I'm sorry."

"Assuming the new defense system passes the field test, how many SRs can be equipped and ready for delivery by Wednesday?"

"Wednesday? As in two days from now? Let's see . . . I have two Sting Rays here in Monterey, but the propulsion unit is shot in one of them. Our plant in San Diego has two units that should be mission-ready—"

"I am dispatching a C-5 transport; it will arrive Thursday to pick up the three vehicles. I am also in need of a pilot. Have Dulce accompany the subs; I'll be sending my private jet to pick up the Taylors. I am extending an invitation for them to join me at Site-B."

"The Taylors? Which Taylors?"

"Jonas and his wife. I do not expect him to make the trip without Terry."

"My God . . . you're the one who sent the acupuncturist?"

Johnny Hon never reacted, confirming her statement. "I want to see the field-test results in twenty-four hours. Have a blessed day."

|||||||||||||||||||||||||||||||||||

78 Nautical Miles West of the Channel Islands
Eastern Pacific Ocean

A gray sky cast its winter pall over a chilly November morning. Wind lashed the surface into foam, creating a snow-like effect over the endless peaks and troughs of ocean spread out before them.

Jacqueline Buchwald stood in the bow of the *Mogamigawa* in defiance of both the elements and her mission. She ran a palm across the crown of her freshly shaved head, wiping away moisture before tucking on the thick hood of her sweatshirt, granting herself a moment's reprieve from the wind. Her eyes remained fixed on the sea and she inhaled its briny scent deep into her lungs. The creature was close; she had known it for days, and this morning she had proven it to her crew, her prediction bonding them to her. In an act of solidarity with her crew, she had shaved her head. When they captured Junior, she had promised to allow them to tattoo her scalp.

The previous nine months at sea had changed the marine biologist, after the first four had nearly broken her. Forced into a position of leadership she had not earned, and a responsibility that did not match her skill set, she quickly found herself at the mercy of an aggressive crew made up of Indians and Middle Eastern men and a handful of women—the latter having been brought on board to cook and service the tanker's officers.

A razor-thin lifeline of sanity kept the pack bridled, and that was the slightest of possibilities that maybe the American female knew how to capture the Lio and earn them all a small fortune.

But the monster, no longer a juvenile, hadn't been seen since the day it had escaped from the *Tonga*, and Jackie's actions seemed born more out of desperation than a strategy to capture the beast. Yes, there was the carnage the creature had left back in the Farallones, and for two months the ship had remained in the Red Triangle—until it became obvious that Fiesal bin Rashidi's replacement knew no more about how to recapture the Lio than the dead man she had replaced.

When another month passed and the creature failed to return, the mood of the crew shifted from skeptical to dangerous. Several of the men began making sexual overtures, forcing Jackie to remain a prisoner in her cabin after sunset.

Warned by one of the women that ringleaders among the crew were organizing a mutiny that would end with her death, she worked feverishly on a plan that would bring the *Mogamigawa* to a populated area where she could make her escape. Two hours later she had met with the ship's officers, a rolled-up map in her hand.

"There was a reason we remained in the Farallones for so long. The Lio's preferred delicacy is elephant seal. These mammals spend ten months of the year thousands of miles from shore, but twice a year they return to land to mate, molt, and give birth to their young. I needed to see if the males would be returning to the Farallon rookery, which it seems they have abandoned. They have to go somewhere; the question is where?"

She laid out a map of the North American coast, detailing the locations of several elephant seal rookeries. "The nearest known elephant seal gathering points are in the Channel Islands. There are eight islands for the displaced members of the Farallon rookery to choose from. They could join an existing group or establish a new nesting area. My plan is to send a stakeout team, armed with a transmitter gun, to each island. We'll tag the Lio, then once we know which island she's stalking, we'll set up an ambush."

The plan was circulated among the crew, earning Jackie a temporary stay of execution. As the tanker headed south along the California coast, passing over the wreckage of its sunken sister ship en route to the Channel Islands, the marine biologist made a list of supplies, instructing the ship's supply officer that they should be delivered to Avalon, a port city on Santa Catalina.

———

The Channel Islands are an archipelago of eight landmasses situated off the southern coast of California, divided into a northern and southern cluster. Elephant seals reside in the four northern islands as well as in Santa Barbara, the five habitats falling under the Channel Islands National Marine Sanctuary. The remaining three islands had small human communities, the largest populace on Santa Catalina.

Jackie ordered shipments of transmitters and harpoon guns to be delivered in Avalon, at which time she would jump ship. Those plans were dashed when the captain, a wily seaman named Cryss Blackwolf, arranged for the supplies to be delivered by helicopter.

Northern elephant seals populate their rookery in shifts that vary among competing bulls, mature females and their pups, and juvenile males. Breeding takes place in the winter months; molting occurs in spring and summer.

The *Mogamigawa* arrived in the Channel Islands in mid-March when the last adults were leaving. For nine days, three-man teams equipped with radios and transmitter guns staked out the northern islands.

The Liopleurodon never showed.

With the rookeries nearly empty and her life hanging in the balance, Jackie altered her plan.

"When these elephant seals leave here, they'll head west, where they'll inhabit the deep waters off the continental shelf. I think the Lio knows exactly where they'll be. If we tag the seals, there's a chance at least one of them will be eaten. Unless the transmitter is damaged, it will continue to send off signals. Once we verify we're following the Lio, it will lead us back to whatever island rookery it will be feeding at during the seals' molting season."

"And how are we to know the transmitter is in the belly of the beast?"

"Bull elephant seals can dive three to five thousand feet deep. If the signal suddenly descends beyond that, it means the Lio ate the seal and its transmitter."

"Most of the seals have left the sanctuary; there are less than thirty left. By the time the transmitters and harnesses arrive, they'll be gone, too."

"Well then," Jackie said, "we'll just have to drug them."

Operating under the cover of darkness, teams of crewmen carrying hypodermic syringes filled with phenobarbital injected the massive mammals using reach poles. Thirteen bulls and four adult cows were kept in a semiconscious state for three days until a supply of harnesses and extra transmitters arrived by helicopter.

The harnesses were pliable plastic adjustable collars that fit loosely around the elephant seals' necks. The transmitter was secured inside a porous titanium sphere roughly the size of a softball that attached to the back of the collar. Each homing device had a range of sixty nautical miles, and their lithium batteries provided ten months of power.

The groggy pinnipeds awoke the next morning, sporting hangovers. Within twenty-four hours only the pups remained on shore.

For the first two weeks, the seventeen elephant seals remained within transmitter range of one another, foraging for food along the seafloor for upward of two hours before returning to the surface to grab a breath. Employing a grab-and-swallow technique, the mammals consumed hagfish and rays, squid and crabs, oblivious to the tanker keeping pace a thousand feet above and several miles to the northeast.

The *Mogamigawa*'s sonar kept a 24/7 vigil on the elephant seals. By the fifth week the bulls had split up from the cows, heading farther out to sea. Jackie chose to shadow the males, since there were far more of them. Several weeks later they arrived at the continental shelf, diving along the vertical slope into depths exceeding four thousand feet.

Still, there was no sign of the Lio.

Spring turned to summer, bringing with it tropical depressions and hurricane season. While most of the cyclone action remained to the west, the ocean grew noticeably rougher. Twenty-to-thirty-foot swells became the new norm, battering the ship and crew while making Jackie regret her decision to head farther from land by tracking the males.

Elephant seals' blood does not circulate to their skin when they are in water; it is only while on land that they grow a new epidermis and hair. By mid-July, the females had begun their trek east to the Channel Islands to molt; their male counterparts lagged a month behind.

The crew's temperament changed with the worsening weather. Jackie knew her days were numbered—if the Lio did not appear soon, the crew would toss her overboard and take the ship.

On August 10, the bulls abruptly abandoned the continental shelf and headed east.

At first Jackie thought this was simply nature's way, the bulls' annual molting bringing them back to land around mid-September. But as she tracked their movements on sonar, she noticed the elephant seals were not foraging on the return trip—they were moving with a sense of urgency.

When one of the homing devices ceased transmitting, she grew excited. When a second unit shut down in close proximity to the first, she ordered Cryss Blackwolf to bring the ship about to intercept.

The captain refused, claiming the seas were too rough and there was no evidence the Lio was anywhere within a hundred miles of the tanker.

She took her plea to the crew. "I was hired to do a job, and I've done it. The Lio is sixteen miles to the southwest of us. If we don't act now, we'll lose it."

By the men's lack of a response, she knew the crew was committed to taking the ship.

"Okay . . . fine. If I'm wrong, we'll end the voyage; you can drop me off at the nearest port."

One of the ringleaders stepped forward. "We'll come about. But if you are wrong, we will drop you off right here."

It is not easy to turn a Malacca-class oil tanker, the degree of difficulty in rough seas increasing tenfold. By the time the ship reached the last known coordinates of the second downed transmitter, Jackie held little hope of locating their quarry.

Scanning the sonar, she targeted the closest elephant seal. The mammal was several miles away, moving along the surface. "There! That's the Lio's next meal."

The ringleader nodded to the captain. "Take us there; our American friend wishes to go for a swim with her seal."

Before she could react, the crew was upon her, their calloused hands groping her breasts and groin as they carried her out of the control room and down five flights of stairs to the main deck—a heaving runway of steel more than a football field long. Towering swells rolled beneath the ship, raising the bow before dropping it. Seasickness combined with Jackie's fear, and she puked her last meal, taking a final moment of pleasure in spewing her refuse over the heads of her intended assassins. They released her and she tumbled to the deck; she tried to run, but there were far too many of them.

Grabbing her by the hair, the ringleader dragged her to the port rail to toss her overboard.

In the predawn gray, Jacqueline Buchwald looked out at the foam-covered waves and spotted the elephant seal as it rode the swell. For a brief second, she experienced a moment of serenity—an acceptance of her fate . . . an end to her anguish—

—and then the beast rose out of the sea.

Crocodilian jaws clamped down upon the fifteen-foot, four-thousand-pound pinniped, crushing it like a ripe tomato. The animal's blood and guts shot through the gaps between the Liopleurodon's teeth as it continued rising out of the Pacific, its immense forelimbs thirty feet from its fang-laced snout, its chocolate-brown back blotting the horizon—seventy tons . . . eighty feet, its girth mocking its would-be captors.

The crew stood in awe as the reptile god slipped silently back into the sea, all evidence of its appearance gone, save for the racing pulses of its eyewitnesses.

The Arab ringleader stepped forward, dropping to one knee. "Forgive us for ever doubting you. Allah has blessed you with a gift; instruct us and it shall be done."

The other men bowed their heads and knelt.

She led them back to the control room, to discover that the dead elephant seal's transmitter had been swallowed whole and was giving off signals.

"You did it . . . you tagged the creature!"

"Yes. Unfortunately, the Lio has grown too immense to capture at sea; therefore, we must capture it on land when it attacks the rookeries. For now, we'll shadow it and allow it to lead us ashore."

That was the last time Jackie was ever challenged, the last time she experienced fear. The crew members were now her royal subjects, and she was their queen. She would find a way to capture the beast, and make each of them wealthy men in the process.

For three months the Lio had followed the continental shelf to the south, until late in the past week, when it abruptly changed course, heading east at a steady 22 knots. The elephant seal rookeries would be heavily populated by now; the beast was returning to land to feed.

Jacqueline Buchwald stood in the bow, staring at the sea. The creature was close: three thousand feet below and less than a mile ahead. A plan was in motion, a trap being prepared—

—the hunter had become the hunted, the slave a master of her domain.

||||||||||||||||||||||||||||||||||

Aboard Global Group International Holdings' Private Jet
87 Miles Northwest of Guam

The brochure in the magazine rack stated that the passenger cabin aboard the Airbus ACJ319 private jet was not only the widest in the industry but also the tallest. Despite these impressive dimensions, after nearly twelve straight hours in the air, Jonas Taylor was feeling as if the walls were closing in.

The last time he had experienced claustrophobia was twenty-five years ago, when the deep-sea submersible pilot had returned to the Mariana Trench seven years after his final, fateful dive with the U.S. Navy. Down on his luck, Jonas had been recruited by Masao Tanaka to escort his son, D.J., to the bottom to recover a damaged seismic drone. The two men had made the nearly thirty-six-thousand-foot descent aboard one-man submersibles scarcely larger than a coffin, so the claustrophobia was certainly justified. The encounter with a pair of Megalodons had not ended well for either Terry's younger brother or the male shark that had killed him.

Jonas had dived the abyss twice more over the years—once to rescue his wife at the bottom of the Challenger Deep, the last time two years earlier to save his son, who had been trapped with Kaylie Szeifert several thousand feet *below* the seafloor in the ancient realm of the Panthalassa Sea. His wingman on that dive had been Angel, and the journey had not ended well for either the Meg or David's girlfriend . . . but still, the claustrophobia had not returned.

So why was he feeling so nervous aboard a billionaire's private jet?

Maybe it had something to do with the information Mac had emailed him an hour earlier regarding one of Dr. Johnny Hon's business ventures. . . .

———

Jonas and Terry had met the billionaire days earlier on a Skype call.

"Professor Taylor, it is an honor to finally speak with you and your lovely wife, who I am so thrilled to see up and about. When I heard Terry was in a coma, I immediately contacted my friend Dr. Chi to see if he could be of service."

"Terry and I are incredibly grateful for what you've done. If there is anything we can ever do to repay you—"

"Nonsense. What I did was simply to plant the seeds of friendship with someone whose work I have admired for several decades. I appreciate your wife cutting her therapy short to meet with me. Time is of the essence, as you will learn.

"The truth, Professor Taylor, is that the three of us share a common enemy. Cancer has robbed me of friends and loved ones, fueling a passion to find a cure. Two years ago, a colleague of mine made an incredible discovery in the field of neurogenesis that has brought us to phase two of human trials. So far, everything looks very good."

Terry had been especially excited. "That's wonderful, Dr. Hon. When will you be announcing your discovery to the rest of the world?"

"Soon. There are still a few small hurdles to overcome before we make it public."

"If there is anything Jonas and I can do to help . . . ?"

"Actually, Mrs. Taylor, I was hoping to pick your husband's brain regarding a few potential solutions. If the two of you would be willing to come to Hong Kong, it would be an honor to share the information with you . . . provided you have no problem signing a nondisclosure agreement."

They had signed the NDA and Johnny Hon had sent his private jet to meet them.

Always suspicious, Mac had done some investigating of his own. He had learned that Global Group International Holdings had made seven-figure donations to several cancer research funds over the years, the most recent monies going to a nonprofit research company run by a microbiologist named Sara Jernigan.

Sixteen months earlier, Global Group had invested upward of a billion dollars into China's number two–ranked science and technology project to construct an underwater lab, the new venture involving an engineering firm in Sweden. This struck Mac as odd, since the project was part of China's five-year economic growth package. Upon further investigation he learned that the Swedish firm was headed by Sara Jernigan's brother-in-law, Jordan Bittel, a structural engineer who was discreetly recruiting members of the Dubai team hired to capture prehistoric life-forms inhabiting the Panthalassa Sea.

Jonas looked up as one of the Chinese flight attendants entered the cabin. "Excuse me, Mr. and Mrs. Taylor. The captain has asked me to inform you that we have begun our descent and will be landing shortly."

Jonas checked his watch. "I must have miscalculated—I don't have us arriving in Hong Kong for another two hours."

The attendant forced a smile. "There's been a slight change in plans. Dr. Hon will be meeting you at the cancer research facility."

"And where is that?"

"I do not know; the location is secret."

"You must know where we're landing."

"Of course, Mr. Taylor. We are landing in Guam."

The private jet eased into a gentle touchdown. Rather than heading for the terminal, the pilot taxied several miles to the east end of the airport and an awaiting Z-18A Chinese utility helicopter.

The attendant opened the cabin door, releasing a short flight of stairs. "The helicopter will take you directly to the cancer research facility. Dr. Hon is waiting for you there."

"No."

Terry turned to her husband. "What's wrong?"

"For starters, we were supposed to land in Hong Kong, not Guam. I don't like last-minute surprises."

The flight attendant blushed. "Forgive me. I should have informed you earlier. Dr. Hon was able to free up his schedule at the last moment and preferred to meet you at the facility, rather than offer you a virtual tour from his headquarters in Hong Kong."

"And is the facility on Guam, or is it on another island in the Marianas?"

"Sir, as I told you earlier, I don't know."

"Jonas, what difference does it make? We're here."

"It makes a big difference. Guam and I don't have a good history together. Guam was our port of call back when I was piloting submersibles for the United States Navy. It's also where Mac and I nearly died trying to prove the Megalodon had surfaced after your brother was killed."

"You're being silly. Come on, I need to get off this plane and stretch my legs."

Jonas paused, not wanting to admit his real fear to his wife. Instead, he followed her down the steps to the tarmac—

—and into the embrace of Dulce Lunardon. "Mrs. T, oh my God, can you believe we're all in Guam? Mr. T—"

"Don't call me Mr. T; Jonas is fine. What are you doing here? Is David with you?"

"Do you think he'd actually leave his pet for more than a day? As for me, I arrived last night in a C-5 cargo plane."

"Carrying what?"

"I can't tell you, Mr. . . . . Jonas. I had to sign all these confidentiality papers."

Terry smiled sweetly. "Dulce, do you still wish to marry my son?"

"Okay, okay. Sting Ray subs . . . three of them. All outfitted with some serious weaponry."

"And why are you here?"

"I don't know. I'm assuming they need me to train their sub pilots."

The helicopter's overhead rotors started revolving, and the captain signaled them to board.

Jonas helped his wife into the sixteen-seat passenger cabin, their luggage already stowed in back.

The Chinese copilot joined them, offering each of them a hot towel and beverage, then a set of headphones. "You'll need these to hear. It's a quick twenty-minute flight—Dr. Hon is excited to meet you."

Terry squeezed Jonas's hand, cutting him off. "And we are looking forward to meeting him."

They flew east over the island before following the coastline to the north. For a brief moment Andersen Air Force Base appeared in the distance, and then the view turned to a stretch of deep blue as far as the eye could see.

Western Pacific . . . the Mariana Islands . . . it's like a bad déjà vu.

Jonas gazed at the tremor in his right hand. Breathing slowly, he inflated his belly and slowly released the breath, repeating the mantra his therapist had taught him over the previous ten months.

I control me. . . .

I control me. . . .

The shaking stopped.

Stay calm and figure this out. What are the chances Johnny Hon built his modern cancer research facility on one of these godforsaken volcanic islands? As Mac would say, slim and none, and slim just got kicked in the balls by the unforgiving boot of reality.

Cancer research, my ass . . . Johnny Hon is building his own version of Dubai-Land in China. Did he convert an oil tanker to stow his catch of prehistoric fish like the crown prince? Or maybe he's got a fleet of frigates linked together by deep-water nets. Either way, if he's deploying the new Sting Rays, he means to capture these creatures either in the Mariana Trench, or worse, in the Panthalassa Sea, and I want nothing to do with it.

Jonas's thoughts were interrupted by the copilot's announcement over his headphones. "Good afternoon. I hope everyone had a nice flight. Please make sure your seat belts are fastened; we'll be landing in the next five minutes."

He turned to Terry. Her headphones were off, she and Dulce involved in a detailed conversation concerning wedding plans. Leaving his seat, he headed forward to the cockpit to get an idea of the kind of ship they'd be landing on.

The copilot motioned for Jonas to sit in the jump seat behind him, then handed him a set of binoculars. "We're about two kilometers out."

Jonas strapped in and gazed through the powerful magnifying glasses.

At first he couldn't see it, its clear surface reflecting the sea and sky. But as the helicopter drew closer, he realized what he was looking at.

My God . . .

It wasn't a ship, it was a massive complex of biospheres, the center object towering at least twenty stories above the surface and twenty below. A dark hoop-shaped framework encircled the object's equator like the rings of Saturn, but appeared to be part of an enormous docking station rather than the biosphere itself. Six smaller spheres were situated around the perimeter of the large ring, each docked within its own oval-shaped berth. A clear tunnel linked these smaller objects to the large biosphere.

Two of the eight smaller docking berths were vacant.

The pilot brought the helicopter to hover over one of the station's helipads. A 20-knot gust of wind rocked the airship as it set down. Within seconds a ground crew appeared, each worker wearing an orange jumpsuit. One crewman quickly secured the chopper's landing gear to the pad while a second opened a metal plate from the helipad and removed a hose, connecting it to the chopper's fuselage to refuel the airship for its return trip.

Jonas rejoined Dulce and Terry, who were being helped down from the cabin by another orange-clad worker while his associate unloaded their luggage.

A woman was waiting for them outside the airship, one hand pressing her iPad to her chest, the other holding her hair bun to her head to keep the helicopter's rotor from unraveling it.

She shouted to be heard. "Mrs. Taylor . . . Molly Wilken. I'll be escorting you and Professor Taylor to Dr. Hon."

"What about me? Dulce Lunardon."

Molly tapped her iPad. "You are scheduled for orientation, which begins in seventeen minutes. Let's go inside so we can talk." She motioned to the biosphere, then led them to an open watertight door.

The women entered the structure. Jonas hung back to inspect the curved hatch. The inside panel was constructed of steel, the outer shell composed of a clear sixteen-inch plastic that appeared seamless.

He caught up with the ladies, who were waiting for him inside an encapsulated interior passage that spanned the ten-foot gap between the biosphere's outer shell and a completely different interior sphere.

Molly pointed above their heads, where the sun was reflecting off a labyrinth of plastic support struts that crisscrossed the gap, buttressing both spheres to one another. "As you can see, the exterior and interior shells are separated by three meters of space that the Chinese refer to as *sheng chi*, which translates into the 'celestial' or 'dragon's breath.' This is where we take on and shed ballast in order to maneuver the sub."

Dulce's eyes widened. "This giant beach ball is a sub? How does it maneuver?"

"There are pump-jet propulsor units mounted throughout the *sheng chi*. Now let me show you a technological marvel that is the twenty-first-century equivalent of the Great Wall of China."

Molly continued through the passage to a second watertight door, its plastic layer twice as thick as the first. They entered another encapsulated passage, only this one was pitch-dark, save for specks of light appearing and disappearing outside the walls of the structure.

Terry gripped Jonas's hand. "There's something out there."

"You are correct," Molly said. "Touch any wall and see what happens."

Dulce was the first to comply, running her index finger along the plastic, generating a neon-violet spark of light along the outside of the sensory-laden wall—

—which was immediately swarmed upon by a school of viperfish, the deep-sea denizens three to four feet long, their frightening jaws sprouting needle-sharp curved fangs that were too long to fit inside their mouths.

Jonas ran his palms along another section of wall, igniting a stream of static blue electricity. Before he could react, a six-foot goblin shark struck the glass with its extended snout, its open jowls revealing chaotic rows of razor-sharp teeth.

A chorus of dull thumps pummeled the exterior as species of anglerfish and snaggletooth charged the barrier, each contact generating more bioluminescent sparks, which only increased the ferocity of the attacks.

"Impressive," Jonas said. "How large is this aquarium?"

"Not large. It's roughly the size of an eighteen-wheeler. It's what we call a mood-setter."

They continued down the passage. It ran another twenty feet before it curved around a bend to reveal the exit, which was framed by the open-fanged mouth of a fearsome yellow dragon, its ten-foot-high marble face animating as they approached, steam pouring from its nostrils, its red eyes blazing brightly.

Terry and Jonas passed through the open jaws—

—and stepped out into the atrium of a five-star hotel. Blue sky appeared overhead, illuminating twenty floors of guest suites set in an open square configuration. Eight bullet-shaped elevators rose and dropped along the interior angles of the infrastructure, guarded by the twisting, curling figure of an eighty-foot-tall Chinese dragon, the statue casting an amber glow over the grand entrance.

"A hotel?" Jonas turned to Molly Wilken. "I thought this was supposed to be a cancer research center?"

"The research center occupies the lower floors. All of your questions will be answered during your virtual tour. Come."

She led them around the dragon centerpiece to what appeared to be the twenty-foot-high curved walls of a giant nautilus shell. Entering the structure, Jonas realized it was a small auditorium, the reclinable seats facing two hundred seventy degrees of blue screen.

"Sit anywhere you'd like. The orientation video is eleven minutes long; when it's over you'll be joining Dr. Hon for lunch. Dulce, if you'll come with me, I'll take you to your orientation session."

Dulce waved good-bye, following Molly out of the circular theater—

—the screen animating as the overhead lights darkened.

A revolving series of images appeared, featuring scientists in white coats working in labs, physicians examining patients, and adults and children lying in hospital beds, their hairless scalps indicative of numerous sessions of chemotherapy.

Actor Morgan Freeman's soothing voice-over accompanied the scenes. "Cancer. One in three people will be diagnosed with the disease; one in five will die. According to the World Health Organization, cancer cases are expected to surge fifty-seven percent worldwide in the next twenty years, with cancer deaths predicted to rise to thirteen million a year. Smoking, alcohol, obesity, poor living habits, environmental pollutants, and an aging populace are all factors in this cancer epidemic—an epidemic that has given rise to a two-trillion-dollar-a-year industry.

"The search for a cure is often dictated by economics. While the molecular ingredients found in certain plants, vegetables, fruits, and animals produce almost no side effects and are far more readily assimilated by our organs, Big Pharma will not invest their research dollars in substances created by Mother Nature, simply because they cannot be patented. This has had a profound effect on research, limiting treatments to artificial medicines that our bodies have trouble assimilating, leading to harmful side effects."

The scene shifted to a female scientist working in a private lab.

"This is Dr. Sara Jernigan, one of the most respected molecular biologists in the world. Dr. Jernigan has spent the past twenty years exploring isolated habitats in order to find natural cures to diseases. Two years ago, she discovered a powerful enzyme produced by the liver of a marine organism that supercharged the human immune system and reactivated the cancer cell's TP-53 gene."

Dr. Jernigan took over, narrating a scene of a cancer cell appearing under an electron microscope. "The TP-53 gene is our cells' anticancer defense system; it prevents the mutation of the genome by causing apoptosis, which is a cell's self-destruct sequence. This is far different from chemo or radiation, which doesn't discriminate and destroys everything, including the body's immune system. When this liver enzyme was introduced to patients with stage-four cancers, it induced widespread apoptosis, killing a hundred percent of the cancer cells within forty-eight hours, without any harmful side effects."

Morgan Freeman continued. "What is the marine organism responsible for producing this natural anticancer enzyme, and where can it be found? To appreciate the unique challenges Dr. Jernigan and her team faced in accessing the species' natural habitat, we must journey back in time...."

An image of ancient Earth appeared, the seven continents grouped together as one.

"Our planet is six billion years old. Life first appeared in our oceans three and a half billion years ago as a single-celled organism, and over the next three billion years or so nothing changed. And then, about five hundred and forty million years ago, something wondrous happened—life evolved."

The scene changed, revealing a vast underwater world teeming with life.

"From multicellular organisms came trilobites and corals, jellyfish and mollusks, sea scorpions and squids. Over the next fifty million years the 'Cambrian Explosion' began making its own design changes. At some point, a new species appeared which possessed a backbone that separated its brain and nervous system from the rest of its organs, and the age of fish—the Devonian Period—had arrived.

"The first of these vertebrates were filter feeders. Because their internal skeletons were composed of cartilage, many species grew a thick, armor-like bony shield that covered their heads as a means of protection. Others developed senses that allowed them to see, taste, smell, hear, and feel within their watery environment. And then, eighty million years after the first fish appeared, a revolutionary new feature came into being—a set of biting jaws. It would be an innovation that would distinguish predator from prey, reshuffling the ocean's food chain.

"For many species of fish, Earth's ocean suddenly became a dangerous place to live.

"One hundred and seventy million years after the first vertebrate hatched in the sea, a lobe-finned fish crawled out of the water and onto land . . . and gasped a breath of air. Over the next twenty million years, these unique creatures—the amphibians—continued to evolve, their gills eventually replaced by lungs, which were ventilated by means of a throat-pump.

"Adapting to a terrestrial lifestyle forced many more anatomical changes, propelled by the need to survive. Sixty million years after the first species of lobe-finned fish crawled out of the sea, the first reptiles were born . . . leading to the age of the dinosaurs, and for hundreds of millions of years these monstrous creatures ruled the land, sea, and air."

A map of ancient Earth appeared, the continents forming one giant landmass.

"The Earth looked a lot different back then, our planet's history going through cycles where its landmasses would merge into supercontinents, only to eventually break apart. The last supercontinent to appear was Pangaea. The rest of this ancient world was covered by a vast prehistoric ocean—the Panthalassa.

"Our landmasses and oceans rest upon the lithosphere—a rigid outer layer of rock, sixty miles thick, that moves along a hot molten mantle. The lithosphere is divided into fifteen to twenty tectonic plates that move, on average, a few inches a year. Mid-ocean ridges are gaps between the plates where hot magma rises from the Earth's mantle to form a new ocean crust—an action that causes the plates to push away from one another. This creates subduction zones—areas where one or more plates collide.

"One hundred and eighty million years ago, volcanic forces caused the tectonic plates to shift, resulting in the breaking apart of Pangaea, leaving two giant landmasses in its place. Laurasia would eventually divide and drift, forming North America, Europe, Asia, and Greenland, while Gondwanaland became Australia, Antarctica, India, and South America.

"It was around this time that the largest tectonic plate on the planet—the Pacific Plate—began subducting beneath the far smaller Philippine Sea Plate, creating the deepest and longest gully on the planet: the Mariana Trench. The resulting volcanic activity led to the formation of the Mariana Island chain and a recently discovered geo-logical anomaly—an isolated sea located between the Philippine Sea Plate and the subducting Pacific Plate, its inhabitants dating back to the Panthalassa Ocean."

A time-lapse animation of the subduction zone appeared, the titanic Pacific Plate wedging itself beneath the Philippine Plate, unleashing billowing clouds of boiling magma. The molten rock rose along the sheer vertical walls of the Mariana Trench, curling out several miles above the seafloor before hardening into a rapidly expanding horizon-tal ceiling that quickly spanned the entire Mariana Trough.

"For tens of millions of years, magma plumes continued rising out of this massive subduction zone. As the molten rock reached frigid water temperatures several miles above the seafloor, it cooled, hardening into a permanent shelf. Hydrothermal vents and nutrient-filled currents en-sured a perpetual food chain that attracted a wide variety of prehistoric life to this warm-water, isolated habitat.

"Sixty-five million years ago, an asteroid struck the Earth, causing an Ice Age that wiped out the dinosaurs and led to the age of mam-mals. As ocean temperatures plummeted, ancient marine life died off—the exception being those creatures inhabiting the warm-water abyss nine miles below the surface of the Western Pacific. Over the last twenty million years, magma gradually sealed up the remaining access points, isolating this tropical habitat.

"Seven years ago, a marine biologist named Michael Maren discov-ered an entrance into this purgatory of prehistoric life and named it the 'Panthalassa Sea.' The *Panthalassa* spans five thousand square miles and resides one thousand, two hundred fifty feet beneath the seafloor. Its inhabitants date as far back as three hundred fifty million years ago to the Devonian Era, and as recently as the Miocene Period, fifteen million years ago."

A twelve-second looped video of a school of fish appeared, the foot-age repeated several times.

"This is *Leedsichthys*, or Leeds' fish, the largest bony fish ever to have inhabited the planet. Adults range from ninety to a hundred fifteen feet in length, weighing in excess of a hundred tons. Like their modern-day mammalian rival, the blue whale, these gentle giants possess gill rakers instead of teeth, which they use to feed on krill and plankton. In his journal, the late Dr. Maren referred to these creatures as the buffalo of the Panthalassa Sea, noting that when a school of Leeds' fish moved across the abyssal plain, their current often dragged other species off the seafloor, trapping them in their wake.

"It was the liver enzymes of *Leedsichthys* that produced the cure for cancer.

"Journeying over nine miles below the surface of the ocean to access this medical bounty comes with many challenges. Water pressure in the Panthalassa exceeds nineteen thousand pounds per square inch. And while the Leeds' fish are plentiful, the selected donor must be isolated from the herd, the creature's liver excised from its body while it is still alive, then transferred within vacuum-sealed containers for processing. Finally, there are the wolves of the Panthalassa Sea to contend with, including some of the nastiest predators of all time, to whom the giant fish's liver is a delicacy."

The scene switched to Global Group, showing Chinese scientists working with vats of clear molten plastic, others testing volleyball-size plastic spheres in pressurized water chambers.

"To combat the problem of water pressure, engineers at Global Group International Holdings turned to aerogel, the lightest, lowest-density solid material ever produced. Aerogels are made by removing all of the liquid from silica gel while leaving its molecular density intact."

A scientist in a lab coat placed a slide of aerogel under an electron microscope.

"Examining aerogel under a microscope reveals trillions of nanometer-size particles of silicondioxide interconnected in a porous labyrinth made up mostly of air. The material is incredibly dense. If you flattened this slide out, it would span an entire football field."

The scene shifted to a massive facility where the large biosphere was under construction. A Chinese word appeared:

黄飞龙
(Yellow Dragon)

"This is Yellow Dragon, the main hub of an amphibious, billion-dollar scientific and medical research platform undertaken by the Chinese government and Global Group International Holdings."

Johnny Hon appeared on camera, seated behind his desk in his Hong Kong office.

"My name is Dr. Johnny Sei-Hoe Hon, and I am the president and CEO of Global Group International Holdings. In the Chinese culture, dragons are considered to be divine mythical creatures that control the rain, lakes, rivers, and sea, bringing abundance, prosperity, and good fortune. The Chinese dragon, or *Lung*, symbolizes power and excellence, valiancy and boldness, heroism and perseverance. A dragon overcomes obstacles until success is his. He is energetic, decisive, optimistic, and intelligent.

"The Yellow Dragon functions as a medical facility, pharmaceutical processing plant, scientific research platform, and—in the near future—a five-star aquatic hotel and entertainment center. Each of our twelve hundred suites comes with an unobstructed view of our surroundings as we submerge beneath the surface of the ocean, transporting our guests to a world very few have ever visited."

An animated sequence showed the entire Yellow Dragon docking platform and its fleet of smaller vessels descending into the abyss, the titanic sphere glowing neon violet, its light attracting swarms of bioluminescent fish. A depth gauge at the top right corner of the screen tracked the dive in meters and feet.

At nearly thirty-two thousand feet, the platform and its vessels passed through a thick hydrothermal plume, a message appearing on screen:

Now entering the Mariana Trench . . .

Sprouting from the seafloor was a petrified forest of hydrothermal vents that spewed superheated, 700-degree-Fahrenheit mineral water into the abyss. The black smokers were surrounded by undulating clusters of tube worms, their tall, albino stalks providing nourishment to an abundance of life.

The neon-violet glow emanating from the biosphere's outer shell powered off, causing it to vanish. From this heart-pounding, suffocating blackness appeared a thousand grapefruit-size orbs grouped in a spherical cluster. These "bait projections" blinked on and off along the Yellow Dragon's hull, attracting the attention of multiple schools of fish, which rushed the darkened sphere from every conceivable angle, only to bounce harmlessly off the unseen aerogel shell.

Rising from its crawl space beneath a rock formation was a giant squid. The fifty-foot beast altered its camouflaged hide to a ghostly albino as it attacked the orbs, its tentacles splaying across the biodome's curved outer shell.

The incredible scene shifted to the inside of a luxury hotel room as a couple observed the action from inside their living area.

As they watched, a sonar image displayed across the top of their smart window, locking on to something very large moving along the dark periphery.

Species identified: *Carcharodon megalodon*

The fifty-two-foot albino shark suddenly turned, launching its attack on the giant squid. Its jaws snatched the cephalopod from the sphere, its teeth shredding the succulent meat as its monstrous snout pressed against the Yellow Dragon's outer shell, but causing no damage.

"As you can see, a Megalodon encounter is nothing to fear. The Yellow Dragon's double aerogel shell is impervious to heat, cold, and giant prehistoric sharks. But we've saved the best for last—our daily excursions into the Panthalassa Sea."

The Yellow Dragon glowed gold like an abyssal sun, casting its light upon one of the tubes, where dozens of people were in line to board one of the smaller spheres. The watertight passage was sealed and the Mini-Dragon rose from its docking berth, its outer shell casting a violet aura—the only visible light in the trench.

Up ahead were blinking red lights marking the circumference of a massive man-made hole—a passage into another world. The entrance was electrified, preventing any prehistoric life-forms from escaping into the Pacific.

Red lights were replaced by green, and the Mini-Dragon plunged straight down into the tunnel. . . .

Jonas blinked as the lights came on in the theater, the video over. "Pretty intense."

Terry nodded. "What do you think?"

"About what? A cure for cancer? I'm all for it, assuming they've figured out how to excise the liver from a ninety-foot, two-hundred-thousand-pound tuna while it's still alive."

"What about touring the Panthalassa?"

"My personal opinion . . . it's insane. By the look on your face, I can tell you don't agree."

"David ventured into the Panthalassa in a tiny Manta sub; you went after him in a craft even smaller. Those Mini-Dragons . . . they're huge spheres, far too wide even for Angel to have wrapped her jaws around. Assuming the aerogel hull can withstand the pressure, I don't see how anything down there could possibly damage it."

"You sound like you actually want to see it."

"If it was safe? Absolutely. To witness these ancient sea creatures interacting in their natural habitat . . . wow. And I'm not alone. Why do you think people climb into aluminum shark cages to observe great whites, while others parachute out of perfectly good airplanes? Remove all the risk and you take all the fun out of living."

Jonas's eyes widened. "Who are you, and what did you do with my wife?"

"She woke up. And now she refuses to live in fear." Terry leaned in and kissed him. "You saved me, Jonas . . . you always save me. Now it's my turn to save you."

"How?"

"I was watching you on the chopper ride out—your hand was shaking."

"Well, if it turns out to be Parkinson's, at least we know how to cure it," Jonas said, referring to his wife's unexpected benefit from having been in a prolonged coma.

"What was it Mac emailed to you that rattled you so badly?"

"Information on Johnny Hon's venture. To be honest, I thought he was building another Dubai-Land. But this . . . this is beyond anything I ever imagined."

He looked up as Molly Wilken returned. "So . . . I hope you enjoyed the virtual tour. I'm sure you have many questions. If you'll come with me, Dr. Hon is waiting."

Tanaka Institute
Monterey, California

David awoke in his office from his afternoon nap at precisely 5:17 p.m., having preset his mental alarm three minutes before the CD alarm clock. For a long moment he stretched out on the leather sofa, staring at the bright orange specks of sunset bleeding through the slats of his venetian blinds. He felt sluggish, having stayed up way too late the night before watching a zombie apocalypse movie with Monty and Monty's new girlfriend. Alexia Rhodes was Dulce's roommate, and David enjoyed having her at his apartment when both girls were there, but with his fiancée traveling abroad, he felt like the third wheel . . . especially with Monty and Alexia going at it in the very next room.

The CD alarm clock went off, playing the Rolling Stones' "The Last Time." He listened through the first chorus, then rolled off the couch and staggered into his private bathroom. Gazing at his reflection in the mirror didn't help. He hadn't shaved in three days—*with Dulce gone, what was the point?* But he knew the dark circles under his bloodshot eyes wouldn't pass Mac's inspection.

Searching his medicine cabinet, he located an old squirt bottle of eyedrops. He leaned his head back and closed his left eye, attempting to drip a few droplets into the right—dousing his cheeks before being rewarded with a burning sensation that caused him to toss the expired container in the trash can.

Returning to the medicine cabinet, he grabbed a bottle of aspirin, twisted off the cap, and dumped five into his palm. Without thinking, he popped them into his mouth and leaned over the faucet to take a drink, before remembering he had skipped lunch.

This is what happens when you mess around with your schedule.

David's stomach was already burning by the time he doused his head in a cold shower and ran a comb through his hair. His new assistant, Shannon Corder, would not be by with his dinner until 5:45—*maybe there was something to eat in his minifridge?*

He left the bathroom to check but found only a six-pack of soda and a shriveled-up plum. He was tempted to text Shannon to hurry up, but that's how he had lost his last assistant, so he turned on his TV to kill some time.

Running a dilapidated aquarium while working with a dangerous animal had quickly proven itself to be an eighteen-hour-a-day, seven-day-a-week job. Mac ran the back end, overseeing repairs and maintenance, but he was getting up there in years, and wanted to spend more time with his five-year-old son, so he set out to train Monty to take over for him.

David's job was to bring the crowds back to the facility, and the first year had been especially difficult. It wasn't that the public wasn't fascinated with Luna; it was simply that the Meg was only a small juvenile compared with Angel, who had set the bar at seventy-four feet and fifty tons. Six years ago, the Tanaka Institute was the only place in the world one could see the most dangerous predator in history—Angel's presence alone had sold out the arena six months in advance. But now Dubai-Land was open, featuring its own mature Megalodon (Angel's only surviving offspring), along with seven other monstrous prehistoric species—all situated in a theme park anchored by twelve five-star hotels.

While Dubai-Land was raking in tens of millions of dollars a day, the Tanaka Institute was barely drawing enough attendance to pay for Luna's daily feeding. The fact that David was personally responsible for capturing three of the species that were now destroying his own business was an irony he struggled with every day.

He had also miscalculated the public's response to his interactions with the Meg. Part of Angel's draw was that she had been so frightening. Watching David swim with Luna may have earned him points with animal rights groups, but it changed the experience for the paying public, who *wanted* to be scared.

It was Monty who came up with a solution. Last week, the institute had quietly announced on its website that future shows with Luna would no longer include David's entering her tank. Two days later, a video shot using an iPhone was "leaked" to the media by an unnamed former employee, showing the forty-six-foot, fifty-two-thousand-pound albino shark attacking her trainer. The video went viral and attendance went up, bringing in desperately needed revenue.

Still, David refused to give up his personal interactions with Luna. The maturing Megalodon clearly appeared to look forward to their private training sessions. And so David would show up at the arena every morning at six and spend two hours in the water with the shark before the institute's handful of employees or the construction crew working on the Meg Pen were allowed to enter.

Shifting Luna's habitat to the lagoon came with its own set of problems. With the sun reflecting off the water's surface, visibility was poor, forcing David to cancel all daytime shows. Instead, two shows were scheduled every night at eight and ten, the Megalodon much easier to see with the underwater lights turned on in her lake-size tank.

The staged video, along with Luna's recent growth spurt, had increased the institute's average weekday attendance to just under thirty-seven hundred visitors a show.

But there were two nights a month when the arena experienced near-sellout crowds. When the moon was full, Luna would rise to the surface and spy-hop for hours, her gently moving caudal fin causing her to sway, her lower jaw opening and closing as if the shark was praying silently to the heavens.

Having survived a challenging first year in business, David Taylor was finally starting to turn a profit. It was a brutal schedule—up at 5:30 a.m., working with Luna from 6 to 8 a.m., breakfast and exercise until 9:45 a.m., business until 1 p.m., when he ate lunch and napped in his office until 5:30 p.m. Then dinner, two shows, and back in his apartment (or Dulce's place) by 1 a.m.

David knew his workweek would not improve unless he could expand the business. That meant more exhibits and an on-site hotel. A few chains were interested, but they would not capitalize the venture with Luna as the institute's only draw.

"If something happens to your Meg, you'll put us both out of business."

———————

David was flipping through the television channels when he came across the ticker-tape news blurb along the bottom of the screen:

Megalodon attack in British Columbia injures three . . .

Retrieving his iPhone from his desk, he Googled the story, his pulse racing.

**Belladonna Attacks Fishing Boat;
3 Injured, 1 Still Missing**

(AP) British Columbia:

A thirty-two-foot fishing boat was trawling the waters off Vancouver Island early this morning when several passengers noticed a four-foot gray dorsal fin trailing in the charter's wake. Captain Scott McLeod immediately contacted the Coast Guard and headed for shore.

"We were less than two kilometers south of Ucluelet when she rammed us from below. Our starboard engine stalled and we started taking on water. I began serpentining back and forth like the Coast Guard advisory instructed, but I think it made the creature mad 'cause the next thing I know my passengers were screaming and the damn thing is gnawing on the starboard bow rail."

> Pamela Hanvey was seated in the bow when the Megalodon rose out of the water and bit the rail. She managed to film this video as the boat started rolling beneath her.

David clicked on the YouTube video, which showed a stark-white shark's head, roughly the size of a minivan, biting down on the aluminum rail—the sea suddenly rushing at the camera.

> Hanvey suffered a mild concussion and a broken pelvis. Two other passengers, Linda Baker of Texas and Shawn Banks of Toronto, were flown to Tofino General Hospital; both are listed in stable condition.
>
> First mate James Martin, a former defensive tackle who played three seasons with the Cleveland Browns, is still missing. Martin was operating the bilge pumps in the engine room when the boat flipped.

David clicked on two more stories related to the attack before he was interrupted by a knock on his office door.

"It's open."

Shannon Corder entered, his new assistant followed by a man in a dark suit and a police officer. "David, these men need to see you."

"David Taylor?" The man in the suit stepped forward, handing him a folded stack of papers.

"What's this?"

"A subpoena. You've been served."

The two men left, leaving Shannon unsure of what to do.

"Are you hungry?"

"Get Tom Cubit on the phone." He sat down behind his desk, opening the papers.

The subpoena had been issued by the deputy minister and executive director of the British Columbia Environmental Assessment Office and the director of the Washington State Department of Ecology, ordering him to report to a 9 a.m. hearing in the latter's office in Seattle in two days, the subject—

—Belladonna.

Aboard the Yellow Dragon
Western Pacific

Molly Wilken led them through the lobby to one of the sets of elevators. She pushed the down button and the doors immediately opened.

The administrator pointed to the inside panel's floor menu. "As you can see, the hotel suites reside above the lobby and are labeled two through twenty. Floors A through T are below the lobby and require a special passkey." She inserted her magnetic card into the slot and pushed "S-Deck."

The bullet-shaped elevator immediately dropped through a second atrium situated in the Yellow Dragon's southern hemisphere, the deep blue of the Pacific at the bottom of the vessel looming into view.

The doors opened to a balcony that looked straight down on T-Deck and the curved bottom of the sphere. Molly led them around the square corridor past administrative offices, the last suite denoted in English and Chinese as belonging to Dr. Johnny Sei-Hoe Hon.

They entered an interior corridor, where a Chinese woman dressed in a business suit was waiting.

"Professor Taylor, Mrs. Taylor . . . this is Catherine Ying, Dr. Hon's personal assistant."

"Thank you, Ms. Wilken, I'll handle things from here." Catherine Ying stepped in front of Molly as she extended her palm to shake Jonas's hand, gripping his fingers painfully. "I am so pleased to have you both aboard our facility. If you'll follow me."

She led Jonas and Terry down a private corridor to a closed polished maple door, a copper plate identifying it as an executive boardroom.

"Prepare to be impressed," she said with a smile as she opened the door.

Jonas's eyes widened as he entered a rectangular conference room, its curved exterior floor-to-ceiling aerogel walls revealing the undersea world. He was so mesmerized by the view that it took him several seconds before he realized there were a dozen people seated around an eighteen-foot-long oval table clapping for him.

A barrel-chested Chinese man in his forties approached, greeting him with a hearty handshake. "Professor Taylor, you honor us by your presence. Mrs. Taylor, I am so pleased you were able to make the trip. . . ."

Johnny Hon followed Jonas's gaze over his right shoulder, where a school of krill were twisting and contorting in the distance, attempting to avoid being eaten by a thirty-foot whale shark.

"Sorry, it's just so . . ."

"Beautiful?"

"I was going to say addicting."

"Yes, I agree. And this is only the appetizer. Speaking of which, you must be hungry. Why don't you fill your plates and we'll talk over lunch."

He pointed to a dozen buffet trays lined up on a narrow table set along the interior wall. At Johnny's signal, a waiter removed the tops, leaving a serving utensil in each offering.

Jonas followed Terry, who handed him a plate, the rest of the executives falling in behind them, Johnny insisting on being the last person in line.

Ten minutes later, Jonas was sitting back in his reclining chair, satiated and once more staring out the window, his eyelids growing heavy.

"You are tired, my friend?"

"It was a long trip."

"This will be a quick meeting. As soon as we finish, Ms. Wilken will escort you to your suite and you can get some rest."

Johnny signaled to one of the men seated at the far end of the table. A moment later the deep blue ocean faded to black, the smart windows converting to a projection screen. A time code, depth in meters and feet, and ocean temperature displayed along the top, and a GPS and sonar screen appeared to the left.

"The footage you are about to see was recorded eleven days ago in the Panthalassa Sea aboard Dragon Pod-2."

The water took on an olive-green tinge as the night vision activated, revealing a blizzard of snow-like particles coming straight at them. The glowing aft lights of a Sting Ray submersible were visible in the distance. A cluster of red blips appeared on sonar, moving steadily on a

northwesterly course, a lone red blip zigzagging away from the group.
Two blue dots denoted the two vessels closing on the target.

A crewman spoke in Chinese, his words translated into English:
"Target has separated from the school; anesthetic has taken effect.
Heart rate: a hundred thirty-three BPM. Range to target: twenty-seven
meters. Sting Ray-2 requesting permission to attach neurological im-
plant."

"No activity on sonar. Fire at will."

The particles slowed as the pod reduced its forward speed.

The Sting Ray appeared up ahead, the submersible dwarfed by the
Leeds' fish. The ninety-six-foot prehistoric giant was tethered to a steel
cable connecting the vessel to a harpoon hanging below the creature's
gills.

"Target's neurological system has been neutralized. We're not in
deep, DP-2 . . . better get the Sunfish in the water."

"Stand by."

The camera angle changed, revealing a section of the sphere's outer
shell as it yawned open, releasing a flat, oval-shaped drone, its design
inspired by *Mola mola*, the giant Sunfish. Twenty-two feet in diameter,
the drone was slightly larger than its namesake and resembled a swimming head that abruptly ended in a tall, rigid dorsal fin and a matching
anal fin.

"Sunfish is in the water. She's all yours, Toshi."

"Engaging signal . . . control established. Stand by."

The drone suddenly accelerated away from the sphere toward the
Leeds' fish, which was gasping huge mouthfuls of sea but had otherwise ceased moving. Hovering directly below the stunned giant's belly,
the Sunfish positioned the tip of its rigid dorsal so that it pierced the
Leeds' fish's anus, the drone inching its way higher and deeper until
half the fin had entered the orifice.

"We're in. Heating up the blade."

The visible section of the dorsal fin glowed brightly, the surrounding
water sizzling.

"Activating internal camera."

The smart window split into two views, the left side continuing to show the Sting Ray submersible hovering in close proximity to the Leeds' fish's tail, the Sunfish attached to its belly—

—the right side revealing a circular lens' view of the species' internal anatomy, lit by the drone's glowing surgical fin.

A woman spoke. "Toshi, this is Dr. Jernigan. You're in too deep. Retract the blade two meters or you'll sever the heart and small intestines."

"Stand by."

The internal camera angle widened as the blade retreated.

"Much better. Proceed with the incision."

"Acknowledged."

The Sunfish's propulsion system activated, pushing the drone dorsal fin-first in the direction of the creature's head—

—its heated surgical blade slicing through the Leeds' fish, eviscerating its belly. A long, dark, snakelike organ slowly unraveled out of the gaping wound.

"Toshi, that's the small intestine. Be ready—the liver should follow."

The small intestine continued uncoiling, followed by a large, flat, meaty, rowboat-size organ.

"Toshi—"

"I see it. Retracting blade . . . activating drone's suction pumps."

Freed from the Leeds' fish's belly, the drone chased after the creature's excised organ. The Sunfish's pucker-shaped mouth opened as its suction pumps engaged, inhaling the liver into the drone's expanding internal cache. With a burst of blood, the orifice snapped shut upon the distal end of the small intestine, severing its connection with the captured prize.

A collective cheer rose from both vessels—

—then gave way to an internal alarm as multiple green targets suddenly appeared on sonar.

"Warning: Unidentified predatory species has
entered the kill zone."

Jonas's pulse raced as several dozen thirty-to-forty-foot sharks attacked the Leeds' fish like a school of ravenous piranha. Not content to simply feed off the paralyzed behemoth, they forced their way into its vented belly, consuming and tearing apart the convulsing creature from the inside out, the gruesome visual disappearing quickly behind a lake of blood. In a span of thirty heart-pounding seconds, the predators had shredded the prehistoric cow into unrecognizable chunks, some of which floated free of the feeding frenzy, only to be snatched up by members of the circling quarry.

Two of the carnivores were engaged in a gruesome tug-of-war with the drone, each writhing twist of their dark triangular heads intended to intimidate their rival. As the Sunfish's cache was torn open and the Leeds' fish's liver released, a far larger shark bulldozed its way into the conflict, the fifty-foot female snatching the drone in her jaws before circling away with her prize.

The Sting Ray fled to open water, only to be chased by five or six of the predators, which bashed and pounded the submersible's depth-resistant hull until it imploded in a brilliant white burst of crushed matter.

So bright was the flash that it left purple spots in Jonas's vision, momentarily blinding him so that he never saw the object that impacted Mini-Dragon-2's viewing window. But he felt the bone-rattling contact, which caused him to jump as the video went dark.

A moment later, the soothing deep blue of the shallows returned, the late afternoon sun splaying curtains of light along the sphere's outer shell.

"Geezus, Johnny—what the hell were those things?"

"We were hoping you could tell us."

"Can you slow the video down? There was so much blood and they were moving so fast, I couldn't tell what species of shark I was looking at."

"Computer, replay the last thirty seconds of the DP-2 attack at half speed."

The smart window darkened, returning to the sequence just prior to the submersible's implosion.

Jonas stared at the swirling dervish of bodies, struggling to discern any characteristics that might identify the species. "They're definitely sharks . . . not as big as a Meg, but using the Sting Ray to determine their size, I'd guess thirty to forty feet and twenty tons."

Terry looked away as the submersible imploded. "Dr. Hon, what happened to the Mini-Dragon? Was it destroyed?"

"Thankfully, no. The last recorded impact vented the outer shell, but the interior shell remained intact. Our sensors confirm that DP-2's life-support systems are functioning, but the propulsion drive was damaged and the biosphere became caught in a current that has carried it forty-seven kilometers to the northwest. We've been waiting for the new Sting Rays and their weapon systems to arrive; now that they are here we can launch a rescue mission."

"How many people were aboard?" Terry asked.

"Six, including Dr. Jernigan. We lost two men aboard the Sting Ray."

Jonas looked up as the light from the implosion faded. As he watched, one of the sharks emerged from the periphery, on a collision course with the Mini-Dragon's control room. It was the big female, the remains of the Sunfish drone still wedged in its mouth.

"Computer—freeze image!"

The playback stopped.

"Rewind to 00:41 and pause."

The scene reversed three seconds.

Jonas stared at the creature's mouth. "Johnny, look at the lower jaw—can you see what it's using to grip the drone?"

Dr. Hon squinted. "Computer, enlarge image by thirty percent."

The still shot expanded, revealing a buzz saw–shaped protrusion of razor-sharp teeth originating from the center of the lower jaw.

"Jonas?"

"It's a tooth whorl. It belongs to a nightmare of creation called a Helicoprion—an ancient species of shark that dominated the Panthalassa Ocean about two hundred ninety million years ago. "If there are schools of these monsters down there, you may have to look elsewhere for the cure for cancer."

Point Bennett, San Miguel Island
The Channel Islands

The number of elephant seals lazing about the beachhead tallied in the thousands. Plump brown bodies were spread out in clusters in the warm afternoon sun, the pinnipeds tossing sand across their backs to keep from burning. Snores rented the salty air, joined by the incessant calls of the seagulls and the heavier grunts of copulation as the male seals spread their seed among the cows in their harem. Every so often a pair of males faced off, the rivals chortling deep throttles as they rose menacingly from their hindquarters to impress their cows.

The four Sikorsky S-64Sky Crane helicopters approached the small island from the west in a diamond formation. Secured to each of the airships' landing gears by a thick steel chain was a corner rung belonging to a two-hundred-sixty-square-foot cargo net.

Jackie Buchwald was strapped in the copilot's seat aboard the lead chopper, surveying the scene up ahead with the aid of a pair of high-powered binoculars. Adjusting her headphones, she spoke into the radio mic. "Remain in formation and wait for my signal before setting down."

––––––––––

The thunderous reverberations had the pinnipeds sitting up and baying at the unknown disturbance. Moments later, the four helicopters were hovering over the beach, the 40-knot winds generated by their six-blade rotors sending the mammals scattering across land and sea.

The airships set down, their engines powering off as each of the six-man teams assembled around the cargo net, which had landed in a heap in the now-deserted clearing. Jackie watched as the entanglement of knotted rope was gradually stretched out to form a tight square.

Shovels were dispersed among the *Mogamigawa*'s crew, the men using them to cover the thick cords of rope with sand while the chopper pilots wrapped camouflage netting over their helicopters' chassis. Finally, fresh fish were tossed over the buried cargo net to entice the frightened elephant seals to return.

Using her binoculars, Jackie scanned the western horizon. The tanker remained out of range, but it was early, dusk still a few hours away. The Lio was out there somewhere; the marine biologist estimated its present course and speed would bring it to the northern Channel Islands between 8 p.m. and midnight. San Miguel would be the first island in its path, the Port Bennett beach the nearest rookery . . . assuming the spooked elephant seals would return in time to serve themselves up as dinner.

She glanced at the men as they filed back inside the helicopter to get out of the sun. They were a scurvy lot, that was for sure—a mixed bag of Indonesians, Filipinos, Arabs, and Indians who had come to the United Arab Emirates through a visa sponsorship known as *kafala*. They had sought jobs in construction and had been part of the manpower that had built the hotels and monorails and massive aquariums in Dubai-Land. Only those who had experience at sea were recruited for positions aboard the two converted supertankers.

The men who had served on the *Tonga* had looked at her the way a hungry wolf eyes a lamb; she knew her fragile alliance with the crew of the *Mogamigawa* was based solely on the promise of bonuses the prince would fund if and when the Liopleurodon was captured and delivered.

But over the past few months she had come to see the crew in a different light, as first the women and then the men had shared their personal stories of abuse.

"My first job was as a domestic worker. I would wake up early to prepare breakfast, then clean, wash clothes, and then cook again. I had to work eighteen-hour days with no rest. The man I worked for abused me sexually. His wife must have known . . . she started hitting me . . . she would strike me in the chest and face and sometimes pulled out tufts of my hair. I complained to the agency that arranged the job, only to find out I was not allowed to switch employers. They held my passport, so I couldn't go home. I had left my family in India just to be a slave."

The conditions the men labored under were often worse.

"They kept hundreds of us in a single barracks with no electricity and only two working sinks, showers, and toilets. We labored in sixteen-hour shifts, barely being fed. Those who tried to leave were beaten; those who couldn't handle the conditions died on the job; their bodies were often buried on the construction site. When I heard they were recruiting sailors, I lied and told them I had served aboard an oil tanker, just to get out of the UAE."

These tales of horror weighed heavily on Jackie. Having already dealt with the crown prince and his warped sense of morality, she knew there was a good chance he would renege on the money due to the crew—not to mention her own million-dollar fee—the moment the Lio was secure in its aquarium.

And so she began formulating a new option, one that would force the crown prince into keeping his word. The first step was to create an alliance with the leaders among the crew—all of whom she had recruited for the San Miguel ambush.

"Karim, gather your team; I want to survey the rookery at Cardwell Point before the sun sets."

"Yes, boss."

Aboard the Yellow Dragon

The twelfth-story view looked out over a moonlit ocean, the ambiance wasted on the suite's two occupants.

Terry laid her head on her husband's silver-haired chest. "You knew this trip would lead to another encounter with the abyss."

"I suspected it, but only after receiving Mac's email."

"Jonas, we're not being held prisoner. Dr. Hon asked for your advice, not your presence aboard the rescue mission. Advise him, and in the morning we'll take the chopper back to Guam."

"And what about Dulce? Our son's fiancée is being asked to pilot one of the Mini-Dragon's Sting Ray escorts. If we leave and something happens to her . . ."

She said nothing, her silence affirming their shared fear.

"Jonas, those creatures . . . the Helicoprion—"

"How would I defend myself if I had to face them? I've been thinking about that all afternoon. My first line of defense would be to illuminate every rescue vessel in bright light. Of course, that only works if the Helicoprion aren't already blind. Even if the light bothers them, they've got far more important senses that will lead them right to those spheres.

"My second line of defense would be to generate an electrical field that would scramble their ampullae of Lorenzini . . . something similar to what David wears when he interacts with Luna, only far more powerful. I'm guessing Helen Emmett outfitted the three Sting Rays with this kind of weapon, but the Mini-Dragons will need similar devices."

"What about conventional weapons . . . torpedoes?"

"If it was only one creature . . . maybe. Against a swarm like we saw in that video—no way. Even if you managed to hit one of the sharks, the blood in the water would drive the rest of them into another feeding frenzy."

"Is that it?"

"That's all I could come up with so far. Of course, the last time I entered the Panthalassa on a rescue mission, I had my own personal escort."

"Angel." Terry thought for a moment and then sat up in bed. "Jonas, if you had an adult Meg as your escort this time around, would that be enough to scare these Helicoprion away?"

"I don't know. There's definitely an intimidation factor that comes into play. It's sort of like a full-grown male lion making a kill, surrounded by a pack of hyenas. The hyenas won't attack, even though they easily outnumber the lion and would probably win the fight if they all charged at once. Animals don't think in terms of winning a battle; it's all about self-preservation. So yeah, if a full-grown female Megalodon was swimming shotgun, I think those Helicoprion would hightail it out of Dodge. Anyway, the point is moot—Luna's far from an adult."

"I wasn't thinking of Luna."

"What other mature adult female . . . oh!" Jonas's eyes widened as he realized what his wife had in mind.

"It'll take time to bring her in . . . at least a few days by transport. Will they wait that long?"

"If they want me to tag along, they'll have to."

"You mean *us*. I'm going with you."

Jonas was about to argue, but the look in Terry's eyes set him straight. "I'd better speak with Dr. Hon so he can coordinate everything with Mac."

"Jonas, whatever they do, they cannot breathe a word of this to David. If he finds out Dulce is involved—"

"Understood."

U.S. District Court
Seattle, Washington

The attorney and his client followed the clerk down a private hall to a closed door labeled MEDIATION 6A. "They're waiting for you inside."

"Thank you." Thomas Cubit held the door open, and David entered the small conference room.

Three people in business suits occupied high-backed leather chairs at the far end of a rectangular table. One of the men and the woman were in their forties, the silver-haired gentleman in his late sixties. A fourth person—a stocky blond woman dressed casually in khakis—was seated off to the side, reading from her iPhone, a holstered weapon strapped around her waist.

The younger man offered a false smile, his New York accent identifying him as an American. "Thank you for coming. My name is Joseph Williams and I am the director of the Washington State Department of Ecology. The esteemed gentleman on my left is Deputy Minister Kenneth C. Webb, executive director of the British Columbia Environmental Assessment Office."

The silver-haired scientist offered a brief wave without bothering to look up from the open file lying on the table beneath his nose.

"Finally, this is Sabrina Agricola, CEO at Agricola Industries. I believe you knew her brother."

David nodded to the slender woman with shoulder-length brown hair seated across from him. "I'm sorry about your brother."

"He should not have gotten involved with Fiesal bin Rashidi."

David motioned to the stocky blonde. "Who's the lady packing heat?"

Joseph Williams replied, "I asked Police Chief Sandra Andrews to join us, just in case mediation fails."

The veins in Tom Cubit's neck appeared to jump beneath his shirt collar. "Are you actually intending to charge my client with something, or is this your way of trying to coerce him through cheap intimidation tactics?"

"Tread lightly, counselor. We've got a small army made up of family members of Belladonna's victims pushing us very hard to charge the Tanaka Institute and its owners with criminal negligence. If we can't work this out, then Chief Andrews will take Mr. Taylor into custody."

Sandra Andrews looked up at David and winked. "Got a nice holding cell all set up for you, sweet britches . . . something private so you and your future inmates can get acquainted."

"What is it you want me to do?" David asked.

Sabrina Agricola took control of the meeting. "My brother's dream was to build a Megalodon habitat in British Columbia. Agricola Industries has partnered with the Vancouver Aquarium to complete construction of a state-of-the-art tank and facility located on two hundred thirty acres of waterfront property situated between the existing park and Vancouver Harbour."

"You want me to catch Belladonna and transport her to her new home."

"Correct. We had originally planned on purchasing a Meg pup from Crown Prince Abu Naba'a—the Dubai-Land Megalodon, Zahra, recently gave birth to two albino offspring—but the ferocity of Bela's offspring is expected to draw far bigger crowds."

"I dunno. Belladonna is much larger than Luna was when I caught her. The *McFarland*'s hopper is way too small to handle a monster this size. What am I supposed to use as a vessel?"

"That won't be a problem," Sabrina said. "The *Marieke* and her crew will be made available to you."

The deputy minister closed the file he was reading and slid it across the table to Tom Cubit. "That's your client's 'Get Out of Jail' pass. Capture that creature and there will be no charges filed against you or the Tanaka Institute and its partners stemming from any Megalodon incidents—past or present—in the Salish Sea."

Tom Cubit scanned the legal document. "This agreement is bubkes, and you know it. Any claims against the Tanaka Institute were based on Bela and Lizzy's escaping from their pen—an act perpetrated by an employee who was working with a radical animal rights group. Our insurance settled all claims pertaining to the sisters six months ago. This document specifically deals with Luna and Belladonna. Those Megs were born in the wild; neither David nor the institute has any liabilities regarding the sisters' pups."

David slid his attorney a note.

Cubit glanced at it and nodded. "I need a few minutes to speak with my client . . . in private." Without waiting for a reply, he stood and walked toward the door, David following him out into the private hallway.

"Don't worry about these barking dogs, kid. Their bite has no teeth."

"I know, but I still want to do the deal . . . under the following terms. First, we agree to set up an offspring exchange program between the institute and their new facility. Second, for capturing Belladonna, I receive twenty percent of their gate."

Cubit shrugged. "I'll do my best, but I expect they'll probably forget about Bela's offspring and buy one of the Dubai pups."

"There are no Dubai pups," David whispered. "Barbara Becker, Jackie's former boss, contacted me last month and told me Dubai-Land had flown her in as a consultant to inspect the aquarium's water supply after Zahra—Angel's surviving runt—gave birth to two stillborn offspring. The crown prince is keeping the story real quiet—"

"Without a Meg, the Vancouver facility is out of business before they even open the doors." Cubit grinned. "I'll ask for thirty-five percent and settle for twenty-five. But I don't want you in harm's way; you're dealing with a very mean, very aggressive fish."

David nodded. "That's exactly what I'm counting on."

Aboard the Yellow Dragon
Western Pacific

The Yellow Dragon's command center occupied the forward compartment of C-Deck's inner sphere. The nerve center for the biosphere was controlled by a central computer that organized and arranged data on navigation consoles as well as the chamber's floor-to-ceiling smart windows. These tactical displays could pinpoint the location of the Yellow Dragon and her fleet of Dragon Pods and submersibles anywhere in the world—except for the Panthalassa Sea.

The tectonic plate that separated the Pacific Ocean from the three-hundred-million-year-old prehistoric habitat was more than a mile thick, rendering GPS satellites useless. Hon Industries' solution was to deploy remotely controlled deep-water drones throughout the isolated sea. Once anchored, these barrel-size robots generated a passive sonar signal strong enough to map out the uncharted domain without attracting any of the Panthalassa's life-forms.

Engineers quickly realized the Philippine Sea Plate was simply too thick for a drone's weak signal to reach the mothership. To remedy the situation, Dragon Pod-1 was converted into an automated deep-water relay system. Controlled by the Yellow Dragon, the crewless vessel was now a permanent fixture within the Panthalassa Sea.

It was through DP-1 that the command center's sonar operators were able to track the damaged sphere. Caught within a powerful current, Dragon Pod-2 and its crew were now located sixty-one kilometers to the northwest of the Panthalassa Sea's access hole.

Among the many challenges of planning a deep-water rescue mission was a ticking clock: The Panthalassa's current was rapidly pushing the damaged sphere to the edge of the drones' fifty-two-kilometer sonar limits. Knowing the DP-2 would soon be out of range of the closest bot, Captain Chau had dispatched the last two drones aboard Dragon Pod-1, positioning them at staggered distances behind the damaged minisphere.

"The most I can stretch the relay is about a hundred and twenty kilometers, and that's pushing it. The reality, Dr. Hon, is that every minute we delay launching this rescue mission brings us closer to a blackout. Once we lose DP-2's signal, we may never reacquire it."

"Understood, Captain. Everything needed for Professor Taylor's Megalodon Defense Protocol has been loaded aboard a C-5 transport and is expected to leave Monterey within the hour."

"Which means it will be at least twelve more hours before it arrives at our location. I sincerely doubt the creatures that attacked DP-2 would have abandoned the Leeds' fish kill had a Megalodon shark arrived. Johnny, my wife is aboard DP-2. . . . I am begging you—dispatch DP-3 now, along with two of the Sting Rays, before we lose their signal."

Dr. Hon contemplated his decision. "What's the soonest DP-3 will be ready to launch?"

"Two hours."

"Make it so."

"Thank you. With Toshi and Jiang dead, I have been struggling to determine which pilot to promote to take over as squad leader. Captain Deng is most qualified as an officer, having served six years in the People's Liberation Army Navy. Duane Saylor—the Ukrainian-American we recruited from Dubai-Land—has logged the most hours in the Panthalassa."

"Who is the most skilled Sting Ray pilot on board?"

"Skilled? I suppose the American trainer, Dulce Lunardon. As she is not part of the team, I never considered her."

"Has she been briefed?"

"She was shown the video of the Helicoprion attack to get her tactical recommendations. She has not been told about the nature of the Dragon Pods or anything about the planned rescue mission."

"Then do it."

"Sir, Pilot Lunardon has shown no respect for authority in the short time she has been on board. She questions every combat strategy, undermining me and my officers while creating doubt in the minds of our pilots. In my opinion, her presence aboard DP-3 would compromise the mission."

"Let me be the judge of that. Where is she now?"

———

There were five submersible berths located along the Yellow Dragon's outer sphere at C-Deck, each composed of a curved watertight hatch encircled by a compression ring similar to the apparatus that had been used on the International Space Station. Guided by cameras located along the belly of the sub, the pilot was required to align the Sting Ray's male adapters to the biosphere's corresponding female clamps, close enough to engage the docking berth's magnetized capture locks, which immediately jammed the two craft together. Once the seal was complete, a green light flashed above both the sub's hatch, as well as in the access tunnel connecting the docking berth to the Yellow Dragon's inner shell.

Two of the Yellow Dragon's five berths were currently occupied by Sting Ray submersibles. A third sub was docked in an inverted orientation along Dragon Pod-3's southern axis.

Johnny Hon entered C-Deck's aft chamber, which housed the pilots' private sleeping quarters, a briefing room, a cafeteria, an entertainment center, and an exercise facility. There were also two simulators, each holding a two-man pod suspended within an aluminum-framed wheel where the crew could train.

Simulator-A was being recharged.

The pilot operating Simulator-B was pushing the machine to its limits . . . and beyond.

As he watched, the oval-shaped pod pitched, rolled, and yawed within the confines of its wheel like a hamster on cocaine, pulling a full G with a cage-rattling, three-hundred-sixty-degree barrel loop, only to level out and throttle up into a stagnant sprint, the 35-knot special effect reserved for its sole occupant.

The third barrel roll, and its accompanying two-hundred-seventy-degree wing-over-wing maneuver, unleashed a blue spark from a floor-mounted fuse box and the scent of burning rubber. As Dr. Hon watched, the machine slowed to a grinding stop. A moment later the hatch popped open along the pod's belly and a Caucasian woman fell out sideways onto the wheel, the greased tracks leaving gray streaks on her orange jumpsuit.

Fighting vertigo, she dragged herself onto her feet, staggered to the nearest plastic trash can, and puked.

When she was through, she sat on the floor, massaging her head.

"Here . . . drink this."

She looked up at the barrel-chested Chinese man and accepted the bottled water. "Thanks." Dulce rubbed the bottle's cold condensation across the back of her neck. "No offense, but who the hell are you?"

"I'm the man who signs your paychecks."

"Helen Emmett signs my checks."

"And I sign hers. Dr. Johnny Hon. It is a pleasure to meet you."

Recognizing the CEO's name, she attempted to stand—

—Johnny catching her as she tumbled sideways. "Easy."

"Sorry. Dulce Lunardon, pilot trainer. Guess you already knew that."

"Since you are our only female pilot or trainer on board, I suspected as much. I've never seen anyone operate a simulator like that before. What were you attempting to do?"

"Keep from being eaten."

"Were you successful?"

"I was until the machine broke down."

"That's impressive."

"It's as useless as polishing a turd."

He looked at her with uncertainty.

"It's an expression. It means you can only do what you can do with the tools at hand. These Sting Rays . . . they were designed for extended missions in extreme depths, not speed and maneuverability. To outrun a herd of Helicoprion, you need a Manta."

"What about the Sting Ray's new defense systems?"

"The simulator isn't equipped with them, so I was limited to tactical maneuvers. Hopefully they'll work when your pilots need them."

"Captain Chau tells me you have been questioning our deep-water strategies."

"I question stupidity. Your former Dubai-Land pilot made it standard operating procedure to engage the Sting Ray's electrical field before the high-beams. I disagreed. When I attempted to explain, Captain Chau cut me off, stating that, as a woman, I wasn't qualified to question his authority. Somehow having breasts renders my opinion moot."

"My sincerest apology. Captain Chau is old school. When it comes to our workforce, China has a long history of treating its women as second-class citizens. When the government instituted population controls, many parents chose infanticide—killing their newborn daughters so they could try again for a son."

"That's barbaric."

"Things are changing. However, perhaps you should not be so quick to dismiss Mr. Saylor's recommendations. After all, he is one of the few pilots who has navigated a submersible among these prehistoric creatures."

"Define 'navigate.' None of the Dubai-Land pilots ever actually got close enough to engage these monsters . . . except my fiancé. He's the one who taught me that an electrical field can scramble a shark's senses up close and personal, but they can also attract them over great distances. That's why I suggested using the lights first."

"Is your fiancé a marine biologist?"

"No. But he keeps a Megalodon as a pet."

"A Megalodon? Oh, I see . . . your fiancé is David Taylor—how perfect."

"I had to agree to marry him; he's the only person ever to beat my score in the simulator. Of course, that was with a Manta. I can kick his ass aboard the Sting Ray."

"Does David know you are here?"

"No. Helen had me sign a nondisclosure agreement when she hired me. David thinks I'm in the Mediterranean presenting the three Sting Rays to the U.S. Sixth Fleet as part of their annual war game exercises."

"What about you? Do you know why we're out here?"

"It's not hard to figure out. If you don't mind me asking, how much are you charging the crown prince to stock his aquariums?"

"What makes you think we are here to capture specimens?"

"Why else would you be baiting the Dragon Pods?"

"Baiting the Dragon Pods? Oh, I see. . . . No, my dear, the Dragon Pods were designed to be used on our Panthalassa safaris. We needed a secondary business venture to justify the massive financial expenditures required to build this complex."

Dulce appeared confused. "I don't understand. You're not using the pods as traps?"

"Not at all."

"Then why did the Sting Ray pilot kill that Leeds' fish?"

"To collect its liver." Dr. Hon quickly briefed her on Dr. Jernigan's discovery and their need to launch a rescue mission with the weaponized Sting Rays.

"The cure for cancer . . . in a two-hundred-million-year-old fish's liver—wow. That certainly explains how you managed to bring Jonas here. I was kinda shocked when I saw him and Terry step off that jet. None of the Taylor men want anything to do with the Mariana Trench or the Panthalassa Sea."

"Jonas agreed to join the rescue mission if we use his Megalodon protocol. Unfortunately, we cannot wait any longer for the C-5 transport to arrive."

"Megalodon protocol? What are you talking about?"

Dr. Hon explained Terry's idea.

"Geez, that's actually pretty clever. How'd Mac manage to load everything aboard a C-5 without telling David?"

"Helen informs me he is out of town."

"Out of town? Doing what? He never leaves Luna alone. That boy's got some explaining to do—"

"Dulce, DP-3 launches within the hour. Join the mission and help us rescue the crew and I'll make it worth your while." Reaching into his pocket, he removed a folded check, handing it to her.

She stared at the figure. "That's a lot of zeros." She handed it back. "No offense, Dr. Hon, but if I'm going to risk my life, it has to be for something more important than money."

"I'm listening."

"David and I have plans: We want to turn the Taylor Institute into an entertainment mecca. To attract hotel chains and major investors, we need to expand, and expansion means we need more than a Megalodon tank. If I were to come home with a few prehistoric species—I don't know, say a few Helicoprion to start—that would be worth risking my life for."

Johnny Hon stared at her, incredulous. "I offered you a million dollars to lead a rescue mission; instead you want Hon Industries to invest a billion dollars to help you and your boyfriend capture these sea creatures?"

"He's my fiancé, and this won't cost anywhere near that."

"I beg to differ. We spent six months and millions of dollars investigating the most efficient ways to locate, capture, and eviscerate Leeds' fish, and that included diversifying the start-up costs to build a Chinese version of Dubai-Land in Chengdu. We'd need nets and subs and adrenaline-junkie pilots like your fiancé, not to mention a vessel large enough to transport these creatures across the Pacific Ocean. There is a reason we chose to build an amphibious hotel. Anything short of committing to build and stock a resort the size of Dubai-Land simply cannot be done. End of discussion."

"Can I at least explain how I'd capture these creatures?"

"No. I have a crew that must be rescued, and you are wasting valuable time." He turned to leave, but she was on her feet and blocking his exit. "You are just as bad as Captain Chau! All I'm asking for is thirty seconds. Are my services worth half a minute?"

He exhaled an exasperated breath. "Thirty seconds."

"You don't need nets or subs or crazy sub pilots, or a converted oil tanker, to haul the captured creatures back to California. All we'd need is the shell of a Dragon Pod and a few basic design changes."

Reaching into the right pants pocket of her jumpsuit, she removed a folded sheet of paper and handed it to Dr. Hon. "This is what I thought you had created the Dragon Pods to do."

He unfolded a rough hand-drawn blueprint of an empty, porous Dragon Pod shell. The end cap located along its south pole was sealed and completely clear, while the north cap was anchored on hinges that allowed it to swing in.

"What is this?"

"It's an animal trap. You bait it and lower it by cable down the access hole into the Panthalassa Sea. The predator smells the bait, swims inside, and is trapped. The cable is reversed, the trap stays in the water beneath the boat's keel, and the next trap is lowered. Remote cameras can be used to target specific species—if you already have enough Helicoprion or Mosasaurs, you simply lock the cage. When you fill your allotment of traps you set sail for home. No nets, no special transport ships are required—all you need is a single Sting Ray to guide the trap down the Mariana Trench's access hole, and the pod does the rest."

Johnny Hon's eyes widened. "Simple, inexpensive, minimal risks . . . genius. I had teams of engineers working on this for months. How long—"

"About an hour. I was lying in bed, trying to figure out the function of the Dragon Pods; this was the only thing that made any sense."

"Incredible."

"It's the breasts—they give me a superhigh IQ. How long would it take your engineers to construct something like this?"

"Not long. We have several empty shells at our plant in Chengdu. As for a surface ship, one of our science vessels returned two weeks ago from the Indian Ocean; it is in Hangzhou and could easily be refitted with cables long enough to reach the Panthalassa. Give me a week . . . ten days at the most. Dulce, this is very exciting."

"But you need my services now. Tell you what: Have your assistant write up a simple agreement, we'll both sign it, and I'll give a copy to Jonas and email one to Mac back at the institute. That way, if anything should happen to me—"

Dr. Hon shook her hand. "I will honor our arrangement. You have my word."

Point Bennett, San Miguel Island
The Channel Islands

They had been camped out on the island for more than seventy-two hours—twenty-four men, four helicopter pilots, two female cooks . . . and Jacqueline Buchwald. Extensive prep work during the first after-noon had hastened the night. From dusk to dawn the tanker's sonar array had tracked the Liopleurodon as it entered the deeper waters to the south of San Miguel and Santa Rosa Islands, the bio-transmitter's pulse flare-ups indicating when the nocturnal predator was hunting.

For twelve hours the four teams had taken up positions behind sand hills positioned around the buried net, each man armed with a high-powered tranquilizer rifle and three injection darts holding twelve ounces of phenobarbital. As temperatures dipped and a 30-knot wind chill dropped conditions to a frigid 36 degrees Fahrenheit, Jackie real-ized how ill-prepared they were for the "Lio stakeout."

By midnight, she was shaking so badly she could barely hold her radio; by 3 a.m. she was running a high fever.

And still their quarry remained at sea.

Sunrise marked the end of Day One's futility—and the presence of the *Mogamigawa* on the western horizon a mere five miles from shore. Was the Lio aware of the tanker's presence? Was that what had kept the creature from feasting upon the elephant seal rookery?

Not wanting to take a chance, she ordered the captain to move the *Mogamigawa* fifteen nautical miles to the northeast into the Santa Barbara Channel. She knew there was risk in distancing the landing party from the ship—especially if they actually managed to net the beast. But with herself and her team already exhausted and weak with flu-like symptoms after only one night, she knew the clock was ticking.

One of the helicopters was sent back to the tanker to bring more blankets and medicine. By midday, most of the elephant seals chased off by their arrival had returned. If the massive pinnipeds were aware of the buried net, they gave no indication.

Having pulled an all-nighter, Jackie and the crew had slept most of the day, some preferring the helicopters' cramped cargo spaces while others dragged their sleeping bags out onto the rise away from the seals. Latrines were initially set up twenty paces behind each airship, but by sunset of Day Two, the crew was digging holes anywhere they could find a vacant stretch of sand.

By sunset the teams were back in place—fed, armed, and ready.

The Lio was moving with the night, circling in the shallows off Cardwell Point, an elephant seal rookery located on the east side of the island. At 1:13 a.m. the creature came ashore, the guttural screeches of the pinnipeds heard miles away by their brethren at Point Bennett.

Several of Jackie's men wanted to go after the Lio, but she ordered them to stay. "Even if you managed to drug Junior, what good would that do? It will take all four helicopters to lift her and she has to be secured in the net, which means she has to come to us."

The sounds of the slaughter mercifully ended forty minutes later, the Liopleurodon returning to the sea just before the eastern horizon turned gray.

Exhausted, but needing to inspect the carnage for herself, Jackie led an armed patrol by foot along the island's southern shoreline. They arrived at Cardwell Point just after sunrise, the golden hue of a new day bathing the bloody scene in its most gruesome detail.

The Lio had not maimed to eat, it had bitten and crushed and bled the elephant seals to immobilize them in order to prevent their escape . . . and *then* it had feasted. The carnage began in the crimson-stained shallows where partially chewed mounds of gushing blubber bobbed in the surf. It continued onto the wet sand where the creature had come ashore. Its immense girth had flattened its victims, splattering their remains in a twenty-foot-wide, three-foot-deep impression that ran up the beach like the imprints of a squadron of tanks.

It had gorged in the dry sand, its immense jaws snatching the slow-moving mammals, which had no choice but to flee inland. Half-eaten carcasses skewered from deep puncture wounds left by the Lio's stiletto-sharp fangs carpeted the beach.

Not all the elephant seals had been eaten. Those that merely had their bones crushed grunted in agony as they waited to die, their remains picked at by cormorants and other seabirds.

Jackie attempted to estimate the Lio's size and weight by the imprints left in the sand while trying her best not to vomit. Hearing her name being called, she looked up to see two of the men waving at her fifty yards inland along the periphery of the carnage.

She did not recognize the remains as human until she was nearly upon it.

The victim was a Caucasian male, approximately five feet, ten inches tall and weighing just under two hundred pounds. From his salt-and-pepper hair he looked to be in his midforties. An expensive Nikon camera with a night-vision lens hung from a strap around his neck.

Jackie did not realize he had been bitten in half until she raised his parka to check his pants pocket for a wallet and identification, finding instead a pile of fly-infested entrails.

"Oh my God—" She turned away, stumbled toward the man's camouflaged tent, and vomited.

One of her crew located the victim's lower body in the tall grass. In his wallet was a New Hampshire driver's license which identified him as Rob Shur. A family photo tucked inside his wallet showed Rob posing with his wife and their teenage daughter and younger son at a Star Wars convention.

Jackie wiped the photo clear of any fingerprints and carefully returned it to the wallet.

The victim's presence at the rookery was a major problem. Had Rob Shur traveled to San Miguel alone? If not, where were the other members of his party? Were they still alive? Were they in hiding? If alone, how had he arrived? Either way, others certainly knew of his whereabouts, which meant that at some point Rob Shur would be reported missing.

That would bring the Coast Guard.

Keeping the Farallon Islands attack a secret was one thing; the death of an American civilian on an island so close to the California mainland was something else entirely. If Jackie could capture the beast before word got out, then there would be no problem; if she reported Rob Shur's death, then the Coast Guard would take over.

Would they allow her to remain on San Miguel to spring the trap or would they force her to leave?

"Damaris, have your crew cover both sections of this man's corpse with seal remains. We're heading back to camp in three minutes—make sure we leave no evidence that shows we were ever here."

Aboard the Yellow Dragon
Western Pacific

Catherine Ying stared at the rough sketch Dr. Hon had handed her, incredulous. "The female pilot created this?"

"Her name is Dulce."

"Could something so simple actually work?"

"My father taught me long ago that the simpler the design, the better the results. Contact Dr. Li at our assembly plant in Chengdu. Tell him I want a prototype loaded aboard the *Kexue* by next week."

"Sir, if this trap actually works and we catch something, what are you going do with it?"

"Let me worry about that, Catherine. Scan the paper and make the calls. If you need me, I'll be in my office watching the DP-2 launch."

"Yes, sir." Laying the sketch flat, she snapped a photo of it with her iPhone, registering the gust of air at her back as Dr. Hon exited the command center.

Pocketing her iPhone, she crossed the chamber to the unisex bathroom and locked herself inside. She entered a stall and sat down, then scrolled her phone for Stefanie Smith's contact information.

"It's Catherine. Are you still working for the crown prince?"

"Yes. What have you got?"

"A means to stock every tank in Dubai-Land with little risk and at a fraction of the cost."

Quatsino Sound
Vancouver Island, B.C.

The twenty-eight-foot fishing boat bobbed gently against the starboard bow of the *Marieke*, the hopper-dredge's bright lime-green hull dwarfing the tiny vessel. The Carolina Classic was powered with twin Volvo KAMD-300 diesel engines. David had selected it from half a dozen other craft offered to him by Sabrina Agricola because it possessed an inboard engine.

He watched as Dawn Hurtienne, a rugged woman with long reddish-brown hair, finished threading a heavy-duty nylon strap through the take-up spool of a ratchet anchored to the transom. The civil engineer had been highly recommended by the British Columbia Environmental Assessment Office to assist David with his plan on capturing Belladonna. She had convinced him it was a two-man job and that she was the best available candidate to drive the boat.

Dawn cranked up the slack on the ratchet, causing a three-foot plastic tubular object to rise out of the water behind the transom, its back end attached to a thick net.

Satisfied, she locked down the ratchet. "Okay, kid, we're all set. Essentially, our boat will be hauling the trawl backward by its cod, or pointy end. The net's two drag lines will trail behind us for about a thousand meters, where they'll feed up through the open hopper to the *Marieke*'s winches. Once we start moving, the current will catch the trawl boards located along either side of the drag lines and the bridles will pop open the net like an umbrella. When Belladonna goes after us—and she will—you'll need to wait until she's right behind us before you pull up on this ratchet. That will release the strap holding the trawl net, and we've got her. The winches aboard the *Marieke* will literally drag that bitch right up into the open hopper."

"This is a big fish. How strong are the *Marieke*'s winches?"

"Strong enough."

David scanned the horizon. The closest shoreline was a good three miles to the south. "You sure this is the area where she's been attacking fishing boats?"

"It's where she got me."

David's eyes widened behind his sunglasses. "You were attacked?"

"Scariest moment of my life. I guess it happened about six weeks ago. We were fly-fishing in Koskimo Bay—just me and Emily Blosser, an old friend. We knew about the warnings, but we were well within the waterway—hell, the shoreline was no farther than we are from the *Marieke*'s stern. Anyway, the salmon had stopped biting and it was getting late—pink sky at night, sailor's delight. We had already landed three or four nice-size Chinook, but Emily insisted we try one more spot, so I took the helm and followed the shoreline when, *WHAM!*

"It was such a jarring impact that I thought I had hit a rock. The rudder shaft started grinding, and then it snapped. So now we're dead in the water, but no big deal—we're close to shore, maybe fifty meters. All of a sudden, Em starts screaming.

"It was watching us . . . this massive white shark, its head as big as the ass-end of a cement truck, and it's just protruding out of the water—so close I could see the pink sky reflecting in its left eye like a devil. After a scary few moments it slipped underwater and was gone."

"It just left?"

"Thank our Lord and Savior."

"How'd you get to shore?"

"We waited a bit longer, then I convinced Emily that we had to swim for it."

She checked her watch. "We've got a few more hours until dusk; I'm going below to catch a few Zs. Make sure I'm up by sunset, will ya, darlin'?"

He watched as she entered the cabin, the boat swaying gently beneath them.

Point Bennett, San Miguel Island
The Channel Islands

A tapestry of stars greeted Jackie as she opened her eyes. With her clothes, boots, and jacket on, the sleeping bag had twisted into a tight cocoon, but she had been so exhausted it didn't matter.

They had become prisoners of the night, bound by the feeding habits of their quarry. And yet none of the crew that had accompanied her to the elephant seal slaughter at Cardwell Point believed the Lio would feed again anytime soon. And so she had split the crew into shifts, assigning herself the 6 p.m.-to-midnight group, hoping to sleep late.

Jackie checked her watch . . . 4:08 a.m. She felt the rumble and prayed it was not rain.

Then she heard the braying.

Unzipping her sleeping bag, she kicked her way out of it as the sounds from the panicked elephant seals grew louder and her team leader rushed to help her up.

"Boss, the seals! Come and see—"

Gaining her feet, she stole a glance below the rise at the beach.

The rookery was in a full state of panic, the females hightailing it up the beach, the males braying as they stood guard over the shoreline—

—the bulls chasing after the cows as the Liopleurodon emerged from the dark Pacific, its size startling Jackie. A juvenile no more, the eighty-foot crocodilian creature weighed in excess of a hundred fifty thousand pounds. Slogging out of the water, it shook its head and gulped the night air multiple times, each wheezed gasp causing the muscles in its neck to squeeze water from its gills even as it inflated its collapsed set of lungs, expanding its chest.

Jackie searched for her radio, locating it in her jacket pocket. "All units, check in!"

"Charlie—green."

"Delta—green."

"Alpha—green."

She waited, her heart racing, as the Lio advanced up the beach. "Tango, report!"

"Sorry, Tango is green."

Using her night binoculars, she searched the rookery for the white flag they had staked dead center of the cargo net. "On my mark, all units fire. Steady . . . steady—

"Fire!"

The pliosaur whipped its head to the right, then back around to the left, its jaws hissing as twenty-four three-inch needles struck its thick hide like a swarm of angry wasps.

"Reload and stand by." She stared through the night glasses, the creature showing no signs that the phenobarbital was working.

Switching channels, she contacted the tanker. "Captain Blackwolf, report."

"We know you have company, Miss Jackie. The *Mogamigawa* is en route. ETA in seventeen minutes."

"Have your men add two more barrels of phenobarbital in the hold."

"Two more?"

"She's a big girl. Buchwald out." She switched channels again, cursing over the radio as the Lio chased after three elephant seal cows, the event taking the creature beyond the buried net.

"Charlie team only—on my mark I want you to fire and then get the hell out of there. . . . Fire!"

The creature spun around, its jaws dripping seal blood, its jaundiced eyes searching for the source of its pain. Spotting the fleeing men, it crossed back over the buried cargo net—

—and collapsed. Jackie held her breath, waiting for the Lio to move. When it didn't, a collective cheer rose from the men.

She stepped out onto the rise, thrusting her left fist into the air. "All choppers—start your engines; all crews pack up! Let's put this baby in the bathwater."

The helicopters' lights illuminated a flurry of activity as the men rushed to clear the camouflage from the four airships. One by one the rotors began spinning, whipping the sand into a blinding frenzy.

Using the Lio as a shield, Jackie made her way across the beach to Chopper-2. She climbed into the copilot's seat, nodding to the pilot. "Are we gonna be able to lift this monster?"

"Hell if I know. It's a lot bigger than you described."

She reached for her headphones, adjusted them over her ears, and switched on the ship-to-ship radio. "All choppers report."

"Chopper-1 . . . Green to go."

"Chopper-3 . . . Go."

"Chopper-4 . . . We're seeing a lot of elephant seals caught in the cargo net."

"Nothing we can do now. Are you green?"

"Affirmative. Chopper-4 is green to go."

She nodded to her pilot, who took over.

"All pilots—make your altitude fifty meters and hold steady."

Jackie held on as the helicopter rose away from the beach, the landing gear dragging the cargo net free of the sand. She could not hear the throat-throttling calls of the pinnipeds, but she cringed as several dozen animals became caught in the rungs of rope, their plump bellies held fast.

The pilot shook his head. "Too much weight—it'll pull the landing gear off."

Jackie spoke into the radio. "All units set down—we're exceeding our weight capacity. Tell your crew we need everyone out; we'll send the *Mogamigawa*'s lifeboats to pick them up."

She held on as the chopper landed, then she climbed back into the main cabin with her team. "Guys, we need to shed some weight, so we're leaving you to be picked up by the tanker. Damaris, have your crew see if they can free those elephant seals from the net—they're weighing us down."

The Indian nodded. Searching through their supplies, he exited the helicopter carrying a chainsaw.

Aboard the Yellow Dragon
Western Pacific

The darkness was heavy and suffocating—he couldn't see his own hand in front of his face. His breathing became erratic as the fear took root, shutting down his muscles . . . turning his blood to lead. He felt the powerless Lexan coffin reverberate beneath his sweat-laced body and realized the movement was caused by his own trembling limbs.

Stop shaking . . . it can feel you.

Lying on his back, he stared out of the clear nose cone into the abyss, the weight of seven miles of water sitting on his downed submersible—sixteen thousand pounds per square inch of pressure searching for the tiniest fissure in which to force its way in and implode his skull.

The pulse in his carotid artery throbbed in his neck as the forty-ton female passed over him, the albino flesh of its swollen belly inches from his face, the claustrophobia drowned in a wave of sheer terror—

"Ahhhhhhhhhhhhhhh!"

Jonas shot up in bed, his T-shirt soaked in sweat, his eyes drawn to the rectangle of daylight framing the bay window's drapes. Still disoriented from the night terror, he stumbled to the floor and tore open the curtains—

—exposing the deep blue horizon of the Pacific glistening beneath a midmorning sky. Below, an enormous AG600 amphibious transport plane sat motionless in the water just outside of Dock-4, a fire hose feeding the contents of its cargo bay into a holding tank located between the outer and inner shell of Dragon Pod-4.

Like his wife, Dragon Pod-3 was missing.

Jonas entered the command center like a mad bull, his mop of gray-white hair uncombed, his face sporting a five o'clock shadow.

Catherine Ying looked up from the command post. "Professor Taylor—"

"Where's Terry?"

"She left you a note. . . . What did I do with it?"

Catherine flinched as Jonas wiped her desk clear of a stack of reports. "Where the hell is she?"

"We were short pilots. She insisted on going with Dulce Lunardon." Kneeling by the pile of papers, she quickly located an envelope with Jonas's name handwritten on the outside. "They're aboard Sting Ray-3."

Jonas tore open the envelope, removing the note.

Dearest Jonas,

Thirty years ago, my father insisted that you accompany my brother on a dive into the Mariana Trench. I fought you tooth and nail, but you replaced me as his wingman—no doubt saving my life. Years later, you returned to this hellhole and saved me again. . . . Two years ago, you rescued our son from the Panthalassa Sea.

The stress from these dives has weighed heavily on your subconscious, the fear manifesting in horrible nightmares. You've endured enough, my darling—now it is my turn to save you . . . and hopefully the millions who suffer from the same disease that nearly killed me.

Please don't worry; Dulce and I will be fine. Nothing scares this girl, and—in case you forgot—I used to be a damn good pilot.

See you in a few days.

> *You are my heart,*
> *Terry*

Jonas turned to Catherine. "Where are they now?"

"We lost them the moment they entered the Panthalassa Sea. We've been waiting for your secret weapon to be delivered so we can dive the platform and reestablish contact." She turned to the Chinese tech seated at the station to her right. "What is the status of Dragon Pod-4?"

"Storage tanks are filled. We're waiting for the transport plane to clear the area before we dive the platform."

Jonas felt his blood pressure rising. "Where's Dr. Hon?"

"He is returning to China on important business." She motioned to her screen, where the cargo plane, its weight borne on large landing skiffs, was bounding along the surface.

"Dive master, open ballast tanks A through M."

"Aye, ma'am. Opening tanks A through M."

For several minutes nothing happened. And then Jonas felt the chamber sinking—

—the underwater view from the bay windows changing as the Yellow Dragon, its diving platform, and the remaining five Dragon Pods began a seven-mile descent to the deepest gorge on the planet . . . and the access hole into purgatory.

Jonas rubbed his eyes, fighting to keep them open. He felt groggy, and wondered if his wife had slipped something into his glass of wine before they had gone to sleep. "Catherine, how long until we arrive?"

"Three hours, seventeen minutes."

"Where can I get something to eat?"

"There's a galley on this floor. Exit the command center and turn left."

Quatsino Sound
Vancouver Island, B.C.

Twenty minutes had passed since the sun had begun its descent, the western sky melding from a golden yellow to crimson red.

Dawn Hurtienne was in the flybridge, conversing over the radio with the captain of the *Marieke*. Large voluminous air bubbles burst to the surface behind the hopper-dredge's stern as the big ship's engines gurgled to life.

David watched the last rays of sunlight diminish into shades of violet dusk. The fishing boat's inboard motor rumbled beneath his feet, and then they were off, the bow bouncing along the surface as the craft headed east doing 8 knots. Using his night-vision binoculars, he scanned the expanse of sea between their boat and the *Marieke*. The hopper-dredge was keeping pace, the trawl net stretched out between the two vessels, the yellow strap securing the ratchet to the cod end rattling against the fiberglass surface of the transom.

Sharks are creatures ruled by instinct—"instinct" defined as a consistently demonstrated behavior initiated as a response to specific stimuli. Conversely, adaptation overrules instinct. It is acquired over time as a result of nature's need to improve upon its design, or learned via trial and error through senses designed to hear, taste, touch, smell, and track electrical and chemical signals in their four-dimensional liquid environment.

As the ocean's apex predator, Megalodon's instinct throughout its thirty-million-year rule was to feed, propagate its species, and avoid confrontation with its own kind. Territorial disputes between two sharks of the same gender were to the death.

Contact with the opposite sex was dictated by whether the larger, bulkier female was in estrus, in which case the male's role was simply to track down a potential mate through its pheromone trail. The act of copulation among sharks is the animal kingdom's equivalent of rape. To position the female so the two were belly to belly, the male is forced to bite down upon the female's pectoral fin, at which time it inserts a barbed clasper inside the ovulating creature's cloaca. Following insemination, it is not unusual for the female to strike back.

For the subspecies of *Carcharodon megalodon* inhabiting the Panthalassa Sea (and to a lesser extent, the Mariana Trench), a diminishing male population threatened the species' survival. Nature adapted by providing the females with the ability to internally self-fertilize their own eggs—essentially cloning themselves.

Angel had been nineteen years old when one of the last surviving male Megalodons had detected her scent and left the abyss to track her down and inseminate her. Eight months into her eighteen-month gestation period, her ovaries had released an additional batch of eggs, only these were already self-fertilized. The birthing event yielded two distinct litters—Lizzy and Bela (born as a result of copulation) being far larger and more developed than Angel's three cloned offspring.

The sisters' reproductive systems had adapted to self-fertilization when their senses could not detect the presence of a single male Megalodon in the Salish Sea. While female sharks reproducing via copulation did not reach the age of sexual maturity until they were fifteen, self-fertilizing females could reproduce within their first four years or even sooner, depending upon the species' populace within a given territory.

As the only Megalodon—male or female—in the Salish Sea, Belladonna was undergoing rapid hormonal changes. As her first ovulation approached, she selected the waters off Vancouver Island's western coast to serve as her nursery.

All that was needed was to vanquish any perceived threats to her future offspring.

Dawn reduced their speed as they approached the deserted inlet, her voice crackling over David's headset. "We don't want to draw it into the shallows. Hang on, I'm going to come about and head north."

Seated in one of the two vinyl chairs facing aft, David buckled himself in as the boat changed course. Salt water sprayed in his face, soaking his night-vision binoculars. Using his shirt, he dried off the lenses—

Whomp!

The boat rolled hard to port as the Megalodon sideswiped the starboard side of the hull, the sudden change in course preventing a direct hit. Ducking beneath the keel, the sixty-thousand-pound shark momentarily hoisted the twenty-eight-foot craft onto its back before the propeller caught ocean and spun the vessel free.

Hanging sideways in his chair, David held on as Dawn pushed down on the twin throttles, the boat accelerating to 22 knots.

"Kid, get up here and switch places with me."

"Why?"

"Just do it!"

He unbuckled his seat belt and climbed the aluminum ladder to the flybridge. "Where is she?"

"I don't know. The damn fish finder's not working. Take the wheel."

He slid in behind her as she vacated the bucket seat. "What are you doing?"

"I know this fish. . . . I've studied its tactics. Stay on this course. She'll come up along our starboard side. When I say, cut hard to port—that'll put her right behind us and I'll release the net."

"Okay."

Dawn descended the ladder, disappearing from his view.

David kept his head on a swivel, searching either side of the boat for Belladonna. *This is no good—she's way faster than this bucket of bolts.*

As he glanced to starboard, his right eye caught a blotch of white torpedoing at them below the surface on a collision course.

He spun the wheel hard to port and then back around to starboard, the S-maneuver preventing the Meg from plowing into the back of the boat. Turning to his right, he saw the Meg's six-foot-tall gray dorsal fin shoot past the starboard bow, the creature's caudal fin slapping the side rail a moment later.

Jesus, she's bigger than Luna. . . .

The powerful shotgun blast caused his racing heart to skip a beat. He stood up to find Dawn leaning over the transom, the barrel of an A-Square Hannibal big-game rifle pointed skyward, its concussive blow having felled her to her knees.

"Damn it kid, I told you not to change course until I said so!"

Picking up the thirteen-pound weapon, she ejected the empty shell, then reached into her shirt pocket and removed another .577 Tyrannosaur cartridge, inserting the 14.9mm, 49-gram monolithic solid projectile into the breech.

The bullet had grazed the right side of the Meg's face, leaving a three-foot-long bleeding gash halfway between her eye and gill slits, the stinging wound chasing her deep.

Shadowing her challenger in a hundred eighty-seven feet of water,

Belladonna's senses homed in on the vibrations generated by the fishing boat's propeller. Through trial and error, the predator had learned that a direct blow to this organ would incapacitate her enemy, and so she ascended, her ampullae of Lorenzini guiding her toward the electric discharge created by the spinning metal blades.

———

"Dawn, what the hell are you doing?"

"This bitch ate my friend—we call this payback. I'm going to blast a hole in her brain the size of a shot-put ball. Now, come about."

"No."

She stood, aiming the barrel of the rifle at him. "Come about, or—"

The fishing boat heaved beneath them, the force of the blow depositing Dawn and David on their backs, the impact snapping the fishing boat's propeller shaft and cracking its keel, opening a six-inch-wide, eleven-foot-long fissure along the bottom of the boat.

David picked himself up off the flybridge's deck. The steady growl of the vessel's twin engines was gone, replaced by a *whooshing* sound as a geyser of salt water entered the lower deck.

"We're dead in the water . . . and we're sinking!"

Raising the butt of the rifle to her right shoulder, she circled the main deck, aiming the barrel of the gun at the surface of the black water. "Turn on the keel lights. Then contact the *Marieke* . . . and tell the captain to haul ass."

David searched the polished mahogany dashboard, flipping each toggle switch until the underwater lights along either side of the boat illuminated, turning the sea an azure green. Locating the radio, he turned the dial to half a dozen different frequencies, his headphones filling his ears with static.

Water seeped out of the boat's cabin, flooding the main deck. "Dawn, what channel?"

"Twenty-six-point-four megahertz."

He turned the dial back the other way as a dark shadow circled just outside the perimeter of lights. "*Marieke*, come in."

"*Marieke* here. We read you."

He was about to respond when a tremendous force struck the starboard bow, tossing him from his seat. Another high-decibel *craaack* of gunfire was partly muted by his headphones; he never heard Dawn's scream or splash, but he was on his feet in time to see her flailing along the portside of the stern—

—the Meg's albino head turned sideways underwater as it bit clear through the woman's lower torso in one stomach-convulsing bite.

"David, are you there? What's happening?"

He stared at the gushing upper torso sinking into the scarlet swirl of light . . . the main deck now underwater . . . the hopper-dredge a quarter mile to the west—

—the trawl net floating behind the rapidly sinking boat.

David slid down the aluminum ladder, landing knee-deep in water. "*Marieke*, retract the net as fast as you can!"

"Did you net the Meg?"

"Just do it!" Freeing the ratchet from the transom, he wound the yellow canvas belt around both of his wrists and dove over the starboard side—

—his arms nearly wrenched from their sockets as the *Marieke*'s twin winches dragged the empty trawl net—and David with it—through the water.

Unable to breathe, he rolled onto his back, his head channeling the sea, allowing him a fragile pocket of air to gasp a few desperate breaths. He was flailing along the surface at 20 knots, the force of his wake stripping him of his sneakers, his pants pried off his waist and wedged inside out around his ankles. He focused his mind on his hands, the canvas strap balled tightly in both fists, the fishing boat disappearing from view, the pain in his arms and back excruciating.

Close to passing out, he was about to let go when the Meg's dorsal fin rose out of the dark Pacific thirty feet behind him, Belladonna following in his wake.

The rush of adrenaline pumped new life into his grip and he held on, his body bouncing awkwardly along the surface even as the streamlined creature effortlessly halved the distance between them, the Meg's albino head breaking the surface, its hideous snout inhaling his scent.

Torquing his upper body, David twisted from side to side and became a moving target, forcing the Meg to alter its line of attack. Seeing the beast lunge at him, he kicked wildly, the heel of his left foot connecting with the monster's upper gums before he quickly tucked his legs to his chest—

—and was suddenly underwater, the keel of the *Marieke* inches from his face. And then he was rising vertically toward a brightly lit surface, the Meg right below him, its jaws hyperextending open, the dark expanse of its gullet summoning him to hell. . . .

David flew onto the hopper and was yanked horizontally from Belladonna's closing maw, which clamped down on the empty night air. Falling back into the water, the thirty-ton shark floundered along the surface before righting itself with a flick of its powerful caudal fin—

—only to collide with one of the hopper's walls as the bottom of the tank sealed shut beneath the disoriented creature.

Barely conscious, David was dragged twenty feet across the net-covered deck before he mercifully passed out.

Aboard the Yellow Dragon
Mariana Trench-Western Pacific

The massive amphibious platform maintained its neutral buoyancy in more than thirty-five thousand feet of water, its oval docks harboring the Yellow Dragon and five of its eight smaller Dragon Pod spheres. Propelled by whisper-quiet pump-jet propulsor units mounted along the outside of its circular undercarriage, the monstrosity of aerogel and titanium trekked east at its maximum speed of 5 knots above a vibrant primal world that harbored the planet's very cauldron of life.

Jonas stared out the command center's bay windows, incredulous. He had dived the Mariana Trench more times than any human, but his trips had been performed in near to total darkness—a limit placed on him by the few external lights afforded him on his submersibles.

The aptly named Yellow Dragon was far more than a deep-water vessel—it was a small sun, the golden hue cast from its smart shell illuminating a valley of hydrothermal vents pumping superheated, 700-degree-Fahrenheit mineral water into the frigid sea. On prior voyages these black smokers had appeared in his night vision as petrified rock forests. Bathed in the Yellow Dragon's radiance, these outflows were transformed into colorful elixirs of chemosynthesis.

A dense vermilion mist dissipated over a Serengeti of tube worms that absorbed the fog's delivered nutrients through their scarlet-drenched tips. Bright emerald particles of magnesium twinkled in the artificial light amid dark violet funnels of sulfur that rose a mile above the valley floor to coalesce into an ominous ceiling of churning minerals—the plume insulating the warmth for exotic life-forms that inhabited a garden of primitive flora and fauna.

Bioluminescent pink jellyfish danced above patches of tube worms, their tentacles searching the ghostly white stalks for fish. Every few seconds one of these carnivores would drift too close to a vent, the hot flow causing the animal's exumbrella to bloom like Marilyn Monroe's skirt above a subway grate, sending it floating upward and away from its meal into the habitat of its awaiting assassins—schools of blind viperfish circling above the flows, waiting to feast.

As the docking station passed over a flat expanse of rock, the geology fragmented into dozens of giant squid, their dark camouflaged bodies changing rapidly from red to translucent white and back to dark brown as they scattered, only to reconvene in another location along the seafloor.

Up ahead, Jonas could see a circular pattern of blinking red lights marking the access hole leading down into the Panthalassa Sea.

The platform's forward inertia slowed, the ship's helmsman maneuvering the Yellow Dragon so that its lower hemisphere aligned with the circumference of the massive man-made hole. Several of the smart bay windows changed to a real-time view looking down into the passage, the ship's radiance revealing a deep shaft with smooth walls that resembled polished glass.

Jonas turned to Catherine Ying. "This tunnel . . . how were you ever able to construct it? It must have taken years."

"Believe it or not, it took less than a week. Hon Industries created an automated boring machine designed to withstand the tremendous pressures of the trench. The subterrene is powered by a compact nuclear reactor that circulates liquid lithium from the reactor core, generating exterior temperatures in excess of two thousand degrees Fahrenheit."

"You literally melted the rock."

"Correct. There is no excavated geology to remove. As the vitrified rock cools, it leaves behind a smooth obsidian-like finish along the shaft walls. The bigger challenge was creating a sensor-activated electrified deterrent to prevent any prehistoric life-forms from escaping the Panthalassa into the Pacific."

Captain Chau entered the command center. "Mr. Li, report."

"Sir, the Yellow Dragon is in position."

"Very well. Deactivate portal shield."

"Aye, sir. Shield is deactivated."

"Lower Comm Link."

"Lowering Comm Link, aye, sir."

Jonas watched as a twelve-foot-diameter titanium sphere was lowered by steel cable into the hole, its blinking yellow light reflecting along the polished walls, marking its descent.

"One hundred meters . . . activating Comm Link camera."

The shaft reappeared on another smart window, the angle revealing a blizzard of particles rushing past the screen as the sphere dropped rapidly through the tunnel.

"Eight hundred meters. No biologics present."

"Activate Dragon Pod-1."

The sound of white noise and static filled the command center.

"Sixteen hundred meters . . . approaching shaft exit."

The static disappeared, replaced by a soft, focused humming.

"Seventeen hundred forty meters. Comm Link has cleared the shaft and has established contact with the DP-1 relay."

"Activate DP-1's GPS. Locate DP-3."

A map of the Panthalassa Sea appeared along four of the smart windows. The shaft, represented by a blinking yellow light, was located at the center of the grid.

Jonas held his breath as the GPS unit aboard the crewless Dragon

Pod-1 searched for the rescue party's sphere. His limbs began to shake as a full two minutes passed without a return signal.

"Captain, where the hell are they?"

"Patience, Mr. Taylor. It's a vast sea, and sound does not travel quickly through the Panthalassa."

"How were you able to track the damaged pod?"

"We had launched relay drones. Unfortunately, the sonar signals stopped transmitting eight hours ago."

"My wife is aboard Pod-3."

"And mine is aboard Pod-2. The Comm Link will find them. . . . Have faith."

Six more minutes had passed, the map continuing to expand outward to encompass more sea, when a green light mercifully appeared in the far left upper quadrant.

"Contact established. DP-3 is located forty-two-point-three kilometers from the access hole."

"Access DP-3's GPS; locate DP-2."

"Aye, sir."

A blinking red light appeared within twenty seconds, the GPS map zooming in so that the two spheres appeared on the same grid.

"Got her, Captain. DP-2 is located nine-point-sixty-three kilometers to the north of DP-3."

"So close?"

"She must have escaped the current," Catherine offered. "Perhaps they managed to effect repairs on one of the propulsor units."

"Perhaps . . . Mr. Li, alert DP-3 that we have established a communication link. Request a status report."

"Aye, sir."

Jonas turned to the captain. "How long will it take to get a response?"

"Now that the GPS unit has established a direct link . . . not long at all."

Aboard Dragon Pod-3
43 Kilometers Northwest of the Access Shaft
Panthalassa Sea

The Dragon Pod submersible spheres were five stories tall and two hundred feet in diameter, outfitted for daily excursions into the Panthalassa Sea. Levels A and E, set at the poles, held the two Sting Ray docking stations, Level B the command post.

Guests were relegated to Levels C and D. The latter held a centrally located food court and service area that was ringed by a thousand-seat viewing area, the reclinable smart chairs facing out to forty-foot-high aerogel bay windows. "Bait lights" could be projected along the inside of the smart glass to entice the Panthalassa's primordial life-forms to come closer. Night-vision filters allowed the spectators to see any approaching creatures, the species identified over headphones.

The person most responsible for tracking and assessing the threat of any biologics venturing within striking distance of the Dragon Pod was in the command post, briefing the rescue mission's four Sting Ray pilots.

Misha Raluca Boltz was not what Terry expected. The tech wizard was in her midtwenties, her brown hair cut in a punk style, tattoos covering her arms.

"So . . . you're probably thinking that I'm some dinosaur biologist or something—wrong. Even if I was, how could I identify critters moving in a pitch-black sea beyond the range of our smart glass using nothing but sonar?"

She pointed to a dark window panel and snapped her fingers—

—causing video footage of pedestrians walking down a major street to appear on the smart aerogel glass. "I'm a computer geek; my background is in security. You've probably seen something similar to this demonstrated before—the video camera locks on to a person's face and the computer recognition program immediately identifies the subject."

Multiple boxes simultaneously framed the faces of dozens of people, a resultant green flash causing the camera to move on, a red flash locking on to the terrorist suspect.

"Pretty basic, right? Using this same technology, I created an identification system with the monsters in the Panthalassa. Check it."

The image changed to an animated shot of Dragon Pod-3 moving across the center of the screen, surrounded by an escort of sixteen bright specks, set in a grid pattern.

"So, this is in real time. See these tiny dots? Each one is actually a drone. Here, I'll do an intro."

She snapped her fingers again, causing the image to zoom in tight on a small aerogel sphere equipped with high-tech camera lenses. "Meet Z.I.G., our Zoological Identification Grid. Ziggy operates in a fashion similar to the Chinese security system, only instead of homing in on the subject's face, it identifies the life-form by its eyes. While eye shapes are species-unique, the animal's cornea markings are as individual as our fingerprints. Z.I.G. not only catalogues the biologic, it can also tag anything within range of our drone, allowing us to track a specific monster across the Panthalassa."

Terry clapped—embarrassing Dulce. "Can you show us what's out there?"

"NP. Ziggy, identify occupants in each sonar quadrant using Standard Triage Protocol."

"Triage protocol?"

"Ziggy prioritizes one quadrant over another based on the threat potential to the ship."

The grid reappeared, the image zooming in on a lone blip heading west in Quadrant-14.

"Species identified: *Tylosaurus proriger.* Length: Seventeen-point-six meters—fifty-eight feet. Weight: seventy-three tons. This animal has not eaten in three days. Threat Potential: six percent."

"How did Ziggy know it hasn't eaten?" Dulce asked.

"There is a specific spot on the cornea that corresponds to blood sugar levels."

Quadrant-13 lit up just ahead of the Tylosaur, revealing multiple blips.

"Species identified: *Cretoxyrhina.* There are eighteen of these sharks present. Average length: eight-point-eight meters—twenty-nine feet. Average weight: five-point-two tons. These animals are being stalked by *Tylosaurus proriger*. Threat Potential: one-point-five percent."

Quadrant-2 lit up, revealing a rectangular blip heading northeast several kilometers above Dragon Pod-3.

"Species identified: *Leedsichthys*. There are sixty-eight Leeds' fish in this school. Average length: twenty-none-point-eight meters—ninety-eight feet. Average weight: ninety-five tons. These animals are stalking krill. Threat potential: seven percent."

"Why seven percent?" Duane Saylor asked. "I thought these over-sized tuna were gentle giants."

Misha nodded. "Cows are gentle giants too . . . unless you find yourself in the middle of a stampede."

Quadrant-5 lit up, flashing on and off every few seconds.

"APEX PREDATOR WARNING: *Carcharodon megalodon*. Length: twenty-four-point-six meters—eighty-one feet. Weight: ninety-five tons. This animal has not eaten in six days. Threat Potential: seventy-six percent."

Misha's expression darkened as she tapped the Comm Link on her shoulder. "Captain, we have a potential threat—"

"Yes, Ms. Boltz, we see her. Let us hope she is after the Leeds' fish."

The pilots and tech officer stared at the smart screen as the oval blip closed on the large rectangular cluster to the northeast.

Terry glanced down at her hands, her right arm shaking. *Eighty-one feet . . . It's bigger than Angel.*

"WARNING: APEX PREDATOR IS CHANGING COURSE. New heading is south by southeast on course One-Six-Three."

Misha's eyes widened as Drone-6 disappeared from the screen. "That bitch ate my F-ing drone."

"She didn't eat it," Dulce said. "The electronic signals were pissing her off, so she destroyed it. Now she's headed straight for us."

||||||||||||||||||||||||||||||||||||

Agricola Aquarium
Vancouver, British Columbia

The tank's dimensions rivaled that of the Tanaka Lagoon—and that was where the similarities ended.

Maintained by the most advanced aqua-filtration systems in existence, the saltwater facility was a pristine, turquoise-blue medium that was oxygenated and fortified with nutrients in accordance with its occupant's own internal needs—all of which were monitored around the clock, thanks to biosensors injected into the Megalodon's bloodstream prior to its release into its new home.

Six-inch-thick aerogel bay windows encircled the lower levels; seventy-five hundred padded, all-weather smartseats were being installed in the retractable domed arena. Two separate feed aquariums, each half the size of the Meg Pen, were stocked with salmon that could be dispersed through connecting underwater channels, the live bait forcing Belladonna to hunt for her food.

Marine biologist Pam Wassom chided David when he described how he had been feeding Luna. "How is she ever going to get any exercise or stimulation if you feed her pre-killed fish? Are you afraid she won't be able to catch them?"

"I don't know . . . maybe."

"Ridiculous." She paused by the next set of underwater bay windows, eyeing David while she waited for the Meg to circle the tank. "Tell you what—why don't you bring me down to the institute for a few weeks; I can reorganize Luna's entire routine for you."

"I can't really afford you right now."

"Let me speak with Sabrina; I'm sure I can get her to cover it. After what you went through to capture Belladonna, I'd say it's the least we could do." Pam winked. "Maybe I can figure out a way to bribe you to take me on a dive with Luna?"

"I already have a girlfriend." *Dope . . . you said that aloud.*

"What did you say?"

"What did I say?"

"That's what I'm asking you!"

"Luna . . . she thinks she's my girlfriend. Putting you in the tank with me . . . she could get jealous. I wouldn't want to risk—"

The Megalodon's impact with the aerogel glass startled both shark trainers.

Belladonna circled back, her right eye peering through the glass at David.

"There's one shark that doesn't think it's your girlfriend."

David nodded, a bit unnerved. *Pleased to eat you . . .*

His new iPhone vibrated in his back pocket. "Hello?"

"David?"

"Speaking." The woman's voice sounded familiar. "Who is this?"

"It's Jackie. David, I need to see you right away."

"Jackie, I already have a girlfriend." He glanced at Pam, who was shaking her head.

Pivoting on his heels, he walked past empty bleachers to the exit. "Sorry, I've had like no sleep. What's up? Are you back East?"

"David, I captured the Lio. She's sedated and in the *Mogamigawa*'s hold. We're heading up the California coast; I'll be outside the canal in four hours."

"Damn . . . look at you! But why are you calling me?"

"My crew and I have taken the ship. Help me and I can force the crown prince to pay you all the money he owes you."

Panthalassa Sea

The Queen of the Panthalassa Sea nudged its prey, the minute electrical fluctuations emanating from the dying creature's carcass causing the tens of thousands of ampullae located beneath its snout to flutter. The "taste bite" that had crushed the strange turtle had immediately determined it was not a source of food. Still, the killer remained curious, its nocturnal vision strangely attracted to the faint sparks of shorting circuits coming from within the turtle's clear, pulverized shell.

The Megalodon that circled the remains of Drone-6 was bigger than any of its ancestors, which had dominated the surface waters for much of the last thirty million years simply because *all* of the subspecies sealed within the Panthalassa Sea were bigger—an evolutionary hiccup of survival that led to a domino effect among the members of this isolated food chain. Size, however, was not the only trait that distinguished the Megs of the Panthalassa from their cousins living in the Mariana Trench. . . .

For all its breathtaking beauty, albinism in the animal kingdom is a curse . . . a birth defect that eliminates the affected creature's ability to camouflage itself from its prey, calls unwanted attention to its pack, and ultimately leads to abandonment, isolation, and death for its victim.

Albinos do not survive very long in the wild.

Albino Megalodons had no chance in the Panthalassa Sea.

The volcanic activity that had created the Mariana Islands was also responsible for sealing a magma shelf that sequestered ancient creatures within the sea's bountiful, tropical depths while concealing it beneath the always evolving Mariana Trench seafloor. Before that separation occurred, all pigmentless life-forms living in the abyss had either relocated to the Philippine Sea . . . or perished.

The albino outcasts would eventually return to the Mariana Trench, lured into the abyss by the warmth pumping out of a new generation of hydrothermal vents and the chemosynthetic food chain it spawned.

The Megalodon circled the drone, creating new angles for its sensory array to search the abyss. Much like the Dragon Pod, the shark generated its own grid, only the predator's was infinitely more detailed and operated over a far greater distance—and in four dimensions instead of three.

Its sense of smell was so acute that it could detect a single speck of blood or urine in ten billion parts of water. The nest of ampullae of Lorenzini located beneath its snout was so sensitive to electrical fluctuations that it could home in on one 10-millionth of a volt over miles of sea or the single beat of another life-form's heart. Its sense of taste could determine the energy content of its prey; its sense of hearing allowed it to maintain perfect balance and equilibrium. And while sight was the least important sensory attribute in a sea of perpetual blackness, its eyes had evolved enough to discern movement in an isolated environment where natural light had never existed.

And then there was its lateral line.

Located beneath the Meg's skin along either side of its body was a channel composed of a gel-like substance containing millions of sensory cilia attached to nerve endings—all of which were linked directly to the shark's brain. As the predator moved through the water, this sensory array detected minute changes in pressure waves occurring between its own body and other objects within its environment, allowing it to "feel" the sea.

It felt the school of Leeds' fish disrupting its kingdom to the north, but the energy expenditure necessary to separate a solitary cow from the herd wasn't worth it. The Cretoxyrhina would scatter upon its approach, forcing it to expend valuable energy for a shark whose entire fat content was limited to its small liver. This left the Tylosaur—an easy kill possessing internal organs that could fuel the Megalodon for several days.

Abandoning the drone, the Meg locked on to its quarry to the south—

—its lateral line suddenly registering the faint presence of an immense object to the east.

Aboard Dragon Pod-3

"All stop."

"All stop, aye."

Captain Simon Ng closed his eyes and listened to his ship. "Tech officer, what is that humming?"

"It's our reactor."

"How long will it take to restart it if we power down?"

"Twelve minutes. We'll also lose our life-support system. If we can't make air—"

"Yes, I know, Mr. Lin."

"Sir, I was going to say we'll lose our ability to maintain neutral buoyancy."

"Captain, these Dragon Pods were built for these excursions," Misha stated. "We're way too big around to bite; there is simply no way for the Meg or any other creature to hurt us."

"I'll reserve my own judgment on that proclamation after we locate Dragon Pod-2. Mr. Zheng, where is the Megalodon now?"

The sonar tech glanced at his screen. "One-point-three kilometers to the northwest."

"Shut down all exterior lights. Restrict interior lighting to emergency lights only."

"Sir, I'm receiving a message from the Yellow Dragon. A Comm Link has been established; they are requesting a status report."

"Inform them that we are about to make contact with a V.L.P."

Terry turned to Dulce. "V.L.P.?"

"Very Large Predator."

"Sonar?"

"She's inside fifty meters, sir. We should be able to see her."

The crew spread themselves out around the bay windows, unable to see a thing.

"Twenty meters . . ."

Terry cupped her eyes, pressing the edge of her hands against the aerogel glass. "I saw something. . . . I think it's circling us."

"I still can't see a damn thing," Duane Saylor said.

"Activate night vision," Captain Ng ordered.

The blackness faded, becoming an empty olive-green void—

—and then they saw it . . . barely.

The Megalodon's eight-foot dorsal fin and its back, from the tip of its snout to the upper lobe of its conical tail, was pitch-black. As the dark camouflage met its mouse-gray flank, it formed rib-cage-like stripes that narrowed to points along the underside of its belly.

As the crew watched in horror, the monstrous shark turned and charged, the underside of its snout's dark pigment wrapping around its upper jaw and mouth like war paint, the effect increasing the fright factor by ten.

Dulce grabbed Terry by her arm and pulled her away from the window as the eighty-one-foot shark struck the aerogel surface, knocking out three of its teeth.

"That's right," yelled Misha, doing her victory dance. "Can't bite us, can't eat us, or mistreat us—we are invincible."

Captain Ng casually wiped a sweat bead from his cheek. "Restart propulsion units. Continue intercept course with DP-2."

Aboard the *Mogamigawa*
Monterey, California

Jackie scooted her chair closer to the laptop's monitor so she could see her real-time image in the lower corner of the Skype video call.

The crown prince appeared a moment later. "Ms. Buchwald, this is an incredible feat. . . . You and your crew have accomplished what many of these so-called experts claimed was an impossible task. How long will it take you to bring the Liopleurodon to Dubai?"

"As soon as you pay us our bonuses, we will be under way."

"Your bonuses will be paid upon delivery of the creature to Dubai-Land, not a moment sooner."

"That's not going to work for us."

"Those are my terms, Ms. Buchwald. Accept them, or get off my ship."

"We'll be happy to leave your ship. . . . We'll dock it in San Francisco right after we deliver the Lio to our other buyer."

"Another buyer?"

She turned the monitor around to face David Taylor.

"Hey there, Prince Walid. How's life treating you?"

The Arab's thick dark eyebrows knit together. "What is it you want?"

"I want my Lio. I caught it the first time and you refused to pay for it; therefore I still own it."

"The creature was hunted down and captured by *my* crew; it is aboard *my* ship! Captain Blackwolf, throw this man overboard!"

David turned the laptop so that it faced Cryss Blackwolf. The tanker's captain was playing cards with four of his officers—guarded by armed men wearing rubber dog masks.

"The crew mutinied, Your Highness. They want to be paid; so do we."

Jackie swung the laptop back around so that the monitor was again facing her. "The wiring instructions have been sent. Ten million dollars will be deposited into my account to cover our promised salaries and bonuses; another fifty million will be wired into David's business account to pay for the Lio. The banks open in Dubai in seven hours. If the funds are not received by 11 a.m. Dubai time, which is midnight our time, the Lio will be released into the Tanaka Lagoon."

Aboard Dragon Pod-3

Captain Ng stood before the bay windows in the command center, his pulse quickening as his vessel continued its descent, the damaged DP-2 located somewhere along the bottom of the Panthalassa.

"Mr. Zheng, increase shell luminosity to a hundred thousand candles."

"Yes, sir." The sphere's soft amber glow brightened, causing the ancient seafloor to bloom into view four hundred fifty-two feet below the ship—along with a frenzy of life caught in the path of the descending sphere.

Hordes of jellyfish were caught in the DP-3's bow wake and flung sideways. Fifty-foot rays were swept up by a school of lancetfish. Moving as one, the gruesome ten-foot-long sailfish swerved to avoid boiling streams of superheated water flowing from a trio of six-story-tall hydrothermal vents, forcing the ten thousand fish to plow through an abyssal jungle of dancing white stalks, each tube worm over one hundred feet tall and twenty inches around, their tulip-shaped, bloodred mouths snapping at the assault, the blind giant riftia attempting to devour the blind prehistoric sailfish.

The sphere leveled out and continued to the northwest. After several minutes the hydrothermal vents and tube worm clusters gave way to a vast plain of gray soot.

As the DP-3 passed overhead, its propulsors swept the thick particles aside—revealing a graveyard of bones.

There were vertebrae belonging to long-necked plesiosaurs like Mauisaurus, Elasmosaurus, and Styxosaurus and short-necked pliosaurs like Kronosaurus and Mosasaurus. Basilosaurus skeletons were piled next to the vacant shells of giant turtles, and there were countless ichthyosaur remains, though the size of these dolphin-like marine reptiles indicated the creatures had been juveniles when they had perished.

"Terry, what is this place?"

She turned to Dulce. "It's a killing field."

Captain Ng pointed to a large mound of gray ash up ahead. "There she is. Mr. Lin, circle the DP-3 and see if you can clear the debris from its shell. Ms. Boltz, any creatures we need to know about on your grid?"

"Lots of peripheral activity," Misha reported, "but no close contacts. They seem to be giving this area a wide berth. Can't say that I blame them."

A blizzard of thick gray flakes obscured their view for the next several minutes while the helmsman attempted to use the ship's propulsors to blow the refuse off the downed pod. When he was through, the sphere and the surrounding seafloor had been swept clean, the DP-2 lying on its side.

"Mr. Lin, circle the DP-2. Use the smart glass to zoom in on the ship; have the computer run a visual inspection of the aerogel shell."

"Yes, sir."

"Captain—" Terry pointed to a massive hole in the seafloor, the smart glass calculating the opening to be thirty-three feet in diameter. A beam of light was quickly directed into the furrow, the smooth rounded walls dropping several hundred feet before gradually curving out of sight.

An identical vent was discovered farther to the west, two more to the south.

"Thoughts?"

"Captain, it could be a lava tube," Quentin Zheng suggested.

Misha agreed. "That would explain the volcanic ash and the graveyard."

"Captain, the computer confirms DP-2's aerogel hull is intact."

"Excellent. Pilots, prepare to launch our Sting Rays. Let's get our people out of there."

There were two Sting Ray submersibles aboard Dragon Pod-3. Lee Deng and Duane Saylor were assigned to the vessel berthed atop A-Deck, Dulce Lunardon and Terry Taylor to the inverted craft mounted beneath E-Deck.

The two women entered the pressurized alcove and resealed the door behind them. Dulce pressed ENTER SUB on the keypad, causing the convex hatch on the floor in the center of the chamber to pop open and swing upward, while the Sting Ray's matching convex hatch dropped inward, allowing the two female pilots to climb down into the belly-mounted craft.

"I've never been inside one of these subs," Terry said, standing on the cockpit ceiling as she struggled to figure out the secret to securing herself into the inverted bucket seat. "They're so much larger than the Mantas."

"Slower, too. But at least you don't have to relieve yourself in a diaper. Here, watch me." Dulce slid her feet between her seat cushion and a roller pad, wedging herself in upside down before buckling the harness across her chest. "Let's do this checklist real fast before I puke up my lunch. Fuel cells?"

Terry scanned the dials and gauges before her as she climbed into her seat. "Fuel cells . . . fully charged."

"Batteries?"

"Batteries . . . Where are the batteries?"

Dulce glanced up and to her right. "Batteries—check. Supplies—check. Sonar, oxygen, carbon dioxide scrubbers—check, check, and check. Hatch is resealed, docking chamber secured. Disengaging docking clamps . . . and we're out of here."

Terry hastily buckled herself into her upper-body harness as Dulce rolled the Sting Ray out from beneath the DP-3's lower docking berth. Righting the sub, she descended rapidly—

—only to realize Sting Ray-4 was already aligning its concave belly with the dome atop the powerless Dragon Pod.

Duane Saylor's voice crackled over the radio. "Sorry ladies. Snooze . . . you lose."

"DP-2's lower berth is inaccessible," Captain Deng said. "We'll take the first load, you get the stragglers. Docking clamps are in place; sealing docking ring now . . . damn."

"What's wrong?"

"I don't know. The indicator light is flickering back and forth from red to green. Stand by, I'm going to disengage and try to get a better seal."

Dulce muted her microphone to speak with Terry. "At these depths, anything less than a perfect seal—"

"I know."

They watched as Sting Ray-4 detached its docking clamps from the titanium oval mounted along Dragon Pod-2's outer shell before slowly advancing again, the sub's five prongs inserted cleanly into the berth's corresponding apertures, the clamps tugging the two vessels tightly together as the O-ring sealed the connection.

"Crap! We're still getting flickering lights. Dulce, did the connections look clean to you?"

"Yes. Deng, it could just be a short in the docking circuitry."

"That's certainly possible. The pod looks like it's taken a beating."

"What about the other docking berth?" Terry asked. "We could use both Sting Rays to roll the DP-2 just enough to—"

"No disrespect, Mrs. Taylor," Duane said, cutting her off, "but the equipment aboard these pods wasn't designed to do one-eighties."

"Is there any way to signal their crew? They probably have no idea we're even out here."

"They should have seen our lights," Dulce stated.

"If the power is down, the smart windows are down," Deng replied. "Emergency batteries are used exclusively for life support after the first seventy-two hours."

A moment passed, followed by the sound of metal clacking against metal.

"What's that noise?" Dulce asked.

"Duane's tapping the hatch with a ratchet. Forget it. If the docking chamber is sealed—which it should be—they'll never hear you."

"Excuse me," Terry said, "but how will you be able to enter Dragon Pod-2 if the docking chamber is sealed?"

"The Sting Ray's hatch can open both doors. Once we get inside their ship, we'll have access to their internal communication system and video monitors. At that juncture we'll know if there are any survivors."

"We're getting a flickering green as well as a red," Duane said. "That means there has to be a sealed connection, right, Dulce?"

"I only pilot them. I don't build them."

"Ng here. The Yellow Dragon has been advised of your situation. It is your call as to how you wish to proceed."

Captain Deng turned to his copilot. "What do you think, Duane?"

"I didn't come all the way out here to let these people die. But if something does go wrong, my wife and kids better be taken care of."

"As is specified in the life insurance policy attached to your contract," Simon Ng stated. "Captain Deng?"

"Dulce, give us some room—we're going in."

"Shit." Pressing both feet to the floor pedals, she turned the joystick hard to starboard, distancing her sub from Sting Ray-4.

Captain Deng powered down the sub's engines while Duane Saylor pressed his ear to the watertight hatch. "Anything?"

"It sounds solid. Of course, there's nine miles of ocean sitting on top of us."

"Shh! Did you hear that?"

Duane listened.

Tap . . . tap. Tap, tap, tap.

The two pilots high-fived.

Deng grabbed the radio as Duane unbolted the sub's hatch. "This is Deng! We have survivors—"

Unbeknownst to the subs' crews, Dragon Pod-2's outer shell had been exposed to a digestive enzyme so acidic that it had melted a quarter of an inch of the eight-inch-thick titanium lip anchoring the sphere's docking station to its aerogel shell. As the Sting Ray's hatch was opened, the Panthalassa squeezed into the narrow void, inhaled a puff of air—and gulped.

The blinding flash was silent—a finality of molecules snuffed between the crushed screeching pocket of existence that had been the pressurized compartment of Sting Ray-4 and twenty thousand pounds per square inch of muted oblivion. The reverberations sent hairline cracks racing along the outer layer of the aerogel sphere, causing it to shed its two-inch-thick epidermis like a snake shedding its skin while preserving the inner cavity of six inches—just as its engineers had intended.

The energy wave rippled outward at a speed in excess of five hundred miles an hour and shook Sting Ray-5 for three terrifying seconds, even as the two-foot-high tsunami of ash raced across the boneyard and throughout the Panthalassa.

Reaching for a plastic-lined air-sickness bag, Dulce leaned over in her seat and retched.

||||||||||||||||||||||||||||||||||||

Aboard the Yellow Dragon
Mariana Trench—Western Pacific

Catherine Ying led Jonas to the small conference room. Captain Chau was seated inside, his expression distant—as if the weight of the world was on his shoulders. Johnny Hon's presence loomed over his left shoulder, coming from a flat screen mounted on the back wall.

"Jonas, we received a communication . . . Dragon Pod-3 about an . . . ago," the CEO stated, the transmission breaking up every fifth word. "The news is not . . ."

"You're breaking up, Johnny." Jonas turned to Catherine, his heart racing, knowing the news was bad. "Would somebody please tell me what the hell is going on?"

She glanced at her boss, who nodded. "The rescue mission located Dragon Pod-2. One of the Sting Ray teams attempted to board the ship. The docking seal on the titanium berth failed and the sub imploded."

Jonas felt the blood drain from his face. "My wife?"

"We don't know. We lost the Comm Link before we were told the identity of the pilots. Our techs are attempting to reposition the drones to reestablish contact."

"Are you recalling Dragon Pod-3? Is there anyone even alive aboard Dragon Pod-2?"

Captain Chau looked up, his eyes rimmed red. "We have confirmation of survivors aboard DP-2."

"DP-2 is lying on its side on the seafloor," Catherine said. "The lower docking berth is inaccessible. Even if it weren't, we couldn't take the risk. The location was described as having a multitude of lava tubes. We believe magma from a recent volcanic event may have melted the titanium seal."

"Okay, so we find another way in."

"There is no other way in," Chau whispered.

"What if we towed the DP-2 back to the access tunnel and surfaced it?"

Chau rolled his eyes.

Catherine answered Jonas. "Dragon Pod-2 is down to its last twelve hours of emergency power, and every volt is being delivered to its life-support system. Without power, they cannot create enough air to achieve positive buoyancy."

Chau snapped. "Why are you even entertaining this ridiculous suggestion? Even if the sphere were buoyant, where are we supposed to find a cable strong enough to tow the DP-2? How would we even begin to rig the two ships? Or maybe we should just push it with your Manta sub?"

Johnny's Hon's expression changed. "Captain, do not . . . me to relieve you!"

Jonas ignored the insult. "Wait . . . you have a Manta?"

Catherine nodded. "We leased it from Emmett Industries while the Sting Rays were under construction. We used it to complete visual inspections of the access tunnel during the excavation phase."

"And?" Jonas could see she was keeping something from him.

Catherine turned to her boss.

Johnny nodded. "Tell him."

"The Manta we leased was Manta-4, the one Zachary Wallace equipped with Valkyrie laser units for your Antarctica mission. Dr. Jernigan used the lasers to kill the Leeds' fish so we could remove their livers. We switched to the more humane method of drugging them before removing their organ once the Sting Rays and surgical bots were delivered."

"How was the Manta docked?"

Captain Chau perked up. "It was wet-docked! Pods-2, 3, and 4 are our surgical units; the wet docks are located on Level-D. Once the surgical drones removed the animal's liver, they returned to the wet dock, where robotic arms vacuum-packed the excised organ in a matching pressurized environment—otherwise it'd have spoiled. The Sting Rays were far too big to be wet-docked, but the Manta . . . Jonas?"

"How far away from the access tunnel are the two Dragon Pods?"

"Fifty-eight kilometers . . . about thirty-six miles."

"How many people are on board the DP-2?"

"Five," Catherine said.

"Six," Dr. Hon said, correcting her. "You forgot Dr. Jernigan."

"Six, huh? That's two in the copilot's seat, one in storage, and three in the glove compartment. I'll have to make a few trips. Where's the Manta?"

"Aboard the Yellow Dragon. There's a wet dock on S-Deck."

"Get her ready; I want to be in the Panthalassa within the hour."

Captain Chau pinched tears from his eyes. "Jonas, you would do this?"

"Just make sure the Manta can trigger the DP-2's wet dock to open. Now, if you'll excuse me, I need to write a letter to my kids before I go."

Catherine waited until he exited the conference room before she spoke. "What if we learn that Terry was one of the pilots who were killed? Should we tell him?"

"Absolutely not," Captain Chau said. "Do that and he might decide to abort the mission. At the very least, his grief would become an enormous distraction."

"If she died, he'll know soon enough."

Tanaka Institute
Monterey, California

Mac opened the conference room door, allowing Tom Cubit to enter. "Have you met my nephew, Monty?"

The attorney shook the Iraqi war vet's calloused hand. "How are you?"

"Ask me in about an hour. Hopefully Jonas Junior over there will be fifty million dollars richer."

David motioned for Tom to sit. "What do you think?"

"When it comes to the prince, I don't trust him—period. Having said that, we know he absolutely wants the Lio, especially now that it's a young adult. Moneywise, fifty million dollars is still fifty million dollars, but he'll earn that back in a week.

"The biggest concern I have is your ex-girlfriend telling him she hijacked the tanker. The prince is no prince, but he is an ally of the United States government, and the boys in the Coast Guard don't take kindly to American citizens hijacking Saudi vessels in California waters. My advice is to move the *Mogamigawa* into the canal. Possession still remains nine-tenths of the law, and he can't commandeer what he can't access."

David turned to Mac. "Will it even fit?"

"She'll be tighter than a virgin on her wedding night, but we can try. You'll have to move Luna into the Meg Pen . . . which brings up another problem. What happens if the prince calls your bluff and tells you he no longer wants the Lio and you can keep her? Last I heard, this beast is now amphibious. Where are you going to put her? Or are you planning to serve up your customers as early bird specials?"

"The MEGheads would love that," Monty said. "A good human feeding always jacks up attendance."

David ignored the comment. "What if we put an electrical collar on her? We could rig the boundary posts around the lagoon; if she tries to exit the lagoon, she gets zapped."

Mac mulled it over. "We'd have to ground the Meg Pen to protect Luna, but it's not a bad idea. I wouldn't be surprised if the governor suddenly changed his mind about expanding the institute. That monster would bring a lot of investors back to the negotiating table."

"I don't know," Monty said, shaking his head. "I still like that early bird special."

Tom Cubit looked horrified. "Do you have brain damage?"

"Little bit, yeah."

Aboard the Yellow Dragon
Mariana Trench—Western Pacific

Jonas stepped off the bullet-shaped elevator onto S-Deck and followed the signs to the wet dock.

The Yellow Dragon was a biosphere contained within a larger semi-permeable outer shell, separated by the containment area the Chinese called *sheng chi*. Functioning as the ship's lungs, this pressurized space held a labyrinth of ballast tanks and bladders that could take on ocean water or expel it in order to adjust the ship's buoyancy.

The wet dock was fifteen feet long and fifteen feet wide, but only ten feet high. Reinforced aerogel walls formed a sleeve that spanned the *sheng chi* before exiting out retractable doors housed within the outer shell. The floor functioned as a massive drain, the ceiling a pressurizing vent.

Sandwiched within these tight confines was Manta-4.

Jonas walked around the sub, a harbinger of bad memories.

The two tubular devices attached to the wings were not part of his and Mac's original design; they had been added by his friend and fellow creature researcher Zachary Wallace in order to pilot the craft in the frozen Antarctic Sea. The two boosters had certainly come in handy in melting the ice, and the lasers had saved his son's life, but the additional weight affected the two-man sub's speed and maneuverability.

What's more important to have in the Panthalassa: speed or a weapon?

He thought back to the video footage of the Helicoprion sharks swarming upon the DP-2's Sting Rays.

The lasers were designed to melt ice, not fend off a school of prehistoric sharks. Plus, they burned flesh only on contact.

Exiting the wet dock, he returned to the biosphere to find something to remove the cumbersome devices.

Tanaka Institute
Monterey, California

The full moon had risen above the cloud-covered horizon, summoning the Megalodon to surface.

David stepped inside the legs of his wetsuit, tugging the tight rubber material up and over his buttocks. He glanced across the deck to the Meg Pen, where Luna was spy-hopping, the sixty-foot albino shark watching him.

"Sorry, girl, I can't play with you now." Grabbing his mask and fins, he crossed the deck to the northern wall of the canal, following the footpath to where Monty was waiting with an air tank and scuba gear.

The war vet spoke into his radio. "We're in place, Mac. You can open the gate."

Rust-infested hinges screeched in protest as the massive doors at the end of the waterway slowly opened inward, beckoning the tanker to enter. Measuring two hundred twenty-six feet across, the canal was just wide enough to accommodate the *Mogamigawa*'s hundred-ninety-six-foot beam.

It was the depth of the ship's keel that would be their biggest challenge.

Monty helped his friend on with his buoyancy control vest and air tank. Securing his fins and mask, David eased himself off the algae-infested concrete wall into the dark water. Monty tossed him an underwater light and then watched as he made his way to the bottom.

Jackie had ordered her crew to empty the tanker's hold as much as they could in order to raise the ship's draft. With no Coast Guard in sight, they had waited until 8:30 p.m. and high tide before attempting to bring the massive ship inside.

David hovered above the muddy bog, directing his light at the slowly advancing bow. The vessel was sitting high out of the water, its keel clearing the canal floor by less than six feet.

Satisfied, he added air to his vest and floated back to the surface.

"Tell Mac we're good. How soon until the banks open in Dubai?"

"Fifteen minutes."

Aboard Manta-4

Jonas's thoughts raced as a deluge of seawater poured in from the floor and ceiling, filling the wet dock's chamber. Bright yellow gauges mounted along the inside of the aerogel walls reported the external and internal water pressure. When the latter reached 16,000 psi the exit door would open, releasing him to fulfill his final mission.

Jonas did not know if his wife was alive or dead, but he knew Captain Chau would not inform him one way or the other before he reached the two Dragon Pods. It was the correct play—Chau's wife was aboard the DP-2—but it still made him angry.

Anger was good. Anger engaged his adrenal glands and kept fear at bay.

Sorrow, on the other hand, was a dangerous distraction.

The yellow numbers on the pressure gauge reached 16,000 psi and turned green. A moment later track lighting along either wall sent arrows advancing to the opening exit.

Pressing down on both propulsion pedals, he accelerated the Manta submersible into the abyss.

Aboard the *Mogamigawa*

The videoconference call had been scheduled for 9:15 a.m. Dubai time, 10:15 p.m. in California.

At 10:19 p.m. (PST) an image of a bank conference room appeared on Jackie's laptop. A moment later the crown prince filed in with a team of attorneys.

"Ms. Buchwald, are you there?"

"We're here."

"We are prepared to advance you and the crew and officers of my tanker the amount requested—provided you make way immediately for the Persian Gulf."

"What about the money you owe David?"

"We do not owe Mr. Taylor any money, as he failed to deliver the Lio on the day of settlement."

"It was on board the *Tonga* for three days!" Tom Cubit snapped, the lawyer's carotid arteries flaring along either side of his neck. "When you took possession, you took ownership. You were supposed to wire the funds."

"Tom, take it easy—it doesn't matter anymore," David said. "I haven't had a chance to tell you, but I've decided to keep the Lio. I spoke to a private investor, who's putting up the ten million to pay Jackie and her team. He's putting together a business plan that will bring in hotel chains, restaurants, and a billion dollars to expand our facility—all because of the Lio."

"How soon will we get paid?"

David turned to Jackie. "The money will be wired tonight. The funds are coming from China."

"Great! What should I do with the *Mogamigawai*?"

"I don't give a damn. Why don't you park it next to the *Tonga*."

"Done." Jackie ended the call. "That was fun. How soon do you think he'll call back?"

"As soon as his heart starts beating again."

Aboard Manta-4

Jonas circled the rim of the 1.7-mile-deep tunnel a half-dozen times in an attempt to regain a feel for piloting the sub. Satisfied, he pulled back on the joystick and executed a three-hundred-sixty-degree wing-over-wing loop above the entrance before dropping into a ninety-degree vertical straight down into the hole.

The sub's lights reflected off the rounded obsidian walls. A minute later the Manta shot out of the accessway and into the Panthalassa Sea.

The sub's GPS immediately started chirping as two dots appeared on the sub's grid about forty miles to the northwest.

Jamming both pedals to the floor, Jonas accelerated to 35 knots, only to cut his speed in half as the debris in the water struck his windshield like a December snowstorm.

Aboard the Mogamigawa

The Liopleurodon had been in a semiconscious state for three days, its gills processing oxygen from the seawater inside its holding tank that was laced with a powerful combination of animal sedatives.

In order to raise the ship high enough for its keel to enter the Tanaka Lagoon's canal, the tanker's captain had drained 35 percent of the water inside the creature's holding tank that served as ballast. In lowering the waterline below the Lio's mouth, he inadvertently bypassed the creature's gills, forcing it to engage its lungs in order to breathe—cutting off the supply of sedatives to its system.

At 9:57 p.m. (PST), the creature awoke from its three-day nap, groggy and in a foul mood.

Tom Cubit looked over the faxed deal one last time. "All right, David, the terms of the agreement essentially state that, upon its execution, fifty million dollars U.S. will be transferred into the Tanaka Institute's offshore account to cover the initial capture of the juvenile Liopleur-odon two years ago. For liability reasons, the prince is leaving the lan-guage regarding Dubai-Land's acceptance of the creature vague, but the fact that he will be paying you places the *Tonga*'s sinking in his end of the pool. So . . . initial here and here, and sign the last page, which I will notarize as a licensed notary . . . and—"

The thunder of pounding metal shook the ship.

Mac slammed the top of Jackie's laptop closed, cutting off the Skype call, as the attorney quickly stamped the agreement and signed his name as notary.

Monty glanced at David. "It's awake . . . and it sounds cranky."

"It sounds like it's using its lungs. Jackie, when you drained bal-last from the hold, did you leave enough to keep water flowing over its gills?"

"You're asking me that now?"

Mac stepped from the control room to the metal staircase looking out over the main deck.

The Lio's enormous crocodilian head appeared as it bit down onto the wood framework of the open hold, its right forelimb wedged out-side of the opening as it struggled to pull itself out.

"Aww, hell."

Mac reentered the control room. "People, we got ourselves a little problem. And by 'little,' I mean a hundred tons of nasty that's climbing out of the hold as we speak."

"Where's the fax machine?" Tom yelled.

"Here, give it to me!" Taking the stack of signed papers from the attorney, Jackie placed them faceup on the fax machine and hit the pre-programmed number.

David ducked outside with Mac in time to witness the Lio climb out of the hold, its belly bloated with air.

"*QUURRRLTURP!*" The deep throttled chirp echoed clear across the waterway.

"Don't look at me," David said. "I'm scared shitless."

"Technically, it's the prince's problem now."

"Unless it goes after Luna."

They turned in unison to the Meg Pen, where the albino shark was spy-hopping, staring at the full moon.

Spotting the Meg, the Liopleurodon scrambled over the side of the tanker and into the canal to attack.

‖‖‖‖‖‖‖‖‖‖‖‖‖‖‖‖‖‖‖‖‖‖‖‖‖‖‖

Aboard Manta-4
Panthalassa Sea

The sonar alarm startled Jonas—in all his years of piloting the Manta he had never heard the bizarre warning sound outside of Mac's workshop.

Glancing at the screen, his first reaction was that the system had malfunctioned. How else could there be thousands of predatory life-forms ahead of him?

Unsure of what to do, he shut down the system and rebooted.

A minute later, the same configuration appeared.

He had avoided using the night-vision optics because it strained his eyes, leading to migraine headaches. But he switched to it now, fearful of what lay ahead.

"Oh, geez . . ."

They were everywhere—dozens of different species, all heading to the northwest. Directly in front of him, blocking the Manta's way, was a school of long-necked Elasmosaurs, and there appeared to be no way around them.

Without warning, a head the size of a utility truck circled back, its mouth filled with two-foot-long, stiletto-shaped teeth.

Pulling back on the joystick, Jonas barrel-rolled the Manta over the plesiosaur's snapping jaws—

—only to be bashed sideways by another and another, the seafloor rushing up at him. . . .

———————

Mac had described Dr. Michael Day as "Eastern philosophy applied to Western fears."

"You need someone trained to deal with these kinds of issues, J.T. His office is in Suite 208; go up the stairs and turn right. . . . He's expecting you."

Jonas exited the Cadillac convertible, angry at Mac's deception in getting him to meet with his shrink.

"What brings you here, Mr. Taylor?"

"James Mackreides."

"I asked 'what,' not 'who.' Surely there must be something in your life that I might be able to offer you a few tools to deal with better."

"All right. How about fear?"

"That depends. There is healthy fear and there is unhealthy fear. For instance, the fear of death is not constructive—death is merely the passage into a higher realm. The key to overcoming the fear of death is to meet this inevitability with a controlled mind."

"What about the fear of being trapped?"

"All fear, Mr. Taylor, comes from our own uncontrolled minds. To quote Shantideva in A Guide to the Bodhisattva's Way of Life, *'All fears and all infinite sufferings arise from the mind. While it is not possible to control all external events, if I simply control my mind, what need is there to control other things?'"*

"And how does one control the fear and anxiety of being separated from the person you love more than anyone in the world? My wife—she's been in a coma for ten months."

"I am so sorry. And how does that make you feel?"

"Angry."

"Because there is nothing you can do about it?"

"Yes."

"The root of all fear, Mr. Taylor, comes from our ignorance of our own existence. Without getting too deeply into this profound subject, life is the dream; what follows is the true reality, and it is our conviction that things exist independently of our mind that is the source of all our fear."

"And how do I deal with it?"

"By understanding that while we are in the samsara—the process of birth, death, and rebirth—we will continuously be separated from all the conditions that make us feel safe: our home, our family, our friends, our money and possessions, and our physical health. If we are not separated from these conditions before death, we will be separated from them at death. What happens to us afterward depends on the karma we have created in this life or in previous lives. This is not something we like to hear, but it is the truth.

"When you are frightened, ask yourself what you are actually frightened of. Our fear of death is unhealthy—death is simply part of the process. A healthy fear of death would be the fear of dying unprepared. Our focus, therefore, should be on the things that we can actually take with us—the imprints of the positive and negative actions we have generated. Instead of fear, our focus should be on purifying our negative karma while accumulating as much good karma as we can."

"And how do I do that?"

"The greatest protector against fear, Mr. Taylor, is love."

Jonas opened his eyes to a throbbing headache and a dark cabin, framed by a soft glow coming from outside. It took several disorienting moments to realize he was hanging upside down from his bucket seat, the Manta buried nose-first in the seafloor's muddy bog.

Pressing the balls of his feet to the dashboard, he redistributed his weight, allowing just enough slack to release the seat's harness. He caught himself as he dropped, the redistributed weight sending the sub's tail flipping over onto its back, pancaking the craft upside down.

"Sonuva bitch!"

Standing on the ceiling, he reached up to the power button and restarted the sub's engines. Unable to climb up and strap himself into the inverted chair, he pushed the joystick all the way to the right and tapped one of the accelerator pedals with his free hand, flipping the Manta right side up while sending himself flying headfirst into the starboard bucket seat.

"Ow . . . damn it!"

Climbing over the dashboard divider, he resituated himself at the port controls and gazed out the windshield—just as the sixty-foot Mosasaur charged.

"Shit!" Slamming his right foot to the starboard pedal, he wrenched the joystick hard to the right, swerving around the charging crocodilian monster.

Jonas quickly buckled in before stealing a glance at the sonar. The creatures were everywhere—all moving in the same direction, as if being summoned to the Panthalassa's version of Mecca.

The Dragon Pods . . . could the spheres be attracting them?

Remaining close to the seafloor, he replotted his course, shadowing a school of enormous Leeds' fish as he raced to the northwest.

Tanaka Lagoon

The Liopleurodon had already entered the lagoon by the time David had climbed down the cargo net hanging from the tanker's portside to the cement footpath running along the top of the canal's north wall.

He looked up as the giant pliosaur shot out of the lagoon like an eighty-foot seal, landing upon the deck of the Meg Pen in one frightening burst of motion. The Lio's presence chased Luna to the bottom of her tank as David reached the inner gate.

Locating the walkie-talkie in his jacket pocket, he fished it out, struggling to catch his breath. "Monty?"

"Yeah, go ahead."

"Contact someone . . . in the control room. Turn on . . . the Meg Pen's lights."

David reached the main deck in time to see the Lio dive headfirst into the dark pool of water. "No!"

The pliosaur was faster and longer than its adversary, but its body was not as powerful as the shark's, its jaws nowhere near as lethal. Gauging the dimensions of the small circular tank, the predator quickly realized it had made a fatal error.

As it spun around and retreated to the surface, the aquarium's underwater lights turned on, blinding the nocturnal creature.

Incensed by the pliosaur's presence in her territory, Luna launched an assault from below, her jaws biting deep into the Lio's right hind flipper. As it whipped its albino head to and fro like a dog playing tug-of-war, its six-inch serrated teeth sliced through sinew and bone, tearing off the entire appendage in a crimson cloudburst.

Disoriented from the lights and in a sudden state of panic, the injured Lio attempted to flee the tank, only its forelimbs weren't quite powerful enough to propel it over the five-foot-high steel guardrail surrounding the habitat. As it attempted to drag itself over the barrier, Luna slammed her hyperextended jaws on the creature's stubby tail, dragging it back inside the tank.

———

David ran to the supply locker and attempted to open Monty's combination lock. "Monty, quickly—what's the combination to the lock on the footlocker?"

"You mean the one with the electric zapper? Uh . . . Oh shit, don't tell me."

David heard someone demanding the cell phone. "David, its Mac. What the hell are you thinking about doing?"

"I'm not gonna let Junior kill my shark—no way!"

"What makes you think she needs your help?"

David turned, his eyes widening in disbelief as Luna's head rose out of the water, her jaws wrapped around the Liopleurodon's soft midsection. Clamping down, the Meg sent a burst of internal organs blasting out of its prey's crocodilian mouth, seconds before its head disappeared beneath the spreading scarlet surface.

"Yeah! Kill that bitch!"

Thirty seconds passed. With a *whoosh,* Luna's albino head broke the surface, its upper torso quivering as it fought to remain suspended above the frothing pink water, the broken remains of its challenger grasped within her bloodstained jaws.

My God . . . she's showing her kill to the moon.

The Meg shook the lifeless Lio from side to side, its serrated teeth tearing through gristle and bone, the action sending swells of bloody froth pouring across the deck of the Tanaka Lagoon in every direction.

"Hey, kid, you okay?"

"Yeah, Mac. Helluva show."

"Aren't they all. Just thought you'd like to know the funds were wired into your account. Prince Walid is now the proud owner of a fifty-million-dollar corpse."

Aboard Manta-4
Panthalassa Sea

Jonas spotted the DP-3 in a clearing up ahead. The glowing orange sphere resembled a blood moon during a lunar eclipse, the object casting its ethereal glow upon a second object located on the seafloor.

"This is Captain Ng aboard Dragon Pod-3. Who is piloting the Manta?"

Jonas reached for the radio. "Jonas Taylor. My wife . . . is she—"

"Jonas!"

"Terry . . . thank God!" Tears poured from his eyes, his limbs trembling. "Is Dulce with you?"

"Yes. Jonas, we're using our lights to communicate in Morse code to the survivors on board DP-2. They're running out of air."

"Have them open the outer door of the wet dock, I'm on my way."

"Jonas, wait—there's a Meg circling the killing field . . . black, with a gray underbelly. Very difficult to see . . . She's bigger than Angel and just as aggressive."

Jonas glanced at his sonar.

The blip appeared in the northeast quadrant, the Meg's presence scattering the clusters of life-forms gathered along the perimeter. His pulse raced as the large animal accelerated straight for him, its intentions clear.

"Jonas—"

"I see her. Tell DP-2 I'm on my way." Jamming both foot pedals to the floor, he raced to the downed pod—

—the sonar blip intent on cutting him off before he reached the sphere.

He arrived ten seconds ahead of her, but still could not see the camouflaged beast. Knowing the Meg queen was close, he looped around the southeast side of the DP-2, his eyes searching the olive-green void for the entrance to the wet dock.

A blinking red light appeared up ahead along the sphere's western flank as the blip closed on him from the south. *How am I supposed to dock moving this fast?*

Jonas passed the flooded open hangar. Pulling back on the joystick, he executed a tight barrel roll to the west, followed by a stomach-churning three-hundred-sixty-degree loop—

—the maneuver placing the open wet dock directly in front of him and the Manta in the path of the charging Megalodon!

Pushing down hard on the joystick, he slipped beneath the shark's massive pectoral fins and shot through the open passage at 20 knots.

Jonas pulled back on the joystick at the last second, raising the Manta's prow so that the sub's curved belly rolled up along the back wall, the impact reduced by a thick protective net.

"Huh?" Jonas opened his eyes to bright lights and bare fists pounding on the Manta's cockpit glass. Reaching his right hand into the central console, he popped open the hatch, the dull ache in the front of his head introducing him to his mild concussion.

Warm, salty air rushed into the cockpit, accompanied by enthusiastic backslaps and "Thank-yous" directed at him in English and Chinese. Introductions were made as the crew hurriedly climbed inside the two-man cockpit.

"Lee Huang, helmsman."

"Bingbing Midway, assistant to Dr. Jernigan."

"Chenli Gan, biologist."

"Dr. Vicky Xu, oncologist."

"Danny Wu, captain."

"Sara Jernigan. This is my mission; if there is no more room I'll remain behind."

Jonas glanced at the three women squeezed in together in the copilot's seat and the two men lying prone in the storage compartment in back. "I guess I'm making a second trip, Doc."

"Excuse me," said Danny Wu, "why could Dr. Jernigan not ride in your lap?"

"I need to be able to pilot the sub. That means two legs and my right arm—unrestricted. Not to mention we're already running heavy. Everyone on board has to be strapped in tight enough to handle a barrel roll without flying free."

"We're good," said the three women in the copilot's seat.

"Good back here," said the two men wedged in storage.

Sara shrugged. "Be careful."

"I'll be back soon," Jonas said. Activating the Lexan dome, he resealed the cockpit.

Dr. Jernigan waved and then returned to the wet dock's control room.

Two minutes later the chamber began filling with seawater.

Jonas grabbed the radio's mic. "DP-3, come in."

Static.

Damn . . . no telling where that Meg is. And we're a lot heavier now.

He activated the Manta's headlights, turning the beams on high.

The chamber began pressurizing: 5,000 psi . . . 8,000 . . .

At 19,460 psi, the chamber's internal lights flashed green, the outer door opening—

Jonas jammed both feet to the propulsion pedals, sending the Manta accelerating out the open passage, the drag on the craft immediately noticeable.

The radio crackled to life.

". . . circling back to intercept."

"Terry?"

"We see you, Jonas. So does the Meg. Come to course three-zero-five; we'll escort you in."

"Escort me in?" He looked down at his sonar screen. The Meg was coming at him from below and to the west, another sub racing in from above.

They're in the Sting Ray. . . .

Dulce pushed down on the joystick, sending the Sting Ray racing past the rising Manta on a collision course with the dark-striped monster. "Charge ready?"

"Ready," Terry yelled back.

"Crank it up!"

The 10,000-volt electromagnetic pulse rippled out from the dual antenna anchored beneath the sub's prow, scrambling the Megalodon's ampullae of Lorenzini. The eighty-ton predator gyrated from side to side before veering away, racing back to the seafloor.

The two women high-fived. "That'll teach that bitch to mess with my man."

"Amen, Mama."

Jonas's face hurt from smiling. "Ladies, that was awesome. I'm dropping off this first group, then I have one more passenger to pick up."

"Roger, dodger. We'll escort you in."

It took twenty minutes to wet-dock the Manta aboard Dragon Pod-3. Alone again in the sub, Jonas accelerated out of the flooded chamber, reaching for the radio.

"Dulce, where are you?"

"On your six. You need to make this pickup fast—something's happening out there."

"What do you mean?"

Terry responded, "Jonas, there are huge holes along the seafloor. . . .
We think they could be magma tubes. The other life-forms are abandoning the area—an eruption may be imminent."

"Geez. Okay, I'll be quick."

The Manta entered DP-2's open wet dock. Jonas set the sub down
facing the exit as the chamber resealed.

Two minutes passed . . . and nothing happened, the compartment
remaining flooded and under pressure.

Come on!

He tried the radio, but there was only static.

Another minute passed in darkness, Jonas on the verge of freaking
out. *Stay calm. . . .*

Metallic clicks echoed inside the dark, sealed space.

The backup generator is shot. There's no power to activate the pumps.

Sweat poured down his face. *You're trapped.*

His limbs began to shake uncontrollably.

You saw this coming when we landed in Guam, yet here you are! He
recalled his high school football coach's favorite saying: "Fellas, do you
know what a shithead is? A shithead is someone who sees a pile of shit
on the sidewalk, knows it's a pile of shit, and steps in it anyway."

Jonas Taylor . . . shithead.

The interior lights flickered on.

Come on, baby!

The pressure gauge illuminated, descending backward from 19,460
PSI.

Thatta girl!

At 0:00 the pumps engaged, the water draining quickly.

Green light! Jonas popped the hatch as Dr. Jernigan dashed out of
the control room carrying a heavy backpack, the chamber already
starting to refill. Tossing the bag inside, she climbed in after it as Jonas
resealed the cockpit.

"Sorry. Backup generator was shot after the first load. I had to drain
the last ounce of power from the life-support system."

"Will that be enough?"

"Ask me again in seven minutes."

The chamber filled with seawater, the internal pressure rising—

—the gauge stopping at 12,729 psi.

Jonas punched the cushioned panel by his left elbow. "Oh, come on."

Sara Jernigan laid her head back and sighed. "Welcome to the last two weeks of my existence. Sorry you were dragged down here with me."

Jonas grabbed the radio. "Terry, if you can hear me—we're trapped inside the flooded wet dock. If there's any way for you to blast open the outside door—do it!"

"I didn't know these subs were armed with weapons?"

"They weren't. They were reequipped after the DP-2 was attacked."

"How long will your life-support system last?"

"Longer than our water supply. The immediate problem is the magma tubes."

"What magma tubes?"

"The ones surrounding this fossil graveyard. An eruption must be coming—the sea creatures are all abandoning the area."

"That means they're back. . . ."

"They? Who's they?"

"Sweetie, you don't want to—"

A brilliant flash ignited as the Panthalassa Sea engulfed the chamber door, the water, and the Manta in one massive gulp.

"Hey, fella, you okay?"

Jonas opened his eyes. The Manta was resting on the seafloor, the Sting Ray hovering above and in front of them.

"What happened?"

"Your friends in that sub must have blasted open the wet dock door. We gotta haul ass—we're right by its lair."

The sonar alert cut him off.

He saw it emerge from the hole and rise behind the Sting Ray, its outstretched jaw nearly dislocating as the hundred-eighty-seven-foot-long *Titanoboa Panthalassic* engulfed the entire sub in one horrific bite, the craft's contours visible as it was propelled down the sea snake's expanding gullet.

For a long second its viperous yellow eyes, translucent in the Manta's headlights, stared at Jonas Taylor.

And then the soulless creature disappeared tail-first into its lair.

Jonas Taylor will return in

MEG

PURGATORY

ACKNOWLEDGMENTS

It is with great pride and appreciation that I acknowledge those who contributed to the completion of *MEG: Generations*.

My thanks to editor Christopher Morgan (Tor/Forge) and Tim Schulte (A & M Publishers) as well as to my friend and personal editor, Barbara Becker, for editing *Generations* as well as her tireless work in managing the Adopt-An-Author teen reading program. My life is made easier thanks to my webmasters Doug and Lisa McEntyre at Millennium Technology Resources. My heartfelt gratitude to my longtime agents and friends Danny Baror and Heather Baror-Shapiro at Baror International. And what would a MEG book be without an amazing cover designed by graphic artist Erik Hollander (www.ErikHollanderDesign.com)?

As this novel goes to press, *MEG 2: The Trench* moves into production—thanks to the incredible work and dedication of my dear friend and *MEG* movie producer, Belle Avery. A very special thanks from both of us to executive producer Jiang Wei for financing *The MEG* and working so diligently with Belle to get the first two movies in the series green-lit at Warner Bros. And a special shout of thanks to Jie Chen, his right hand in Beijing, for her tireless efforts, and to Belle's hubby, Tim Risch, for being a saint.

To my wonderful wife and soul mate, Kim; our children—Kelsey, Branden, Amanda, and Chad; and our grandchildren—Savannah, Leanna, and Alexandra.

Finally, to my MEGheads, the most loyal group of fans an author could ever hope for—your support and caring mean the world to me.

—Steve Alten, EdD
Meg82159@aol.com

To personally contact the author
or learn more about his novels, go to

www.SteveAlten.com

MEG: Generations is part of Adopt-An-Author,
a free nationwide program for secondary school students
and teachers. For more information, go to

www.AdoptAnAuthor.com